# A SEASON

# AMONG

# PSYCHICS

For Mary,
It was a pleasure meeting
you and reading to you.
All best wishes,
Elizabeth

a novel by

## Elizabeth Greene

*inanna poetry & fiction series*

**INANNA PUBLICATIONS AND EDUCATION INC.**
**TORONTO, CANADA**

We gratefully acknowledge the support of the Canada Council for the Arts and the Ontario Arts Council for our publishing program. We also acknowledge the financial support of the Government of Canada.

Cover design: Val Fullard

*A Season Among Psychics* is a work of fiction. All the characters, situations, and locations portrayed in this book are fictitious and any resemblance to persons living or dead, or actual locations, is purely coincidental.

Library and Archives Canada Cataloguing in Publication

Greene, Elizabeth, 1943–, author
    A season among psychics / Elizabeth Greene.


(Inanna poetry & fiction series)
Issued in print and electronic formats.
ISBN 978-1-77133-501-0 (softcover).— SBN 978-1-77133-502-7 (epub).—
ISBN 978-1-77133-503-4 (Kindle).— ISBN 978-1-771335-04-1 (pdf)

    I. Title.  II. Series: Inanna poetry and fiction series

PS8563.R41737S43 2018          C813'.54          C2018-901529-2
                                                 C2018-901530-6


Printed and bound in Canada

 MIX
Paper from
responsible sources
FSC
www.fsc.org
FSC® C004071

Inanna Publications and Education Inc.
210 Founders College, York University
4700 Keele Street, Toronto, Ontario, Canada M3J 1P3
Telephone: (416) 736-5356 Fax: (416) 736-5765
Email: inanna.publications@inanna.ca  Website: www.inanna.ca

*For the teachers*

ALSO BY ELIZABETH GREENE

POETRY:
*Understories*
*Moving*
*The Iron Shoes*

EDITED AND CO-EDITED COLLECTIONS:
*The Window of Dreams: New Canadian Writing for Children*
*On the Threshold: Writing Toward the Year 2000*
*We Who Can Fly: Poems, Essays and Memories in Honour
of Adele Wiseman*
*Kingston Poets' Gallery*
*Common Magic: The Book of the New*

*Beyond this, men think and feel certain things and see certain things not with the bodily vision.*
—Ezra Pound, letter to William
Carlos Williams, 1908


*Nel mezzo di camin de nostra vita....*
—Dante, *The Divine Comedy*


*Just because there's no word,*
                    *no reason*
                                *no proof*
    *doesn't mean it isn't*
                    *true.*

# 1. PSYCHIC FAIR

WHEN I WAS FIFTY and thought my life was over, I let my best friend, Claire, persuade me to attend a psychic fair. It was a bright blue January morning, forty below, the snow plowed into bobble-edged cliffs by the side of the road. Everything was frozen except for the plumes of exhaust from car engines, if they started. It was an insane time to go out. I could have made coffee and snuggled into the couch with a book—lavender shawl around my shoulders, black cats curled on the rug, fire burning in the fireplace. But Claire was my best friend, and I was ready by ten, dressed warmly, when she came for me in her sturdy aging Volvo, a leftover from her marriage.

Claire was maniacally punctual, and we were much too early. There was a sagging red ribbon across the entrance to the room where the fair was to be held. We sat in the hall on a discouraged vinyl couch and tried to pretend we weren't tired of waiting. We were sitting in the dark looking into a hall bright with light, promising forbidden knowledge.

"Look," whispered Claire, "there's one of them now."

The woman looked like a middle-aged angel from the top of a prison Christmas tree—short, neat blonde hair, shading toward brass, with bangs that could have been cut from under a bowl, pristine white sweater over slim tan wool trousers, otherworldly light blue eyes. I introduced myself and Claire with a confidence that was mostly assumed. Psychics had always seemed glamorous to me. I thought of them as having the inner freedom of writers, artists, and magicians—a freedom I had always longed for.

Luck is having what you want or being grateful for what you have. I was trying to be grateful, but I was twisted with discontent. Two years ago I'd been married to a colleague, had a tenured job, and a son—all things I'd wanted. But I'd found myself in a place where all the doors seemed shut. I thought of that Robert Frost poem "The Lovely Shall Be Choosers," about all the joys that were actually confinements and pushed you down from the radiance of your younger self.

I'd never been married before so I couldn't tell when a marriage needed more work to get through rough spots, or if it was simply going bad. Henry and I had been very happy before we'd gotten married. We'd had summers in England, long afternoons on tennis courts, coffee and sherry late at night in our offices. Later, I was home with Davy a lot while Henry worked or played tennis or went hunting or went out to coffee. Most of the hall closet was taken up with Henry's eighteen coats. I was exhausted and depressed. Henry had started throwing bills at me—big ones like the oil bill—furious that I hadn't paid them yet. I remembered reading a new advice columnist saying, "My marriage was no bed of roses." But whose marriage was? And who would want to sleep on a bed of roses with all those unexpected thorns? But after fifteen years, the thorns seemed more frequent, and the petals fewer and farther between.

One February night I woke up, shaken, after a vision of Henry weeping crocodile tears over my grave. By June, I'd announced that I wanted to separate, and, by September, after a summer of bad fights, he was gone.

Before that, even my job, which I'd always loved, went sour. Like my marriage, it went from bad to worse. I was suddenly teaching an array of courses in areas I'd never studied, and although I was lucky to teach, I was scrambling to get my classes together. Henry had taken up as much of my time as he had the coat closet, so I couldn't really prepare. Mostly, I did it between two and four in the morning, when Davy was in bed and the house was quiet. When Henry did come to bed, I didn't want to be bothered with him. That was my working time. But it felt hopeless, because heads of departments then didn't count teaching as actual "work," so it looked as if I wasn't doing anything, even though new courses are a lot of work to organize and teach.

Henry could have stood up for me, both when I was cut out of courses in areas I did know something about, and later, when the head of my department, the partner of Dottie Driver, a colleague who had vowed to destroy me (English departments can be like that) tried to fire me ostensibly for not publishing (though some of my male colleagues had published less). It occurred to me he might want to hire someone of his own choosing to replace me.

Add to the mix one disturbed child who had started withdrawing when I put him in day care at age two and who, at three, became prone to angry, sometimes violent, outbursts, hitting other kids or me or his teachers. By the time he was five, he'd been assessed with autistic elements. He also had huge separation anxiety (another reason why I'd prepare for my courses between two and four in the morning).

And finally, my writing. Since I'd started teaching at Royalton, most of my writing was looping back to me with rejection slips (*like dead babies*, Sylvia Plath said). To be fifty and mostly unpublished was even more depressing than my messed-up job or dealing with Davy's autism. So, after a good beginning in my twenties, and writing in secrecy in my thirties, by my late-forties, I was beginning to feel that the road of my life had been smudged out. Nothing was working out. Maybe a psychic leap of faith would carry me over the gap and land me on a new path.

"I'm Rosetta Kempffer," the blonde angel said with a slight lisp and a Germanic accent.

"I've heard of you!" I was surprised. "You teach at Roy- alton!" She was a friend of a woman I didn't like much and who I thought would be the last person in the world to hang around with psychics.

"Taught," said Rosetta. "I'm retired. Now I'm doing healing work, and I love it."

I was jealous. Imagine loving your work and knowing you were good at it!.

"This is my first psychic fair," Rosetta confided. "Please come see me!"

Then she vanished abruptly into the bright room.

"Well, that was something!" said Claire.

"Yes," I nodded. I was still thinking how unexpected it was that an academic could also be a psychic, and about what it might be like to be doing work that you loved, and doing it well, no doubt. Even to be able to say, *That was when I was working on such and such,* and have it done and then move onto something else, something new and more fulfilling, not teaching classes and having no idea whether they were effective or not, and then starting all over again in September. Sherlock Holmes said, *For me there remains the cocaine bottle,* but at least he had quickly, and brilliantly completed cases. Of course, he had Watson (or Sir Arthur Conan Doyle) to help him. Maybe I needed a Watson.

Claire put her hand gently on my arm, trying to get my at- tention. "I broke up with Sergei last night," she said.

"What, again?"

"I'm pretty sure this time it's final."

"He seems pretty doleful to me."

"He was sweet," Claire said defensively, though she had slipped into past tense. "But I couldn't see that we had any future."

I couldn't understand how Claire, who was a blonde, blue- eyed snowflake beauty, managed to find all these sad-sack men and cast them as leads in her story. They always liked her immediately of course—she was so pretty, so clear, so attentive. The problems came later. Ultimately they didn't measure up to her ex, Raymond, a nice-looking lawyer from a good family. I had met Claire when she was still married, chatelaine of a sprawling old house full of antiques on sloping waterfront land fifty miles outside of town. Claire did volunteer work, baked spectacular muffins, commuted to complete her university degree part-time, and was bringing up her kids. She was happy—happy enough—until she discovered that Raymond was having an affair. She was a good wife; he would have stayed married, as long as he could keep his mistress. Claire didn't go for that, but she grieved; she still had dreams about Raymond, still mourned the loss of her marriage. Now a single mother looking for job, she was taking courses in education. Compared to Claire, I was hard-hearted; I had no regrets about ending my marriage, whatever else I might regret.

"We went for coffee last night, and we had nothing to say to each other," Claire lamented.

"Do you think that's because Sergei's native language is Russian?" But then what had they been talking about for the past two months? Claire would have known the limits of Sergei's English—he was a student in her English as a Second Language night class. Should they even have been dating? Even though they were both adults? And I had taught Claire ten years before—was it appropriate for me to befriend her? What about Brian, who I was still yearning for, and had been my teacher for two weeks at Banff? He had made sure not′ happened between us, but even though I hadn't seen ¹ nearly two years, I could still hear his voice insid╭ *you know you're mine.*

*Yes, but Brian, I'd like to talk to you in re* *see you in real life. Am I just making all ′*

I told people I'd fallen in love wit╲ fallen in love with me. There was r *heart, he's under my skin his voice* and I had spoken on the phone a few days before—for the first time in months—and I could feel his arms around me right now, could see him smiling.

*This guy doesn't have enough money.*

*Dry up, Brian,* I thought now. *Who asked you? Claire isn't like that.*

*Just wait—you'll see I'm right.*

*Go take a hike.*

I shouldn't have said that—he was gone.

Was I just talking to myself? Had we just connected? I wished I knew someone I could ask about telepathy—was it real? Once, when I'd tried to ask Brian about it, he'd just looked or sounded scared.

I turned toward Claire, "How do you feel?"

"Well, I miss him already, but I'm relieved too."

"But it was only last night."

"I know it's over. Have you heard anything more from Brian?"

"Not since we talked." I'd told her about the phone call a few nights ago. Brian didn't call often, and of course there had been nothing since. I didn't want to tell her about his telepathic commentary on her love life.

"I think things will happen very slowly with Brian, if at all." Claire had said this before.

"He's too damaged."

"I couldn't have said it better myself. Look, something's going on!"

A woman in a maroon uniform appeared at the entrance and uncovered a cash register. I could see movement inside the room. Finally, someone took down the barrier. The woman in maroon took our money, and we passed easily from darkness to light.

st of the tables were still empty. Maybe all the psychics en up late at psychic parties or maybe some of them hard to negotiate the cold and snow, and didn't have over from their marriages to get them here. But the enormous table in the centre of the room was laden with hundreds of books shining like jewels with their bright covers. There were books on runes, on the Tarot, on the Kabbalah, on Tibetan wisdom, on Medieval mystics, on Celtic legends, on Egyptian mysteries, on Feng Shui, on shamanism, astrology, aromatherapy, crystals, herbs, and, of course, yoga. It was overwhelming. I felt like Dorothy in *The Wizard of Oz*; at the beginning there are so many roads in front of her that she can't begin to choose which one to follow.

I reached timidly for an astrology book and looked up my sign and then Davy's, searching for the keys to who we both were. But it was confusing. According to my astrological sign, I was neat, orderly, reticent, talkative, explosive—well, people *are* contradictory—but I felt there must be something more, some mystery that wasn't in these books.

I riffled though a book on runes, but somehow having read *The White Goddess* made everything in it seem stale, even though I loved the idea of letters that whispered, letters that both singly and wound together could speak secrets. The secrets of our own alphabet long buried, like country underneath a highway. In runes, sigel/sun is s; beorc/birch tree is b; mann is m. The letters reflect the world they are rooted in—trees, cattle, the sky, water, the weather. Nyd—necessity. Words and letters make my mind spin, but right then I wanted to find something less rational. I knew that somewhere here was the perfect book, but I couldn't navigate the jumble on the table to find it.

Claire was on the other side of the table, and I joined her. "Did you find anything?"

"I'm thinking about this one," she held up a book on feng shui. The very idea made me shudder. Virgos are supposed to be orderly, but I was incorrigibly messy. Every time I invited someone over, I had a cleaning crisis. I admired that Claire's house was always tidy, and I enjoyed being in it. The colours were dark and peaceful, and Claire shone in her living room like a golden-haired star.

I also admired that Claire found it easy to have people over. Claire had *friends*.

I mostly stopped having friends when I came to Royalton. I had a job, I had a lover, then a marriage, then a son—but I hadn't made many friends since I'd started teaching. There'd been no time to nurture new friendships.

"But your house is already lovely."

"I could make it more harmonious," Claire said thoughtfully. "And you can arrange your house to encourage things to happen—I know of a woman who put pictures of lovers all over her bedroom, and it was great for her romantic life. And a friend of mine rearranged her kitchen to favour prosperity, and she got a good job. I think I'll buy this book and see if it works. And look, I see people starting to line up for readings. Should we each go to someone and meet here after?"

What would encourage Brian? I wondered. He'd probably never even see my house, and I'd probably never see his.

Claire went off to make the book on feng shui hers, and I started to wander around the room, even more overwhelmed by the choice of psychics than by the choice of books. At forty dollars for a reading, they all seemed expensive.

I found Rosetta Kempffer at the back of the room. "How about an African bone throw?" she suggested. "Three questions for fifteen dollars."

My imminent mortgage payment was always peering over my shoulder, but I could afford fifteen dollars.

"Okay." I sat down at her table and eyed the collection of tiny bones, stones, and feathers in front of her. It didn't look very promising. There was also a large green binder in one corner of the table, and a pair of brass rods with white handles across the top. I decided to trust Rosetta. She gathered up the collection of bones, stones, and feathers.

"What's your first question?"

I took a breath. "I want to know about my writing." My voice cracked.I'd wanted *to write* since I was nine. Forty years later, I'd had a few things published in journals, but I hadn't yet published a book. Why was I even *asking?*

Rosetta nodded, as if the question were perfectly natural, and shook the bones.

Then she motioned to me, and I cupped my hands and took the bones from her. They felt light and fragile as I shook them, like the spirit of a baby bird.

*Oh, please, don't let me do it wrong,* I thought as I let them scatter on the table.

I like languages; I like translation, but I couldn't make heads or tails of the pattern I had scattered. The bones weren't quite parallel; one red stone was near them, while one was further away. I waited for a breath that seemed like forever.

"You're close," said Rosetta. "You just need to quit your job. Then the bones will fall straight, and then you'll do it."

"I couldn't do that," I said. "I'd be begging on the streets."

"There are ways," Rosetta said, but I couldn't imagine a single one. At the same time, something inside me seemed to spread its wings at the very thought of quitting. I breathed air I hadn't tasted for years.

"You don't have to quit this minute," said Rosetta. "But keep it in mind."

I knew I couldn't afford to quit; I was supporting a son and three lovely, black, unworried cats, who, even if I set them out on the streets with a hat, wouldn't bring in much money. Mice maybe. Henry said he would only pay child support if forced to by law. Even so, I had a fleeting vision of blue sky stretching above me.

Rosetta gathered the bones. "Your second question?" she asked as she began to shake them.

"I'd like to know about my son." *Should I say anything about the autism?* I decided not to.

"Hold him in your head," Rosetta instructed as she emptied the bones, stones, and feathers into my hands. I shut my eyes and thought of Davy, cute as a button, even at the awkward age of fifteen—silky brown hair, deep brown eyes, generous mouth. But he still "spoke funny," sort of mechanically, and he repeated things he said (the Thearaputic Nursery School had called it "perseverating"); he twitched sometimes the way special kids do; he didn't have friends, didn't play any sports, didn't have a part-time job. When other mothers bragged about their kids, I felt left out. But Davy had managed to get to ninth grade. He was passing his first term courses and had managed without a teaching assistant. He was in Grade 6 piano and would be in the Kiwanis Festival and do his exam in the spring. He had learned to go to the piano, adjust the seat, play, bow, and leave, which he couldn't a few years before. I wasn't holding Davy's accomplishments or lack of them in my head, though—I was holding his energy, bright as a candle flame.

I threw the bones, holding my breath. Once again, I couldn't tell anything from the scatter they'd settled in.

Rosetta pored over them.

"He's been affected by your separation," she said.

That must be true, although we'd talked about it. Davy seemed to understand it, and he hadn't regressed as he had in other stressful situations.

"His father's been very absent," Rosetta continued.

*Tell me about it*, I thought. Henry hadn't even taught Davy how to throw a ball.

"Your son will start seeing more of his father, and there will be things you don't like, but just bite your tongue. It will all turn out in the end."

No tragedies or failed grades, anyway, nothing to indicate that Davy's life was off the map.

"It'll be fine," said Rosetta. "Now, your third question?"

"Love?" I asked tentatively. This was ridiculous. I was much too old for anything to happen. I wasn't interested in anyone but Brian, who was unattainable, who I scarcely knew, and hadn't seen for nearly two years. Still, he'd sent me a Christmas card; and when he called, he'd said this year we'd have a chance to meet. If it weren't for the telepathic moments (which I surely imagined!) and the heart connection (which he might not feel at all), I would have forgotten him.

Rosetta didn't act surprised or judgmental. She just shook the bones and handed them to me to shake and throw.

*Sort of a pretty starburst*, I thought, but one bone was directly across the other, and Rosetta giggled.

"Is it that bad?" I asked.

"Hold him in your head," she said, with the steadiness of someone confronting a crisis. She took off her necklace with the smooth clear crystal, held it by the chain, and swung it gently a few times in front of me.

It was easy to hold Brian in my head. He was there so much anyway. I'd looked into his eyes; I'd felt his arms around me—he'd been teaching us individually and in groups, and he was big on hugs. He had a very fluid walk—he'd been trained in movement as an actor. But what did I know about him really? No wonder the bones were crossed.

Rosetta put her necklace beside her and said, "He's strong. He's as strong as you. That's why you like him.

"He's got a military walk," she continued, "but he's not military."

*An actor's walk,* I thought.

"He's got children, but you don't need to worry about them."

Well, yes, he did. They were in their twenties, and he wasn't close to them. He'd had to fish around for his son's age, *a bad sign*, I thought. Would I ever have to think for a minute about Davy's age? Even if by some miracle Davy became independent?

"He's very sensitive," Rosetta said, "very emotional. You have to be careful of him."

*Oh, fine,* I thought. *Doesn't he have to be careful of me? Whose side are you on?*

Rosetta picked up her necklace and began swinging it again.

"Physically, he's a ten; you're about a four." *Encourage me more.*

"Emotionally he's about an eight. Mentally, you're a ten; he's about a seven."

*My tiresome, good mind; my only strong point. Who cares about minds in romance anyway?*

"I don't get it," said Rosetta. "You should be well-matched. If you ever worked together, you'd be unstoppable. I think it's a destined relationship. I don't see what the block is."

She took her rods from the cover of her binder, muttering, "Tunnel, heart, trust, light, recognition of perfection, gate to oneness—the block's at the gate."

"Excuse me?"

But she was continuing. "Mm, accessibility, allowing, positioning, programming, transportation—"

For someone with a supposedly good mind, I was totally lost.

"It's about rights," she said. "But you're very close to being in the Oneness together. Do you have any questions?"

I gulped. My four-letter question had led to this roundabout baffling answer, which, in spite of Rosetta's best efforts, didn't sound exactly like a confident yes.

"Will I see him again?"

"Oh yes, you'll see him again."

She held her rods till they swung. "In April."

April wasn't so far away—I could wait. Or maybe Rosetta was picking up on our meeting in April two years ago. Or it might be April five years from now? I didn't ask. I felt as though I'd been on a trip and that I wasn't quite the same person who had sat down at her table fifteen or twenty minutes before.

"Thanks very much." I pulled out my wallet to pay for the reading.

"Wait," said Rosetta. "I do lots of other things too—I do healing. Here, take my card. Call if you need anything. I don't think you and I have completed yet."

Even though I had no intention of calling her, I took her card and nodded.

I thanked her again, and made my way through the suddenly much more crowded and noisy room to look for Claire. I craned my neck, searching. I didn't find Claire but recognized someone else I knew—my hairdresser. "Talitha!" I called out.

"Judith!"

"I didn't know you were into this sort of thing."

"Oh yes, it's my passion. What about you?"

"This is my first psychic fair," I admitted. "But I just had a great African bone bone-throw reading by someone named Rosetta Kempffer."

"Really? Where is she?"

"All the way in the back of the room," I pointed.

"Is she expensive?"

"Fifteen dollars," I replied, with the pride of discovery.

"That's very interesting. Thanks, Judith. I'll see you later."

Talitha had been cutting my hair since before Davy was born, and I never knew she was as interested in all this as I was.

I cut across the swirl, back toward the book table, and there, waiting for me, was the book I was going to buy: *Initiation* by Elisabeth Haich (who I'd never heard of). I liked the idea of initiation, and, browsing through a few pages, I warmed to the narrator's voice. I grabbed it and was heading toward the cash when suddenly I ran into Claire, cool and collected, considering books on Celtic myth.

"Guess who I saw? Talitha!"

Claire had also run into Talitha (who cut her hair too) as well as a few other acquaintances—but then Claire was more social than I was, better connected.

"Did you have a reading?" I asked.

"Yes," said Claire. "It was okay. Let's go have coffee, and I'll tell you about it. Did you?"

"Yes, with Rosetta. She's *really* good. You should go to her."

"Let's have coffee first."

I suddenly realized I was dying for a coffee. In spite of my reading with Rosetta, which had given me reassurance that my paths weren't totally hopeless, in spite of finding what I was sure was the right book, I felt limp without that first jolt of caffeine. I waved my book. "I have to buy this first so I don't get arrested for shoplifting."

We made our way to the cash at the entrance. There was a short wait to pay—other people had found books too. Then we went back through the dark hall, up the stairs, snaked around corridors, and found the coffee shop. It was just an ordinary coffee shop with plastic tables and moulded seats that you had to fit yourself into, but we were lucky to get them because it was crowded, and a line was forming behind us. Now I was glad we'd arrived early.

"So tell me about your reading."

Claire smiled a little. "He said I would meet someone!"

"Well, that's no surprise!"

Claire had everything going for her—she was beautiful and clear-minded. She could make any man happy—share trips, concerts, art galleries, books and music, talk about important things—the wonder was that she hadn't met anyone yet except for all those sad sacks.

"I know it's important to be a strong woman, but I'd really like to be in a relationship again. Wouldn't you, Judith?"

"I don't know," I said. "I haven't really been attracted to anyone except Brian, and he hardly knows I'm alive. And Davy still needs a lot of bringing up. And I'd like to have my name on a book. In some ways, I'm not out of the marriage I was in—Henry's still not speaking to me, we're still dickering over the value of the house through our lawyers."

"I thought you'd resolved that."

"Not yet, but we're close. At least Henry isn't asking for sole custody of Davy anymore."

"Why did he want custody? It's not as if he's ever spent much time with Davy. It's like Raymond—he's never spent much time with Megan and Scott, but he never asked for *custody*—"

"If he had custody, I'd have to pay child support." Claire knew my post-marriage grievances against Henry, how upsetting I found it that Davy had to bring his own pasta when he went to his father's for dinner, his own duvet when he stayed overnight. Why had I married this man? But he'd been different twenty-five years before, when we'd been lovers. He'd gotten more selfish after we married. In separation, he became money-obsessed. He'd said, "Love's gone; all that's left is money." I'd been shell-shocked for two years. I felt like an octopus clinging to the sandy ocean bottom so I wouldn't be pulled up and consumed.

"Where do you think our coffee is?" asked Claire.

We'd been talking long enough that it should have come, but one overworked waitress seemed to be waiting on everyone at the same time. I motioned to her, and she gave a harried look but didn't veer from her course.

"She must be run off her feet," I said. "I bet this place isn't usually so crowded."

"But she could just bring us a couple coffees," Claire said reasonably.

I looked around, saw the coffee on the hot plate, the cups stacked next to it. I got up and went over to the station, took two cups, poured the coffee, and found little containers of milk for Claire.

"How could you just *do* that?" Claire asked.

"Some things aren't worth waiting for."

The coffee certainly wasn't. It was thin and watery, like ground up sawdust dissolved in boiling water. It was hot, at least.

"I think you should see Rosetta," I said, as Claire added her tiny container of probably artificial milk to the coffee.

She considered my words as she drank her coffee. I thought she might be trying not to wince. "Would you sit with me during my reading?"

"I'd love to. Do you want to go now?"

"Don't you want to finish your coffee?" My cup was still nearly full.

"I've insulted my insides enough."

We left money on the table—there was no point enduring another wait for our bill—unwound ourselves from the plastic and threaded our way out the door. The hall and the stairway down to darkness seemed spacious and liberating after the closeness of the coffee shop.

I led Claire through the crowds to Rosetta's table. Unfortunately, there were now seven people ahead of us. It looked as if today was Claire's trial by waiting (which she hated) just as it was mine by absence of coffee. She hesitated, then put her name down on the list.

We sat at chairs within sight of Rosetta's table, and Claire filled me in on all the gossip—what stores were opening and closing, who was buying and selling houses, what marriages were ending, who had gone on dates with whom.

"I was surprised to see Talitha here," I said.

"Oh, she's very interested in all this. She's been to see a psychic in Ompah who sounds very insightful. I'd go myself if it weren't so remote."

"Maybe we could go together sometime."

"And she's done past life therapy."

'Wow, who was she in past lives?"

"Lots of people—men, women. She and Rafe were together in a lot of them. Sometimes one of them killed the other. A few of her past selves drowned. That's why she's afraid of water."

How did Claire know all this? When Talitha cut my hair, I mostly sat silent. One of the things I really liked about her was that she didn't make me feel bad for not having anything to say. At the end, she always said, "Better?" and I always said, "Much better, thank you!" and I'd pay and take my gorgeous hair out for coffee or lunch. But Claire knew how to ask the right questions, how to draw people out.

Rosetta's table was suddenly empty. She stood up and beckoned us. "My client didn't show, and the others aren't around. Do you want your bone throw now?"

"I'd like that." Claire got up, graceful, unhurried. We crossed the few paces to Rosetta's table.

"What a beautiful day," Rosetta said as we were about to sit down. "I'd rather be skiing, but my guides told me I should be here, that there were people I needed to meet."

My jaw dropped, and I have to admit I felt envious. Guides! Speaking to you! I wondered who the people were that Rosetta needed to meet. Talitha, probably. Maybe Claire.

"So what's your first question?" asked Rosetta.

"I want to know about my career." Claire sounded young and uncertain. I was surprised.

"What do you *want* to do?" Rosetta was careful and professional.

"I don't know. I want to help people."

"You could take my course and become a healer." Rosetta betrayed her own interest just slightly.

"I don't know," said Claire. I loved Claire, but I could shake her for being so vague. Needless to say, the bones didn't offer much further guidance about her career.

But the bones were positive about her kids. They were both fine and I couldn't help feeling a little wistful since Davy so obviously wasn't. Claire's son in particular was also feeling his father's absence and needed Claire to be both father and mother, and to bring new male influences into his life.

Claire nodded. "Yes, that's true."

"And your third question?"

"Will I find another relationship?"

"Yes."

"When?"

Rosetta swung her brass rods. "In two months."

I was amazed. That was so *soon*.

"That's so *long*," sighed Claire. "Do I have to wait that long?"

"For a relationship of the *quality* you want—" Rosetta lingered on the *l* of quality.

Claire dimpled. "Is it someone I know?"

"No, but you probably know some of the same people."

"So he lives in Prince's Harbour?"

"Yes."

"What does he do?"

"He's a professional man. He'll appreciate you."

Claire tried to tease out more, but even psychics have their limits.

She tried one last time. "And I don't know him?"

"You'll know him when you meet him."

"Thank you very much." Claire rose to go, and it was good timing because someone else was waiting—in fact the line had formed all over again while we'd been at Rosetta's table.

"Goodbye," said Rosetta. "Good luck. If you decide you want to learn about healing, here's my card."

As we emerged into the sunlight, I noticed that the day wasn't as frigid and brittle as it had seemed earlier. The top edges of the drifts had melted in the sunlight. Claire was wondering about the man she was going to meet, and I was thinking about Brian.

But then I was home, unlocking my front door, back in my everyday life.

## 2. DAVY

DAVY WAS SITTING in my late father's Harvard chair, which was pulled up right next to the fireplace in the living room. Even at fifteen, he didn't much like being alone, but he could manage in the living room with a fire leaping and breathing, and the cats asleep on the couch or on the rug. He probably hadn't stirred from the chair since he'd gotten up, except to put wood on the fire.

"Hi," I said weakly.

"Hi, how are you?" Davy's speaking was better, but still a little mechanical.

"I'm sorry I'm so late," I said. "Claire was waiting to see someone and there was a line."

"Okay."

"How were things here?"

"Fine." But there was an edge of anxiety in his voice, as if he might erupt into anger or retreat into loops any minute. I'd been gone too long; he'd been worried.

"Are you enjoying the fire?"

"Yes."

"The cats?"

"Yes."

"Would you like me to make you a sandwich?"

"Yes." His tone was a little firmer at this.

I hurried into the kitchen to make Davy's usual lunch, a smoked turkey breast sandwich on brown bread with lettuce and green onions. In summer, I'd throw in arugula or chives or oregano or thyme from the garden, but in January, there were just a few feeble rosemary leaves from a plant that wasn't wintering well.

"Do you want to eat in front of the fire?" I called.

"Yes."

The fireplace was one of the best things about our house—it was large, with a generous hearth, and as long as the chimney was cleaned every year and heated before each fire was lit, it drew well, and it was safe to leave a fire burning for a long time. I threw a couple more logs on the fire, left Davy with his sandwich, and made my long-awaited coffee, hot and strong.

With coffee in hand, a purring black cat next to me on the couch, and with Davy calming, I felt relieved. Still confined— *oh, when would I be able to go out the door without it being a big deal?*—but relieved.

WHEN DAVY WAS TEN MONTHS OLD, we took the boat to England. Davy was a cute baby, and lots of people spoke to us. One woman said that she had never left her daughter until her daughter went to school. I was horrified, and it made me suspect that I didn't know anything about mothering. I still needed to get out of the house, needed to have adult time, hadn't yet surrendered to motherhood. And the rest was even more horrifying—her perfect daughter had died at sixteen.

What was the message? That she had cared for her daughter with every ounce she had during her daughter's short life? That the care had been a dead end? Davy was not even a year old, and I'd already left him a lot. I was working full-time (Royalton didn't have maternity leave then), so I left him with Henry or a sitter every time I had to teach a class. Henry and I were still playing tennis, going to movies and concerts, eating out. Davy had been fine with babysitters. Maybe if I'd been more attentive and hadn't left so often, he wouldn't have regressed between the ages of two and three. Maybe if I'd taken another year off and hadn't put him in daycare, which he'd hated, he wouldn't have become suspicious of most foods (except for nuts, seed, chickpeas, fruit he could pick himself, and Five-Alive), given up books, started hitting other kids or screaming at them, and maybe wouldn't have vanished behind what Barry Neil Kaufman, an expert on autism, calls an "invisible wall" in his classic book *Son Rise*. I didn't see it at home right away. But Davy was repeating things. And he completely mixed up pronouns, a marker of autism. When he asked for something, he said, "d'you want some?" as if *I* were the one asking *him*.

Now, a little calmed down as he ate his sandwich and drank his mug of warmed cider, he asked, "Why was Mummy so late?"

"I'm sorry, Davy. Claire miscalculated right and left. First we went for coffee, and that took forever; then we were waiting for this psychic, and that took forever too. We should have gone to the psychic first, and then left and had coffee downtown. I had a good time, but I was pretty dragged out by the time we left." I didn't tell him I enjoyed being out, and that it was nice being with Claire, even though we'd spent a lot of our time simply waiting.

"Do you want to put another log on the fire?" I asked.

"Yes." Davy loved fires, was good at making them, good at warming the chimney, good at tending them. Some of his early pictures, when he was about six, were of fires in the fireplace. Now he took photos of the fire blazing. I loved the fires too, and so did the cats.

Davy carried in an armful of logs from the porch, deposited them next to the fireplace, and then tossed one in so that the sparks flew upward. The coals were hot; the log caught right away.

After lunch I asked, "Do you want to practice?"

"*Yes.*" I loved that about Davy—he always liked to practice piano. I never had to ask him twice. He sat down at the piano at the far end of the living room and began with Bach.

Davy had started piano late, at ten. He hadn't been able to

sit still and concentrate well enough to have lessons before. Claire had given me the name of her daughter's teacher, who was kind, patient, unflappable. She got him playing "Twinkle Twinkle Little Star" and its variations, and then later songs like "Love Somebody," simple, warm, and catchy. The teacher had recitals in her home on a country road north of Prince's Harbour. I worried through the first several that Davy wouldn't sit still through the whole recital, that he would talk when other kids were playing. And he did strain to get up, and he didn't quite know how to bow, but the teacher took it all in stride, and Davy learned. The only really bad time was when he wanted to take pictures of the other kids playing, which would have made some of them even more nervous, and we both had to spend a lot of time explaining why he couldn't do it.

Davy was never nervous about performing. He liked it. Mistakes didn't flap him—but he also practised enough that he usually rose to the occasion when he performed. Even at his first recital, playing pre-Grade 1 pieces and a duet with the teacher, he played well—better, I thought, than Claire's daughter, Megan, who was three piano grades ahead of him. So even though I worried about his behaviour, I never had to worry about his playing. And while Davy lurched from year to year in school, his piano had always proceeded smoothly through the Royal Conservatory syllabus. He was behind most kids his age, but acquitting himself respectably in Grade 6. He hated reading books, but he read music fine—worked it out hand by hand, stumbled hesitantly, then got it to soar off the page.

I put my feet up on the coffee table and settled back to listen. "Don't just play with your hands, Davy—remember what that judge last year said, sing the notes to yourself as you play. Try it again."

Davy always tried it again, and it always improved, and I told him so.

Reading was something else. He hated it. It was my fault. I'd read to him starting when he was ten months. He'd been picky, hadn't liked anything sentimental, but loved being read to between the ages of ten months and two years old, when we were all in England on Henry's sabbatical. He'd known when to turn the page; he'd point at anything I asked him about, and sometimes he'd point to things so I'd read them again and talk about them. We had a big book of nursery rhymes with great pictures, and I read it so often that it wore out and I had to buy another. He especially loved *The Patchwork Cat*, a story about Tabby, who had a patchwork quilt she loved and always slept on. The mother of the house threw it out. Tabby found it in the dustbin, crawled inside, and went to sleep, only to be swept up with the rest of the garbage and taken to the dump. She was scared being in the dump at night when it was cold and dark, but in the morning, when the dump gates opened, she dragged her quilt to the gates and escaped. Then she pulled the quilt along the streets until the family milkman saw her and gave her a ride home. The family was relieved to see her! And the mother washed and dried the patchwork quilt, and when Tabby went to sleep on it, everything was restored. It was a story of loyalty, but also a story of, *be careful what you throw away!*

When Davy was just over two, we came back to Prince's Harbour with not much time to spare before classes. I couldn't find a sitter, and I'd had to put Davy in daycare. He was okay at first, but then he hated it so much he got mad at me. He stopped singing (he'd been singing in tune before he was two— no words though), became afraid of playgrounds and other kids, and, especially sad, he gave up reading. I was the one he associated with books, and I was the one who had put him in daycare. By the age of three, he was withdrawn.

I tried to talk to Henry. "Davy seems unhappy. I don't know what to do."

"Davy is fine," said Henry. "You're worrying too much. Let's have dinner, and then I have to set my essay topics for tomorrow." Maybe my marriage began to end right there.

One day in the summer, on the way home from the daycare when Davy was starting to talk and I wasn't quite so exhausted, I asked him, "Do you like daycare?"

"Daycare," he echoed.

"Daycare yes, or daycare no?"

"Daycare yes," he said.

"Oh, I thought you didn't like it. Do you want to stop? You don't have to go."

"Daycare," said Davy.

I was sure he didn't like it, but that sounded like yes. Did he know what he was saying?

I decided to cut back on daycare in the fall to six hours a day, three days a week. But it didn't do any good. By the following May, Davy was a wreck, screaming at everything, unwilling to try new things, including foods. His development had stalled, even regressed. People were thinking autism. No one said it, but I knew they were thinking it. He was resistant to books; he wasn't eating much; he refused toileting; and he screamed if I tried to leave the house. The Child Development Centre, who had been assessing him for months, thought he had serious problems, but they weren't saying what.

So it really was my fault, or at least that's how I felt, and it was up to me to get Davy out of it. I addressed his lacks one by one. I started by getting him to brush his teeth. Then travelling with him. Visiting playgrounds. Science museums, if we hit a town that had one. Childrens' concerts. Bit by bit, Davy opened to the world.

I thought, *Where are all those wonderful people who are supposed to emerge when there's a crisis?*

I did meet a friend crossing City Park and cried on her shoulder. She recommended the nursery school her son had gone to a few years before.

Well, it was a start, and I called the teacher. She thought maybe Davy could manage the class for two-year-olds, but he didn't do well there. He was the least competent kid in the group—worse than simply not competent though, because he screamed and hit other kids and wouldn't do much of anything.

"He likes cleaning," the teacher said pityingly.

"He doesn't get it from my side of the family," I assured her. He liked crayons, finger paints, too, but his squiggles and pictures had been better, whatever better was, two years before. When he wasn't having a tantrum, he liked music.

I did eventually meet other mothers and started to arrange play dates. Davy didn't socialize, but he came to enjoy those afternoons. He started liking playgrounds again, although he wasn't interested in the other kids the way he had been in England.

Gradually, I started reading him simple books again. He still liked *The Patchwork Cat*. He still liked nursery rhymes. He liked *When We Were Very Young* and *Now We Are Six*. By the time he started kindergarten, at six, there were about a dozen books he liked, and he wanted all of them read to him every night. Sometimes we both fell asleep during the process. Sometimes Davy would wake up and insist I finish the rest.

He wasn't especially slow to read in first grade. He liked the book about the foolish beaver who built a house with too many windows—Davy was always interested in houses. But in second grade, he had a teacher who emphasized reading. She'd been a gym teacher, and she was trying to prove that she was rigorous in the classroom. And she was mean. Davy went off reading all over again. This time I recognized the signs. Even though Davy agreeably said that this woman was his favourite teacher, I didn't believe him, and pulled him out of her class in November. Still, the damage was done. Davy was once again resistant to books. He retreated, and, when he was in school, you couldn't tell that he had a brain in his head. Luckily, by this time, he had a teaching assistant who'd been with him for two years and knew him, and he had former teachers who knew he could do better.

Autism is a learning disability. Learning had to be part of an antidote. Skating, swimming, pottery. Davy liked all of them.

In third grade, in a different school, Davy made a friend, Gillian. Gillian had a whole circle of friends, so Davy had kids to eat lunch with and be on the playground with, and he even got asked to parties. By fourth grade, he was better behaved, but the reading got much harder—it was chapter books. By spring, Davy and I read before school, after school, and after dinner, but we were still behind. Gillian, unfortunately, had transferred to another school, so Davy didn't have help from her or the daily boost of her friendship. Davy got his last book report in on the last day of school—not the last day of classes, the very last day when the teachers were in school, but the kids were not. But in grade school, effort counts for a lot, and he passed.

Davy did like to write. But he didn't like to write about books he read. He always had trouble synthesizing (another symptom of autism), but was good on detail (maybe still another symptom).

In daycare, and in nursery school, Davy's teachers had suggested I put him in a special school either in Prince's Harbour or Ottawa. "If he were my child," said one of the teachers in the therapeutic nursery school, "I'd want to give him every chance." Henry thought this was a great idea, since it would give us both time to work, but Tabby hadn't given up on her patchwork quilt, and I wasn't giving up on Davy. And even though school had often been rocky, and I'd held my breath, Davy had passed every year and was almost through the first term of ninth grade. His piano progress was smooth. He'd sold photographs.

Davy hadn't had another real friend after Gillian. He socialized some with adults, but he was still awkward or silent with kids his own age.

In his last elementary school, he hadn't learned anyone's name. In ninth grade he still wasn't returning hellos—and when he did talk, he sounded jerky, as if English wasn't his native language. But he'd come a long way since daycare. He'd had great teachers.

This term Davy had taken Science, Math, Art History, and French, all things he could learn by memorizing. He wasn't losing his temper, even without a teaching assistant, and he was passing everything. When we'd gone to Toronto, he could tell me which members of the Group of Seven had painted what—he'd had a good teacher!

It was probably a terrible idea to ruin a perfectly good afternoon with unnecessary reading, but I thought maybe it would be a good idea to get a jump on it before Davy started exams for his first term courses.

I pulled *Julius Caesar* from a shelf—I knew that would be the hardest thing he read—I hadn't gotten into it myself in high school—and I didn't see how Davy was going to get into it either.

We put another log on the fire and sat on the couch, *Julius Caesar* between us.

"Julius Caesar was Roman," I said hopefully. "He spoke Latin." Davy had worked his way through Latin grammar two years ago. When I'd been at Banff, we'd talk on the phone about past perfects and imperfects and subjunctives.

"Interesting," said Davy politely, drawing the word out to gain another couple seconds.

I skimmed quickly. "Let's skip the first scene. It's confusing."

"*Yes*." Davy would have been happy to skip the whole play.

"Let's start where Caesar appears."

"Okay."

It took fifteen minutes to get from the beginning of the scene to the soothsayer's "Beware the Ides of March." No wonder Davy was having trouble synthesizing. He read Shakespeare like an ant, carrying one word-crumb at a time. At least he was mostly reading the words correctly and not leaving out the middles so that it would go faster.

"What's a soothsayer?"

"Sooth means truth. A soothsayer is someone who speaks the truth."

"Can't you speak the truth if you're not a soothsayer?"

"Soothsayers predict. They're like psychics, like the ones I went to see with Claire. This one's sort of ragged, though, I think. Like a street person. Sometimes when you're busy pulling things out of the air, you neglect things of this world, like clothes and haircuts." I thought, *Maybe once you start living for something beyond the pragmatic, you've jumped into a different value scale.* If you're looking for the perfect poem, you may not find the pot of gold at the end of the rainbow. Then again, you may not find the perfect poem, either, but at least you'll have died in its service. The medievals knew that the essence of a person was who or what they served, and even Alexander Pope, so many centuries later, living with the last bits of the medieval structures of thought and belief, said "I have loved the brightest eyes." I thought, *Yes, I have too, Brian's and Davy's. In different ways.* That was enough for Pope, and it would have to be enough for me.

"Soothsayer," Davy read dutifully. "Beware the Ides of March. What are the Ides of March?"

"It's a Roman way of marking the month—it's March 15."

"Why don't they just say so?"

"Shakespeare's trying to make it sound Roman. But Caesar doesn't believe him."

"Why doesn't Caesar believe him?"

*Well,* I thought, *the whole problem of believing psychics!* But I didn't want to get into that, so I settled for classism, which I knew was a copout. "If a raggedy street person came up to you and said, *Be careful on March 15,* would you believe them?"

"No...."

"The whole first part of the play is full of omens, and Caesar doesn't pay attention to a single one."

It was a long scene. I'd forgotten how talky *Julius Caesar* could be. It wasn't very predictive of Davy doing well in ninth grade English, whatever else it might be.

"Okay," I said after an hour of glacially slow reading. "That's enough for now. You need some hangout time and so do I." Shakespeare probably could have written three plays in the time it was going to take Davy to read this one.

"Yes." Davy leapt off the couch and started hopping around the room. He hadn't hopped when he was young, but he did now.

I felt chilled and worried all over again. If Davy couldn't get through English, he might not be able to stay in high school. I didn't want Davy in one of those classes of special kids who just looked as if they were killing time. I wanted him to have a life.

There were people who thought he'd be okay. Brian, who'd never met him, did; so did a family friend who had raised a difficult grandson and worked with children at the Bank Street School. A man on a plane on the way to Banff two years ago had been encouraging. And now Rosetta. Psychics thought he'd be okay. Well, that might be enough to make me a follower of psychics. I certainly would rather be in the soothsayer's corner, rags and all, than Caesar's.

As Davy twitched and hopped, he did look as if he might be at home in one of those special classes. I was never far from worry about Davy, and I started to worry all over again. But then I told myself there was nothing more I could do at this minute. I pulled out my own books and started making notes for Monday's classes.

# 3. I AM THE ICE WOMAN

WHEN I'D BEEN IN CRISIS BEFORE, I'd always been able to work my way through it. F. Scott Fitzgerald said, "It is in the thirties that we want friends. In the forties, we know they won't save us any more than love did." From the outside, he might not have looked as if he were in crisis—he was, after all, one of the great writers—but his wife was in an asylum, he was scraping by as a screenwriter, and he was constantly worried about money. He had had everything and lost most of it—only his daughter, Scottie, at Vassar, was turning out well; he did find a second love; and his writing, though not well-paid, was incorrigibly eternal

I'd never had Fitzgerald's brilliance or his heroic romanticism, but it probably looked from the outside as though I were managing fine too. I had a secure job (no matter that I'd almost lost it). I hadn't had to worry about money, but that was probably coming to an end. People survive marriages coming apart—Fitzgerald did—but there's still the sorrow of the great love of your life fraying, not being enough to carry you through middle age. It's not the end of the marriage—it's the getting there. At any rate, the things I'd thought would support me, my marriage and my job, seemed to have dissolved out from under me.

I still believed in teaching, but I'd never been an orthodox teacher, and I was afraid I was dreadful at it. At the same time, teaching means you're responsible for your students' inner life and growth, and I couldn't change simply to be like everyone else. I couldn't say to my colleagues, *I went into this because I thought literature was the most wonderful thing in the world and I wanted to help students see that.* It was like when I'd started teaching and was thinking about the difference between poetry and prose, and had ventured to say a few things about that to a colleague. *Oh, no one thinks about things like that,* she'd said with complete disinterest (though I know people do now). Teaching is an obscure job, but I felt the weight of its responsibility even more than when I'd started, and I had even more worries now that I wasn't making the books alive enough for my students. I tried to be careful of their inner lives, though. My students might complain that I assigned too much reading or that my classes weren't organized, but I could see in their essays that they were finding their own voices and own thoughts in the course of a year, and many of them would tell me that they'd really loved a particular book. You can't always tell what you might have accomplished with teaching. If your students are still reading in ten years, you've done it. If they're still clear-eyed and clear-voiced, you've done it. Of course, it might not be *your* teaching. But at least you haven't gotten in the way. And then you start again the next year with the next group. It's a privilege, but it's also a push.

I KNEW THAT LIFE OFTEN BROUGHT YOU to places you didn't expect. I didn't expect my late forties to be such a slog, a seemingly never-ending process of putting one foot in front of another without having much to show for it. I hadn't expected to be watching my son through one-way glass in a therapeutic nursery school so resistant to learning that it all seemed almost hopeless. I could tell from Davy's eyes that even though these teachers were supposedly experts with special kids, Davy wasn't being well-taught. I hadn't expected to be married to a man who woke me up in the middle of the night to ask, furiously, to sort through all the mail on the hall buffet—it was a mess. The house was a mess. "Let's clean it up together," I suggested groggily, since some of the mess was his. But I had to paw through unsorted mail, only seeing what I'd done later when some bills and bank statements were gone, I must have thrown them away in my near sleep. And why did Henry have to wake me up to sort through the mail, sort through old keys? I had never expected such bad temper, especially in the middle of the night when I was sleep-deprived anyway. And I hadn't expected bad temper to the point of abuse. Even now that we were almost legally separated, Henry was still lying in wait for me on street corners and bursting into fury with me. Sometimes I yelled back. Sometimes I went numb. I wondered if inside I were turning to ice. But I couldn't stop to deal with it. Davy had to be brought up day by day; my students had to be taught day by day; even the cats had to be fed and cared for (even though they gave it all back in purrs). I could manage the daily work, but I was still numb and couldn't see beyond it.

I realized then that the numbness I felt had also been there in my late teens when my mother was yelling at me, but I hadn't recognized it until I was travelling in Europe, communing with cathedrals and great art, discovering that men found me attractive. I was on a boat tour of Lake Como when I'd felt my frozen heart begin to melt. I hadn't known that it needed to. But this, now, was worse. I was more stuck. I had more obligations. My mother had died, and I hadn't completed with her. We'd had a few moments of resolution, peaceful conversation that reminded me of my long ago caring mother who made up stories when she put me to bed. After she'd died, I learned that she'd had a brain tumour for twenty years, but I was still processing the difficulties between us. In her afterlife, she was still a critical presence. And there was nothing I could do about Henry's anger, which I was pretty sure had nothing to do with a brain tumour.

This was where I was when I met Brian—numb, blocked, stalled, though still working at mothering, at teaching, at writing, with only minimal results, and with the conviction that nothing would ever change.

# 4. BRIAN

W HEN I WAS NOT QUITE FORTY-NINE, Henry and Davy, who was then thirteen, drove me to the Prince's Harbour airport late Easter morning to get a plane to Toronto, another plane to Calgary, and a taxi to Banff. By some miracle, I'd been accepted into a six-week writing program, and, by another miracle, Henry didn't say I couldn't go. It was a miracle because it was a program for writers, published writers, and I had barely published anything. It was also a miracle because Henry was hardly letting me out of the house in those days. I could go to classes, but he'd come home five minutes before they started and then I'd arrive at the university late and unsettled. Henry didn't think anything but work was a good use of my time, and he got angry if I left him with Davy for anything other than work, so I'd started lying about going for coffee with friends, saying I was going to the library. I'd meet Claire Saturday mornings in the midst of shopping, when half an hour more or less wouldn't show. If I went out for what might be perceived as something fun, Henry would lose his temper with Davy, I suspected, because Davy would be a wreck when I got home. Davy wasn't speaking enough to say what had happened, but his change of mood told me a lot. I hoped he would be all right for six weeks. I'd hired babysitters to be with him at home several hours a day every day, and he'd also be in school. I also promised him—and myself—that I'd call a lot.

So there I was on the tiny plane that flew between Prince's Harbour and Toronto, bouncing as the air currents chopped around us. I took in the great expanse of the lake before we climbed above the clouds. I managed to read some poetry, but mostly I was gripping my armrests, especially when we bounced so much my head hit the ceiling (it was a very small plane).

*That's what I get for wanting to leave*, I thought, and hoped I wouldn't die in a plane crash. But the plane bounced forward, then sank beneath the clouds. Toronto came into view. We skittered to a landing.

I hadn't travelled much for several years, so I felt as if I'd crawled out from under a rock as I made my way to the Toronto-Calgary gate. I waited, boarded, found a seat near a window. About ten minutes before takeoff, a man slid into the seat next to me. When we started to talk, he told me, among other things, that I was unhappily married.

"How can you tell that?" I asked.

"I can just tell. And I'll tell you something else: he's got a temper. It's bad for your son. That's why he's slow. Get him out of there. Get him out and he'll be fine."

For a moment, the worry lifted, like a gap in the clouds. Leaving my marriage seemed a small price to pay. True, I wouldn't know what to do with the garden. But a garden seemed like a bad reason to stay married. And when I thought of it, although Henry was a good gardener, he didn't do much. He didn't cut the grass till it was knee high. Or he'd hire boys to cut the grass and go off to have coffee and leave me to pay. We had an agreement that I would buy plants and he would plant them. But more often than not, he left them to die.

"I'll tell you something else," the man said just before we landed in Calgary. "With very little attention, someone could get you very interested. You could have a nice romance."

*Oh, fine*, I thought. *How sad do I look?*

"I kind of like you myself."

We landed, and he rushed to get his connection to Victoria. I went to look for the taxi I'd booked to go to Banff and had a few breathless moments when I felt I might be stuck overnight in the airport. Finally, the driver appeared and we were on our way.

There was still light as we drove along the Bow River, the Rockies growing larger by the mile as we drove west. But it was dusk by the time we got to the mountains and dark when we finally arrived in at the Banff Centre. I knew from being there the year before with Davy that the centre was nestled in a bowl of mountains, ancient sacred space.

I got my room key, found my room. Single bed and a desk long enough for many revisions of manuscripts. My computer and printer, which Henry had helped me pack (was that a good enough reason to stay married?), had arrived. I unpacked and looked out the window into darkness.

Being away, among mountains, even if I couldn't see them, I felt filled with clarity. I had vowed not to give up on Davy, but years of unhappiness had eroded my feelings for Henry. It does take two. I was unhappy; Henry was bad-tempered. I took off my wedding ring and put it in a pocket of my luggage.

I WOKE THE NEXT MORNING when the light was still blue and rushed to my window. Below, a deer browsed on young aspen leaves, and then I spotted another deer nearby. In the middle distance great firs lined a path down to the road. Far off, at the horizon, was a picture-perfect mountain range.

"Hello deer," I said. Of course they couldn't hear me—they were three flights down and my window was closed.

I finished liberating my computer and printer from their boxes. I left my wedding ring where it was. I showered, went to get photographed for my artist's card—my artist's card!—and went down the hill to look for breakfast, so entranced by the tall firs and the ravens flitting to and fro in the first slanting sunlight—and by the far-off snowy mountains—that I almost forgot there would be food at the end of it. I knew this was a place I had always wanted to be.

At breakfast I sat alone and wondered about the people around me, and which ones were the writers. Some writers do look writerly; some don't. I didn't recognize anyone when I got to the lounge for our first meeting. But the sun was streaming in the windows; you could see that the world outside was bright and alive,

We were welcomed, and then we went on a tour. Walking through the woods, looking at the beautifully architected studios of the Leighton Colony, I could feel the sun, so much warmer than it had been yesterday morning in Prince's Harbour. I didn't want to go in, and when our guide said, "Brian is waiting." I thought, *Who cares?* It was the first time I'd felt spring this year; it was a new world and I wanted to stay balanced on the edge of possibility forever.

But our guide led us inside and left us at Brian's room, a large dance studio with mats and mirrors. Brian had on a comfortable-looking, large-stitched green sweater and moved easily around the room. He got us walking, even jogging a bit, stretching. He had long, silky brown hair and deep brown eyes. I thought he might be dismissive of me—men often were—but he engaged with all of us, as engaged as you can be with a class of twenty-two. He didn't give us much time to think about his looks. He had us grab mats from the side of the room and lie down with our eyes closed. then led us through a meditation. I think we were all a bit skeptical—this seemed to have nothing to do with writing—but we were polite. Once the meditation started, I realized he had a lovely voice. He took us out to the edges of the universe and then back to the room. I've always loved the idea of space travel, and I liked this trip, past the moon, past the planets and the edge of the solar system, past the stars to the very edge of being. I wondered if he'd written the meditation himself. This was a place where even the non-writers could write, I thought. Then the class was over, and it was time for lunch.

"Well," said a woman with short, curly grey hair, who might have been five years older than I was, "What did you make of that?"

"I thought it was interesting," I said.

"I could see you were right into it," said another woman, tall with dark hair and pale skin, sort of lily-like. How could she tell I was into it if our eyes were closed?

"Do you think he's married?" asked the first woman.

I considered. There was something in Brian's eyes that suggested he'd known love and he'd known hurt, but he also looked a little careless of himself. "I think he's been married but he's not now," I ventured.

Brian had told us to sign up for his private classes, and even if it all seemed a bit weird, I thought my writing could use all the help it could get—and so could my reading out loud—so, after lunch I signed up for every other day.

By my first class, Wednesday, I was pretty intimidated. Most of the writers in the group were published, and they almost all had writing lives. I wasn't sure what I was doing there. I climbed the steps to Brian's studio just before one, unexpectedly heavy with terror. I got more and more scared every step I took.

What if Brian told me I was absolutely hopeless and sent me home? If I hadn't signed up, I wouldn't have had the courage to knock at the door. And I had to knock twice because the first time I'd knocked so faintly (I was always doing that and then feeling discouraged that doors didn't open).

"We were just finishing," said Brian as he opened the door. A tall, slender,woman whose name I hadn't yet learned was lounging against a table.

"I'm sorry," I said.

"No, it's past time. Come on in."

He and the writer—I think she was one of the poets—hugged lightly. She thanked him. He said, "See you next class," and she was gone, leaving me feeling very awkward and as if I shouldn't have come.

"Did you bring any writing?" he asked.

I gave him my story. I thought, *Here I am, alone in a room with a perfectly attractive man, and I don't have a crush on him. I must be dead.*

He looked through the story then gave it back to me. "Read a little out loud."

People had told me I read well, so I launched into the first page.

"Not bad," Brian said. "You're forcing a little. You want to let the words float out of you. We'll work on that."

He asked for the story back and had me lie down on the mat and close my eyes. "Now say the words after I say them."

The weirdest assortment of words came hurling at me as if from outer space. I said them again and again: Car, renting, directions, drive. *What idiot would use prosy words like that?* I wondered, and then I realized they were from the beginning of my story. Why hadn't I chosen words that were more beautiful, had more resonance?

The story was about Davy, and I remembered how worried I was about him, and suddenly I started to cry in a flood. I couldn't stop. Then I realized that the story was also about my renting a car, and driving by myself, so it was about the end of my marriage. Those ugly words were appropriate.

"Don't worry about crying," Brian said. "If your emotions are blocked, your writing will be blocked. If you release emotions, it's better for your writing. Some people have a lot of stored anger, and they let it out when they are here. Are you okay?"

I sniffed and nodded. After all, I was nearly fifty. I should be able to take care of myself.

"Can you read me the beginning of the story again?"

I did.

"Better," he said. "Let yourself linger on the l's and r's. And maybe the m's and n's."

"The liquids."

"It's a place to start." He gave me a stack of papers about three inches thick. "These are hints for reading."

I tried not to look appalled. It seemed like a lot to take in. "Thanks," I muttered, stuffing the papers into my bag.

We were just about at the end of the hour, and I didn't want to put the next writer through the awkwardness of having to wait for me. I picked up my story and prepared to leave.

"Sign up for more classes," said Brian. "You could sign up every day."

I didn't think I could go through another class like this one every day. "I've signed up for more," I said. "My next one's Friday."

"Good," he said. "I'll see you Friday."

We hugged goodbye, and I left, thank goodness just as the next writer was arriving.

"How was it?" she asked.

"Good," I said, realizing that I was about to cry again and hoping it didn't show. "Have a good class."

I couldn't work, so I dropped my stuff in my room and walked in the woods to what was already my special spot, overlooking the Bow River many feet below and Sulphur Mountain and Mount Rundle in the distance. I sang all the songs I knew and cried. Then I walked into town, went to the museum and looked at historic Banff pictures, and cried some more. Then I went for coffee and cried. Then I walked along the banks of the Bow and found the four-leaf clover patch I'd discovered when Davy and I were here the year before and cried again. I'd have to come back to pick a clover—I didn't have anything to press it in, even temporarily. I went back to my room and cried. I cried for my dead parents and their friends who were also my friends. I cried for worry about Davy. I cried for having worked so hard and not having gotten anywhere. About midnight, I stopped crying and went to sleep. Maybe I felt a little less numb inside, but there was still a lot left.

I wasn't quite so scared when I walked up to class Friday. Whatever happened couldn't possibly be as bad as what had happened on Wednesday.

"Are you okay?" asked Brian. I was surprised by his kindness. My experience in my marriage, and at the university, had made me think that people weren't really kind to people when they were down. And also, I was old enough to take care of myself. "Yes, I'm okay, thank you."

I'd brought the same story, and again he had me start by reading. "You've been practising!" he crowed.

I had. I was surprised he could tell. And glad he was so pleased.

"You're not forcing as much, and you're enunciating better."

We spent the hour working on my reading, and, at the end, as I stood in front of him, he held his hands over my head and said, "I ask that you be given a new life."

*Oh, sure,* I thought. No one could unscramble the mess I'd made of my current life.

But after I left the class, I felt better. Did Brian have that power? Was it just the power of suggestion? He seemed so unassuming, except for being a bit of a megalomaniac about everyone taking as many of his classes as they could fit in.

The next day, Saturday, a group of us went to the Cave and Basin. It was sunny and warm, and it was lovely being out, and under the sky, mountains rising on all sides. I was getting to know the other writers, though I was still intimidated. But, talking to them, I was beginning to get a sense of the writing life and realizing that even if I hadn't been much published, I had at least been writing.

On Monday, I brought a different story to Brian's class—not so autobiographical, with better words. I read the epigraph from Richard Fariña's song:.

> *Well, if somehow you could*
> *Pack up your sorrows*

*And give them all to me*

*You would lose them*
*I know how to use them*
*Give them all to me.*

"I should sing it," I said to Brian, "but I can't."
"How does it go?"
I hummed it.
"Now with the words."
I froze. I'd stopped being able to sing with words. When I sang songs in grad school, my voice had started to crack—something got tight in me, and it went to my voice. After Davy was born, I could sing out loud to him, but nowhere else. But with Brian's encouragement, I tried. This time, surprisingly, my voice held.
"Oh, you've got to sing it!" said Brian.
This time being on the mat and hearing my words come out of nowhere, I wasn't so surprised. It was easier to give them depth, and even though the main character was also a mother of a small child, I had some distance from her.
Then I got up and read—and sang. I had read about a page and a half when I saw that Brian looked moved, hit in the eyes, vulnerable.
"Darling!" he said, and I fled the classroom, down the stairs.
It probably happens all the time, I thought. He's a great teacher, and he loses himself in his students' work. And they're all such good writers. Still, I was amazed that my work might have that power. Maybe it wasn't so hopeless after all.
By then I'd had three classes. One led to an eleven-hour cry; one gave me a new life; one included an instant of falling in love. What was left? I thought I'd have to be careful.
I went to dinner that night feeling better and talking more. But by the end of dinner, I'd socialized enough. At home I usually stayed in with Davy, so I wasn't used to being out

after seven-thirty. That was probably one of the reasons my therapist said there was a power imbalance in my marriage, and I would have to either change it or end it.

"Why don't you just go out when you want to?" Claire had asked more than once.

"Davy doesn't like being left alone, and when I leave him with Henry, it takes a long time to calm him down. And if I'm out late, Davy's not in bed *and* he's upset."

"That's passive-aggressive," Claire always continued. "Not Davy, Henry. You shouldn't stand for it."

But what can you do when you come home and your kid's a wreck? Of course, I was worried about being gone for six weeks. But Davy did have school, and babysitters for the afternoons and on weekends, and I was calling home every couple of days—we were talking a lot about Latin grammar.

I did some work on my story and went to bed. I slept fitfully, and when I finally sank into a deeper sleep, I became aware of three or four grey presences by my bed. They got me up and hustled me out of the room. I thought, *Don't I get a choice in this?*

The next thing I knew I was on a ledge halfway up a cliff. Below, in a valley, or a dip in the land, were a group of men (spirits, maybe?) in work clothes.

Another group of grey figures brought Brian to the ledge, and when they'd set him down, he fucked me. It wasn't making love; it was fucking, and it was wonderful. My dreams aren't usually tactile, but I could feel him inside me. I could feel the ecstasy between us.

The spirits gave a huge cheer.

And then I was back in my room, awake, shaken. I'd never had a dream like that. I looked at the clock. Three-thirty.

Was it a dream or a vision?

*How pathetic,* I thought. *A man seems to like your writing, and you tumble into bed with him, even if it's not on a bed, but rather on the ledge of a cliff, and only in your dreams.*

I WOKE WITH THE BLUE LIGHT, not really rested, too groggy to rush to the window and look for deer. As the light grew clearer, I heard Brian's voice as though he were inside my head: *Get up right now, and you'll see me at breakfast.*

*Oh, come on, Brian,* I thought back. *That's absolute crap. I'm imagining the whole thing.* Why on earth did I think he could hear me?

*No, get up right now.*

I got up, showered and walked down to the dining hall, not hurrying. It was not quite seven, too early. At least the guardian firs and the fairy tale mountains were breathtaking in the tender early morning light. I was the first person in the dining hall. Of course Brian wasn't there. *I told you it was total nonsense,* I thought.

But as I settled at a table with fruit, coffee, and a muffin, he came in. When he saw me, he looked so shocked that I thought maybe it hadn't been simply my imagination after all. What do you say to someone who may, or may not have, had sex with you a few hours before in front of a valley full of spirits?

We both fell back on manners and small talk. He looked so appalled that I didn't tell him I'd dreamed of him. We were speaking commonplaces, but we were also speaking a language of the eyes. I thought, *So that's what it's like.*

Other writers joined us. After a week, the group had started to gel, and meals, even breakfast, were always full of laughter. I've always loved sociable breakfasts, and I lingered after Brian was long gone to get ready for his first class, long after almost everyone else. Then I went back to my story.

I THOUGHT I FELT BRIAN'S PRESENCE when I was alone in my room, that morning, and in the days following, especially at night, especially between three and four in the morning.

At Banff, maybe because there were always so many writers around, maybe because of the vibrations of the high peaks, the days passed like years. My class with Brian on Wednesday seemed ages away from my class on Monday.

I was a bit wary. I wasn't sure if I wanted another unpredictable session that tore the covers off everything. I tried to choose a story that wouldn't unleash an explosion, a gentle fairy tale that I'd dreamed just after Davy was assessed. It held a hope for a happy ending, even when everything seemed against it. I didn't get to the bad-tempered uncle (probably a stand-in for Henry) who turned into a grouse at the end. The class passed without incident. I learned some things about reading without forcing, sinking into my text.

Toward the end of the hour, Brian said, "I'll give you colours. See if you can tell what they are. One's in your aura."

I stood with my eyes closed, afraid this was a test I would fail. When I opened my eyes, I told Brian that I saw yellow and dark blue.

"Yes," he said. "And lavender. You've got lavender in your aura." I noticed his deliberate lips and that he seemed pleased, whatever lavender in my aura might mean.

When we hugged to mark the end of the session, I don't know why, but I suddenly threw my arms around him.

"Nice," he said. "Trust."

I summoned my courage. Weren't we both adults? "You know I have feelings for you," I whispered.

He looked scared. "Not here, not now. It will interfere with your growth."

So we hugged lightly, and I left, feeling rejected, but set straight that our feelings weren't equivalent, which wasn't so surprising. I was surprised, however, that he'd been so considerate as he set his boundaries. There were so many gifted and lovely writers at this retreat, some unattached. I was the least likely person to be matched with Brian. I couldn't help it, though. I longed for him. But I had lived long enough to know that feelings aren't always returned.

My mother, who was wise when she wasn't being critical,

used to say, "You can't help how you feel, but you can help how you act." I kept my feelings to myself and tried to act correctly.

We still saw each other at meals—we still spoke a language of the eyes—but we were never alone. I never had a chance then to ask what he thought about telepathy, though I did later, when he called. The vision I'd had of having sex with him before a valley of cheering spirits was never repeated.

At one point, though, near the end of Brian's two weeks with us, I told him I was thinking of leaving Henry.

"That's a good idea," said Brian. "He's blocking your growth. You're young—you'll meet someone else."

Would I rather have a romance or growth? Luckily, probably, it wasn't left to me to choose.

At the end of my last class, we stood close together, and he said, "This is a beginning."

*Of what?* I wondered. We hugged lightly, comfortably, as if we'd known each other forever.

At the end of our last group class, Brian said, "You were all meant to be here. You were chosen. And not by people."

I'd had some more glimpses of the Banff spirits by then, so I didn't find this quite as mysterious as I would have two weeks earlier, I'd find that thought consoling in the next few weeks when I agonized about my writing and missed Brian, not just as someone I was longing for, but as someone who believed in my writing, who, just for a moment, had fallen in love with it.

The next morning I looked out my window and saw him making his way toward the bus stop, swinging a small travelling bag. Was that all he'd needed for two weeks? The bus came. He got on it. He was gone. Would he ever think of me? Banff already felt emptier without him. I wasn't sure how I'd survive the next four weeks without his encouragement.

I thought I heard his voice, *You've got to believe.* But I couldn't tell if it was telepathy, or if I'd imagined it.

IN THE WEEKS THAT FOLLOWED, the woman who looked like a lily told me that Brian had been in a car crash when he was fifteen. His parents had been killed, and he had spent months in the hospital. His left forearm had to be reattached. He'd been in a coma for weeks. I didn't hear much about his marriage, but I guessed he'd been too young, and he might not want to be married again.

One of the poets, who was part Coast Salish, asked, "Who heals the healer?" I wondered if I could.

I began to understand that although I was the wrong person for Brian's dramatic side, I might be careful enough for his wounded side. I thought I felt him thinking about me, thought I felt him taking me over cell by cell, which I didn't like at all. I was still longing for him, but he didn't write. He'd given me someone's play to read—"then you'll have to write me!" he said triumphantly—and I did read it and write him, but he didn't write back.

*Okay,* I thought, *I just imagined it.* That night I had a vision of a skeleton marrying us, and a voice saying, *Forever.*

I woke up shaken, but thought, *I don't need to deal with this now. If it's forever, I've got lots of time.*

As I got closer to the end of six weeks at Banff, I wondered how I was going to break the news to Henry that our marriage was over. Emotionally it wouldn't be hard. I'd spoken to Davy regularly (he was into some of the fine points of Latin grammar, like future subjunctive), but not much to Henry. Henry hadn't asked once how I was. He'd just assumed I'd be ecstatic to be away. In fact, I wasn't ecstatic. There were a lot of ups and downs, even without Brian. The biggest up was when our group had our reading. Everyone was wonderful, and I felt as though my writing belonged. Another up was my editor suggesting a few places to send my manuscript when it was done—as if it might be publishable. The downs were absolute despair. I was writing new stories and revising old ones, and agonizing that they might be dreadful.

Somewhere, between the ups and downs, was the confusion I felt about Brian. I had become psychically attached to someone I hardly knew at all. I could hear Brian saying, *Darling*, and, *You gotta believe* (again). I half did and half didn't. But I didn't think I could have imagined anything this weird all by myself.

I came home from Banff on a high—I was in love, even if it wasn't returned—and I had the beginning of a writing life.

The night I got back, Henry and I broke open the champagne he'd bought to celebrate my getting accepted into the writing program (we'd been quarrelling too much to drink it then), and when we were about three-quarters of the way through the bottle, I heard Brian's voice,

*Tell him. You've gotta tell him now.*

I took a deep breath. "I think we should separate," I said hurriedly, glass still in my hand. *Okay, Brian, I've told him.*

"You're either clinically depressed or you've got a malignancy," Henry said. "You should see a doctor."

He didn't believe me for a couple weeks, then he got mad. Separating wasn't easy, but after Henry finally moved out at the end of the summer, I never had a single regret. Davy was better with Henry's temper out of the house. Even the cats were happier.

I still felt connected to Brian, but I had lots to do, and I knew he did too, since he also taught. Once that fall, I thought he came to get me by astral travel (was that possible?) and we flew to his house (a big white house with big windows—you could see in the moonlight), went through a second-floor window and down a hall with an antique lamp on a small antique table, and into his room. Brian's body was lying asleep in his bed (so it must have been his soul that had come and gotten me). Somehow, I started touching him, but then he woke and was furious, and instantly I was back in my own bed. It was twenty to four.

Sometimes at movies or at concerts, I felt him sitting in the next seat, especially when the next seat was empty. He'd give his great smile, and I'd almost reach for his hand, forgetting he was a thousand miles away.

He finally called in November., and it felt as if we'd known each other for years.

"My play opens next week," he said, as if I'd know exactly what he was talking about.

"Your play?" I asked. .

"Yes, I'm doing *Under Milk Wood.*

"Great choice." I thought I'd give anything to see it

"I'm trying to work on the invisible gesture." As if I knew what he was speaking about. But it was like the lavender in my aura. He threw things out.

"How are you?" he asked

"Okay." I tried to think of something else, but I couldn't. "Putting one foot in front of another."

"Are you writing?"'

Henry would never have asked that. "Some. It's harder during term."

"There's so much to teach and so little time," he agreed. "And then doing the plays—they're exciting, but I'm at the end of my energy."

"I'm tired too," I offered. "And I'm not also directing a play."

"I should go," he said. "Please pray for the play to go well."

"Of course," Then I took a breath and asked, "What about the telepathy between us? Isn't it strange? "

"Shh," he said, sounding frightened. "We can protect each other."

Brian was cryptic and I wasn't sure whether what I'd been sensing was actually happening or not. His palpable fear suggested he might be feeling, sensing, intuiting the same things I was, but his evasiveness made me doubt everything.

We sent each other love—*love*, did he mean it? Or was it just the way he was with people? And then he was gone, leaving me wanting more. Who knew when we'd speak again? Even when he wasn't busy, Brian often didn't answer the phone or return calls. And neither of us were comfortable with email in 1994.

Afterwards, I walked along the lake contemplating the gauzy clouds in the late afternoon sky, the flame-coloured trees, and thought of him. Well, protection was something—in fact, if you're going through a messy separation, it's a lot.

But even though we'd just talked, Brian seemed a million miles away. Connection in real life was hard. The psychic way seemed the only way to get to know him. *If I followed that path,* I thought, *I might get closer to Brian.*

# 5. CLAIRE HAD MET SOMEONE

CLAIRE HAD MET SOMEONE, ahead of Rosetta's schedule. She'd been visiting a friend who had one of those homes on lots of land east of town and had backed into someone's car as she was leaving. "A BMW," she said ruefully. Claire was still driving her old Volvo and making it look chipper and well-preserved, but she really wanted a new car. In a way, her car had chosen for her.

She had offered to pay for the damage, but when the man saw the little edges of rust on her Volvo as well as Claire's golden hair and forget-me-not blue eyes, he said it was okay, he'd let it go.

He'd mentioned his name, something Scott, maybe Jesse? but since there'd be no insurance claim, they hadn't exchanged anything formally. Claire had called every Scott in the phone book until she finally reached an answering machine for a Josh Scott that she thought was probably his. She left a message; he didn't call back. After some agonizing, she called again, and got him in person. They agreed to meet for a drink. At first they'd had to look twice to recognize each other, especially without the layers of winter clothes, but they lingered over their drinks, white wine for Claire, scotch for Josh. He was nice-looking in a slightly repressed way. He did something with computers, so he was more established than the men Claire had been dating since her marriage had broken up. He was also deaf in one ear—surprisingly for someone in his late forties. He liked movies, but wasn't interested in music, one of Claire's passions. They did have a lot to say. Claire loved the excitement of new relationships, and, within a week, they were going out to dinners and planning a  trip to Quebec, maybe in Josh's plane.

"Imagine!" said Claire, "he's got a *plane!*"

I couldn't believe how easy it was for Claire to go out two or three nights a week  But her daughter, Megan, was Davy's age and very responsible, even though she complained about having to babysit after the third time in ten days. There seemed to be no glitches. They liked each other and were willing to see where it went. Claire hoped that at some point Josh might like her well enough to take her to concerts, in spite of impaired hearing making him lukewarm about music.

No wonder Claire didn't think Brian was real—she couldn't believe anything could be so hard. Why was Brian so elusive? Yes, she thought Brian might be damaged, and I might half-want some one unavailable so I wouldn't have to commit. Still, it seemed thankless to pursue something so unlikely. I wondered about that myself. But, sometimes, I still felt Brian with me at night. Indeed, except for the thousand miles between us, we almost could have been in the same bed. I still heard his voice. I could still get his attention (telepathically) by telling him (telepathically) that I was his—I could actually feel a jerk at the other end of the line.

But then, if Shakespeare was right that the course of true love never did run smooth, what Claire and Josh had between them might not be true love.

# 6. REPATTERNING

FEBRUARY SLUSHED ALONG. I taught my classes. I helped Davy with his homework and listened to him practice (which I always loved). I didn't hear from Brian. It was all striving without arrival.

I was seeing less of Claire. She wasn't entirely sure about Josh any more, but they'd gone to dinner a couple of times, to movies a couple of times, and up in his plane, briefly, during a short clearing in the weather.

I was getting more and more depressed. One dreary afternoon, when I picked up my journal to write about how depressed I was, Rosetta's card fell out. Maybe she was right—maybe we hadn't finished with each other. I called her and made an appointment for the next Monday, when I didn't have classes.

I drove to her apartment through grey February rain. She'd said, "When you get to Loeb's, turn left and follow the driveway all the way back to my building." So I did, tentatively, inching along the driveway past an alley of bare trees. It led to a white brick building, very private, set far back from the road. The parking spaces in front said "Reserved for Visitors," but I wasn't really a visitor, I was a client, so I went around back and found a parking space in the large lot invisible from the front.

I felt shaky, pushing past the unfamiliar into the unknown, but Rosetta had given excellent instructions, and they made sense once I was inside the building. I opened the heavy door into the vestibule, pushed the top button and got an answering buzzer, which allowed me to open the next set of doors into a very dark lobby. The elevator was at my left. It came slowly. Rosetta's apartment was on the top floor, she'd said. The elevator was lit only by dim lights until it got to the fourth floor, where I spied boots and plants outside the door to someone's apartment and a little grey light streaming in from the window at the end of the hallway. Nice that the landing was an extension of their space. Finally the elevator let me out at the top floor, and I stepped out into a surprising pearly light.

The entrance to Rosetta's apartment was enormous, carpeted but unfurnished, with a window on the left that let in that subtle light. A short flight of carpeted stairs was the only way to go, so I followed them up. At the top, at the entrance to the expansive living room, was a lovely bronze statue of a girl, long-limbed and lithe, her head slightly down as if she were reflecting on her inner world or looking into the depths of an invisible forest pool. A gauzy white shawl was draped over her slender shoulders, a circlet of stars perched on her bronze hair.

Rosetta appeared. "You found it," she said.

"Your directions were excellent," I said. "I love your bronze girl."

"I love her too."

"Did she come with the shawl?"

"No, I dress her differently, depending on the day. Would you like some coffee?"

"Yes, please."

I followed Rosetta past the lovely girl, through the large living room, also filled with light, a dining area, which had a long wooden table, probably an antique from Quebec, into a comparatively small but serviceable kitchen.

Rosetta, who wasn't much taller than I was, stood on tiptoe and rooted around on the top shelf for coffee. "I wasn't drinking coffee for a while," she said. "I thought it interfered with my energy. Now I drink a little. I like the taste."

"I do too," I said. I couldn't imagine not drinking coffee for a while.

"Found it!" Rosetta said triumphantly, clutching a jar in her hand. I saw with a shudder of revulsion that it was instant, but it was too late to back out now. "Do you take milk?"

"No, just black."

She boiled water, let me help myself to the instant coffee so I could get the right strength, poured the hot water, and then led me into the dining room. I sat on one side of the long table, facing the large fireplace on the far wall of the living room. Rosetta sat at the head of the table, facing a wall of glass, and her large balcony. I took a sip of the coffee. It was terrible. I'd made it much too strong. I thought if coffee were always like this, I could give it up easily. I noticed that Rosetta had her large folder and her rods.

"Are you right-handed or left-handed?" she asked.

"Left."

"If I rolled a ball exactly between your feet, which foot would you kick it with?"

I experimented under the table. "My left foot."

"Make a small triangle with your fingers—smaller than that—and look at my nose through it."

"Okay."

"Now close your right eye." I did. "And my nose disappears." It did.

"I need your fingers for muscle testing. Make a circle with your thumb and little finger. Good. Think of something you really, really like."

Of course I thought of Brian as Rosetta tried to pull my fingers apart.

"Good," she said. "Nice and strong. See how they stay together? Now think of something that stresses you."

Pick one! I thought, but I thought of my job.

"See?" said Rosetta. "Your fingers come right apart."

"Is that good?"

"Well, it's accurate. All right—hang onto an ear with your other hand. Left ear—" she pulled at my fingers. "Right ear. You're left-eared." She circled something on a sheet. Actually, she'd been writing everything down, but I hadn't noticed before. "Put two fingers to a temple. Left." She pulled my fingers. "Right." she pulled again. "Now put two fingers to the other temple and count. Now put two fingers to a temple and hum."

"Out loud?"

"Sure."

I felt really foolish—and I couldn't decide on a song. I grasped at straws and found myself humming "You Are My Sunshine," one of Davy's favourites, but not one of mine.

"Other side."

Life does give second chances, I thought, at least in small things. I hummed "The Otter," a song I liked better. I've always loved otters.

"All right," said Rosetta. "You're left-brained."

"I thought I was right-brained because I'm left-handed."

"No, your dominant hand is left, but the left side of your brain is also dominant. And you have left dominance in your ear and foot. You're right-eyed. So you have a brain-eye flow, but the rest of your brain pattern is blocked."

I was alarmed. "How bad is that?"

"Well, it makes things harder if you're stressed. The brain"— she lisped a little on the "r" of brain—"fires from one side to the other. So with your eye, there's no problem taking things in. You have a good flow. But with everything else, you've got to work a little harder at connecting with the outside world. With this brain pattern, you were probably shy as a child."

"Yes."

"You have a rich inner life." A slight lisp on the "r" of "rich."

"Your logic is in your left brain, which is where it is for most people. So you're strong on logic."

I wasn't sure that was true.

"Your gestalt, or feelings, are in your right brain, which is where they are for most people, but since you're left-brained, you have trouble accessing your emotions and your intuition. Is that right?"

"I guess so," I said. *But if I had trouble accessing my feelings, why was I crying all the time?* I didn't ask.

"Your first strength is your eye. You can always take things in with your eyes. And with this brain pattern, you might be clairvoyant."

*Oh, sure,* I thought.

"Your ear might be your second strength. You probably aren't very verbal."

"I guess not," I agreed, although that wasn't really very hopeful for someone who wanted to write. I thought if I ever did this for other people, I wouldn't make pronouncements that made them feel so awful about themselves.

"Exercise time," said Rosetta, and I felt a moment of panic I hoped I wouldn't have to do anything like a headstand. Luckily it was just marching in place, and then another finger test. "Strong," said Rosetta. "You like that. Now march lifting your left arm and right leg, your right arm and left leg, so you're going across."

I was immediately confused, and my finger testing said I didn't like it.

I repeated after Rosetta, "I want to succeed." My fingers said I did. "I want to fail." My fingers said I wanted that too.

"You're sabotaging yourself!" said Rosetta. "Now say, 'I want to be well.'" I did.

"I want to be sick." I didn't.

Then peripheral vision. Rosetta stood behind me and opened her arms, and I was supposed to say when I saw them.

"Okay," I said.

"Step forward and turn around to face me." Rosetta's arms weren't terribly far apart.

"Lady," she said, "You've got a bad case of tunnel vision."

I must have looked woeful because she said, "That will all change. Soon."

We sat back down. "I don't think we need to test your Reading Brain," she said. "You don't have trouble processing reading, do you?"

"Only manuals."

"Well, that's action, and you're not strong on action."

Rosetta swung her crystal. "It says we're ready for concrete base. Your concrete base is a belief system you formed at a period of your life when things were stressful. Before it was formed, you were unlimited. Your concrete base helped you get through that period, but it limited you later, and it's limiting you now, as if it had been set in concrete. Put your thumb and little finger together, no, not your index finger—" as I offered the wrong one.

"Good," she pronounced, as I made the correction. "Now I can finger test." She pulled at my fingers, and when they came apart, she said, "Yours was formed when you were thirteen, fourteen, fifteen. Can you remember what was going on for you then?"

I began to tear up. I thought of my mother losing her temper with me and suddenly becoming so critical. All of a sudden, nothing about me was right, not my body or my mind. She didn't like Henry (maybe she was right about that), but she basically wanted me to take him back and exchange him as if he were a dress from Bloomingdale's. I learned just before my mother died that she'd had a brain tumour, and that probably explained a lot, but by then the damage was done. I cried more. Rosetta pushed a box of Kleenex toward me, and I took several.

When I'd used them all, Rosetta said, "What belief system do you think you formed then?"

"Oh, that I was completely imperfect and I'd have to live with it."

"That's it," said Rosetta, and I sobbed again. She left the room and reappeared with another box.

When I came up for air, Rosetta said, "Can you say, 'I love myself and my body'?"

I said it weakly, still sniffing.

She said, "You don't believe it. But that will change. Can you say, 'I do my best, and my best is good enough'?"

"I try to do my best," I said, "but it isn't good enough."

"All right," said Rosetta. "Miracle time. You've chosen to be repatterned by the magnetic field. Pick a place to stand where you're comfortable, face me, and I'll walk into your energy field. Think about everything you'd like to happen in your life. There's no limit—this is not three wishes. I will pull down energy from the forces that control the universe. Just be ready to receive."

There was a large fig tree in the corner of the dining space I hadn't noticed before. I stood near it, facing the length of the living room and the fireplace, and closed my eyes.

I could feel when Rosetta walked into my energy field. I felt the strengthening quality of the energies. I felt flooded with golden light and white light. It reminded me of Brian. What I wished for—what I always wished for—Davy to grow up into his own life, my writing to turn out (whatever turning out might be), seeing Brian again. Then I thought of the wishing cloak in *Queen Xixi of Ix* where the little girl heroine just wants to be happy again and wishes for that. Maybe I should have wished that Brian and I would be together. But I didn't really have much idea of who he was. And I knew from my own teaching that what you see of a teacher is just the tip of the iceberg. I wished for an equal relationship, which Henry and I hadn't had. I could have stood there forever, just taking in energy. It felt like forever, timeless time.

When Rosetta said, "Whenever you're ready, open your eyes."

It felt as if days had passed, but the light outside the window suggested it was still morning, and when I looked at my watch, I saw that I had only been at Rosetta's a little over an hour.

Rosetta retested my marching, my same side crawl and

cross crawl, and this time I liked the cross crawl better. I no longer wanted to fail. When she stood behind me to test my peripheral vision and when I stepped forward, her arms were spread much wider.

"That's the best," said Rosetta, "because you can really see the change."

I now believed that I did my best and my best was good enough. At least for now I loved myself and my body, even if weakly.

"Let's drink some water," Rosetta said. "These are real changes, but they are like seeds. They're the beginning of growth. You can stabilize them by drinking lots of water. You should drink seven glasses a day."

*Seven glasses a day!* I'd float away.

For now, we both drank, and when I'd finished my glass, she poured more for both of us. The instant coffee sat cold, neglected, barely touched, at the side of the table.

"I think you need a meditation," Rosetta said. She motioned to a couch at the side of the dining area, which I hadn't noticed before. I lay down on it and closed my eyes. I plunged so deep that I was practically asleep, but I remember Rosetta's voice telling me to be grateful for my body, my toes, my knees, my shoulders, my head, all the parts.

When she finished, I opened my eyes with a start, barely aware of where I was, the graceful branches of the fig tree hanging over me, as if I were in the tropics, or at least in summer.

I felt so much better I almost forgot it was February.

Rosetta scanned my body by finger testing and said everything was fine, and I should be grateful.

"In the next few days, you may have memorable dreams," she said. "Pay attention. As I said, you need to work at these changes to make them  grow."

I thanked her—thanks seemed inadequate for such an intense but unhurried session—and paid her—pay also seemed inadequate for so much transformation. I took the elevator down, found my car in the back parking lot, and drove back into my own life, feeling lightened. Just for now, the constant barrage of criticism was gone.

"I WAS REPATTERNED!" I told Claire over the phone that afternoon. "It was great!"

"I might try it sometime," said Claire. She didn't really have time to talk. She and Josh were going out to dinner and then to a late night spot for jazz.

"I thought Josh was deaf in one ear?"

"He's still got the other ear. He said if I wanted to go, he would come with me. Let's have coffee Thursday or Friday. I want to hear about your repatterning."

"Thursday afternoon at Stuart's Place?"

"Around two?" I was thankful for being separated (if not officially) all over again. I could get out! I didn't have to lie!

"Great."

# 7. IT WOULD BE THE BEST GIFT

I SOARED FOR A COUPLE WEEKS on the strength of being repatterned. By this time in the year my classes usually had momentum and were almost running themselves. Davy did well in the Kiwanis Festival—especially with his Bach, and had gotten an A, First Class Honours. His entrances and exits were fine—Jane Austen might have said unexceptionable—except that it had taken some coaching to make them so.

Claire wasn't feeling great about Josh. She'd hinted that she wanted to be sent flowers for Valentine's Day, but what he'd sent was a large pot of green plants.

"It must have been expensive," Claire said respectfully, but regretfully. "But it wasn't *roses*. It wasn't even lilies or gerbera daisies. I want to feel *cherished.*"

And they did go out, but just to a good restaurant, as she had suggested—he didn't *plan* anything.

"At least he took your hints and remembered," I said.

"But he might not have if I hadn't made such a big thing of it. I don't think Rosetta sent the right man."

"She didn't *send* him," I objected. "She *saw* him. She didn't say he'd be the be-all and end-all. She said it would be a relationship of the quality you required."

"Well, I think I require more quality. The sex is good, but that's not enough."

"Why don't you introduce him to any of us?"

"He's not housebroken. Besides, he uses porn."

I'VE ALWAYS LOVED THE GREAT slanting fields of light in March. I loved that I could walk home in light at five-thirty after my late class. But after the Kiwanis Festival I felt let down. The weather turned cold and rainy, so the fields of light were behind clouds. My classes were okay, but everyone felt dragged down by the weather and probably also by end-of-year work—piles of essays—and since the class reflects the teacher, it was up to me to pull us all through.

By the third week of March I was exhausted, deep in essays and depression, and I couldn't think of anything to do but call Rosetta and make another appointment.

I went on one of those snowy March days when the flakes seem almost like cotton. March snow can be heavy, but it usually doesn't last. It felt a little lighter than the depths of winter, but it was still winter.

I was looking forward to another long, leisurely session, maybe another deep meditation waking up under the fig tree, but, this time, Rosetta didn't seem as relaxed. She offered coffee, but this time I knew better than to accept.

We sat at the long wooden table with our glasses of water, Rosetta across from me. She had her book and rods. "How have you been?" she asked.

"I was great after I was repatterned," I said. "And I did have interesting dreams." I paused to see if she wanted to hear them. She didn't. "But now I'm discouraged about my job. I seem to work and work and never get anywhere."

"You feel like a failure," Rosetta said. It was true, but it wasn't exactly what I wanted to hear.

"One of my colleagues vowed to destroy me, and when her partner became Head of Department, he called me into his office and told me I hadn't done anything worthwhile for the university. Then, he tried fire me."

"Maybe you hadn't done enough," suggested Rosetta. I remembered that this was a healing session and managed not to slug her.

Maybe I hadn't, but many men had done less. I'd been assigned all those new courses in areas I'd never studied. And I
had taken a lot of unpaid leave because of Davy. I didn't want
to say I'd been in a life crisis because at Royalton University,
professionals didn't have life crises. That was what wives were
for. But my Head went through what I had done and dismissed
it. The courses I'd originated in Women Writers didn't count,
because they were just women writers. The reviews I'd had
published didn't count because they were just reviews, even
though there were a lot of them. The book I'd co-edited didn't
count because it wasn't in a field taught in the department. The
stories I'd published and the writing I was doing didn't count
because, he said, you'd have to get a Nobel Prize for creative
writing to count in our department. I couldn't teach anything
because I "wasn't qualified" to teach any of the courses offered in the department, and there was no question of offering
new courses now, even though the courses I'd originated in
Women Writers were now established electives. The article I'd
published in a top of the line anthology was all right, but it
was only one article.

"But you had tenure," said Rosetta.

"I had tenure, but it was a rough ride, and I'm not over it."

"You have to forgive," said Rosetta. "You have to forgive
your colleague, and your Head of Department," she said as
she swung her crystal, "and your ex-husband, and even your
son a bit."

That seemed like too much too fast. How could I forgive
before I'd healed?

She led me through a short meditation, trying to get me
to forgive, and anchoring the belief: "Together my job and I
provide our highest possible service to the universe."

I certainly didn't believe it when we started, and I didn't
really believe it when we finished. If my job and I were pro-
viding our highest possible service to the universe, why was
I getting such terrible merit raises? Well, yes, it was the same

department head I was supposed to be forgiving. I wasn't sure he'd forgiven me for not lying down and dying when he tried to get rid of me. I had tenure. I got people to write letters for me, for which I was grateful, but they were so glowing that they seemed to be about a completely different person. I don't think they convinced my Head, but they did get the Dean to think maybe there was another side to the story. And Davy was now enough on track that I could come back to full-time teaching. They did manage to find courses for me to teach without adding anything new to the department's offerings. I embarked on a course in Contemporary Literature, which I didn't know anything about, but which was exhilarating. I had my sights set on a course in Contemporary Canadian Women Writers, but I needed to gather my strength—I knew the department wouldn't go for it. I'd have to wait a bit before asking for a new round of letters.

I definitely didn't feel healed. I felt let down on the sidewalk with a thump when Rosetta announced that she had an appointment and had to leave.

"Wait," she said. "You have a question."

"I do?" *Which one?* I wondered. "What comes next?"

"I'm giving a two week course in May for people learning to do the healing work I do, to be Results Facilitators. You should take it."

"How much is it?"

"A thousand dollars."

That seemed like a lot, especially for someone about to assume a huge mortgage on her own.

"You should take it," Rosetta repeated. "It would be the best gift you could give yourself. Now I really have to go."

"I'll think about it," I said. "Thank you."

I paid, gathered my coat and left, probably one run of the slow elevator ahead of Rosetta. I was disappointed. I didn't feel healed at all, and all my feelings about my job were now flying around like wasps. Forgiveness might be great in theory, but you have to move on from woundedness before you can forgive. Or you have to get to the right space. Sometimes this New Age stuff seemed much too simplistic.

After repatterning, I'd felt like a princess who'd gone to the underworld and done everything right and come back with a golden ring. This time I felt like the wicked stepsister who'd done everything wrong and come back with a sack of coal.

But as March ground to an end and lightened into April, and I got more and more tired and discouraged, I felt there was no other way out, so I called Rosetta and signed up. She said I could bring the cheque to the first class in May.

"Talitha's doing the course too," said Claire when I told her.

"I'll ask her about it the next time I get my hair cut. At least there will be someone I know." I didn't usually have a lot to say to Talitha, but I did like her.

"Are you looking forward to it?"

"All I need is one more profession I'm not any good at," I said ruefully. "And, I've never had any desire to be a healer."

But then I remembered that one of Henry's former students had read my palm after we were married and said I had healer lines on my palm. But he has also said there were lines for continued success in the arts, which obviously hadn't happened. He hadn't said anything about my marriage, which made me wonder what else he might have seen.

But Brian was a healer, and if I took this course, I might understand him a little better. That decided me.

# 8. THE PSYCHIC WORLD BEGINS WITH THE BODY

I WAS LATE, TO BEGIN WITH, and everything looked surreal in the soft grey fog. The first pink blossoms and green leaves glimmered through the haze like a dream of Paris in the spring. Saturday morning, early May, roads nearly deserted. The car clock said eight-twenty. Class started at eight-thirty. Should I run this red light and make up for some of the time I'd wasted dawdling? I thought of Davy sleeping deeply at home. The cats were also sleeping deeply, curled up like black commas on my bed. I could still turn around, but I didn't. I didn't run the red light either. I opened my heart to the mistily blossoming trees, then drove forward through the haze, turned the corner onto Princess Street, and passed the walled Sisters of Providence Mother House with its hidden greenery and Loeb's large, green, box-grocery store, marking the turn into Rosetta's driveway.

It seemed to take forever to get an answer to my ring, for the door to open. The elevator was slow as usual. I was already frazzled by the time I arrived at the top floor and made my way into the light. The foyer was empty and quiet. The bronze girl, today with a purple shawl around her shoulders and a silvery crown, stared blankly at me. The living room was empty, but I heard voices murmuring, so I turned into the kitchen and saw Talitha and a couple of other women lounging against the cabinets, mugs in hand.

Talitha was lovely and vibrant in a soft pink sweater and jeans. I was so used to seeing her dressed up for work that I suddenly realized how much I didn't know about her life. One of the other two women looked kind and shy, with light-filled, blue-grey eyes. She reminded me of a deer; I could imagine woods around her, seeing her through trees, ready to take flight.

"Hello, Judith," said Talitha in her distinct, unhurried voice. "This is Deirdre. She's a massage therapist. And this..." she nodded at the other woman, who was short, with dark eyes that looked eager to please, "...is Sharon."

We all said hellos. We were all wearing sweaters, even though it was May. This was one of Prince's Harbour's recalcitrant springs.

"Would you like coffee?" Talitha flicked a switch on the kettle.

"Is there time? I thought I was really late."

Talitha handed me a mug. "We're the only ones here besides Rosetta."

"Thanks." I remembered the dreadful instant coffee and fished around for herbal tea. I found something called blushing peach.

The buzzer sounded. Talitha answered.

"Thank you, Talitha." Rosetta appeared around the corner, unexpectedly in a one-piece fuschia jumpsuit, cut a little low for teaching, I thought. She welcomed me in an embrace. Then she clapped. "Everyone into the living room. I know we're not all here yet, but we have a lot of material to cover today."

We drifted into the living room and settled into chairs. Talitha took a comfortable chair by the fireplace. The woman who looked like a deer, Deirdre, took a smaller chair on the other side. The dark, eager woman, Sharon, settled into a corner of the couch. I perched on a not terribly comfortable chair and noticed that the mist outside was dissipating.

In the centre of the circle, a pile of large binders waited like logs in front of a campfire. There were also stacks of papers with smeary, dark printing on them.

"First, welcome," Rosetta said, "to a course that will change your life. In two weeks you'll find you see differently—your friends will be different and you will be on a different path."

*Oh, sure*, I thought. Anyway, I didn't really want different friends. I was happy with Claire.

The woman Talitha had buzzed in appeared at the edge of the circle. She was short and brunette. Blonde highlights. Her hairdresser wasn't as good as Talitha. She looked vaguely familiar.

"Andrea," she offered. "I'm sorry I'm late."

I searched my memory, had a flash of the colour red, a memory of weight and awkwardness.

"We sold you a vacuum cleaner!" I said. Prince's Harbour was small enough that you were always running into people unexpectedly.

"The red one? I'm still using it. I love all the attachments."

I had hated that vacuum cleaner. It was too heavy. The gadgets were too fiddly. There was even a tool for fluffing up a rug after you shampooed it. We'd bought it when Davy was a baby. A salesman came to our door while Davy and I were napping, and Henry woke me up to look at it. I was so sleepy I'd bought it just to get back to bed. I placed an ad in the paper and sold it a few months afterwards.

Andrea was wearing a gold sweater and a tight, brown tweed skirt that rode up above her knees when she sat down (on the other end of the couch from Sharon). She was the only one in the room wearing makeup.

Rosetta told us that our first task was to choose a binder—I chose blue—and to transfer the pages into it. She could talk while we worked. But the pages confused me. I had no idea what came first.

I scarcely noticed when a very small, timid woman slid into the room. "I've seen you before," she said to me.

"Oh?" I was embarrassed. I didn't remember her.

"At the Golden Rooster," she said. "I go there with my daughter sometimes, and you were there with your son."

"Yes, we go there a lot."

Davy almost had an eating disorder. For years he ate nothing but nuts, seeds, and crackers, and Five-Alive. I didn't like it when he rejected my cooking, so we'd go out for pasta or Veal Milanese. Recently, he'd started making his own pasta and sauce at home. I didn't want to explain all this in front of the group. But I cast my mind back and saw a beautiful little girl, fine, light hair flying back from her face as she spun around like a butterfly in the aisles of the Golden Rooster. "Oh yes! You're the mother of that lovely little girl!"

"Yes, my daughter, Lily. I'm Elaine, and it's nice to meet you. I'm late because Lily isn't well, and it is always so hard to leave."

I understood that! I looked over for Rosetta, but she wasn't there. "We're supposed to put notebooks together," I nodded in the direction of the binders and papers.

"Lily's sick so often," said Elaine. "I did get a sitter, but it's not the same."

I understood that too. Autism is not the only problem.

"I'm sure she'll be fine," I said. "You can call at lunch time and check in."

Elaine gave me a relieved look. She was very pale and thin, with blue eyes. There was a trace of childhood freckles on her cheeks.

"Which sheets come first?" she asked.

"I don't know. They aren't numbered. Rosetta didn't say they had to go in any particular order." I thought, *Maybe we're supposed to do it psychically.*

Rosetta reappeared. "We're almost all here," she said. "You can finish the notebooks on break."

Elaine raised her hand. "Please, Rosetta, which pages come first?"

Rosetta pulled a picture of a skeleton from a stack on the floor across the circle from me. "This comes first. Then this group." She pointed. "Then this one."

So there was an order, even if there were no numbers.

We sat back on the chairs and couches. Elaine settled into

the centre of the couch between Sharon and Andrea. Prince's Harbour is small, but I was still surprised that in this class where I'd expected to know no one, I already knew Talitha and I'd met (even if I hadn't remembered them) Andrea and Elaine.

"Now," Rosetta began again. "This is a course in a complete system of healing, from the physical through the emotional to the spiritual. How many of you have done healing work before?"

Deirdre raised her hand, then Elaine.

"Good," said Rosetta. "Deirdre is a massage therapist. Elaine does reflexology. How many of you have experienced healing?"

The rest of us raised our hands.

"Tell us," said Rosetta. "Talitha?"

"I've done sessions with you and some past life sessions with Jess Gillis."

"Jess has done this course. She's a gifted healer. Judith?"

"You repatterned me and gave me a session, then suggested I do this course, so I'm here. I really don't know much about healing."

"By the end of the week, you'll be repatterning people yourself."

I gulped. "That seems awfully fast."

"This system gets results. That's why it's called Results. In two weeks, you'll all be pros. Andrea?"

"I've had massage and shiatsu, and sessions with you."

Rosetta nodded. "Sharon?"

"I haven't done anything. I'm just here with Andrea. I'm sort of nervous about it."

At least someone else was inexperienced too.

Rosetta was about to say something, maybe even something reassuring, which I didn't think was her style, to Sharon, when there was a whoosh of air and a young man appeared, heavyset, in a tan jersey which bulged a bit over his khaki shorts. He was carrying a cup of Tim Horton's coffee, which I looked at longingly, and he was out of breath.

"Sorry, ladies. It's just too soon. I'm not awake yet. Oh, do I need this coffee!" He lifted the cup to his mouth, and I could almost taste it.

I expected Rosetta to ream him out for being late, but she only said, "This is James. He's a gifted energy worker. There's one more person coming, but I think we can start." It was twenty past nine. I could have stopped for coffee too. James took the empty chair beside Rosetta, next to the couch.

"As I said, this course is very intense. It's a hundred and fifty hours, which is equivalent to a three-credit course in university. By the end, you'll be certified Results Practitioners. Your lives will be changed, and you will be able to change lives. And you will have a set of skills that people will pay for. Now I think we should introduce ourselves and say why we're here, what we expect." She swung her crystal. "Talitha, you start."

"This is my passion," said Talitha in her silky but decided voice. "I'm interested in the psychic, in healing, in past lives, in angels. I read about it all the time. I wanted a chance to learn more."

Rosetta beamed. "Welcome. You're definitely supposed to be here. In fact, I foresaw you all, except for Judith."

*Thanks, Rosetta.* So was I supposed to be here or not?

Elaine was next. "I'd like to add a modality to my reflexology, and I thought this would be a good one. I want to make more money. I'd like to buy Lily a bike. I think if she were out more, she might not be so sick."

Rosetta swung her pendulum and looked at me.

"My life's stalled," I admitted. "Everything's stalled. I'd like at least something to start going forward again. I think I need a lot more healing, and I hoped this would help."

Rosetta nodded, so although I'd revealed myself, I hadn't disgraced myself.

Rosetta's pendulum indicated Andrea next. "I'm having trouble with my boss," said Andrea. "I'm trying to get up the courage to quit my job and look for something else, but it's hard. There aren't so many jobs out there. And I'd like a boyfriend."

"Male energy," said Rosetta. "You probably need to deal with your father issues."

"I don't think so," said Andrea.

Rosetta said nothing, but turned toward Sharon, who said hesitantly, "Next year my youngest son will be going into first grade. I've been at home for ten years, so I'm looking for part-time work. We could use the money. But I think I'm also looking for some direction."

"Do you have any idea what you'd like to do?" asked Rosetta.

"I know it sounds crazy because I've spent the last ten years mothering, but I think I'd like to work with children."

Rosetta nodded and turned to Deirdre. "I don't have as much energy as usual," said Deirdre. "I'd like physical healing. And I'd like to be able to add this system to my massage practice." She had a soft voice; it was hard to hear her.

"It's good to have more than one modality," said Rosetta. "We'll do a lot with the physical."

Deirdre nodded. I winced, in spite of having anchored "I love myself and my body."

"James?"

"I need to make some money! I've got my eye on two gorgeous big crystals at Treasure Garden, but I can't afford them. I LOVE crystals! I'd like to take a reiki course. And I'd like to move into my own place. My mother's a bitch."

"Your mother pushes your buttons," Rosetta corrected. "Sometimes the people who push your buttons are your greatest teachers."

"I think I might have learned enough by now," said James.

I looked more closely. James' face was still forming. His eyes were almost the colour of flint. His skin would have been improved by more exercise. I couldn't tell his age. He was younger than the rest of us, but his presence had an authority that no one else in the room had, even Talitha.

"I can understand that," I said. "Mothers can be difficult."
Even years after her death, I was still working things out with
my own mother.

James looked at me gratefully. "Twenty-two years is enough,"
he said.

"Are you only twenty-two?" Talitha asked.

"Twenty-one. Twenty-two next month. I like roses, if any
of you want to send them."

"Twenty-two's a power number," said Deirdre.

"What colour?" asked Talitha.

"A mixture," said James. "I'm a Gemini. I like variety."

"This is a very good group," said Rosetta, to my surprise.
Every one of us seemed so lost, except Talitha. Obviously,
the psychic world had different measures than the ones in my
experience.

"Now," said Rosetta. "The psychic world begins with the
body. For the next two weeks, I ask you to do a gentle cleansing—no alcohol, no sugar, no caffeine. Meat is full of additives
and hormones, so please try to avoid it."

Sharon put up her hand. "We raise our own cows. Is that
meat all right?"

Rosetta beamed. "Yes, organic meat is fine. But don't eat
too much of it. You don't want to overload your digestion.
Digestion takes energy, and you'll need your energy."

"Our milk is really good too," said Sharon.

"Maybe you'll bring some in," said Rosetta. "But mostly,
for these two weeks, you should try to be vegetarian."

My heart sank. No coffee? Now I really wished I'd had one
last coffee and been later. No sugar? Alcohol I could take or
leave.

James looked troubled too. "So what can we drink in the
morning?" he asked.

"Hot water."

James made a face. I did too. Hot water reminded me of my
mother when she was sick.

"Herbal tea. Ordinary tea has caffeine. It's almost as bad as coffee. No soft drinks."

"What about just one cookie?" negotiated James.

"James, I know you are a gifted energy worker," said Rosetta. "But just for these two weeks, see what happens if you don't gum up your system with sugar and caffeine. Your body has carried you this far. Be respectful of it these two weeks."

I sympathized with James. I hated people telling me what I could and couldn't eat. That also had something to do with my mother.

"Now please look at your sheets on food combining. These"— she brandished the sheets with the tabloid-smeary type.

Then, confusion. I riffled through my book for the sheets and couldn't find them—for a few moments I was in a bad dream—I *had* put the pages out of order. But then I found the bleared type. Rosetta was talking about something called food-combining and reading from a page headlined LIVING HEALTH. The typeface made it look like an insert from the *National Enquirer*. It warned us that if we didn't eliminate SUGAR, FATS, ALCOHOL, VINEGAR, CAFFEINE, MEAT, and DRUGS from our diets, ill health and misery would take over our lives. Reading the sheet and listening to Rosetta, I was astonished I hadn't died ten years ago.

There was also a diagram with a lot of boxes and arrows about food combining. Meat (if you insisted on it) should be eaten with green vegetables, but not with carbs. Carbs could be eaten with green vegetables, but not with fats. Meat could be eaten with fats. Green vegetables went with everything. Melon should always be eaten by itself. Fruit should be eaten separately too.

Rosetta paused for questions. I had plenty, mostly, what was I doing here? Only two days ago I'd been frantically grading exams and a few late essays, discovering that some of my second-year students didn't know what an elegy was, and that some were pretty confused about aesthetics. This couldn't be further from the world of aesthetics and elegy—unless someone suffered an untimely death from eating prosciutto with melon and needed a poem to be written about them.

James raised his hand. "What happens if you eat meat with potatoes? Will the earth open up and swallow you?"

"Of course not," said Rosetta. "You'll just use more energy digesting and have less for healing. You won't be as clear a channel. I know you have a lot of energy available to you now—but see what happens if you take better care of your body."

"What about just one piece of chocolate cake?" James persevered. My heart, or at least my gut, was with him.

"Chocolate cake's another story. There's too much sugar in it, and sugar's a cell destroyer. And white flour gums up the villi, the tiny hairs inside your intestinal tract. If your digestion isn't working well, food starts to rot in your stomach."

*Charming*, I thought. I was sure, in addition to all my other problems, that the chocolate bars I'd consumed to get through my grading were rotting inside.

"Carob?" asked James hopefully.

"Chocolate, carob—it doesn't make much difference."

Talitha raised her hand. "How much time should you leave between meat and carbs?"

Rosetta considered. "About twenty minutes."

"I can't live without my coffee," said James.

"What about decaf?" asked Andrea.

"No decaf. It's just as bad as coffee. No sugar substitutes either, especially not aspartame. It's bad for the brain." Rosetta's lisp emphasized the "r" of "brain."

She continued, "You may think that caffeine and sugar and alcohol"—she said each of these with a curl of distaste—"give you energy, but it's a short-term jolt, and the body is actually depleted. I cut down on coffee when I started this healing work. For a while I switched to decaf, but now I don't miss either."

*That's fine for you*, I thought.

"What sweeteners can you eat?" This from Sharon.

"Maple syrup is best because it's vegetable. Honey is second best."

"We make our own syrup from our own trees," said Sharon. There was another whoosh of air, and a tall woman in a black cloak swept into the room, long brown hair flying behind her to its own rhythm.

"How'd you get in?" I asked. No one had been in the kitchen to answer the buzzer.

"Magic," she grinned. Her eyes gleamed silver-green, like a cat from the moon. She turned to Rosetta. "I'm so sorry I'm late. My car died, and I missed the bus, and I had to walk for an hour before I could get the next one."

"Try to come earlier tomorrow," said Rosetta, her mouth pulled tight. "Do you want to introduce yourself before we take a break?"

"I'm Vivienne." She was still a bit out of breath. "I'm an artist, but none of my paintings are selling, and I thought this course might clear away some blocks. If not that, at least give me a way of making money besides retail."

"We'll take a fifteen-minute break," said Rosetta. "Finish assembling your notebooks if you need to. There are almonds and apples on the table."

The almonds were unpeeled and unsalted and looked stale. I tried the door to the balcony, found it unlocked, and breathed the cool May air gratefully. The balcony was huge. A crowd of fifty people would have fit there easily, but it was mostly bare, with only a few chairs and a table in the middle. I wandered to the railing and looked down on the soft May trees, the new grass, birds flitting, not having to give a thought to food-combining—just building nests and raising families. Simple. Brian would say, "Don't forget to breathe," so I breathed in the fresh air. Maybe the whole thing was worth it just for the view. What would Brian say about the rest of it? I knew he didn't drink, tried not to eat sweets ("My mother baked all the time, and my immune system was wrecked.") But he did drink coffee—lots of it—at least when he was teaching at Banff. What would he say about Rosetta? Probably that she was right about a lot of things, but dogmatic. I sighed. I would have to change what I ate for these two weeks.

Break was over, and I drifted back inside.

The circle was much more electric with Vivienne. She had folded her cloak over the back of her chair and was wearing a gorgeous dress. with a vivid, purple top. It was black at the waist, and had a flowing green and purple skirt broken by black stripes coming from the waistband. She looked as if she'd just come from the moon. Her face was exotic with its high cheekbones. But before I could figure it out, Rosetta began. "How many of you have experienced finger testing?" We all put up our hands, even Sharon.

"Now you're going to learn how to do it. Everyone find a partner."

I turned to Elaine, who nodded.

We agreed that she would do the finger testing first since she knew a little bit more about it, from reflexology.

The person who was being finger tested was to put her thumb and little finger together in a circle (the way I had during sessions with Rosetta), and the person who was doing the testing would pull them apart.

"You're using telepathy," Rosetta said. I pricked up my ears at this. So there *was* telepathy. *Maybe I hadn't imagined Brian's voice in my head.*

"You're talking to the person's body/soul without talking to their conscious mind.

Their fingers will come apart when you ask them a question. If they're too tight, the person is a control freak. You need to check to make sure you can reach them without words, so before you start, ask them to think of something they really like and see if their fingers are strong or weak."

Okay, I remembered this. I thought of Brian, and my fingers tested strong.

"Good," said Rosetta. "Now switch."

Elaine's fingers were soft and floppy. I definitely didn't feel I was communicating with them.

"I can't do it," I said to Rosetta. She came over and took Elaine's hand.

"Put your fingers closer together," she said. "Closer than that. Now think of something you really like." She pulled. "Nice and strong. Now you do it, Judith."

I had to be gentle with her fingers, but I could feel that they were closer together, and, if I didn't pull too hard, they stayed together.

"Now think of something that stresses you," I said, and yes, her fingers did come apart.

The next thing was to get the fingers to answer yes or no—open fingers meant "yes," and "no" fingers were closed. I was starting to be in touch with Elaine's fingers, had some idea of when they were just floppy or when they were giving me a message. Then we had to do it with our own fingers.

"Let go of your inner knowing," Rosetta said, but it wasn't just letting go of our inner knowing, it was trying to figure out what we consciously knew. It shouldn't have been that hard, but I was lost.

"Now you can do brain patterns," said Rosetta.

Well, some could. Luckily Elaine was person A. Luckily, Rosetta also gave us a checklist—hand, foot, eye, ear, brain, logic, gestalt (synthesis).

I was definitely left-handed and left-footed. Right-eyed. But when Elaine asked my brain dominance, I cheated. I held onto my fingers for my left brain and opened them for my right brain. I thought, *here's my chance to be right-brained*, like I thought I was. And for good measure, I also made my logic right-brained and my gestalt right-brained.

After we finished, we compared our results.

Everyone in the class was right-brained except for James, who was left-brained, right-handed, right-footed, right-eyed, right-eared, with logic in the left brain and gestalt in the right brain.

"James is one of the fortunate ones," said Rosetta. "He has a complete flow with the world."

I was dying for approval as if it were chocolate, and hoped Rosetta would like my revised brain pattern better than she'd liked my poor unfortunate blocked one.

But when Elaine announced the brain pattern of the person she'd been working with, Rosetta looked very grave. "This person is very confused!" she said. "It's bad to have logic and gestalt in the same hemisphere. This person is strong on feelings, but very weak on logic. Unbalanced, in fact. When you find a brain pattern like this, you must repattern immediately. This person is totally out of sync."

Even though neither Rosetta nor Elaine had named me, I wanted to go through the floor. I wanted my old brain pattern back, even if it was left-brained and blocked. At least I wasn't totally unbalanced.

"I might have made a mistake finger testing," said Elaine.

"Maybe," said Rosetta. "Check again before lunch." She turned toward Vivienne's brain pattern, which, like most of the class, was right-brained, left-eared, right-eyed, right-handed, right-footed, with logic in the left brain and gestalt (synthesis, feelings) in the right. So very strong on hearing, possibly clairaudient, with a strong inner life, strong feelings, weak on logic. That was Talitha's brain pattern, and Rosetta's too. And yet Talitha seemed strong on action—after all, she gave great haircuts and was always working on her house. And it looked as if Rosetta was strong on action too.

"Remember," Rosetta said. "Brain patterns are simple. People are complicated." She also recommended that we find peoples' second strengths, in fact rank all their abilities from strongest to weakest. I didn't think I could figure that out from the information brain patterns gave me. Hadsn't Rosetta said that practically my greatest weakness was verbal? Even though I tended to accept what people said of me, especially when they were psychic, I just wasn't sure that was true.

At lunch, Elaine retested my brain pattern. I didn't cheat and returned to being left-brained, with logic in my left brain and gestalt in my right, where they are for most people. So that meant I was strong on logic (was that true?) and found it harder to access my feelings (that was true, and probably accounted for my iced numbness). It also indicated I was shy, and I had trouble with action. It wasn't the world's greatest brain pattern, but it wasn't deeply troubled, either. Rosetta looked relieved when Elaine told her.

As we headed into the dining alcove, Vivienne said to me with a wicked grin, "So you've got a screwed-up brain pattern?" From her, it didn't sound so bad.

"I was cheating," I admitted. "I wanted to be right-brained and creative like everyone else."

Vivienne chuckled. "So what *is* your brain pattern?"

I told her. "I'm afraid I'll never be able to get a single thing accomplished with a blocked brain pattern."

"You're just not like everyone else," said Vivienne. "That's not a bad thing. I don't want to be like everyone else."

"On you it looks good," I said. "I love your dress."

"Thanks. I made it."

"You *made* it? You must be strong on action."

"I'm not actually. But I have to have some sort of brain-hand flow. I'm an artist."

I said, "I'm the only one in the class with a blocked left-brain. I'm inner but not intuitive. It's not comfortable not being like everyone else."

"*Comfortable?*" said Vivienne. "You don't get anywhere by being *comfortable.*"

I turned my attention to lunch. Of course it was all rice and vegetables with some almonds thrown in. An uninspired salad with carrots and beets. A bean salad. A side dish of carrots. No herbs, no spices. Boring. And the rice was a little stale. But everyone said it was delicious, and I was grateful for the food, even if it didn't feel nourishing. It didn't feel like love. I liked the almonds, but I would have toasted them or sautéed them in butter. I wouldn't have overcooked the beans in the rice dish. I liked the carrots, but I would have squeezed orange juice over them.

Rosetta instructed us. "Almonds are good for your bones and for parasites. Brown rice feeds your brain. Beets are good for your liver."

"What about dessert?" asked James.

"Have an apple," said Rosetta sternly. "The fibre's good for digestion. We're cleansing."

Talitha and Sharon were doing the dishes. I carried mine into the kitchen and then headed for the balcony.

Really, if there were nothing more than the view of lawn and trees below, it would have been enough. The sky had cleared to blue with big white clouds. I could look down on birds flitting from tree top to tree top. It soothed me and I was ready to get back to the work.

After lunch we looked at charts of parts of the body and what food was good for each of the parts. It was almost all fruits and vegetables, of course. It was like being on a merry-go-round. Things were repeated so often that my head began to spin, so I looked for things I liked: cherries were good for adrenals; blueberries were good for eyes. Peaches were good for lots of things, surprisingly. So were green beans and leafy green vegetables. Almonds had calcium, as did broccoli. Almonds and pumpkin seeds destroyed parasites. Green peas (which I loved) were full of vitamin E, and you should eat all you could while they were in season. I felt a little hopeful. Sweet potatoes were full of beta-carotene and potassium, but you shouldn't have them with butter, and certainly not candied. Tomatoes were good for the prostate, if you had a prostate. I guess the lesson was that we were all chemical soups, and some things were really good for our chemistry and some not. I had enough trouble with trying to think of cottage cheese as good and of desserts as bad, without having to worry about which vegetables I should be eating for my lungs and brain. I'd been up early, and now I was really missing coffee.

"What about vinegar?" asked Vivienne, waking me up. She had a low, memorable voice with an interesting undertone of hoarseness.

"Well, vinegar is fermented, like wine, so it's not ideal. Lemon juice is better."

"I make my own vinegar with rosemary and herbs."

"That's better," Rosetta said grudgingly, "but it's still something rotting in the body. I'd use it sparingly."

Vivienne nodded. Then, when Rosetta had turned her attention elsewhere, she winked at me. "I saw your eyes close," she mouthed.

"Thanks for waking me up," I mouthed back.

Rosetta must have seen me nodding, because she said, "I won't go over what all the parts of the body do. You can read that in your notebooks tonight. The important thing is that it's all connected. If your hips are out of balance and you don't correct them, your whole body can torque and one leg can end up shorter than the other. If your head is off its axis, you won't be able to think properly. We'll go into some of that tomorrow.

"For tonight, practice your finger testing and study your food combining."

After a much-too-short break, we did a meditation on the body and the miracle of each of its parts working together, much like the one I'd done when I was repatterned. Then Rosetta produced a deck of medicine cards, and we each drew one.

To my disappointment, I got Ant.

"Patience, order, discipline," Rosetta read from the book. "The reward is just over the horizon."

*Oh, fine.* But would I ever get to the horizon?

But then Elaine got Turkey, the giveaway card of self-sacrifice, and Deirdre got Antelope, which performed a shamanic dying so others could live—and that seemed worse. Vivienne got Skunk and grinned. "Skunks aren't life-threatening," Rosetta read, "but they are threatening. Skunk teaches you that by walking your talk and respecting yourself, you can create a position of strength and honoured reputation."

"So watch out!" said Vivienne.

Rosetta got Wolf, the teacher, pathfinder, listener to trees, plants, rocks, wind, rain. "You should all be learning this way," said Rosetta. "Nature is the great teacher."

Just what a teacher of literature wants to hear. Cancel class and send your students out to the lake.

Finally, the day was over and Rosetta let us go. I staggered into the elevator with Vivienne. "I'll drive you home," I said.

"It's way past the end of the bus line."

"That's what cars are for."

The elevator released us, and we emerged into the late afternoon light, the green, flowering, ordinary world. "I parked illegally," I apologized as I headed toward my car in Visitors Parking.

"Illegal's more interesting."

I unlocked the car, a Subaru (I'd bought Henry out of it when we split). "I'm wiped," I said.

"I'm annoyed," said Vivienne. "This is such low-level stuff."

We settled into the car. Vivienne looked authoritative in her flowing cloak.

"I guess you do have to start with the physical," I said.

"Maybe, but you could make it interesting. There are so many connections. The big toe is connected to the brain. When your back goes out, it's a sign that your life isn't supporting you. I've got arthritis in my hands from painting. That's self-criticism."

"I'm self-critical," I said. "I don't have arthritis."

"It might manifest somewhere else. Maybe your hips."

"Probably my hips," I said with regret. "Where do you live?"

"Turn on Concession, then left on Division. Hips are parents. Left, mother; right, father."

"My left hip must be totally messed up." I negotiated the

jumble of stores and unlovely buildings that lined upper Princess St., swerved left just before the LCBO, teetered through an unpretentious residential neighbourhood, and came out past the Cataraqui Conservation area.

"This is a long walk!"

"It was. I hitched part of the way, and then I got a bus on Princess, but there was a lot of walking. I think they'll have my car fixed Monday."

"Okay, now where?"

"Right on Bur Brook Road. When I grew up, this was all country. I liked it better."

"There are still bits of green."

"Not enough. If it wasn't for my daughter, I'd move back up north."

"Why?"

"Not so many people. Also, I might find a shaman if I don't find a magician."

"Why are you so keen on finding a magician?"

"I want to learn everything. I need someone to transform my art."

"Why does it have to be a man?"

"Alchemy, the lightning flash, sex. I wouldn't get that with a woman."

"That's what happens in *Moon Magic*, sort of. And in *Initiation*." Maybe that's what had happened with Brian. But it wasn't enough. I still needed something to transform my writing.

"I love *Moon Magic*. I haven't read *Initiation*."

"I just read it this winter. It's wonderful."

Vivienne directed, "That cluster of houses over there on the left, the one with the big trees. That's mine." It was a neat little white house hidden behind huge spruces.

"Nice house," I said as I pulled into the driveway. For an instant I thought that it didn't look like a penniless artist's house.

"It was my mother's. She's in a nursing home. Hey, thanks a lot for the ride!"

"Sure. I'll pick you up tomorrow if you think you can stand another day."

"Can you?"

"I don't like it, but I think I'll be there. Ten past eight?"

"We'll probably be pathetically early, but someone has to get there on time. See you then. Thanks."

I watched her go into the house, black cloak swishing, then backed carefully onto the road and drove home. I was exhausted. It was a relief to be back in my neighbourhood of assorted nineteenth-century houses with their reassuring bricks and stones. This streetscape had barely changed in a hundred years.

My house was a semi-detached limestone, the front built in 1842, the back, later, but probably not much later. It had high ceilings and a lovely hall, as well as a great fireplace. We'd bought it eleven years before, when we were a two-income, one-kid family, when things were better between us, when my career still seemed more or less on track, when Davy was still afraid to go outside. I knew I'd probably have to sell it at some point, but not yet.

I dragged myself, on autopilot, into the kitchen and fed the cats, who purred and wound themselves around my ankles, then settled into their tuna.

I cut a slice of cheese for myself, careful not to have it with bread (food combining), and then went upstairs to throw myself on my bed and sink into sleep before Davy came home. It wasn't quite five-thirty. Before the cats could even jump up to keep me company, I heard our loud raspy doorbell.

I saw the golden top of Claire's head through the window as I staggered downstairs to the door. She swept past me and then asked, "So, how was it?"

"Exhausting. Lots of stuff about what you should and shouldn't eat. Lots of stuff about what food is good for different organs."

"Did Talitha like it?"

"I don't know. She seemed pretty unruffled, but then she always does."

"Were the people in the class interesting?"

"Not very. One guy was a gifted healer, everyone said, but we were too busy being lectured about food for me to see it. There was a woman I liked who's painting, but not selling. And I think I did my notebook all wrong, and I've got no idea how to make it right because there aren't any page numbers."

Usually I loved seeing Claire, but now I just wanted her to leave so I could go back to sleep. "Sorry, Claire, I'm exhausted. If anything interesting happens, I'll let you know. For now, if this is psychic, I'll take vanilla."

"I just wondered—"

"Fine, and I'm just telling you."

I saw her out the door and went back to bed, this time protected by loudly purring cats. If the psychic world began with the body, I thought, the least I could do was give my body the sleep it needed.

## 9. THE PSYCHIC WORLD INCLUDES TRANSFORMERS

THE NEXT MORNING I WAS AWAKE EARLY enough to make a pot of Lapsang Souchong, which wasn't herbal tea, but at least wasn't coffee, and a couple pieces of toast. I felt nourished, and I was early enough to pick up Vivienne at ten past eight. It was a lovely sunny morning, quiet because it was Sunday, and all the blossoms and tiny new leaves were reaching up to the sky, almost dancing as they went about the serious business of growing.

Vivienne was waiting on her front step in her cloak, which was ruffling slightly in the breeze. "You look great," I said as she got into the car. "You look as if you could summon a broomstick and fly to Rosetta's."

She grinned. "How I'd love to be able to do that! And teleporting. I don't suppose we'll get to that in the next two weeks. How are you?"

"Better," I said. "I had a really good sleep."

"Ready for today?"

"I don't know. What else can she throw at us?"

I parked in the Visitors' Parking a little more confidently, and we rode up in the elevator. The empty apartment didn't bother me this time, and I led Vivienne straight to the kitchen. There was Talitha, all in black today (good with her blonde hair); Sharon, in blue; Andrea in an orange sweater and jeans with sparkles n them; Deirdre, in grey. So we were almost all there.

"I was practising finger testing," Talitha was saying. "Do I want to be here? No. Am I supposed to be here? 'Yes.' Hello, Judith. Hello, Vivienne. Help yourself if you want instant coffee..."

"We aren't supposed to have coffee," said Sharon.

"I wouldn't ruin a cleanse with instant coffee," said Andrea.

"...or tea," Talitha continued. "The water's hot."

"I'd like a tea," said Vivienne.

Talitha waved at the cupboard. "It's on the top shelf."

Vivienne was tall enough that she could reach. "Peppermint," she decided. "Do you want one, Judith?"

Peppermint sounded pretty good to me. "Yes, please."

Vivienne extracted two tea bags and mugs, poured the water, and returned the tea to the top shelf, all with surprising grace. I couldn't help thinking she'd be good at mixing potions.

Rosetta appeared and motioned us into the living room.

I settled into my chair and sipped my tea. I liked it. "It's good," I said to Vivienne. "Thanks. I didn't think I'd like herbal tea."

She nodded, unfurled her cloak, folding it deftly and placing it at the side of the room by the window. She was wearing a flowing lavender blouse with sequins on it.

"Great blouse," I said, worrying that I was gushing.

"It's a galabia. A friend brought it back from Egypt."

"Egypt?"

"Now there's a place of mysteries. My friend says you haven't lived until you've lain inside the Great Pyramid and listened to the ghosts in the King's Chamber."

Rosetta clapped us to order. "Has everyone heard about the Earth changes?"

James bounded into the room. "Yes!"

"What Earth changes?" asked Talitha.

"They're really wild," said James. "It's like the apocalypse!"

Rosetta pulled out a large map of the United States and Canada with very different shapes. "Over the next twenty or thirty years with increased global warming, the polar ice caps

will melt and the seas will rise. There will be floods. Most of
what is now the Eastern Seaboard will be washed away along
with a lot of the land around the Gulf of Mexico. Hurricanes
and tornadoes will be more severe. There will be earthquakes
and tsunamis. We are living in a time of transition. These
weather events are part of the transition between this age and
the next, which will be one of peace and prosperity for those
who survive to see it."

On the map, New York was gone. That's what I minded
most. Oh, that couldn't happen. Those old brownstones,
those streets where I'd walked, Central Park, the galleries
full of art and antiques, the museums—what would happen
to Rembrandt's Self-Portrait at the Frick? Or the Comtesse
d'Haussonville? And the few friends I had left, so rooted in
New York intellectual life—I couldn't imagine them homeless.
The map showed that all the places of my younger life would
be gone—eastern Pennsylvania, Connecticut, eastern Massa-
chusetts—I couldn't believe it.

"It's a cleansing," Rosetta said. How could she be so heart-
less? It was people; it was homes. It was history. But mostly,
it was people.

"And when the earth has changed, other things will change
too," said Rosetta. "For instance, there will be no money."

I didn't hear the buzzer, but Elaine came in just as Rosetta
was finishing. "I'm sorry," she said. "Lily's still sick, and I
don't like to leave her."

"You have a sitter, don't you?" asked Rosetta.

"Yes, but it's not the same," said Elaine.

"I've got a really bad headache," said Talitha.

"It shows your vibration is being raised. Any other questions
or comments before we start?"

Sharon raised her hand. "I still don't get finger testing. I'm
still confused about strong being closed and also meaning
"no," and how you do it to yourself."

"When you finger test yourself," Rosetta said, "You usually

ask for a 'yes' or 'no' answer. You make a circle with your thumb and little finger and see if the index finger of your other hand can open the circle. If it can open the fingers, then the answer is 'yes.' If not, it's 'no.' It's a little confusing that it's the opposite for strong and weak, but sometimes things have multiple meanings."

"How do you know it's right?" asked Sharon.

"You have to let go of your conscious knowing," said Talitha. "It took me hours to get it, but I finally did. This morning I asked myself, 'Do I want to go to class?' and my finger testing said 'no,' but then I asked 'Should I go to class?' and my finger testing said 'yes'."

"That's exactly right," said Rosetta. "You have to let go of your conscious knowing. And it's important to ask the right question."

I wanted to ask, *How do you know when a headache is your vibration being raised and how do you know when it's just being sick?* but I felt everyone else was learning, and I was just confused.

"So then why do you have to learn how to distinguish strong and weak?" asked Elaine.

"It's mostly for repatterning, to make sure that you can communicate with someone's body/soul without contacting their mind. It's telepathy. Although you can ask for 'yes' and 'no' by telepathy too."

Rosetta seemed to take telepathy for granted. So, for now, one of my questions, at least, was answered.

"When you do a physical check, strong is good and weak means something needs rebalancing. Can I have a volunteer?"

I felt that I was doing too much lurking on the edge, so I raised my hand weakly.

"Judith. Come stand up here."

I felt very awkward in the middle of the circle.

"Give me your thumb and little finger." Rosetta grabbed my hand and pulled at my fingers. They stayed shut.

hold them so tight. You're being a control freak. ter."

_..c pulled at my fingers again. I had no idea what she was asking. "Your brain's fine. Your eyes are fine. Your ears are fine. See how she tests strong? Your heart's fine."

My heart felt pretty roughed up (I thought) between worry about Davy and missing the ever-elusive Brian. And, I wasn't letting myself feel how much I hated Henry coming downtown where he knew I'd be and then yelling at me, but I did. He'd always said that if people wanted to separate or divorce, they should do it amicably. I didn't realize there'd be such a gap between his theory and his practice.

Then she pulled and my fingers sprang apart. "Your adrenals are way down," she said with concern. "Wait here." *As if I were going anywhere in the next two minutes.*

She came back with a medium-sized pill bottle and a glass of water and grabbed my hand again. "You need two core adrenals. Now. And two more after lunch."

The core adrenals were huge. It took several tries before I managed to swallow them.

Rosetta returned to pulling at my fingers. "Let's see about your other glands. Your pineal gland is all right. Your thymus is off; your parathymus is off; your parotids are off. Your pancreas is stressed. Your liver needs support—not as much as your adrenals. And you've got yeast. You need to eat fewer carbs and cut out sugars. Yeast bloats you. But the real trouble with yeast is that it travels to the brain and causes Alzheimer's."

Rosetta was pulling my fingers and pronouncing on all my glandular deficiencies. As with everything in Results, it was so fast, I hardly knew what was happening. "I'm a basket case," I said, feeling again as if I didn't belong in the group.

I hated being told what was wrong with me. But this scared me too. I was afraid I was going to lapse into Alzheimer's any minute. Maybe I wouldn't be able to find my way home. I was also embarrassed. Who could have more wrong with them?

"You can do this for your clients," said Rosetta to the class.

I thought, *it's the beginning of the second day and already we've got clients?*

"And when you find something that's off, you ask whether you should give a nutritional supplement or just continue counselling."

"How do we know about nutritional supplements?" asked Deirdre.

"Well, that's a separate course, but you might want to do it if you think you're going to have clients with physical problems. Or you could call a nutritionist or herbalist—we have some good ones in Prince's Harbour. Or you could look in your book for supportive foods. Now for adrenals: cherries, dandelions, dates, figs, nuts, sweet potatoes, brown rice, seeds—they're all good for adrenals. She took my hand again. "Judith wants cherries, dates, sweet potatoes." (Finally, food I liked.) "Brown rice is good for everything. We'll have that for lunch. And take some almonds now."

I went to the table and scooped up three or four almonds. They were dry and uninspired.

"Cherries are good for most glands," Rosetta continued. "Lemons, nuts, seeds, green leafy vegetables. When a client tests weak on something, you can look in the book to see what foods they need and then finger test for the best ones."

I started for my chair.

"Let me finger test you one last time," said Rosetta, interrupting me mid-step. I had no idea what she was doing.

"There!" Rosetta was triumphant. "Your adrenals were an eight for stress; now they're down to a six. They should be better after lunch. Thank you, Judith. Let's have one more volunteer."

I collapsed back into my chair. My adrenals might have been better, but I wasn't sure about the rest of me.

"I'll do it," said Talitha. She looked like a priestess—all she needed was a white robe instead of a black sweater.

Rosetta pointed to each part of Talitha's body as she finger tested. Everything was fine except for her jaw—TMJ—and shoulders. "That's where lots of people hold stress," said Rosetta. "You've got too much responsibility, and you're holding a lot in."

Talitha shrugged. "I'm the breadwinner."

"You should leave him."

"I don't want to."

"My guides say you should. There's stress around your heart."

*What nerve,* I thought. I'd be careful about breaking up someone's marriage if I were psychic.

"I don't *want* to," said Talitha again.

"Well, just be aware of what your body/soul is saying," said Rosetta. "You're more wounded than you think you are. Anyway, that's how strong and weak work. You'll need them for body alignment."

Whatever body alignment was.

"Finger testing depends on intention," said Rosetta. "It replies to what you're asking.

"I like pendulums better," said James. "I've got a pendulum that was once used by Aleister Crowley. It's very powerful."

"Aleister Crowley!" It just burst out of me. "Wasn't he the one who was so neglectful of some of his children that they died?"

"He really knew his magic," said James. "His Thoth deck is awesome."

"Why didn't he use some of his magic on his kids?" I couldn't believe I was saying this. I didn't want to quarrel with James! But when you have a kid like Davy, it changes everything. Maybe when you have any kid, it changes everything.

"I don't want kids," said James. "I want to find a boyfriend and start a restaurant named Hecate's Cauldron with a room for healing and maybe a massage parlour at the back."

"What food would you serve?" asked Sharon, ignoring the massage parlour.

"Soups, stews," suggested Talitha. "Anything you can make in a cauldron."

"Mushrooms, carrots," suggested Deirdre. "Potatoes. Other things that grow underground."

"Devil's food cake," said Andrea.

"*Dulce de leche*," said Vivienne. "It's not underground, but I bet Hecate would love it. Nettle soup."

"Paella," said James. "Chicken Marbella. Roasted lamb. I'd like to have an open fire with a spit to roast things. Pomegranate juice."

"We could sell you organic beef," offered Sharon.

"That all sounds great, James," I said. "But I think you should be a little careful about using Aleister Crowley's pendulum. You don't know what could be coming along with it."

"It's really powerful," said James.

"Power can go in a lot of directions," I said, thinking of my disastrous department head.

Rosetta clapped her hands in an attempt to end the discussion. "We'll get to pendulums soon," she said. "Now it's time for a break."

I DIDN'T WANT TO FACE the one-day-older apples or the almonds again, even if they were good for my adrenals, so I headed out onto the balcony.

Vivienne joined me. "Well, that was fun." She produced a pack of cigarettes as if by magic. "Want one?"

"No thanks."

"Don't tell Rosetta."

"We'd better go to the other end of the balcony."

"So what did you think of this morning?" Vivienne lit her cigarette and took a grateful puff.

"I thought I'd go through the floor if I didn't die first. And I hope James isn't mad at me. It's as if we've all been together for months, and it's only the second day."

"It's not really what I want to be learning," said Vivienne.

It wasn't exactly what I wanted to be learning either. "What do you want to be learning?" I asked.

"Spells. I wouldn't mind curses. You can find some of those in books, but they don't work unless a teacher tells you what's been left out."

"The psychic world begins with the body," I said. "At least I've got a good excuse to buy cherries."

Break was over. Vivienne stubbed out her cigarette under her shoe and tossed the butt off the balcony. "If it starts a fire, we can go home early."

After break we each found a partner and practised checking all the places in the body that could be strong or weak. There was lots of room in Rosetta's apartment—the long living room ending in the dining room, two extra bedrooms, and the bright sitting nook as you came from the elevator. I went into one of the guest rooms with Andrea, who seemed just as confused as I was.

We both had trouble with what was strong and what was weak, but eventually we muddled through each other's bodies from head to toe. Andrea's brain was stressed—no wonder! My glands didn't test as weak for Andrea as they had for Rosetta—maybe it was the core adrenals.

Rosetta came by to check. She vanished and returned with a white pill for Andrea and some drops for me, and we both tested stronger. "Healing can be that fast," she said.

I didn't feel any different.

As for lunch, the brown rice was starting to taste suspicious, and the vegetables were tired. Rosetta had announced that tomorrow we would start taking turns bringing lunch, which I dreaded. ("It's so personal making food for someone's insides," says Gwendolyn MacEwen.)

"YOU CAN SEE THAT FINGER TESTING is the basis of everything else," said Rosetta when we'd reconvened in the living room after lunch. Talitha said she would start. "It's the way you communicate with the client's body/soul, and it's more accurate than speaking. Once you've done the work, you check by finger testing to see if you've done it properly. If not, you go back and do it again. You can do it with pendulums"—she looked at James—"but we'll get to them later. There's something to be said for having the physical contact of finger testing. Now we're going to do transformers. Does anyone know what transformers are?"

"They're like little chakras," said James. "They're energy centres."

"Right." Rosetta looked pleased. "We take things in through our senses, but we also take in information and energy through our transformers. Look at the diagram in your book. They're where your energy field intersects with the greater energy field. They're sort of sub-chakras where you take in energy from the universe. They're a little like windshields. Like windshields, they get dirty, and you have to clean them, energetically. That's what we're doing now. Can I have a volunteer?"

Well, certainly not me after this morning.

Deirdre volunteered, and Rosetta showed us where the transformers were: hands, feet, eyes, and ears. You cleaned them with a circular motion of your hands, not touching the person you were working on, four to six inches away. Then you finger tested to see that you'd cleared the transformer. If you had, you went on to the next one. If not, more cleaning, like silver polish.

"It feels nice," offered Deirdre, "like your edges are being smoothed. I think I could do this for my clients."

"You have to pull down the energy from the forces that control the universe and ask it to come through you, sort of put it on your energetic cloth and buff." Rosetta took Deirdre's hand and finger tested several times. "Your transformers are clear. There's something else, but we'll deal with that later."

"Thanks," said Deirdre. Her energy seemed so clear and quiet that I couldn't imagine anything might be wrong with her. But we were probably all here because we needed healing, weren't we?

Rosetta instructed each of us to find a partner. I didn't want to work with Andrea again—it was too much like the blind leading the blind—so I summoned my courage and turned to James, who I thought was much too good for me and would be bored by my ineptitude.

"Let's go in one of the guest rooms," he suggested.

"Good idea," I agreed. That way Rosetta wouldn't see me unless she checked.

Rosetta had set each of the guest rooms up with a massage table during lunch. There were a couple in the living room too.

"I *love* energy work," said James.

"Great," I said. "You do it first."

"Okay. Start face down."

I climbed onto the table. "Tell me what you're doing. Otherwise I'll have no idea. How did you learn all this?"

"I hang out at Treasure Garden. And my guides tell me."

"I wish I had guides."

I could feel James' energy, his hands moving over my back. It was nice. "Wow, there's a lot of stuff here," James said, not judgmentally. "Was anyone trying to hurt you?"

I started to weep. "There was this woman I thought was a friend, and she vowed she would destroy me and turned people against me so that no one was speaking to me. And her partner nearly fired me. How could I expect a not-quite twenty-two year-old to understand all this when four therapists hadn't? And Rosetta hadn't really, either.

"That's a bitch," said James, his hand circling back all the while. "I just put a stone on your back. Obsidian, to repel negativity and return it to senders."

"You just *have* that?"

"I love stones. I forgot to bring my big crystals, but maybe tomorrow. I keep smaller stones with me. Obsidian isn't a crystal, but it's useful to have around. You never know when

you're going to run into negativity. Okay, I'll do your feet."
He made a few circles over them, and I peeked to see how he
did it. "They're fine."

"That's odd, considering how much I walk."

"It's not the use, it's the energy. Now your elbows, the backs
of your hands. You can turn over now."

"What about the obsidian?"

"I'll put it on your power centre. That and a quartz crystal
for clarity."

I turned over, felt the slight weight of the stones just above my
navel. It seemed to me that if Brian were doing this to me, we
might both consider it sexy, or at least his unconscious might.
But I knew from Rosetta, and now from James, that healing
can be intimate without being sexy. And that you have to be
careful with anything that intimate.

"There are your hands, your face, your ears, all okay. Your
third eye's wide open."

"I didn't even know I had a third eye. I thought it was a myth."

"No, you've got one, and it's wide open. Don't you ever see
things not with your physical eyes?"

"Of course, doesn't everyone?"

"That's your third eye." James made a few more circular
motions around my heart, and I felt less frozen, the beginning
of tears.

"All done," James said cheerfully.

"Thank you," I babbled. "Thank you. I feel much better."
And, to my surprise, I did.

"Energy work," said James.

I got up slowly. "I'll never be able to do that for you."

James lay face down on the table. I gulped, had no idea of
what I was doing, in spite of Rosetta's demonstration, in spite
of James' gift of healing to me. I circled my hands tentatively
over the back of his head, looked at the curly brown hair,
the broad back, the pasty skin, and didn't see any trace from
looking at his body of the care I'd felt when he was cleaning

my transformers. I of all people ought to know that peoples' outsides can be very different from their insides.

I felt a little silly waving my hands around in the air, but Rosetta said that a lot of healing was intention, and my intention was to clean James' transformers.

"I can feel the space around my head getting clearer," James said from the depths of the massage table.

I was surprised, but I didn't let it distract me. I worked my way down to his elbows and feet, and asked him to turn over. I had no idea if his third eye was open or not. I thought if this were Brian, who was also a Gemini, also split between head and heart, I'd want to bring the fragments together. So I concentrated on that, paying special attention to James' hands, a healer's hands—when suddenly James said, "I died!"

"Oh my God," I said, "Are you all right?" Oh what had I done? I grabbed his hand.

"I'm shaken," he said, sitting up. "I was going down a dark tunnel and I saw Mama Isis at the end standing in light. She said, *What are you dong here? You're not supposed to be here yet.* So I turned around and came back."

"I think we should get Rosetta," I said

"I came back, didn't I?"

I dragged him into the living room where Rosetta was working with Sharon and Andrea. "Are you done already?" she asked, looking up at us with obvious irritation.

"I died!" James reported the whole vision with obvious enjoyment. "Mama Isis said it wasn't my time yet."

Rosetta looked grave. I thought she was going to throw me out of the class for psychic violence.

"I was trying to concentrate on cleaning his transformers," I said apologetically. I imagined that everyone was going to hate me the way they did after Dottie started her campaign against me.

"It's a shock," said Rosetta to James.

"No kidding!"

Rosetta spoke, not just to us, but to the class. "To cross the boundary between worlds is a great gift. Judith's care created a space where James could travel. It's a journey not everyone could make."

Sharon raised her hand. "Was it real or was it just a vision?"

"Just because you are not travelling with your body doesn't mean it's not a real journey," Rosetta said in her teaching voice. "Think of all the adventures we have as we sleep. Just because our bodies are in bed doesn't mean our spirits aren't travelling. But it's important to have someone ground you so you can come back."

"It felt like home," James said. "I won't mind going back there, crossing into that light at the end of the tunnel."

"It's not your time," Rosetta reminded him. "Now I think you and Judith should take a walk outside. Don't hurry. Take the time to be here, in these moments."

We went down in the elevator and wandered around the grounds. The sun was just starting to slant into afternoon, and the puffy clouds were tender with golden light. We walked under maples with their young green leaves, under apple blossoms, looked at robins and blackbirds flitting. We took it all in through our newly-cleansed transformers.

I wasn't sure what we were supposed to do. "Tell me about Isis," I said.

James brightened. "She's my mama. She doesn't nag. She's not critical. She opens her arms and enfolds me in brightness."

"My mother was pretty naggy and critical," I said. "I guess that's the trouble with only having one child. You want them to be everything." (Though surely I didn't feel that way about Davy.) "Your mother should be grateful to have a son who's such a gifted healer."

"She just thinks it's a waste of time."

"What would she like you to be doing?"

"I don't know. Go to college. Find a career."

"What would you like to do?"

"Learn reiki. Find a boyfriend. Start that restaurant."

"Maybe you should start with reiki."

"I can't afford it. My mother won't pay for it."

"Would she have paid for college?"

"Probably. But she thinks reiki's too *woo-woo*."

"My mother would have a fit if she knew I was doing a course like this. That's sort of a comfort."

James gave a watery smile. "What did she think you should have done?"

"Oh, have a super career, a super husband, super children. Like I could wave a magic wand and they'd all appear."

"Is she still with us?" James asked delicately.

"No, she's been gone about fourteen years."

"Do you feel her spirit?"

"No—and anyway, she didn't believe in spirits. She hated anything mystical."

"Mine does too."

"I guess some mothers are just born to be obstacles. I hope my son doesn't ever feel that way about me."

We walked along some more and watched a robin bringing a worm back to her nest. Mothering can be so simple. Well, the feeding's the simple stage.

I tried to get James to say more about his guides, about the Egyptian gods. "So who else besides Isis?" We were walking behind the back of the building where there were more trees. I pulled down an apple blossom branch for us to smell, the way I would have for Davy.

"Nice," said James.

I breathed it in myself and was surrounded with sweetness.

A heron flapped by us, the unhurried flap of creaky wings, a glimpse into what the world must have looked like thousands of years ago.

"Thoth," said James. "Well, really, Thoth's bird is the ibis, but herons are as close as we get here. Thoth's one of my faves, bringer of alphabets, trickster, magician, writer."

"James, I hope I know you when you're forty," I said. "You'll be a master. You're pretty amazing now."

The heron flapped out of sight. Off to its nest, I'd guess.

"I'm feeling more grounded," said James. "I think we could go back."

We turned the corner of the apartment building and walked unhurriedly toward the parking lot and the entrance, letting the sun soak into our arms. It really was a lovely day, too nice to leave this world for another.

"Why are you taking this course?" I asked as we turned the last corner. "You know so much of this stuff already."

"This is a system. The stuff I know isn't organized. And, I might be able to make some money if I can hone my skills. Why are you taking the course?"

"I need the healing," I said. "But there are times when I feel the cure's worse than the disease."

We were close to the entrance now, in the shadow of the building, and the day grew darker.

"Besides," I added, "at some point I feel the world is going to fall apart. You heard what Rosetta said about the earth changes and that there won't be any more money, I'll need something to barter with. No one's going to want lectures on English literature."

We walked through the outer doors and left the day behind. I rang the buzzer. No answer.

"Let's think to them that we're here," said James. "Really concentrate. Okay, now I'll ring again."

To my surprise, I heard Talitha's voice on the other end of the intercom. "Come in," she said, and James grabbed the door as she buzzed us in.

I WAS BRACING MYSELF for another onslaught of food-combining, but instead Rosetta told us about our three minds—conscious, subconscious, and superconscious—our alignment with the world around us, our psychic connections in the ether, and our connection with the Divine Mind. All three were meant to be aligned, but they weren't for any of us.

When she finger tested me, I discovered that my conscious mind was off—I just wasn't in tune with the world around me. I was the only one in the class, which once again made me feel like a misfit. My subconscious could use strengthening. My superconscious was surprisingly strong, as was Deirdre's.

Then we did a meditation in which we met ourselves as a child. I was afraid I'd let my three-year-old self down. "You haven't done so badly," she said.

Then we met our parents, and that was difficult—my mother ever more critical, making me feel that I'd wasted my opportunities, my father not contradicting her.

I was wrung out by the time Rosetta told us to come back to the room and open our eyes.

When she retested me, my superconscious was still fine, my subconscious was better, and my conscious mind was still off.

Rosetta said, "By the end of the course, you'll find your three minds aligning."

*Good heavens*, I thought, *in just twelve more days?*

Rosetta must have read my mind. "This system works quickly," she reminded us. Then she added, "For homework, find someone and practice body alignment."

*Yuck*, I thought, *just what I need.*

We ended with a circle, with a great moon song that started "Smiling Virgin, Shining Crescent/, Waxing fullness, luminescent/ Sickle of silver, reaper of bone/Maiden, Mother, and Crone"—but I didn't remember the rest of it.

"YOU LOOK PALE," said Vivienne as we made our way to the elevator.

"I had a difficult meditation," I said. "It started fine, but then I remembered how critical and bad-tempered my mother was."

Vivienne shrugged. "My parents didn't want me to be an artist. My father's long gone. My mother's still alive, but she's very ill, poor thing. I'll go see her after the course is over. What about when you brought your highest energy form into the meditation?"

I searched my memory for the highest energy form, which had come toward the end of the meditation. "It said that everyone had the right to strive."

"I think that's probably true."

The thought left us in silence, and the landscape rolled by till we got to Vivienne's home.

"Thanks," said Vivienne as she got out. "I'm pretty sure my car'll be ready tomorrow, so you won't need to pick me up. Thanks for ferrying me."

I got out and we hugged goodbye. It felt as if we'd gotten awfully close in two days.

WHEN I GOT HOME, Claire called. "How was it?"

"Don't ask," I said. I couldn't face saying, even to Claire, that I nearly killed someone, that I might be at risk for Alzheimer's because my yeast was so high, and that I was visited by the ghosts of my parents and that it had upset me. "We ended with a great song about the triple Moon Goddess," I said, "but I can't remember the words. If life gives me second chances, I'll sing it to you. How are things with Josh?"

"Up and down—more down. I think Rosetta was wrong about him."

"She didn't say he'd be the love of your life."

"Maybe I should go back and see if she can foresee another man that is a better fit for me."

I suddenly felt exhausted.

"I've got a few minutes before Davy gets home," I said. "I want to sit and sort things out."

"Okay, I'll call you tomorrow."

# 10. ALL IS IN DIVINE ORDER

B Y THE FOURTH DAY we were settling into a routine, arriving between eight-thirty and nine, making herbal tea, and, instead of hanging out around the kitchen, drifting into the living room. I had discovered ginseng tea, and thought I could manage for the rest of the two weeks with it and peppermint. Vivienne's car was fixed, so she didn't need me to drive her. I missed her sardonic comments. I wasn't quite so exhausted. (Maybe this was because the core adrenals that Rosetta had fed me were helping, or maybe it was because I was another day away from end-of-year marathon marking.) Elaine and James were still the last to arrive; Elaine because of her concern for Lily, who still wasn't well, and James because he was a night owl and only really woke up around noon.

We had started taking turns with the lunches. Talitha had volunteered to go first. "I like to cook," she said.

I wanted to put it off as long as possible. It wasn't that I didn't like to cook—I just didn't think I could manage a vegetarian lunch for eight. The very thought made me queasy.

We were getting used to Rosetta grabbing our fingers and then telling us what they'd said.

This morning she grabbed James' hand as soon as he arrived and said, "All is in Divine Order, and I am accepting of that order now."

"If everything were in Divine Order, I'd have a boyfriend," James objected.

"Me too," chipped in Andrea.

*Me too*, I thought, and Brian slipped into my mind with his lovely brown eyes and his sweetness.

Rosetta moved on to Deirdre. "Can you say, *All is in Divine Order, and I am accepting of that order now?*" Deirdre's fingers opened. "Good for you! You believe it."

As Rosetta continued to finger test us, it turned out that Deirdre was the only one of us who believed in it. Even Sharon, who was usually so in tune with everything in this course—possibly because she lived such an organic life—wasn't really there.

Deirdre said, "You can wish for things, but you can't control what happens."

"But can't you work toward things?" asked Talitha.

"Of course," said Rosetta. "But you can't control the outcome. But I think some of you are also being modest and not seeing yourselves as part of the Divine Order."

"It sounds awfully Christian to me," objected Vivienne.

"Not just Christian," said Rosetta. "Now close your eyes, but keep pen and paper handy in case you want to write something down."

"How can we write with our eyes closed?" asked James.

"Open your eyes; write; close them again." Rosetta was usually patient with questions, but I thought I caught an undertone of exasperation. She took a breath.

"Imagine you're on a beautiful beach." Her voice was softer than usual. "The temperature is perfect, the sun is caressing your shoulders, and the sand is warm under your feet."

I pictured Tofino, the beach with the rocks and caves and the many-coloured starfish: orange, purple, red. Some of them were spangled. I went to Tofino with Davy and Henry before we split. We had all loved it.

"The water is the perfect temperature," Rosetta continued. "You wade in, and, if you like, you start swimming."

The tides were strong in Tofino, and the waves, gathering momentum all across the Pacific, were too fierce for good swimming. Even in my head, I didn't want to be swept out to sea. I jumped to Sanibel, where we took Davy when he was seven, eight, nine. A lovely sandy beach with a gentle slope, pelicans flying overhead, shells washing up on the shore. Once, after a storm, it looked as if the sea had thrown its treasures all over the beach. I was six, seven, eight years younger, and it wasn't so fearsome wearing a bathing suit.

"You feel the water lovingly surround you, and you see a beautiful school of fish. They invite you to follow them."

I thought of my mother saying, *Don't go anywhere with strangers,* but these were fish for heaven's sake, so I followed them to a cave where a big wise fish waited.

I vaguely heard Rosetta's voice telling me I could ask this fish anything, but I was so in the vision that I didn't really hear it. There was the fish. I asked for Davy to grow up well. Then, I asked to see Brian again (was that possible?). I asked about my writing. I thought the fish was nodding and thanked him.

"You give him a gift in return," I heard Rosetta saying through the haze of fish vision.

I panicked. I had nothing to give! Then I felt something in my right hand—a lapis scarab—where did that come from? I placed it in front of the great fish's throne and kissed the sea floor.

"Then the school of fish escorts you back to the beach," Rosetta said. "You climb out of the water and feel the sun once more before you travel back to this room. When you're ready, open your eyes."

My mind was still full of water, shells, starfish, and hope. It was a shock to be back in Rosetta's pale living room in the semi-comfortable chair that seemed to have become my place.

I thought we all looked a little dazed with the vision world we'd been in.

"Anyone want to share?" Rosetta asked.

James raised his hand. "I'm not sure where I was—the beach was on a curved bay—maybe an island. The fish were golden, and they led me to Zeus in the shape of an enormous porpoise, and I felt very safe and filled with light. The water was like green crystal, like being inside an emerald."

"Lovely," said Rosetta.

"Oh fuck, I forgot to bring my crystals," said James. "I will tomorrow."

"I was on Big Sandy Beach on Wolfe Island," said Talitha. "I couldn't believe how warm the water was. While I swam, I heard the lake singing to the shore and the trees and the sky, spring music, growing and lapping and flowering."

"Beautiful," said Rosetta. "And the fish?"

"The big fish was a huge bass. He told me I belonged to this land and I needed to work to preserve it. Usually I'm afraid of water—I think I drowned in some of my past lives—but I wasn't afraid this time."

"What did you ask him for?" asked James.

"I think I don't want to share that," said Talitha.

"I saw colours," said Sharon. "I didn't see a fish. But I felt I was swimming in rose pink."

"Love," said Rosetta.

I thought for a meditation that had started so sternly with Deirdre's admonitions that Divine Order wasn't about our being granted our hearts' desires, it had all been unexpectedly upbeat.

Rosetta turned to James. "All is in Divine Order, and I am accepting of this order now."

He repeated it easily, and she retested him. "Now you believe it."

"I guess I do," said James, "but I'd still like a boyfriend."

Rosetta retested each of us. "All strong," she said with satisfaction. "But drink some water at break to anchor it and maybe again after you get home. This is a belief system that many others rest on."

"It still seems awfully Christian to me," Vivienne muttered. If Rosetta heard it, she ignored it.

"Actually," said Rosetta, "Let's take a short break now for water."

"I wouldn't mind wine," Vivienne said to me as we headed toward the kitchen.

"At ten-thirty in the morning?"

"Okay, gin."

"I *liked* the meditation." I was defensive.

"It was okay. I've done better. I can't believe she thinks we're going to make money from this."

"I'm not in it for the money. I need the healing."

"It *might* work." Vivienne sounded doubtful. "Why did you like the meditation?"

I dutifully chugged my water and headed for the balcony. "The fish granted my wishes. He didn't make fun of me for asking."

"Haven't you ever wished for things that happened?"

I thought of Henry. I'd wished for him, and we'd been together. Some good years, some hard. Maybe I should have let the Divine Order take its course. I thought of Davy. I'd wished for a baby, and there he was, cute and cuddly and (surprisingly) blue-eyed, at least for the first few months. I wouldn't have wished for the autism, but as I still tell Davy, the stork brought the right baby. I'd wished for a teaching job, and I'd gotten one. Now it felt like an atrophying appendage—not my students, but the job. Maybe Divine Order could have done better for me if I hadn't asked so specifically.

"Yes," I said, "but some of the things were mixed blessings." I leaned on the balcony and looked down at the trees. I could feel Brian at my other shoulder. Oh, was I making all this up? Would I even like him if I ever saw him again? I thought of Sylvia Plath writing in her journals at the end of her year in Boston, "I am a serene, confident, and happy writer." Imagine!

"And I still have wishes," I said.

"That just means your life isn't complete," said Vivienne. "Mine isn't either. I need to bring up my daughter, and my art has a long way to go. And I need money to support both of them. And I'd like to go back up North and spend some time with Elders again. They really see into the heart of things. I'd need money for that too, and I can't believe I'll make it doing this stuff."

"Maybe it's a transition," I suggested. "Maybe it will lead to something. Isn't that part of Divine Order too?"

"Would you still have liked the meditation even if your wishes hadn't been granted?"

"I think so. I loved the beach. I loved being in the water and seeing all the shells. I liked swimming with the other fish. The big fish was a little scary, but ultimately I felt blessed. It felt as if something had lifted, that some wall, holding me back, had dissolved. "

"You have problems with authority," Vivienne said.

"No," I said. Then, "I guess you're right."

"Break's over." Talitha beckoned from the door.

"Too bad," said Vivienne.

We trooped back to our chairs. I knew something about Divine Order from having been a medievalist, but there's a difference between looking at the stars and feeling that you're an essential (though infinitely small) part of the universe they shine in. I'd think about it later. I'd think about having problems with authority. My mother, my department head, even Henry—it was probably all of a piece.

"We need to move on," said Rosetta. "I want to talk about the heart."

My heart. Brian's heart. When I breathed, I felt they were connected. But why didn't he call?

"The heart is the most important muscle in your body. It works with the lungs to keep cells nourished, to keep them breathing and hydrated. Fat is bad for the heart because it clogs it. Exercise helps burn fat and keeps the heart running effectively.

"Nutritional supplements that help the heart are water soluble vitamin B complex, Vitamin C, Vitamin E, selenium...."

"Do we have to take all that just for the heart?" James was appalled, and so was I.

"You can get some things in foods—carrots have beta carotene; peas have Vitamin E. Look in your book for other examples. What other foods have B vitamins?"

"Brown rice," guessed James.

"Garlic," said Talitha. "Garlic's good for nearly everything."

"Green leafy vegetables," Deirdre chimed in. "Potatoes. Fish."

"That's why it's so important that you know your nutrition," said Rosetta. "If you eat properly, you won't need so many supplements. Heart disease is caused by free radicals. And free radicals are produced by the action of oxygen on fat molecules."

Rosetta looked straight at me, and I felt I was going to drop dead instantly of heart disease. Maybe I'd be healthier if I took up scotch or heroin. At least I'd be thinner. People think that if only you put your mind to it, you can lose weight. Like if you only put your mind to it, you wouldn't be depressed.

"Water is also very good for combating free radicals," Rosetta continued. "That's another good reason to drink eight glasses a day. Co-enzyme Q-10 strengthens the heart." She paused. "But what most people don't know is that heavy metals—like mercury, lead, and cadmium— also clog the heart. They're even worse because they're harder to get rid of."

"Where do heavy metals come from?" asked Sharon. "They're not in food."

"Not usually," Rosetta agreed, "but they can be in the water you drink. They can leach into your blood stream from dental fillings. Industrial waste puts a lot of pollution into the air."

"There's not much industry in Prince's Harbour," said Sharon.

"Where does our weather come from?" asked Rosetta. We didn't need to answer—we all knew: Windsor and Detroit. I once walked by the river in Windsor and my eyes started to burn so badly I had to go inland.

"But the good news," Rosetta went on, "is that heavy metals can be removed from the blood by a fairly simple procedure called chelation therapy."

"What?" we all asked at once. It made me think of ice cream.

"Che-lation," Rosetta broke it down. "A synthetic amino acid is slowly dripped into the patient's veins over three or four hours. It acts as a plumber. It removes harmful metals from the body, as well as yeast."

She looked at me again, and I wanted to vanish.

"What's wrong with yeast?" asked Talitha.

"Well, yeast really belongs in the intestines," said Rosetta. "In the rest of the body it gobbles up everything it can—"

"Like a pac-man," James said helpfully.

"And it migrates," said Rosetta. "It gets into the vagina, the brain. You can't treat it with antibiotics—they kill off the good bacteria that are supposed to keep yeast in check. You just have to change your diet and cleanse."

I was feeling gloomier and gloomier.

"Chelation therapy is fairly simple," said Rosetta, "but it isn't easy to find. There's a clinic in Chicago. And a few other places. If you ever want it, let me know, and I'll give you the list. Deirdre, you might want it sometime."

Deirdre, so gazelle-like, so thin, so otherworldly. Why would she need chelation therapy? She didn't look as if she had a health problem in the world.

"Deirdre's mother, grandmother, and sister all had bad hearts," said Rosetta. "They all died young without much warning."

I looked to see how Deirdre was taking this—I would hate being so exposed. But she seemed placid and just said, "Yes, I'm very careful about what I eat. Lots of beets and celery and alfalfa sprouts."

"Cabbage and grapefruit for blood vessels," Rosetta added.

"I do yoga," said Deirdre.

My first thought was, *So I wasn't the only one who had*

*something wrong with me.* My second thought was, *No wonder Deirdre said those things about Divine Order not being what you wished for.* How could she be so serene? I know people are complicated—your outside is not your inside. But her outside certainly didn't provide any clues.

My third, unsettled thought was that I really wasn't careful about food. And I was pretty conflicted about it. One of my mother's friends had said to her, "Food is not love," but I knew my mother did think food was love, and maybe I was in agreement with that, too.

"And your healing work helps," said Rosetta. "When you heal others, you also heal yourself."

Rosetta was saying something about food absorption being important because it gives the cells their magnetism, and allows them to carry electricity, one of the basic transformations of life—but I wasn't really listening. Maybe I needed more healing than I thought. Maybe even though I didn't belong here as a potential healer, I had a lot to learn. I was chagrined.

And then it was time for lunch.

TALITHA'S LUNCH WAS DELICIOUS. She had made bean burgers with onions and tomatoes; a good salsa; a pasta dish with almonds, sun-dried tomatoes, and green beans.

"This is wonderful!" I exclaimed. "Where did you find the recipes?" I tended to think of health food as tasting like sawdust or being heavy with cheese.

"They're in the back of our books," said Talitha serenely. "I just wish I'd been able to find beets—there's a good recipe for citrus beets. But by the time we left yesterday, a lot of stores were closed."

"Did you do dessert?" asked James hopefully.

"Sorry, James." Talitha's voice was silky.

"Have an apple," Rosetta said grimly.

As we got up from lunch, I went over to Deirdre. "I'm so sorry about your family. Especially your sister."

"I still miss them a lot," said Deirdre. "And it's scary. I might look into that chelation therapy. I wish it weren't so far away."

"Didn't you mind Rosetta talking about your heart in front of all of us?"

Deirdre shrugged. "I do have a weak heart. I have to be careful of it. I think this course will give me some help with it." She wasn't exactly warm, and I felt a bit rebuffed, as if I shouldn't have been so intimate.

Deirdre drifted over toward the pile of books Rosetta had left out, while I followed Vivienne out to the balcony.

"What do you need healing for?" I knew I could ask Vivienne, although I half knew what she would say.

"Poverty. Men. I have men around, but they're all twits. I'd like people to be buying my art. What about you?"

"I can't get anything to turn out well."

"Well, that's a belief system that needs changing."

"You mean, like my imperfections and I provide the highest service to the universe?"

"You know that's not what I mean. Besides, if all is in Divine Order, which I'm not sure I completely believe, these are just stepping stones toward arrival."

"I thought you didn't believe that stuff at all."

"Scratch a lapsed Catholic and you'll find someone who believes in Divine Order, more or less. I always liked the incense."

"Too much to take in," I said.

Sharon appeared at the door. "Rosetta says it's time to start."

"Okay, okay, we're coming," Vivienne muttered.

"HOW DID YOU GET INTO THIS ANYWAY?" James asked Rosetta as we took our places in the circle.

"I had a very happy marriage," said Rosetta. "My husband and I worked together at Royalton University. We loved our jobs. When he retired, I retired—we'd planned to travel. But almost as soon as he retired, he was diagnosed with Alzheimer's.

It went very quickly. I was beside myself until I discovered this system and started doing classes at Smith Lake in Virginia. That helped. Not that it has been easy. He doesn't recognize me most days when I visit him. But I can do sessions on him, which he might or might not be taking in, and I hope they're healing in some way. And, once again, I'm in a space where I love my work."

We all sat, stunned.

Talitha said, "I'm so sorry, Rosetta," and gave her a hug.

No wonder she had talked so much about yeast going to the brain and clearing away toxins. She'd probably been through it all with her husband. I had a former student who had a part-time job taking care of a woman with Alzheimer's. Her mind was like a flickering lamp—sometimes the connections were there, and sometimes they weren't. What is left when the brain is gone? Something, some non-verbal core, maybe? I had seen that with my mother in the days before she died, when she had lost most of her words but could still talk of love, could ask if the baby was all right. What did she know behind the silence? What did Rosetta's husband know? My mother's brain tumour was fast, at least, once it was diagnosed. I didn't have to watch her deteriorate slowly. She wouldn't have wanted that either. I felt like I knew Rosetta better now than I had before.

She didn't let us stay in a space of feeling sorry for her, though.

She said, "Tomorrow a client is going to come in for repatterning, and she's agreed to be repatterned in front of the group, so I want to go over some things first." She looked around, and we all waited for her to speak.

"First, you want to make your client feel comfortable," said Rosetta. "Ask her a bit about her life, what she does. Then take down her birthday so you'll know how old she is—you'll need this for the concrete base: the belief system that allowed her to survive at a stressful time but then limited her.

"The facilitator's belief is the most important ingredient in healing," Rosetta continued. "You are creating a space where your clients can heal, but they have to do the work. Always get permission to do the work, even at long distance." I thought of Brian's brother being so indignant that I'd knocked on the gate of his soul.

"Say things out loud," said Rosetta. "That allows the client to get involved. "The best facilitator is the one who lets the client feel she's done it all by herself."

I knew about not getting in the way. In Junior Lifesaving, we were told to downplay any role we had in saving someone's life—oh, I saw you were a little tired, and I just gave a little help. I read in an article that therapy's supposed to be like that too. And students too—I wanted them to remember what they'd read and thought and written, not my teaching.

As she talked, I realized how methodical and thorough Rosetta was. I wasn't exactly enjoying the course, but she was a real healer, and she built her healing on a clear structure— no mess, no loose ends. "So that's what we'll do tomorrow morning," said Rosetta. "Now we'll review body alignment."

"Oh good!" said James. "I think my head's been off—I've been getting headaches."

Rosetta finger tested him. "Your liver is off. You need two core liver tablets right now. And some radishes. There are some in the refrigerator."

"Not ice cream?" asked James.

"Radishes," said Rosetta sternly. "Fats stress the liver. Go."

When James had taken his core liver tablets and radishes, Rosetta said, "It's hard to tell with headaches. They could be blood pressure. They could be fatigue. Or your head could be off. But remember, your vibrations are all being raised. You are expanding. That causes headaches."

"How can you tell what is what?" Talitha asked. "I've been getting headaches too."

"You finger test," said Rosetta. "The body/soul will tell you, even if it's your own body/soul. That's why it's so important to let go of attachment. You have to really hear what the body/ soul is saying. Later you'll have pendulums and energy rods. They are more powerful. But finger testing is fine—in fact, it's better if you're working with a client because you're in actual touch with them. But James, this time it's your liver. It's not absorbing well, so your brain isn't getting enough nourishment."

"Rats," said James. "I wanted my aura to be expanding."

"I'm sure it is," said Rosetta; she was always surprisingly gentle with James. "But your aura will expand even more once you cleanse your liver. Squeeze half a lemon into a small glass of water and drink it every morning before breakfast. That will help."

James climbed onto the massage table and Rosetta swept her hand over his prone body. "First, you scan." She lifted his legs so that they bent at the knees. "Now let them go," she said. "More than that. Don't be a control freak."

James' legs needed aligning—one was shorter than the other.

"It's very important to do this," Rosetta told us. "If legs and hips aren't corrected, one of them can hike up and the unevenness will make it harder to walk, and then you'll need an operation. It's much easier to correct it right at the beginning before it gets serious. Your sacrum's off. That suggests that you don't feel supported in your life."

"You wouldn't feel supported if you had my mother either," said James.

"Now, now," said Rosetta. "The people who push our buttons are our greatest teachers." She'd said something like this to us before; it was a reminder.

"You do the whole sacrum at once," she said to us. "Like this." She swept her hand over his sacrum and then finger tested. "Good. But that's an area of weakness, and you'll want to anchor belief systems for it." James heaved a bit as he turned over and she finger tested again. "Okay, James, everything else seems fine. You can turn over on your back."

Rosetta turned toward us and nodded. "I start with the head,"

Rosetta explained. "In fact, his head is off axis. That's easily corrected." She did something I couldn't follow and then finger tested once more. "Fine. Your mind should be much clearer."

Rosetta scanned and finger tested quickly and expertly.

"Your ribs are fine. It's important to be very careful with ribs both in front and in back. If you're not gentle, you can do some damage."

Just what I needed to hear.

"Your hips are off. Your left hip's pretty torqued. That's your mother."

"What about my right hip?"

"That's not so bad. That's your father. You probably don't find your father so difficult."

"He's not around," said James. "Besides, I get my cooking skill from him."

"Maybe you'd like to cook tomorrow?" Talitha suggested.

"Sure. There's a black bean stew I want to try." Enthusiasm coming from someone lying on a massage table sounded a little incongruous, but welcome.

"Your hips are aligned now," said Rosetta. "Usually when your sacrum's off, your hips are off too. Not always. You should check them at least three more times during this course."

The only other thing she found was a cramped muscle in his right thigh. Rosetta corrected it.

"Thank you!" said James. "I feel great." He almost bounced. He had loved the attention. I had hated it.

Then we broke into pairs for reviewing body alignment. I was with Sharon. "I don't really get this," I said to Sharon.

"I don't either."

I said, "I'm afraid one of us has to get up on the massage table. Do you want to or should I?"

"I will." Sharon climbed onto the massage table and lay face down.

"I'll try to be careful," I said. I picked up her lower legs from the ankles and let them drop. She wasn't holding on to them and they fell evenly. "Your hips are aligned," I said. "At least, I think so. And you're not a control freak."

"You can't really be with three sons," said Sharon.

"How old are they?" She might have said, but I'd forgotten.

"Thirteen, eleven, and five. I think the thirteen-year-old is fine, but the eleven-year-old, Rory, isn't doing very well in school. He's not interested in reading. All he wants to do is draw all day."

"He's only *eleven*." When Davy was that age, he was in fifth grade, and I still held my breath in case he had a tantrum and the school sent him home. I took a breath and confessed, "My son's fifteen and he's a hopeless reader. He reads one word at a time—painfully—and he sometimes skips the middles of words so it will go faster."

I did the checking and realigning, remembering to be very careful of the ribs, and said, "Do you mind if I give you a massage even though it's not part of the system?"

"That would be great," said Sharon.

"I'll do it quickly before Rosetta comes and checks up on us."

I kneaded Sharon's shoulders and then went down her back.

"That feels nice," said Sharon.

"Good." I'm vain of my massages. "Don't tell anyone!" This was my first inkling that maybe you could go outside the system. After all, wasn't intention more important than the actual letter?

"Okay," I said. "You can turn over."

Rosetta appeared in the doorway. "How are you doing?"

"Sharon's very aligned," I said.

"Everyone's being very slow," said Rosetta. "This isn't supposed to take forever."

But we did take the rest of the afternoon.

Class ended just after five-thirty, and I left with Vivienne, sorry that she didn't need a ride home.

"What did you think of today?" I asked when we were safely out of the building.

"More pop healing. A little of this, a little of that. I'm never going to make money from it."

"I don't think I will either. But you said it might be a stepping stone to wherever we're going."

"I'm don't think I should have said that. Right now it feels like a dead end to me. I've half a mind not to come back."

"Don't you dare! This is hard enough without having to go through it without you!"

We were standing in front of our illegally parked cars.

"Okay," said Vivienne. "I'll see you tomorrow unless I get really cold feet. You know what I want. I want to make money to support my painting. I'd like to meet a magician who teaches me everything he knows. At least you've got a job."

"But Rosetta thinks I've got to give it up if I ever want to write anything decent."

"So do you think you will?"

"I don't know. I'm lucky in my students. And, I *am* writing, but it's not going anywhere."

"I think I *am* painting decent things, but they're not selling."

"Rosetta would say you can't be attached to outcome. It's hard though."

"What happens if you stop?"

"Then you *never* arrive."

We both considered.

"People used to know more," said Vivienne. "Think of the instant travel the great rabbis had. I think there's real telepathy, not just this finger testing stuff."

"I think I know a real telepath." I thought of Brian.

"Is he magic?"

"I think so."

"Why don't you go study with him?'

"I did study with him. That's what got me into all this. But I don't think he likes me much. He didn't answer my letters. We've only spoken on the phone a few times. I have dreams of being in the same place with him, and he's always going out

the door I'm coming in. He's looking for his sister." Suddenly
I missed Brian so much I could hardly stand it.

"There's got to be something going on under the surface if
you're still thinking about him," said Vivienne.

"I think there's telepathy. But I asked him about it once, and
he just seemed terrified. At least he didn't laugh it off."

"That's the sort of teacher I want."

"If he isn't scared of you."

"He should be scared. I want everything."

"Where do you find someone like that?"

"Where you'd least expect." That was certainly where I'd
found Brian.

"We could talk about this forever," I said. "I devoutly hope
I'll see you tomorrow."

"I'll come tomorrow. I don't know about the next day."

We got into our cars and drove home, at first in the same
direction until Vivienne diverged north.

I drove home, hoping Vivienne would stick with the course,
missing Brian so much I could barely concentrate on the road.
I wanted to drive the thousand miles that separated us and
fling myself at him, except that he'd probably shut the door
in my face, and I wouldn't be back in time for Davy's dinner.
Also, James was bringing lunch, and I wondered what the son
of a chef would make.

"VISIONS BRING FORTH THE HIGHEST in you…" Rosetta was
saying as Vivienne and I came in, the next morning, both a little
late (maybe we were starting to be telepathically connected?).
Vivienne was wearing a blue sleeveless dress with red trim at
the ankles and pockets, and a matching red shawl. Rosetta
nodded to us and continued, "—but they don't necessarily
happen. They're like golden carrots."

Was that all? Couldn't visions be moments of pure truth?
Even if they never happened?

"How many of you have read Carol Pearson's *The Hero*

*Within?*" Rosetta changed the subject. I'd heard of it, but hadn't read it.

"It's about archetypes," said Rosetta. "The first one is the Magician."

I listened more attentively. I've always been fascinated by magicians—Brian was one, I was sure. And I loved the Tarot card of the Magician with his wand raised to the sky, the other hand pointing toward the ground (as above, so below), an infinity sign over his head. I saw that Vivienne was listening attentively too.

"Magicians have to learn to trust fully enough to let the future unroll as it will," said Rosetta. "Magicians need to deal with their shadow side." (I thought of *The Wizard of Earthsea*.) "Magicians, by naming the unacknowledged parts of themselves, allow growth—first anarchy, then chaos, then growth. And they can then help others find their true names, their true selves. Often the people we have the most difficulty with reflect the shadow side of ourselves."

It was interesting, but it seemed like a scatter of non-sequiturs, and I wondered if Rosetta was just filling the time before her client came for repatterning.

"Wise love transforms," said Rosetta. "That is what healing should do—that and put you in touch with your shadow side, so that you will then be able to help others get in touch with their shadow sides."

Okay, but that seemed very advanced. I felt off-balance, and I think I probably wasn't the only one.

"What a great dress, Vivienne!" said Talitha out of the blue.

"Thanks, I made it."

"You could sell those," Talitha said. "I'd buy one. Wow, there are even pockets!"

"Let's get back to healing," said Rosetta.

"A great dress *is* healing," said Talitha.

"Just like a great haircut," I chimed in.

"Our client will be here in half an hour," said Rosetta, "and there are things I want to go over before she arrives."

We settled back in our chairs.

"Your clients are your teachers," said Rosetta. "You will find that they mirror you, especially as you begin to work with them. It's up to you to put them at ease, create a healing space, and find what the body/soul needs. Just don't be too attached to outcome. You do the best you can, with healing intention, and it's up to the client how much she accepts, how much work she does."

At this point the buzzer rang. The client was early. Talitha jumped up and let her in. Rosetta led us to the small light-filled sitting room near the elevator

A wren-like woman entered the room—her presence was centred in her upper body and head. She hardly seemed to touch the ground. She might have been in her late thirties or early forties. She was neat and well-dressed; her hair had been well-cut. She held herself with confidence. She didn't look like she needed healing.

"This is Céline," said Rosetta.

"We spoke about this on the phone, but I will remind you." Rosetta said. "Do you mind if my class observes what we do?"

"No, it's okay," said Céline. She had the barest trace of a French accent.

"So you're not from Prince's Harbour?" Rosetta asked, surprisingly gentle.

"No, Québec City. I've been here twelve years." Her voice caught.

"I'll just tell you a little about the Results system," said Rosetta. "It's fairly new, about ten years old. It releases stress, and it brings results quickly."

Oh come on, I thought, she's here for healing. Don't give her the *brochure*!

"Now," Rosetta continued, "I need your fingers for muscle testing—either hand, your thumb and your little finger, like this." She tested and said, "You need emotional replacement. You need to replace a negative belief system with a positive one."

Céline nodded. This wasn't surprising, since if you don't need to replace a negative belief system—or five, or ten—then you don't need healing.

"Since your last birthday, what stresses have you felt? You don't need to tell me in detail, just a few words."

Céline found a Kleenex in her purse and dabbed at her eyes. "It's my boyfriend," she said. "We've been living together twelve years, but something's changed."

Rosetta turned to us, "Now you ask, possibly silently, 'Does she need to say anything more about this? Is there some related stress from some other age?'"

She turned back to Céline and finger tested again. "You want to be repatterned."

Céline looked blank, just as I had at my first session.

"We choose a preference for using one side of the brain more than another. This method will balance your brain better. Things will suddenly click into place; everything will be easier; and your brain will say, 'Why didn't you show me before?'"

Rosetta kept finger testing. "You're left-brained. You're logical. You need the next step, but you don't see it. That's why you're here. Now put two fingers to a temple and count."

"Out loud?"

"It doesn't matter." Céline counted to ten. "Good. Your logic's in your left brain, where it should be. Now put two fingers to a temple and hum. Now the other side. Now the first temple."

Rosetta looked grave. "Your gestalt's stuck in your left brain—you're denying your intuition in order to control things. You're overusing your left brain."

Céline looked stricken.

Rosetta continued. "Taking in information is easy for you. Physical activity is easy for you. You probably like dancing. You're comfortable in your body. But you don't like looking inside, and this situation is forcing you to. That's the silver lining. Your eyes are stressed looking up and down, but fine looking right and left."

*What did that mean?* I wondered. *What was the point of a test if there was no meaning?*

Céline was strong on the same-side crawl (marching), and weak on the cross crawl, which most people were before repatterning.

"You're ready for concrete base," Rosetta said. "When we're young, we're unlimited. But during a period of stress, we form a belief system that helps us through at the time, but then limits us. For the rest of your life you danced that dance. Yours was formed"—she finger tested—"I'm impressed, I really am. You held out till you were twenty-four. Most people accept limitations much sooner. So what was going on when you were twenty-four?"

Céline cried quietly.

"Was there a guy in your life? Were you married?"

"I got pregnant. He left. I had an abortion. Later in the year I met Robert and came here. Now it feels like the same thing all over again, except I'm not pregnant; I'm much older; and I'd like to have a child."

So she was only thirty-six. Thirty-seven at most.

Rosetta nodded sympathetically. Had she ever wanted a child? I loved Davy, but it was hard to give up my adult life—I hadn't had much of it—teaching before motherhood, travelling, nice clothes. I didn't think I'd wish anything so hard on anyone. Then again, Davy took a lot of mothering.

Rosetta said, "How would you say in a few words what you were feeling then and what you're feeling now? It doesn't have to be a lot."

"I feel I'll never get the love and family I want."

"That's your concrete base," said Rosetta. "Repatterning will break that and substitute new belief systems. Your body/soul will choose the very belief systems that are right for you." She swung her energy rods, and I knew she was going down the list. "Can you say 'I am worthy of a successful and happy relationship with a successful and happy man'?"

Céline said it tremulously. Rosetta finger tested. "You don't believe it."

I thought, *I need that belief system too.*

"And this one," said Rosetta as the energy rods crossed: "'I am now attuned to the Divine Plan of my life.' Can you repeat that?"

Céline faltered. I didn't believe it either.

"You don't believe it," said Rosetta, "but you will."

Céline chose the magnetic field for repatterning.

"That's really the best," said Rosetta. "People aren't always receptive to magnetic field, but if you are, that's the best. Just stand, be relaxed, and ready to receive. And ask the universe for all your wishes."

Céline closed her eyes, and Rosetta walked into her magnetic field and channelled energy. From the outside it didn't look like much, but I remembered what it felt like during my repatterning, and I was reminded that you can't always tell about things from the outside. Céline looked very concentrated, even with her eyes closed, and she looked younger. I wondered what it was like to be Rosetta. I thought, *I'd like to repattern people.*

I remembered the actual process of repatterning feeling like forever. But during it you are in what H.D. calls "timeless time." Watching from the outside, it didn't take long at all.

Céline opened her eyes, and Rosetta retested her same-side crawl (weak now) and her cross-crawl (strong). Her peripheral vision was wider, and her eyes weren't stressed looking up or down (whatever that meant). Then Rosetta retested the belief systems: she believed them. Being attuned to the Divine Plan of her life seemed possible now to her, no matter how odd it sounded to me.

"Now you believe it," said Rosetta. "You've changed. Now put a hand to your right temple and hum. Good." She finger tested. "Your gestalt is now in your right brain where it belongs. That should make life a lot easier for you."

Céline smiled

"We're reaching solutions now," said Rosetta, "but this is just a beginning. Make sure you put the belief systems you've anchored where you can see them. And drink lots of water. Drink some now." They both drank. "And you might want to do the cross-crawl to keep your brain better balanced."

"Thank you very much," said Céline.

"Do you have any questions?"

"Should I stay in Prince's Harbour?"

Rosetta swung her energy rods. "No. Your guides will tell you where to go."

"And will I have a child?"

Rosetta swung her rods again. "The chances are nine out of ten. And give us a timeline"—she swung the rods—"within two years."

"Oh, thank you so much!" Céline sparkled with hope. But then, I had sparkled with hope after the Psychic Fair, and I hadn't seen Brian; nothing had happened with my writing; Davy might be better, but I was still worried that he wouldn't pass English and go on to tenth grade. Still, I was in a different space.

She thanked us all, and we thanked her, and she left.

"Do you think she'll really have a child?" asked Sharon.

"The future is always changing," said Rosetta. "But if she stays in this space, if she continues to anchor those belief systems, and continues to evolve, yes."

"How can you know it's part of the Divine Plan of her life?" asked James.

"I think we often intuit what our life's purpose is," said Rosetta. "It's true that life sometimes surprises us, but we know pretty young that there are things waiting to unfold. And she has a lot of faith. Remember, her concrete base wasn't formed until she was twenty-four."

"What about a relationship?" asked Andrea.

"She didn't ask about a relationship. She needs to heal from the two she's had."

"She really changed while she was here," said Talitha.

"Repatterning does that—you've all experienced it. This client had to change a bit more because of her gestalt being in her left brain—that's a real block. With her gestalt in her right brain, she'll be able to access her feelings more easily. Now just a few things before we move on. You can see that you don't need to go into great detail about the stresses—a few words will do. Make sure you always retest everything after the repatterning. And make sure you close the session. I didn't do that out loud. I asked the energy rods if we needed anything else, and we didn't. Sometimes there's a comment the client wants to make—it might be as simple as 'thank you.' Sometimes there's something you forgot to say. So before you end, always ask for questions, comments, discussion, from you and from the client. Then ask if the session is complete. But never end the session before the energy rods say it's over."

"What happens if you forget to close the session?" asked James.

"The energy isn't sealed. It's like a tap that isn't turned off. For homework tonight, find someone and repattern them."

"Tonight! Isn't that awfully soon?" I asked.

"I don't think I can do it," said Andrea. "Where am I supposed to find someone to repattern between the end of class and tomorrow morning?"

"You're all ready or you wouldn't be doing it," said Rosetta. "If you need a client, Andrea, go to Treasure Garden and ask someone in the store if you can practice on them. Now, let's take a short break. I need coffee."

"I thought we weren't supposed to be drinking coffee," said James. [

"There are always exceptions," said Rosetta. "I don't drink it much, but I need it now. Besides, I'm not cleansing, you are."

"Does repatterning take that much out of you?" asked Talitha.

"Sometimes," said Rosetta. "It's harder with transposed hemispheres—even half transposed, like hers. The gestalt shouldn't be in the left brain. You can't function properly when your feelings are jammed together with your logic. It shows how strong she is that she's done so well."

"Do you think now that her feelings are put back in her right brain she'll find a better relationship?" asked Andrea hopefully.

"It's possible," said Rosetta. "I don't see it clearly. I have to recharge." She headed for the kitchen, and we followed like a school of fish.

"I was planning to head to Treasure Garden too," said James. "We can't all do that."

"You can find someone in the street," said Rosetta. "When I see someone whose energy is down, I grab them, and if they need repatterning, I do it."

Vivienne and I exchanged looks.

"Who are you going to repattern?" I asked.

"I'm not sure yet. What about you?"

"I'll probably find a neighbour. They think I'm sort of weird anyway, and they'd probably go for it if I threw in a glass of red wine."

"You'll interfere with the energy."

"I'll give them the wine after."

Rosetta put a heaping spoonful of instant coffee in a chunky blue mug, added boiling water, and sighed with relief.

Even from across the kitchen, I could taste the bitterness. "Isn't that awfully strong?"

"You're right," said Rosetta. She reached in the fridge for some milk.

"I think you need some energy," said James.

"Yes." Rosetta set down the mug. "Now watch, all of you. Usually you shouldn't give energy outside the system, but there are always exceptions." She closed her eyes.

James reached out his hands toward Rosetta and moved them up and down as if he were weaving spells. It was quite a lot like giving energy to someone's magnetic field except for the way his hands danced around her. I could see Rosetta starting to relax.

"Lovely," she said, opening her eyes when he was finished. "Thank you. You are a really gifted energy worker."

"I'd like to learn reiki," James said.

"Well, don't become a junkie. Some people go from course to course and they get scattered."

I didn't have to worry about that. I planned never to do another healing course.

FINALLY, LUNCH. It had been an interesting morning, but it had taken a lot of concentration, and I couldn't believe that I'd be repatterning someone in less than eight hours.

James did some fiddling in the kitchen to get everything ready, but he emerged with a really wonderful Brazilian black bean soup, sourdough bread, and falafels. Talitha had made a salad.

"James, you've outdone yourself!" said Vivienne, and we all chimed in praise and gratitude.

"I thought I didn't like vegetarian food," I admitted, trying not to be bothered by Rosetta's stern look, "but this is great!"

James beamed. "I'll bring in the recipes tomorrow. And when I open Hecate's Cauldron—"

"This soup would be perfect for Hecate's Cauldron," said Talitha.

"Wild mushroom soup with rosemary," said Vivienne. "There are lots of wild mushrooms in the woods, so it wouldn't be expensive. I grow rosemary."

"Beef stew," suggested Sharon, "with potatoes and carrots. All organic."

"Dark chocolate," said James, "fondues with strawberries. Mousses with peppermint. I thought of making a mousse, but we're not supposed to have desserts."

"Dark chocolate doesn't have much sugar," said Rosetta, "and it's full of flavonoids. It's actually quite healthy."

"Now you tell me!"

"Still, chocolate mousse is not exactly appropriate for a cleanse," said Rosetta.

"Okay, okay," said James. "I can dream. And Hecate's Cauldron will be after the course."

"But you'll still want to eat correctly," said Deirdre.

I finished my soup and falafel, and, even though they were delicious, I felt the prospect of correct eating stretching ahead of me like a prison.

"I still wish I'd made a dessert," said James.

I wished he had too.

"This was fine," said Rosetta. "I don't want anyone on sugar highs all afternoon. Back to the living room in ten minutes."

ROSETTA BEGAN WITH SOME RANDOM thoughts about nutrition. Three almonds a day would keep off parasites, but if you were using them for parasites, you should soak them the night before.

If you ate unwashed grain, it would expand in your stomach, so it was better to stand a bit first.

You shouldn't do dairy first thing in the morning.

The best choices were cereal, fruit, and brown rice—especially brown rice with pineapple juice.

Why was Rosetta telling us all this after James' large, very satisfying (and vegetarian) lunch? My thoughts drifted to chocolate. I thought that after the course ended I would drive right to the Sleepless Goat and order one of their desserts. It was just hard to decide which one. Maybe the three-layer mousse cake with white, medium, and dark chocolate.

I looked around the room. Everyone seemed replete with black bean soup and falafels. Sharon and Elaine had closed their eyes. Talitha looked polite, but glazed. James was fidgeting with his pocket crystal. Even Deirdre, who was interested in health but probably knew most of this already, was nodding off.

Rosetta switched suddenly—maybe to wake us up. "Become

ever more aware of the places you put yourself into. Create a sacred space in your home. Be aware of the vibrations of the people you surround yourself with. Surround yourself with music that nourishes your soul. Books do that too. And nature." She paused lovingly on nature. "You want to raise your vibration. If you do things that are highly vibrational, you will become higher vibrational."

Maybe I half-understood that. At least I was listening.

"If you're living alone, it's best to eat one food at a time," Rosetta went on, and for a moment I thought she must be lonely. "If you live in a family group from whom you're becoming different, you may want to eat some of the foods they do to keep the vibrations the same.

"Let spirit guide you to appropriate food," Rosetta added abruptly. But how could that be right? Spirit was guiding me to chocolate.

"That's enough of that for now. But never forget that nutrition is the basis of energy. That's why I keep talking about it."

She opened her book and swung her pendulum, then grabbed Talitha's fingers. "Can you say 'I am trusting of nourishment and support in this universe'?"

Talitha repeated it serenely.

"Good for you! It's a little shaky, but you believe it. And 'I now attract to me loving, healthy, and happy relationships'?"

Talitha's voice shook a little, and I could see from her face that her fingers had answered "no."

"You don't believe it!" Rosetta sounded almost accusing, the way she always did when you weren't strong in a belief system. "You should leave that husband of yours, you know."

"But I love him."

Rosetta didn't argue, but went on to Vivienne, who didn't believe either one, and to me—I didn't either and felt exposed and hopeless, all over again.

In fact, as a group, we were weak on these belief systems. Elaine didn't believe either one—I wondered if she might be slightly anorexic—nor did Andrea, who looked as if she might be waging a perpetual battle with her clothes not to pull or ride up (though I would say mostly she always looked stylish, only that her clothes tended to look a bit strained). Deirdre didn't believe either of them, which surprised me, because she was smart about food—but I thought she might be a bit lonely too.

"Well, these belief systems need anchoring," said Rosetta. "Is anyone cold? Does anyone want blankets?"

Elaine, Sharon, and Andrea raised their hands. Rosetta vanished into another room.

"Where does she get off?" whispered Vivienne. "Telling Talitha just like that that she should leave her husband—and in front of all of us!"

"It did seem weird. Do you think she's right?"

"How can I tell? But it's not appropriate to do it like that."

*I wouldn't want the responsibility of breaking up a marriage,* I thought, then shuddered involuntarily as Henry popped into my mind.

Rosetta came back with fleecy blankets. Sharon, Andrea, and Elaine wrapped themselves in them and looked ready to sleep.

"I'd like a blanket too," said Deirdre.

"I would too," said Talitha.

If my chair had been more comfortable, I would have asked for one too.

"I could go to sleep," said Talitha once she'd wrapped her blanket around her. "Does it matter if we go to sleep during a meditation?"

"You're still taking it in at the cellular level," said Rosetta. "It's not your conscious mind that's doing the healing."

*I wouldn't like it if half my class slept through any of my lectures,* I thought, *but then you can't read poetry without your conscious mind.*

"This is another meditation on forgiveness," said Rosetta. "Old anger gets in the way of relationships—you can't move on—and it's a block between you and the universe. Close your eyes and imagine a movie about a person you need to forgive. Move your eyes down and to the right and think of the person that caused you stress."

I closed my eyes and thought of Dottie, the way I'd first seen her in a department meeting—long, wavy, dark hair down the middle of her back, leather sandals snaking up her legs like Margaret Trudeau's, the freedom of travelling in Spain still around her shoulders. Dottie had been an undergraduate at Royalton just before I arrived She'd come back with an almost Ph.D. from Princeton. Because she'd been an undergraduate here, she had a confidence unusual for women in our department.

I wondered if we'd be friends, but then realized that the women I'd become friends with in the past five years had all lost their jobs—maybe not so surprising since they were all adjuncts and sessionals—and I didn't want to jinx her.

We did have her over for dinner a few times, and she had me over once when Henry was in England on sabbatical. Her apartment was neat but otherwise unmemorable.

We never got close, but I'd thought of her as an ally. She was an immensely popular teacher, but students who loved her courses usually liked mine as well. And she got tenure on schedule—she knew the department from the inside, and had lots of political savvy.

"Now," said Rosetta, "move your eyes to centre. Include the same feelings and experience of stress, but without the other person."

I panicked. I hadn't even gotten to the stress yet: Dottie had gradually become more distant and allied herself with people who were more powerful in the department She was the woman in the department on all the important committees.

Originally she'd wanted no part of Women's Studies or the introductory course I was organizing. Most women faculty were afraid to be associated with Women's Studies—they were afraid men would see them as second-class. But once the program and course were approved, Dottie changed her mind and became part of the group. We had agreed at a meeting, when Dottie wasn't there, that we should write a letter to the Principal urging not just the appointment of more women, but more efforts to keep the women we had. (Royalton had lost some excellent women in several feminist fields during the years when we were trying to originate a Women's Studies program.) I volunteered to write a letter and circulate it.

I was astounded when Dottie accosted me in the hall between our offices and tore a strip off me for the draft of the letter I'd written to the Principal.

"You should have consulted with the faculty," she said. "I won't sign a letter like that."

I was so shocked that all I could manage was a stammer, "You don't have to sign it. And I thought circulating it for comment was consulting. What's wrong with keeping women faculty?"

"I'll destroy you," she said, "I'll go to Carol Campbell. She's a friend—she'll believe me." And she swept off, leaving me speechless and mystified. Believe her about what?

When I told Henry, he said, "Dottie's envious. Indira is younger, prettier, smarter. She makes Dottie look bad. Of course she would want her gone."

"That's crazy," I said. "Dottie has tenure. Why wouldn't she want to keep someone like Indira who's on the way to being at the top of her field?"

"Jealous," Henry shrugged. "You'll see I'm right."

I guess she had gone to Carol Campbell and said something about me because not long after a group of women summoned me to a meeting of the embryonic women's studies course I'd been working on for two years, and one by one told me how inefficient I was, making it clear they were taking charge of the course and the program, if the course indeed turned into a program. Davy was being assessed then, and I was beside myself. I said I was having a crisis at home, but another woman I'd considered a friend said coldly, "Everyone has something."

I was too embarrassed to say that Davy was too fragile to be left with sitters and that Henry wouldn't stay alone with him, so the wonder was that I'd been getting anything at all done in twelve and a half hours a week that I was at the university. I was embarrassed to say, *If any of you had helped me, even if I'd gotten some secretarial help calling meetings, I would have been more efficient.*

I learned later that Dottie had been on a committee charged with making a counteroffer to a brilliant woman colleague, Indira, who had been offered a full professorship in the States. Dottie had been instrumental in the committee's final offer of more money but no promotion. Indira had published more than most of the full professors in the department. Of course she left.

"She would have left anyway," Dottie said to me later, I knew that wasn't true. Indira had told me that she would have preferred to stay, but not as an associate professor.

If the principal had gotten my letter, he might have put two and two together and realized that Dottie was not exactly on board with keeping women faculty at Royalton.

It seemed like a poor reason to destroy someone—as well as a friendship—but it is not entirely out of the ordinary to follow ambition, in academia or anywhere else for that matter.

I tried to imagine the stress without Dottie and all those other women, and I'd almost managed it when Rosetta moved on. "Now turn your eyes down and to the left and run the same movie. Keep the feelings of stress, but eliminate the other person. This time speed it up."

But I was already way behind. I wondered if Dottie had talked to my department head, who happened to be her partner, and if that was why he had tried to get rid of me. Henry wouldn't stand up for me because he said he didn't want to alienate any of his colleagues. Really, our marriage had ended right then.

It had just taken five more years to play out.

"Turn your eyes up and to the right," Rosetta said. "Allow yourself to forgive that other person for choosing to participate in your perception."

I was still way behind. I wasn't sure I was doing it right. Hadn't Dottie managed to dislodge a professor who had been her lover when she was an undergraduate? She hadn't gotten rid of him—he was a tenured full professor after all—but he had no more power in the department, and he didn't really recover until he retired. (My neighbour said, "I saw him at a funeral, and he was a changed man.") Henry must have been right that Dottie was jealous. The dean had told the committee they could offer Indira anything in order to keep her. The poor counteroffer of a raise but no promotion ensured Indira wouldn't stay. I wasn't supposed to know, but secrecy was porous at Royalton, in fact in Prince's Harbour generally. Indira had taken the full professorship and had gone on to become the superstar she was destined to become. She might have thanked Dottie for making her choice clear—and maybe I should too—because I decided then and over and over again, as you do when you make a life choice, that I would put my time into raising Davy first and my teaching second no matter what the consequences.

When you've done that," said Rosetta, "turn your eyes up and to the centre. Forgive yourself for having this perception."

But, it wasn't a perception of harm— it had been real harm. If I'd been a different person, I might not have incurred it. Anyway, this meditation was a wipe.

"Now," said Rosetta, "turn your eyes up and to the left. Call the other person to mind again and visualize yourself standing side by side with him or her."

I cried a bit, but I managed to hold Dottie in my head, not so much now as earlier when we'd been friends. Okay, there we were standing side by side. I still felt raw, but there we were.

"Keep visualizing yourselves standing side by side. Then

visualize the light as it radiates love, warmth, and forgiveness from the universe to both of you."

I tried to visualize, but all I saw was a great purple sock. It sort of spread over us, and, as it did, I did feel a bit better. I guessed it was like all of these healings—the meditation itself was a seed, and you had to nuture it.

"And when you're ready, open your eyes."

I was still crying a little, but Vivienne was sobbing. Talitha went to her and hugged her. I reached for her hand. James went to her and put his hands on her shoulders. "It's all right," he said.

"I've got to go," said Vivienne.

"Do you want to share?" asked Rosetta.

"No, I want to leave."

"I'll follow you home," I said.

Still holding her hand, I led her toward the elevator.

"Fuck," said Vivienne, once we were in the elevator. Her eyes were still teary. "I was afraid that would happen. I didn't want to go to pieces in public. And I've forgotten my fucking stuff."

"I'll go back for it."

"No, I want to get out of here."

"Sit in your car and let me go back for it. Too bad your car's fixed—I could just drive you home."

"Okay, I'll wait. You don't have to do this, you know." Vivienne settled into the driver's seat of her broad-beamed old Chevy, a car that looked as if it might be able to fly, if you knew the right spell.

The door to the building was locked, of course. I rang, but no one heard. I was about to give up when an elderly woman came out, and I grabbed the door. "I forgot something," I said. "Thanks so much."

She looked suspicious, but she didn't stop me, and I slid into the dark elevator, pressed the top button, and started the slow journey up to the light.

Except for our empty chairs, it was as if we'd never left. It seemed that people had finished sharing whatever they'd wanted to about the forgiveness meditation, and Rosetta had moved on to acupressure. I gathered up Vivienne's binder, pencils, shawl.

"Don't forget about the eclipse tomorrow," Rosetta said.

"Eclipse?"

"It's a total eclipse of the sun. Bring eclipse glasses if you've got them—I have a couple pairs—or prepared glass. I've got some of that too."

"Okay," I said, the sort of yes-yes I had no intention of following through on. Henry was a master of it. "See you all tomorrow."

"Is Vivienne okay?" Talitha asked.

"I don't know yet."

"Tell her we're thinking of her."

"It's a healing crisis," Rosetta said serenely.

*Oh, fine,* I thought. As if naming it was dealing with it.

I got back to the parking lot where Vivienne was looking tearstained.

"Talitha says they're all thinking of you."

"Talitha's okay." Then, turning to me, she asked, "Judith, can we just go for coffee."

"Okay." But it was more than okay—it was better for me, not so out of the way.

"What about the Laundry? It's sort of on your way home." The Laundry used to be a Chinese laundry before the current owners turned it into a café. It had stellar cheesecakes, which we shouldn't have during our cleanse, and great scones, too, which were on the far edge of allowed. We started our cars and eased out of the parking lot, along the tree-lined driveway out to Princess Street, crawled through traffic downtown and, lucky for us, found parking on Clergy, the nearest cross-street.

"I feel better already," said Vivienne as we settled into a table near the front window. I wasn't surprised. The Laundry did have a good vibe. "That apartment's starting to give me the creeps," she added.

"The view—"

"Yeah, I know, the view—but we're inside except for breaks."

After we'd ordered coffee and scones—I know, it should have been tea, but this seemed like an exceptional occasion, calling for caffeine—I asked, "Who was the person you were visualizing?"

"My ex. Gord." Vivienne said. "He was a piece of work. I think he killed me in a few past lives. We were definitely connected, but I'm not sure that was a good thing."

I was impressed. I'd wished I knew something about my own past lives.

"I don't think I knew Henry in any past life."

"I hope I won't know Gord in the next one."

I tried again. "Rosetta thinks you can forgive in an instant, but it takes longer than that."

"Yeah, she doesn't deal with the tidal wave of stuff that comes up when you're trying to cope with something. Did you figure out the person who was stressing you?"

"Sort of. It all went too fast for me to keep up, and in the end I saw a great purple sock and felt better, I don't know why.

"Rosetta doesn't get it," said Vivienne. "She thinks you can just tap a few ribs and do a meditation, anchor a few belief systems, and you'll be healed."

"It's just a beginning," I heard myself saying. Where had that come from? From Brian—when he gave me my last class, that's what he said. Was it? But it had only been the barest of beginnings. Nevertheless, if it weren't for him, I wouldn't be here—so maybe it was.

"So what upset you so much?" I asked.

"I thought I was over that marriage, but I guess I'm not."

"What went wrong?"

"I guess what usually goes wrong. You start with sex, and you think you'll be happy forever, but then you're stuck together, and it gets more and more unkind. And then there are the putdowns and sometimes the slap-arounds and the broken arm. It's not a perception of damage—it's real damage. And your family thinks it's your fault for not making the marriage work, and you feel lucky to escape with your life—but then no one believes in you." There were tears in the corners of her eyes.

I took a sip of my coffee, which had arrived when we were talking. She did too, a little shakily. "You are an artist," I said, hoping that I sounded encouraging. " Maybe that's what you need to focus on."

"I don't know. I try. I think I'm on the right road, but I don't sell anything, or not very much. And I can't change my paintings just so they'll sell. Gord was so nasty about my art at the end. He thought I should be cleaning. Or going out and getting a job. Or both. Maybe he was right."

"Of all the people in the world you shouldn't trust with an opinion, it's ex-husbands."

"I guess," Vivienne sniffed. "But it sure brought it all back, and I felt like a fish dangling on a line. I want more magic in my art. I want to meet a magician, but I know I won't here."

"But you might be doing the work here."

"You're such an optimist, Judith. So why are you taking the course exactly?"

"I got roughed up with my job. I've had more therapists than Elizabeth Taylor had husbands, and they haven't done much good."

"So it's not about your ex?"

"My marriage was over long before it was over, at least for me. Deciding to end it was like stepping out of a ragged old coat and giving it to the Salvation Army"

"Sounds like fun."

"Better than being married when the marriage has gone dead. What about your ex?"

"I try not to think about, Gord but all this made me realize I'm not over him. Oh, I'm over the loss of the love, but I'm not over the damage  the relationship caused."

"How long has it been?"

"Twelve years."

"Time to move on." I sounded like the man on the plane. Maybe it was true for me too, though. Maybe it wasn't just our clients who were our mirrors.

"Gord was a prick, that's all. He made me feel like crap, but he still kept acting as if he owned me. And I try to forget the way he hit me."

For a moment I didn't know what to say. Then, I added, "I think you should come back and keep healing. Sometimes it's easier in a circle, even an imperfect circle."

"I'll think about it."

I turned my attention to my scone. It was light and flaky; the jam was homemade and delicious. It wasn't what we were supposed to be eating these two weeks, and maybe it *would* interfere with what we were learning, but maybe it was even better for being off-limits, and for a few moments there was nothing in the world but the scone, the butter, the jam, and the coffee.

When I came to, I asked, "What about your father?"

"He wasn't around much."

"You know, except for maybe Sharon, I don't think anyone in the class has been well-parented. That's why we all need healing."

"Rosetta?"

"She never mentions her father, and her mother pushes her buttons."

I thought about my father. I loved him, but he'd never protected me. Maybe it was no surprise that I'd married someone who would never protect me either.

"I'll give you energy," I said. Maybe it was too soon, but we were supposed to be repatterning someone tonight for homework, and Rosetta thought the magnetic field was the best way.

"*Here?*"

"Maybe outside." St. Andrew's Church was opposite. We

finished our scones and crossed the street to St. Andrews, a comfortable, sprawling, nineteenth-century church with enough lawn that no one would be particularly curious about two women standing to the side of it, one with her eyes closed, the other with arms outstretched

We stood next to the brooding spruce farthest from the street. I walked into Vivienne's energy field, asked for light to come through me, and closed my eyes.

I could feel that she wanted golden light and violet light, so I pulled those down and gave them to her. I could feel the tangles in her heart, in her power centre. I had to reach to get to the top of her head, to pour the energy through it, but her head didn't need it as much as her heart. I felt her heart wanted lavender roses, which made me think of Brian, but I brushed the thought off. Her power centre wanted a bonfire. Her third eye wanted a pair of white birds—I saw seagulls, but maybe there were other less raucous, more elegant white birds—flying free.

"When you're ready," I said, "open your eyes."

"I felt it," said Vivienne. "You're good."

I told her what I'd seen. "Did you see anything?"

"I saw roses—those roses with pink on the outside and yellow on the inside. I saw ibises."

"So that's what they were! I didn't think gulls were right. That's amazing."

"It's not that amazing. Don't you believe in telepathy?"

"Not sure." Again, I thought of Brian. "Why didn't Rosetta tell us that you could feel what was going on in people?"

"Maybe she's not a good enough listener."

"I thought she knew everything about this stuff."

"There's a whole universe out there. One thing about this course is that it gets you looking. And when you start looking, you'll see everything differently."

"So you'll come back tomorrow?" I ventured. I couldn't imagine another nine days of the course without Vivienne.

"I'll consider it. I'd still rather be studying with an Inuk shaman. But I doubt one will magically appear in the next nine days."

"Are you okay going home alone?"

"I'm fine. Thanks for the scones and the energy."

We hugged. After a session like that you have to.

# 11. ECLIPSE OF THE SUN

AN ECLIPSE OF THE SUN! I'd been aware of them, but I'd never really seen one. Either it had been cloudy or I'd been studying. I thought the next one would be sometime in my nineties. I was not going to miss this one.

I arrived in fairly good time, made a ginseng tea ("Ginger's good too," Sharon had said. "You pour boiling water over sliced ginger and add honey"), and settled into my chair.

I saw with a sinking feeling that Vivienne's chair was empty. But so was Elaine's—she probably was putting off leaving Lily until the last possible minute.

"What do you think of the floods in Holland?" Sharon asked Rosetta.

"It's a cleansing."

"But those poor people—"

"There's going to be a lot of loss before the earth readjusts. Tidal waves, earthquakes, droughts. We just need to hold down the vibration as best we can. Now tell me about your homework. Did you all repattern someone?"

We all looked blank.

"I gave someone energy," I said tentatively. "It seemed to work."

"You should never give energy outside of the system," Rosetta admonished. "It's too powerful."

"I didn't have time to repattern anyone," I said.

"Well, do it tonight. Anyone else?"

"I repatterned my mother," said James. "I don't know if it will do any good."

"You can't be attached to outcome," said Rosetta. "You offer what you have to offer. You create a healing space. That's all you can do. How did she want to be repatterned?"

"Meditation," said James. "It surprised me."

"How many belief systems did she anchor?"

"Three."

"After all, she is your mother. Your gifts don't come from nowhere. Your ancestors live in you."

I wondered what ancestors might be living in me. My parents had never talked about their families much.

"That said," Rosetta added, "I don't think I could ever repattern my own mother."

"I couldn't have," I said. I wondered if you could repattern someone after they were dead—but even then, you'd have to have permission, and my mother would hate stuff like this. Knowing that was enough to keep me in the class.

Vivienne swept into the room. She was wearing a dark green dress with an electric green shawl wrapped around her shoulders, silver bracelets jingling. I jumped up to hug her. "You came back!" I said quietly enough that no one else could hear.

"I didn't want to," she whispered, "but my finger testing said I should."

"Thank goodness! I missed you already!"

"Another great dress," Talitha said. "I love the shawl."

"The shawl's Egyptian. A friend gave it to me. I made the dress from old curtains."

"Curtains!" I gasped.

"It's material—you might as well use it."

"Did you repattern anyone last night?" asked Rosetta, carefully not to mention that Vivienne was late.

"Sorry," said Vivienne. "I made dinner for my daughter and helped her with her homework." She settled into her chair as if there'd never been any doubt.

We hadn't done very well with repatterning. Sharon had repatterned her middle son, the artist, and said he was receptive, but she'd forgotten to retest at the end. She'd also forgotten to check for attitudes, and she hadn't closed the session. "You'll have to close the session when you get home," said Rosetta.

"What happens if you forget?"

"You've got unstructured energy hanging around, and you can't tell where it will end up or what it will do. You always close."

"In magic, you always close the circle," said James.

"Yes, it's the same thing," Rosetta nodded.

Sharon was alarmed. "Should I go to Rory's school and do it now?"

"No, it can wait until you get home."

Elaine had crept in noiselessly. "I repatterned my neighbour's dog," she said.

"How did you finger test?" asked Talitha.

"I used my pendulum." That wouldn't work for most of us—we hadn't done pendulums yet.

"What about the homolateral and cross-crawls?" asked Deirdre.

"I didn't do those."

"How did you repattern him or her?"

"I used the magnetic field."

"Did you close the session?" asked Rosetta.

"Yes. He didn't want any more. No questions, comments, or discussion."

"Good," said Rosetta. "But overall, this is dreadful! Repatterning is the gateway to this particular healing system. Try it again tonight. If you already did it, do it again. The practise won't hurt you. No dogs or cats."

She continued, "I want to do one more thing before we go out to wait for the eclipse. Sit back and close your eyes."

We all did as we were told.

"What's the first thing that comes into your mind?"

I panicked. Again, I was sure I was doing it wrong. I emptied my mind and saw my big blue double-columned *Chaucer,* edited by F. N. Robinson—the Robinson *Chaucer*—with the oak leaves I'd put in it, the notes, the cards. If you held the oak leaves to the light, they still looked a little like red stained glass. Time hadn't yet taken all the colour out of them—or the book, which was clothbound and faded.

"All right," said Rosetta. "Open your eyes. What did you see?"

"Crystals!" said James. "Especially my favourite large crystal. I promise, I'll bring them in tomorrow."

"We'll believe it when we see it," said Vivienne.

"I was in my kitchen," said Sharon, "just about to start dinner."

"Robinson's *Chaucer*," I said.

"A magic wand," said Vivienne, "a real one, with an emerald at the tip. And a paintbrush."

"A red vacuum cleaner," said Andrea.

"What? The one we sold you?" I was shocked.

"I love that vacuum cleaner."

I'd hated it—it was so heavy, and it stood for all the times Henry had woken me up and I'd had to go through the day terribly sleep-deprived. It was good that Andrea loved it.

"It's *powerful*," said Andrea.

"Lily dancing," said Elaine.

"A forest," said Deirdre, "with deer in it."

"A white horse," said Talitha. "I used to ride a lot."

"What you saw is your power symbol," Rosetta said. "Now that you know it, you can visualize it when you need it. Of course Judith would see a book"—she said this without rancour—"and Sharon would see the heart of her home, and James would see a crystal. Each of you remember your symbol so that you can use it."

No wonder I felt so powerless without a book! I didn't hear the rest of what Rosetta was saying, but it all made perfect sense.

"Now," said Rosetta, "Get your sunglasses, and I'll get my prepared glass, and we'll go out on the balcony."

"I didn't bring sunglasses," said Vivienne (I'd forgotten to tell her).

"I've got some extra," said Rosetta.

The sun was shining; the trees still had some of their petals, although some were scattered on the ground; the birds were singing. It was a perfect May morning.

"Well, this is exciting," said James.

"It hasn't started yet," said Rosetta. "Open your hearts and be ready to receive."

"It's amazing to look down at robins," said Talitha. "They must be making their nests."

Ever since I'd met Brian two years ago, I'd watched the birds and butterflies in the spring and thought, *The world is coupled.* Well, not really everyone. Vivienne wasn't at the moment— not until she found her magician—though she could be if she wanted. Andrea wasn't. Elaine wasn't. James wasn't. Deirdre wasn't. Sharon was. Talitha was, though Rosetta thought she shouldn't be. (Where did Rosetta get off?). Rosetta herself had a husband with late-stage Alzheimer's and a boyfriend—we had seen him mowing the grass.

"I think it's getting darker," said James.

"In your dreams," said Vivienne.

"It *is* getting darker," said Talitha.

"You're right," said Vivienne. "Sorry."

At first it was hardly perceptible, but now it was getting darker fairly quickly. And colder. I rushed inside for my sweater. Vivienne had her shawl wrapped closely around her.

It wasn't quite night, but it was pretty dark. The birds stopped singing.

"You can see why people used to worship the sun," said Deirdre.

"Anyone want to look at the sun through the treated glass?" asked Rosetta.

We all did. "Keep your sunglasses on," Rosetta added. "And don't look directly at it too long."

"It's amazing," said James, who (of course) went first. "Like the sun in an Egyptian crown."

"Beautiful," said Talitha.

When it was finally my turn, I saw the dark disk of the moon obscuring the sun, the ring of fire surrounding it. I was inside a moment I had only known from pictures before.

"Don't look too long," said Rosetta, and I handed the smoky glass to Andrea.

For those few moments, we stood in the footsteps of people who had lived before us—centuries ago, millennia ago—powerless in the dark, but also awed that day could turn so untimely into night.

"It's awesome," said Sharon, when it was her turn for the smoky glass. Yes, awe was the right word.

"You can see why the ancient Maya were so careful with their calendars," said Vivienne. "So they'd know when there were eclipses like this. Maybe also to remind us that our lives are small in the great circle of time."

"Can I have the glass?" asked James. "I don't know when I'll ever see this again."

"I think it's getting lighter," said Talitha.

"Give the glass back," said Rosetta. "I don't want anyone going blind."

Minute by minute it got noticeably brighter. As the light returned, the birds started singing, and the robins went back to building their nest. We were all quiet.

"Someone famous will probably die," said Rosetta. "It happens after comets, but also after eclipses."

"I don't want anyone to die," said Sharon.

"No one does. But the age is changing; their time here is finished."

We filed inside, silent, still in the spell of that darkness, leaving the restored light outside, but newly grateful for it.

I hoped we'd just hang out before lunch—Sharon had brought it today—but Rosetta clapped us to attention and said, "Now we'll start on pendulums."

She reached into a box beside her chair and drew out some necklaces, serviceable metal chains with stones on them, none as beautiful as her crystal.

Rosetta must have seen the look on my face. "These are for practise," she said. "When you know how to use them, you'll get your real pendulums. But pendulums are powerful. They gather energies from the air. You must be sure that you use them responsibly."

"What about energy rods?" asked James. "I love energy rods."

"Those are even more powerful," said Rosetta. "We'll get to them next week."

She gave us each a pendulum, except for James, who had his own. It was a crystal set in silver. I couldn't help being jealous.

My practise pendulum was pink quartz. There was nothing wrong with it—it simply didn't feel special.

"First," said Rosetta, "hold the pendulum chain in one hand, like this"—she demonstrated—"so that the stone is hanging down. *Don't move your hand!* With your mind, tell the stone to go back and forth."

*I can't do this*, I thought. But sure enough, the pink quartz was going back and forth, and I hadn't moved my hand.

"Good. Now tell it to go in a circle." Andrea had trouble, but the rest of us got it, even me. "Now tell it to stop. When it's stopped, tell it to go in the other direction. Now you're communicating with it by using your energy, and not your hand."

"I think this is a writing exercise too," said Vivienne.

"I don't get it," said Andrea.

"You just need a little more time," said Rosetta. "Practise after lunch. The next step is a little harder. Look in your books—"

*Oh no—my book! With its pages all in the wrong order!*

"You can ask your pendulum a question where the answer is probability from one to ten."

"Like, what are the chances of my meeting someone?" asked James.

"Yes, it gives you more options than a simple 'yes' or 'no.' Look at the circle diagram in your book. Half of it is divided into angles from one to ten. When the pendulum goes to that angle, that's the probability."

I riffled through my book until I found the circle.

"Practise asking it to go from one to ten."

I was a bit lost.

"*You* don't do that," said Talitha. "You just swing your pendulum, and it jumps. Or it doesn't."

"That's the next step," said Rosetta. "When you get more comfortable, you can ask your pendulum for a 'yes' or a 'no.' Or for what the answer to your question is on a scale of one to ten. When it's 'yes,' it jumps. Otherwise, it's inert."

I dutifully tried to get my pendulum to go from zero to ten (each was at a slightly different angle), even though I wasn't sure what I was doing.

"Now ask it a question," said Rosetta, "with an answer from one to ten."

I thought, *How likely am I to actually repattern someone tonight after class?*

"Let go of your conscious knowing," said Rosetta. "Don't be attached to outcome."

Okay, I thought. Let go of conscious knowing. Not attached to outcome. I emptied my mind. My pendulum went to nine. Okay, I would repattern someone. The universe would provide.

"Did you all get answers?" asked Rosetta.

I nodded.

"Yes!" said James. "I use pendulums all the time. But—" and his face fell—"I only got a five."

"What did you ask?"

"I asked if I would find a boyfriend."

"You shouldn't ask a pendulum anything that important at this stage," said Rosetta. "It's good for choosing belief systems.

Or you can ask it which is the best fruit in a supermarket bin or whether you should go to something or stay home."

"Does it mean 'no' forever?" James was plaintive.

"You didn't give it a timeline. It didn't say 'no.' It wasn't giving an answer. Sometimes things haven't been decided. Anyone else?"

"Aren't zero and ten awfully close on the diagram?" asked Talitha.

"Yes, it's a bit hard to distinguish. But common sense will probably tell you whether it's zero or ten. And, as I said, once you get used to pendulums, you won't use this method—you'll just throw it out—like this!" She threw out her pendulum, and it jumped. "If you need a one to ten, you'll probably count in your head and see where it jumps."

*Oh, fine*, I thought. It still seemed confusing.

"Vivienne?" asked Rosetta.

"I've used pendulums before. Painting's not so different. They're both getting to your inner knowing, or channelling a higher knowing, through your hand. There's more to painting. But you're still letting go of your conscious mind and letting things flow from your brush and your hand."

I was impressed. My writing was so agonized. I could barely string two sentences together without stopping. I mentioned this to Vivienne when we broke for lunch, and she said, "You just have to let go of your conscious knowing. If it's all wrong, so what? You can always paint, or write, over it."

"But how do you know?"

"Ask the painting what it wants. That's probably true for writing too. Anyway, pendulums are good practise for making art."

It occurred to me that I'd been trying too hard to enter some magic world before I wrote. I had ideas about high style, but if you aren't Keats or Shelley, high style can be pretty boring.

"This shepherd's pie is delicious," said Talitha as we started lunch.

I thought it was too bland, but at least it was meat.

"It's all organic," Sharon said proudly. "Our beef, our potatoes from last year, our onions, our carrots."

I wish she'd thought to grow some rosemary or thyme.

"Thank you," said Talitha, and, like a group of ducklings, we all chorused our thanks as well,

"This is a wonderful lunch," said Rosetta. "You can tell everything's been grown with love."

"It's all better with butter," said Sharon. "I put in a little, but there ought to be more."

"Butter's hard to digest," said Rosetta primly. "It interferes with your energy, and we're going back to pendulums after lunch. I don't think everyone got them. How many need more work on them?"

I did. Talitha, Sharon, and Andrea did too.

"Who's making lunch tomorrow?" Rosetta asked.

"I will," I heard myself saying. Then I wondered how I'd fit it all in after class—the shopping, the cooking, not to mention helping Davy with his homework and reading, which could spill over into the morning. Oh, and the repatterning, which my pendulum had assured me—nine out of ten—that I'd manage.

No one seemed to think I'd done anything extraordinary, just assumed, yes, lunch would be on the table tomorrow. I hoped I wouldn't serve everyone charred eggplant. Well, there was always takeout Indian food (a good Indian restaurant had recently opened in Prince's Harbour, which had been a restaurant wasteland when I'd arrived). Souvlakis, good grilled cheese sandwiches, indifferent steaks, hamburgers, and shrimp cocktail. For a while there'd been a good fish and chips restaurant, but it closed. Then there was a lovely, elegant, fresh ingredient and good wine restaurant in a converted fire hall—Henry and I had gone there when I discovered I was pregnant. We'd had salmon and lots of good white wine (probably not a good idea)—but it had also closed. Thank goodness for the pasta place that had broken the stranglehold of Davy's eating disorder. I thought I'd go there. Or, I could make a vegetarian casserole with onions and carrots and herbs. *Usually,* I thought wistfully, *I'd add chicken, but the vegetables can carry it off.* And a salad. Now there was the shopping and the repatterning.

We gathered and reviewed our pendulums for a short time.

"You can take these home to practise," said Rosetta. "But bring them back. I'll need them the next time I teach this class."

James raised his hand. "We've had the eclipse, but I don't feel like I've changed."

"It doesn't necessarily happen the same day," said Rosetta.

"It's more like plus or minus a week, even two," said Vivienne.

"How do you know that?" I asked.

"My astrology teacher told me."

"Is there an astrology teacher in Prince's Harbour?" I was surprised. Usually you could tell who was around from the cards posted in Treasure Garden or the ads in *Complete Health,* but I hadn't seen any sign of an astrologer.

"No, in the Yukon."

"I'd like to learn astrology." I knew I was pulling the conversation way off to one side.

"I'd like to learn reiki," said James, for the umpteenth time.

Rosetta looked stern. "Don't add too many modalities too fast," she said. "You'll dissipate your energies. You'll get split. There's enough in this system to last you for a while."

"I love what we're doing," said James. "But I really want to learn reiki."

Points to him! He was the only one in the group Rosetta couldn't swerve.

Rosetta read us a poem, "An Invocation to the Light," which seemed appropriate after an eclipse.

*Brian would have liked it,* I thought.

"We are all connected," said Rosetta. "We are all connected by the Light. Any thoughts? Judith?"

I shook my head. I didn't want to break the spell.

"All right," said Rosetta. "We'll take a short break, and then we'll come back and do a meditation."

I went out on the balcony with Vivienne and hung over the edge with the most trees below.

"Do you do horoscopes?" I asked Vivienne.

"Yes, but not often. They're hard to calculate."

"Could you do mine?"

"Not during the course. They take too long."

I hadn't realized how much I'd wanted my horoscope done until Vivienne said she wouldn't. She must have felt my energy plummet.

"After the course, let's meet for coffee, and I'll bring my ephemeris, and I can show you where your planets are."

The door opened a crack. "Thank you." I didn't want to gush, but I said it again. "Thank you."

"And I should tell you," Vivienne added, "My paintings may know what they want, but they're not selling. Or I wouldn't be hoping to make money with this."

ROSETTA GATHERED US AGAIN in our circle. I felt overloaded and wanted to sleep. I pulled down my power symbol, my faded blue Chaucer with its oak leaves inside, to keep me awake, for now. Maybe I could sleep during the meditation.

"Life is about relationships," Rosetta said. "We each have our own energy entity, but there is also an energy entity for a relationship. When a relationship goes wrong, we have to heal ourselves, and, as far as we can, the other person, and then we have to heal the energy entity between us. That's what we'll be doing in this meditation. This is another movie, another forgiveness meditation, but choose someone else and concentrate on the energy entity between you."

I looked over at Vivienne. "I think I'm okay," she whispered. "I just won't do it."

Rosetta began, "Close your eyes and think of a time when you were completely loved."

I closed my eyes and thought first of being three years old and playing on the screen porch while my parents were reading their newspapers. Summer. I knew I could go down the porch steps and hide behind a huge clump of orange day lilies. Then I thought of my first years with Henry, having sherry and coffee and chocolate in our offices late at night, the feeling of being next to him as we travelled together on planes and trains.

The man on the plane had said, "You had some good times. Time to move on."

Brian had said, "He's blocking your growth."

I focused on the last leg of our travels, coming back from England before Davy was born, my head on Henry's shoulder, the feel of my arm against his, knowing we were coming back to our own sixth-floor apartment with the view of the lake. This was home, both the moment and knowing that we'd still be home when we arrived. As I remembered, I was entirely in the present. The present was enough.

Rosetta instructed us: "Ask the body what the movie needs to be about. Turn your eyes down and to the right. Run the movie full length. Allow yourself to feel what you felt."

I'd sort of already done that. When had we lost what we had?

I remembered Henry waking me up one night around two in the morning—Davy was still fairly little—and hauling me downstairs and shoving a small ornamental box at me and saying, "What are these keys?" Why he had to choose two in the morning to declutter, and why he had to start with a *box* was beyond me. I was still half-asleep. I couldn't figure out what the keys were, and I threw most of them out. Two were the keys to my safe deposit box, which I later had to have broken open at great expense; one was the key to my ancestral cabinet—irreplaceable. I forget what the others were. But I lost the sleep, and I threw away the keys, and Henry still wasn't happy.

"This house is looking like a garbage pit!" he said, not for the first time.

"Well, let's clean it up together," I said groggily. "But not now. If we do it now, you'll have to get up with Davy at five-thirty."

I went back to bed, and was still half-asleep when Davy woke

Okay, that was the movie. And the house never really got cleaned up, though it was better with Henry gone. He wasn't so neat himself.

"Now turn your eyes down and to the centre, and run the movie faster."

By the third time, when I turned my eyes down and to the left and ran the movie as fast as I could, it seemed like a cartoon, Henry being so furious about those poor unoffending keys, which were, after all, safely stored in a box, and me being so sleepy that I didn't know what I was doing. I would have preferred not to throw away the keys to my safe deposit box, but it seemed funny from this distance. And I remembered my father telling me that my grandfather never locked anything because he said the furniture was more valuable than anything in it. I'd unwittingly thrown away the key to my ancestral buffet. It wasn't a big deal to leave it unlocked, but the key was lovely and old, and the buffet didn't look quite the same without it. Maybe that was the moment I realized, in my half-asleep state, that kindness had been replaced by anger. I don't know if I forgave, but at least I was distanced. I heard someone giggling—it might have been me—and some other sounds I couldn't identify.

"Now turn your eyes up and to the right, breathe, and notice what you see."

I had a glimpse of my mother, at least I thought so, telling me civilization would end if I didn't clean out my closet—and then I heard sobs. My eyes flew open, and I looked at the group.

It was James. Talitha, Sharon, and Vivienne rushed over to him and placed their arms around him. Rosetta tried to go on for a sentence or two, but James was wracked with sobs.

"Can you say what's the matter?" Talitha asked softly.

James shook his head.

"When you're ready."

"Just breathe," said Vivienne.

James heaved and snuffled, but gradually the sobs stopped.

"It ... was ... in high ... school. Maybe about seven years ago. November. I've always hated that month. I'd just discovered I was gay. A bunch of guys jumped on me after school in the playground and held me down and raped me. I can still taste the cement. Yellow and brown sodden leaves plastered to it."

"That's just evil," said Vivienne.

"It's horrible," said Talitha.

I felt sick. I didn't know what to say.

"They didn't even speak to me," said James. "Not before, not after. They just fucked me and laughed and left."

"So then what did you do?" asked Talitha.

"I pulled up my pants and went home."

"What did your mother say?" asked Sharon.

"You don't think I told her? She wouldn't like me being gay. She certainly wouldn't like me being raped. She'd of had a cow."

"I didn't tell my mother when I was raped either," said Vivienne.

"*You* were raped?" James looked incredulous.

Vivienne nodded.

"What would you want your mother to say if you had told her?" asked Talitha.

"Oh, I'd want her to make a big fuss over me, say it wasn't my fault—"

"It *wasn't* your fault."

"I'd like her to say the guys were dorks," James continued.

"They were worse than dorks," Talitha was emphatic.

"James," I finally spoke up, "those guys were wicked. No one deserves that. It makes me sick to think about it. But what I want to know is, who do you forgive? Them for being evil? Your mother for not facing it and standing up for you? Yourself for being in such an awful situation?"

"You should forgive everyone," Rosetta said. "Or you won't move on."

"Sometimes you can't give up wounds until you've searched them, understood them." I felt, not for the first time, that Rosetta was too simplistic about this. "You have to be ready to forgive."

"We might try this meditation again another day," said Rosetta. (Twice seemed plenty to me.) "James, do you want to talk more about this?" she asked politely.

"No thanks. It was bad enough reliving it. I'd nearly forgotten."

"What about the other stuff?" I said. "I wouldn't have gone to my mother in a crisis either, certainly not after I was about fifteen. I wonder how many of us would have."

No one likes to think that they haven't been well-mothered. We were all, unusually, silent.

Then Rosetta said, "Let's form a circle and sing 'We Belong to the Goddess.'" It was another song that everyone seemed to know but me, but I really liked it.

*We belong to the Goddess*
*And to her we must return*
*Like a drop of water in the ocean—*

I had to scramble to keep up, but by the end I had the tune to the chorus and a jumble of the goddesses—Isis, Astarte, Diana, Hecate, Demeter, Kali, Inanna. The fast-moving line sounded like Diana running through the woods.

I hoped Vivienne would teach me the song properly after class ended. Songs are like people—you can lose them forever if you aren't careful. But sometimes they wait for you.

"Mama Isis," said James contentedly when we had finished.

"Remember," said Rosetta, "Sometimes there are truths that you can't see. Sometimes hurts get you searching."

Mercifully, she let us go early. I had to shop, find someone to repattern, and practise with my borrowed pendulum, not to mention sitting with Davy over pasta, listening to him practise on the piano, and helping him with his homework.

"That was quite a day," I said to Vivienne as we rode down in the elevator. "I'm wiped."

"It was about par for an eclipse of the sun," she smiled.

We reached the first floor and stepped out into the late May afternoon.

"See you tomorrow," I said before I got into my car, grateful that I could still say that.

"Don't forget to dream of goddesses."

FIRST, SHOPPING. Pasta and tomato sauce from Pasta Genova. I was there anyway to get pasta for Davy. It was sort of cheating, but I'd add onions and garlic and mushrooms and carrots. I also picked up foccaccias—they wouldn't be as good tomorrow, but I couldn't help it—and vegetables at Tara. Next, cheese. Okay, I thought, I can do this. Grapes. Cashews. I thought we needed something to make up for those stale almonds. Yes, almonds were healthier. But there's something pious and depressing about stale almonds after five days. Salad stuff— lettuce, tomatoes, green onions. We had chives in the garden, and the cilantro had reseeded and was coming up.

When the phone rang, I thought it was probably Claire asking how things had gone, but I was busy practising with my pendulum, wondering if the universe would send me someone to repattern (it did—my neighbour's eleven-year-old daughter) and didn't answer. Sometimes you just can't explain.

## 12. CRYSTALS

WHEN I ARRIVED THE NEXT MORNING with my casserole, as well as the focaccia, cashews, grapes, and salad—two trips from the car—I saw that James had brought his crystals and was showing them off in the living room. After I'd stored the food, I saw there were several large crystals that you could see little eddies of clouds in—James said these were particularly fine—a large amethyst crystal, a thunder egg, and a cluster of small crystals. These were mostly clear, but some had rose in them, some purple, some yellow. Everyone gathered around *oohing* and *aahing*.

"They're so gorgeous," said Talitha.

"I love the big ones," said James. "I'm going to have a crystal garden at the entrance to Hecate's Cauldron. A pool with goldfish and crystals around it."

"I love the purple one," said Sharon. "I could live with a crystal like that."

"Let me show you something," said James. "Just stand there, Sharon, and I'll walk into your aura."

"What?"

"Just stand there." He went to the far end of the living room and pulled out his pendulum, a real one, not a practise one. "It'll jump when I get to your auric field." He held it out and walked slowly toward her. The pendulum jumped maybe eight feet away.

"Good. Now pick up the amethyst crystal, the purple one,

and hold it in your hand." He went back and walked toward her again. The pendulum jumped maybe sixteen feet away.

"See how it extends your auric field?"

"Is that good?"

"Well, yes. It's your presence in the world."

"I bet yours is huge, James!" said Sharon.

"It's bigger when I've got crystals. That's one reason I love them."

Rosetta appeared suddenly. She was wearing a green velvet jumpsuit. "You can also expand your aura by drinking water."

"And by putting crystals in water," said James, "and then holding them."

"I'm sorry," Rosetta said, "I was out late with Mark."

I felt a twinge of yearning for Brian.

"What a great outfit!" said Talitha.

"Great colour," said Andrea. "You've got to have long legs to wear it, though."

"We're doing crystals and auras," James announced, perhaps unnecessarily.

"Everything has an energy field, not just crystals," said Rosetta. "Wait a minute."

She vanished and came back with a few pairs of rods like the ones she used sometimes. "These are energy rods," she said. "They are more powerful than pendulums and more accurate. It's the same idea. Let go of your inner knowing and see if they want to close. Closing means 'yes.'"

She handed the energy rods over to about half of us, and then instructed us to choose a partner and measure each other's aura.

I turned toward Vivienne, who had appeared unobtrusively (unusual for her). How had she gotten in? She mentioned that she had used energy rods before, but she didn't say where. "You can use them to find water, too," she said. "And energy vortexes. I found an energy vortex once and brought it home."

I was impressed. "Do you have it now?"

"I left it up north. You take the energy rods. Ask them to respond to my aura. Now walk away."

I walked about fifteen steps, held the rods loosely, and they closed. "Wow, you have a big aura!"

"Did you need energy rods to tell you that? Now back up till they open, go back further, turn around and walk into my auric field." I did. "See how they close just at the point where they opened going the other way? Now I'll do yours."

My aura was not as expansive as Vivienne's. I wasn't surprised. "Not bad," said Vivienne kindly. "Now take one of James' crystals." She had to walk much further back. "You LOVE crystals!" she said.

"I love this one. It feels comfortable."

We spent some time measuring all our energy fields. James, Talitha, and Vivienne all had huge energy fields. Elaine's was extremely small. Deirdre's was larger than I might have thought, given how quiet she was. Andrea's was also larger than I might have expected.

"If you put Elaine with her daughter, her energy field would be much larger," said Rosetta.

"Everything has an energy field," Rosetta repeated. "You can do this with cleaning products too." She whisked out a bunch of cleaning products from her storage closet—Comet, Mr. Clean, SOS pads, Javex—put them in the hall, whipped out her energy rods, retreated and walked into their auric fields, which were surprisingly large.

"Is that good in a cleaning product?" asked Sharon.

"Not really," said Rosetta. "It shows that they do get things clean, but it might be a good idea to explore alternate products with less reach. It's a hard choice."

It was. I used Comet in my bathroom, the rare times I tried to clean it. I had tried other, gentler products, with Davy's encouragement, but they didn't eat up the grime.

"It's like apples," said Rosetta. "There's a trade-off between the fibre and the vitamins and the toxins from the spray. You can wash apples, but you can't get all the toxins out—they're sprayed as the fruit's just beginning to form. Cleaning products are problematic. But don't get your clothes dry-cleaned. That's thoroughly toxic."

I didn't use most of the cleaning stuff, but I did get my clothes dry-cleaned. I remember my mother telling me to get my clothes cleaned and stored over the summer, and I did it for years. Did I have to give up dry-cleaning so my work would turn out? Or to be lucky in love? It was strange how widely different things were connected. At least I wouldn't have to give up apples. Especially not if I bought organic.

We all took turns with the energy rods again, testing the cleaning products and the crystals.

"Why do we have to practise with pendulums?" asked Talitha. "Energy rods seem so much simpler."

"You may not always have energy rods with you," said Rosetta. "But you can easily wear a pendulum or put it in a pocket. You might run into someone who needs an answer—you never know."

I remembered Rosetta had said she sometimes repatterned people she met in the street.

"Anyway," she continued, "a pendulum is just one more tool, one more way of accessing the universal energies. If you don't have a pendulum, finger testing is fine. Except some people may have arthritis, and it will be painful for them."

Rosetta started toward her chair, and we followed her back to the living room. "Homework check," she said as she sat down. "Any problems with pendulums?"

"I'm still confusing one and ten," said Andrea. "And I can't always tell what number is what."

"You probably won't use the numbers," said Rosetta. "That's just to get you used to pendulums. I don't do angles. They're too picky. If I want to know what something is out of ten, I count toward ten silently, and my pendulum will jump at, say, seven. Did you all feel you were connecting with your pendulums?"

"Sort of," said Andrea. "But I don't see how all this stuff is going to get me a new job or a boyfriend."

"You can't be too attached to outcome," said Rosetta.

I saw Brian drifting even further away and sighed.

"But if you change, other things will change around you."

Andrea looked rebellious, as if this wasn't what she signed up for, and I couldn't help feeling a bit the same way.

"Practise your pendulum tonight. Then you'll get it. And we'll practise in class later. Any other problems?"

"I didn't think my pendulum liked me," said Talitha.

"That's because it's a practise pendulum. When you get your own, it will like you. Now, repatterning. Did you all repattern someone?"

We all nodded.

"Anyone want to share?"

"I repatterned a woman I met in Treasure Garden." James was restored to his ebullient self. "They have that curtained-off space at the back of the store where Theadora does Tarot readings. I anchored seven belief systems."

Rosetta didn't look enthusiastic. "Don't anchor too many," she said. "You're making physical changes. The body can't usually deal with more than three. Sometimes one is enough. We're doing two and sometimes three at a time, but this is a high-vibrational space."

"My pendulum said she wanted seven. I've been doing five, seven, ten on myself since we started the course."

"You don't need to do them all at once," said Rosetta. "You'll get healing indigestion."

"Okay," said James, looking remarkably uncrushed.

"Anyone else?"

"I repatterned my sister," said Talitha. "She only wanted two belief systems. It was interesting because some of her stuff was some of my stuff."

Stuff? I wondered. Talitha always seemed so together and cheerful—of course, when she was cutting my hair she was in a professional situation—but then you wouldn't be taking a healing class; you wouldn't be passionate about reading healing books if you didn't have *stuff.*

"Any problems with brain pattern?"

"No, we've got the same brain pattern."

"Never forget that your clients are your mirrors," said Rosetta. "You're healing yourself as well as healing them. You'll tend to attract clients with your issues, especially at first. Anyone else?"

"I had someone with transposed hemispheres," said Elaine. "I don't think I managed to set them right."

"Transposed hemispheres are pretty rare," said Rosetta. "If you have them, you're marching to a different drummer. You might seem eccentric. Did this person seem like that?"

"I'm not sure. I don't think so."

"If you get a chance, check again. It can be hard with finger testing. Sometimes people are hard to access. I think the weak connections are the worst—it's hard to tell if they're saying 'yes' or 'no.' You can check with your pendulum or with your energy rods when you have them. Deirdre?"

"I repatterned one of my clients," Deirdre said softly. "She came in for a massage, and I threw in repatterning. And some body alignment. She has chronic fatigue and fibromyalgia."

Rosetta beamed. "It's nice to give the first session free. I like to do that."

She certainly hadn't for me. And I thought a thousand dollars for a fifteen-day course was pretty pricey. If I kept giving healing sessions away, I'd never get that money back, let alone make any. It certainly wouldn't pay off the huge mortgage I was about to assume once I bought Henry out of the house—our lawyers were close to settling—and did the last of the marriage cleanup—at least the legal marriage cleanup. But then I thought of Danile, the blind basket-weaver in *Crackpot*, who gives his first thirteen baskets away, to the despair of his wife, because "when you have a gift you give it." And I certainly hadn't charged my eleven-year-old neighbour, Evelyn, a slender, serious girl who tended to cling to her mother and didn't laugh much. I wouldn't have charged her even if it hadn't been practise.

What I'd learned: repatterning was like teaching. You had someone's inner being in your hands, and you had to be careful of it. You could do a lot of damage.

I'd learned that Evelyn wanted to travel—she emphasized the "ra" as she said it, which made it seem rolling, essential. Her concrete base was about her father not being around much—he had important positions at the university. She wanted two belief systems, and they were anchored. I'd done it in the back garden, which was a little untidy but pleasant, with the looming willow still that fresh spring green—a guardian, but also a nuisance, because the yard was always filled with willow wands.

"Judith, what repatterning method did your client call for?"

It was weird to hear eleven-year-old Evelyn called a "client," and I had to think twice. "Magnetic field."

Rosetta nodded. "Magnetic field's the best. Did you like doing it?"

"I felt like it was a big responsibility. I didn't want to do it wrong."

"With repatterning, and with all of this healing work, you have to trust that whatever happens is meant to happen. If your intention is good, you will offer healing. You can't tell what your client will do with it. As I've said, you can't be attached to outcome. All you can do is set your intention. You create the healing space, but your client is the one who does the work."

"Then what are we doing?" asked Talitha.

"Learning to create the space. Asking the energies to become available. Making ourselves channels so that healing comes through us. Anyone else? Andrea? Sharon? Vivienne?"

"I did my girlfriend," said Andrea. "She just wanted more fun. We're going dancing tonight."

"Sounds great," said Sharon. "If my kids were older, I'd come too."

"What belief system did you anchor?" asked Rosetta.

"Life is a joy!" That was all she wanted."

"I did my neighbour," said Sharon. "She didn't need a lot of healing—she didn't have attitudes or anything—but she felt better after. But I think she'd like to do something outside the home, and this didn't really solve that for her."

"She might need a few more sessions," said Rosetta. "But it might not be the time for that yet. You start with the work that is closest to you. How did she want to be repatterned?"

"Cross- crawl."

"Good." Rosetta nodded. "Vivienne?"

"I repatterned a poet who hangs out on the streets. He'd murdered his wife. He'd never be able to afford this if anyone charged. He wanted a lot of healing. It took a couple hours."

"How did he want to be repatterned?"

"Magnetic field. He's got this pillar of sustaining faith, like a shaft of light inside his Salvation Army clothes. I want to see if his poetry changes after this." She said it defiantly, as if she expected us all to gasp, and I sort of did. She'd gone to the edge.

"And how was he your mirror?"

"I'm poor." Vivienne was still defiant. "My art could use some changing and opening up. I never murdered my husband, but I thought of it." Her look said, *I don't care what you think*. I admired her honesty.

"Did he *really* murder his wife?" Probably we were all thinking it, but it was Andrea who said it.

"Yeah, bad karma. He did his time. He changed. That doesn't mean he doesn't have a right to the life he's got left."

I was shocked. But isn't every bad marriage a fight to the death? Hadn't I died in a whole bunch of ways—giving up friends, feeling stranded in my job, losing confidence, not being able to get out of the house during my marriage? And I'd certainly made my share of snarky remarks. And I knew Henry didn't like my crying. Not that he ever felt an urge to do anything about it.

"Good," said Rosetta. "You're ready to move into the rest of the system. We'll start that tomorrow—you might want to read ahead tonight."

*Oh, sure*, I thought. It felt as if we'd been through a whole day, but it was only a little past ten. We took a short break, which we all used to examine James' crystals.

"Put them in water," he said, "then measure the water's aura."

"Can you scry in them?" asked Vivienne.

"What's scry?" asked Andrea.

"See things," said James. "Sometimes see the future. No, I can't. Yet. Can you, Vivienne?"

"A little. I'm out of practice. Let me try in that big crystal with the whirlwinds in it."

"This one?" James gave her one of the large crystals with cloudy swirls in it.

"Energy vortexes," said Vivienne. "Like God appearing to Job."

She held the crystal in both hands. After a few minutes, she apologized. "I'm not seeing much. I haven't done this in a long time. It's a great crystal though. Want to sell it?"

"No way," said James. "It might be hard to scry with all of us around."

"I do see a rainbow," said Vivienne. "That might be for after the class is over."

I looked. "I don't see anything," I said. "I love the crystal. I'd like my soul to look like that."

"Your soul is not a rock," said Vivienne, then added, "You have to let go of your conscious knowing, and let the shapes come to your inner eye. Now I see a dog."

"Stacey. Our golden retriever," said Sharon. "What's she doing?"

"Walking in the woods."

"Our woods."

"Some wild animal's chasing her," said Vivienne. "Don't let her go out alone for a while."

"Do you think she's okay now?" Sharon worried.

"These are just images. They might or might not come true," said Vivienne. "But this is toward the surface of the crystal, so, soon. You might want to call home, just to check."

Sharon rushed to the phone in the kitchen.

Vivienne kept searching. "Judith, I see you in a cottage by the sea, maybe in the next three months. I see wild roses."

"Nice," I said. "Thanks." Though really, I didn't think it likely.

"Time to start again," said Rosetta.

"We should wait for Sharon," said Andrea.

"Can I borrow the crystal till lunch?" Vivienne asked James. "I really love it."

"Sure."

"Can I see?" I asked. She handed it to me. Its heaviness in my hand played against its lightness to my eye—it looked like a northern snowfield on a sunny day, sun streaming through it, wind kicking up whirlwinds. But I couldn't see the smallest trace of a rainbow (well, maybe if I held the crystal to the light) or a dog or a cottage with wild roses—or anything else.

"Stacey's all right." Sharon returned to the circle relieved. "My husband brought her inside."

"Just keep an eye on her," said Vivienne.

"Oh, we will!"

"Light," said Rosetta, trying not too successfully to call us to order. "Light keeps us connected to the universe. We bring it in, and it circulates through our blood. If you have a circulation problem, you aren't getting enough light."

My mother had bad circulation. Mine wasn't great either. After I'd been sitting a while, preparing classes or reading essays, one of my legs sometimes went numb—it felt as if it weren't there. It was always awkward getting it to feel alive again.

Andrea looked uncomfortable. Maybe she had bad circulation too.

And I remembered the darkness in my father's face just before he died.

"Light is our life force," Rosetta continued. "It's what keeps us alive. It's important that our bodies be good vehicles to carry the light. Good nutrition is the simplest way."

"What about ghosts?" asked James.

"Ghosts like light too. When you encounter a restless spirit, send them into the light where they belong. Often if they're still wandering, they're scared to go into the light."

"I live next to a graveyard," said Talitha.

"No kidding," said James. "I bet there are spirits who want to come into the light. I should come over one day, and we should help them."

"Do they come back?" asked Sharon. "Do you believe in reincarnation?"

"Yes," said James. "But not enough to die for it."

Everyone burst out laughing. We were dangerously close to insubordination. I was enjoying every minute of it.

Rosetta clapped her hands to call us to order. "We're going to do a short meditation before lunch."

I hoped it wasn't another movie on forgiveness.

She went around and finger tested "I am a radiant light of love." I not only didn't believe it, I could hardly say it, it sounded so pious. When I tried to say it, I saw tubercular Victorian heroines, beautiful but frail with illness, swooning in sentimental gorgeousness. The other belief system, "I am naturally enlightened." sounded a little more eighteenth-century, filled with high windows and polished silver. Well, both light, anyway.

I don't remember what Rosetta said. I closed my eyes and I was gone, inside an enormous crystal, like the one Vivienne had borrowed from James, but much bigger, with a series of caves, light streaming through the ice, like swirls on pillars. It was a great, bright, ice palace—not cold, though. I walked through rainbows—the crystal was prismatic in spots. Somehow, I knew Brian was there, somewhere, in some room. I saw two deer on the other side of a crystal wall. I saw a shower of stars, even though it was daylight. Finally, there was Brian at the end of a long hallway. "Brian!" I called. He was too far away to hear me, and he vanished. "He's looking for his sister," I heard a voice say, but when I turned, no one was there. *I could be his sister,* I thought. But of course, I wasn't. And although I'd always wanted a brother, Brian wasn't that to me either.

I kept going. I knew I was approaching the edge of the crystal. I saw fir trees and ravens. Banff. I came to a building and I suddenly knew Brian was in it.

And then I opened my eyes—with a start. I was shocked to be back in Rosetta's living room—but *oh, heavens! Lunch!* I had to warm the pasta and dress the salad!

"You went deep," said Vivienne.

"I did," I said. "I can hardly drag myself to the kitchen to heat the pasta."

"Do you want help?"

"No, but thanks."

I did drag myself to the kitchen, wishing I could have taken those extra steps before the meditation ended, climbed the stairs to Brian's room, and knocked on his door. I turned on the oven, cut up some focaccia, stirred the salad dressing, put the pasta in the oven to heat, dressed the salad, and started to set the table, still a little drugged by the meditation. In the living room, people were sharing what they'd seen, but I was focused on looking for silverware, and opening cupboards for plates. You'd think by now I'd know where everything was, but I was still dazed.

Suddenly Talitha was in the kitchen with me, reaching out in a smooth motion for the plates—which she found on her first try—and gliding them to the table.

"Thanks!"

"It's faster with two."

*Especially when one is efficient,* I thought.

"Water," she said. "Glasses. And a pitcher."

"Is there a bread basket?" I couldn't believe how helpless I was. She found it, and I put the focaccia in it. Salad on the table. I'd used my large salad bowl. Pasta finally warm enough to serve. Serving spoon? Talitha found one. Salt and pepper stayed on the table, though Rosetta didn't encourage salt. Pepper was acceptable.

"It looks delicious," said Talitha.

"It's just stuff I make all the time," I said. "At least when I actually cook. I don't do it often."

"Okay," Talitha called into the living room, "Judith has made us lunch."

"Just a minute," said Rosetta. "I have to see if your belief systems are anchored." I quickly threw the pasta back in the oven, so luckily she didn't do mine.

When everyone else was retested and sitting at the table, I brought the pasta out again and set it down in the centre of the table.

"What did you think of the meditation?" Rosetta asked me.

"I liked it," I said. "I was wandering around inside James' crystal. I saw lots of rainbows. I wasn't ready to come out."

"That's scrying," said Vivienne. "It doesn't matter if you're inside the crystal or outside."

"I couldn't do it again, though. I couldn't do it without the meditation."

Rosetta said, "Meditation is a guide to getting deep inside or high above. Everything we need is already within us. We'll anchor that belief system in a couple of days."

"I can't believe this is still the first week." Sharon helped herself to more casserole. "Judith, this is delicious."

A surge of relief. I realized I had huge performance anxiety about my cooking.

"In a way, it feels like forever," said Andrea. "It *is* good, Judith."

"This is very intense," said Rosetta. "Remember, you're doing a year-long course in two weeks."

"I can't believe we won't be here all summer," said Elaine, "although I'll be glad to get back to Lily. I want to take her swimming."

"I'm not sure I could concentrate this hard all summer," said Talitha. "Judith, thank you. This is great."

"It's really simple," I said. "It's just pasta and sauce with onions, mushrooms, carrots, and rosemary. You can add chicken if you're not a vegetarian."

"What are we all going to do after this course is over?" asked James.

"Don't go jumping ahead," said Rosetta. "There's still a lot of this course left."

"What's left?" asked James.

"The rest of the system, for one thing. We'll do that after lunch."

I went into the kitchen and brought out the grapes and cashews as a dessert of sorts

"Cashews!" said James, and reached for a large handful.

"Almonds are really better," said Rosetta. I didn't say that I didn't want my cashews mixed up with her stale almonds.

"I thought we could have them at break too," I said and got up to clear. The best thing about cooking was overcoming fear. The second best thing was having food with herbs—rosemary in the casserole, chives and coriander in the salad. The worst thing was having to clean up afterwards, so I missed my subversive moments on the balcony with Vivienne.

"Gold star for you," said Vivienne, accompanying me to the sink with a load of plates. She scraped them into the compost and put them in the sink.

"Thanks." I scraped the leftover salad into the compost and wiped the bowl with a paper towel. "I'll let the casserole  soak and wash it when I get home."

"What about the salad bowl?"

"I don't wash the salad bowl. It's wood. I'll oil it when I get home."

The dishes went quickly with two people, and we took our places in the circle.

"Now," Rosetta said, "We'll consider what comes after repatterning Remember, this is a complete system of stress management, beginning with the physical and going right on up to the spiritual. Repatterning is the usual first session. But you can have a session with someone who hasn't been repatterned—they might not be ready. Then you just deal with what comes up and close the session. Have any of you done this before?"

We all shook our heads.

"But some of you have had sessions after you were repatterned. I know you did, Talitha. And you, Judith."

"I couldn't tell you what happened, though," said Talitha.

I couldn't either. All I remembered was the anguish of being told to forgive when I hadn't healed enough to do it, and then Rosetta having to rush to a doctor's appointment.

"Okay," said Rosetta. "First of all, you ask if you have permission to enter the system. It's a little easier with energy rods, but pendulums are fine. Now look in your books for the page with the pictures of hands in it—those are the directional indicators, and you use them each time you go from one part of the system to the other."

We all looked blank.

"To begin with, put all your fingers over your thumb, like this"—it was like a fist, but relaxed.

We all did it.

"Do I have permission to enter the system?" she asked. Her pendulum jumped. "Questions, comments, discussion?" She put her fingers lightly over her thumb, and her pendulum jumped again. "Someone has a question or something they want to say."

"Don't the hand signals just make everything more complicated?" asked James.

"This is a very extensive system," Rosetta said again. "We're doing Basic Results, but there's also Universal Peace, Groups, Business, and Relationships. Most of you won't need to use all the indicators, but they show you exactly what is stressing the client. The hand signals are sort of like road signs so you won't get lost. They also pull down certain energies."

"Don't the hand signals make it hard to hold the energy rods?" asked Talitha.

"Well, you can put the energy rods down in between or only use one. I only use one."

*Growth is hard*, I thought, but luckily Rosetta's pendulum didn't pick that up when she asked again for questions, comments, or discussion. Her pendulum glided out and back.

"Can we go on?" This time Rosetta's pendulum *did* jump. She made a circle with her thumb and first finger. "Is it physical?" We all looked confused, and the pendulum stayed inert.

"That's the first indicator," said Rosetta. "Look at your sheet. Repatterning is first because it *is* a physical change and clears physical stress as well as other stresses. And repatterning is stronger when it's done within the system, but you can do it outside.

*I'll always do it outside*, I thought. *This sounds way too complicated.*

Rosetta continued. I got more and more confused. A couple things stuck. The hand indicator for negative energy was bending down your third finger while all the others stayed straight. I could do that.

"Most people can do that," said Rosetta.

But the indicator for positive energy was bending down your pinky, your spiritual finger, while all the others stayed straight, and I couldn't do that for love or money.

"What if you can't hold your little finger down?" Once again, I felt inadequate. Maybe all my problems were due to my weak spiritual little finger.

"You can do exercises and affirmations," said Rosetta. "But in the meantime, just hold your little finger down with your thumb—or hold it against a table. You probably won't need to use that indicator. The most common ones are physical, nutritional, emotional, and sometimes spiritual."

I felt a jump of recognition when she said "emotional" as if I were a pendulum myself. That's probably what I'd be doing if I ever actually worked on people.

The other thing she said, repeating as she went through, was "always check your indicators. Always make sure they've cleared." It was like body alignment—and that was one thing I could appreciate about body alignment—you worked on one thing at a time; you didn't want to carry unfinished business from one area to another. When you ended a session, you always asked if there was anything else—questions, comments, discussion?—and then if you could end the session. It was very thorough.

"Okay," said Rosetta, "Now break into pairs and we'll try it."

I paired off with Sharon, and we went to the small table by the window at the entrance to the kitchen. "Do you want to facilitate first?" I asked her.

"No! Maybe we should ask our pendulums."

We each swung our practice pendulums, and they said that I should be the first facilitator.

"Okay, what's the first hand signal?" I looked in my book and touched all my fingers to my thumb, gentler than making a fist. "Do we have permission to enter the system?"

Yes.

Thumb making circle with index finger. "Is it physical?"

No. And Sharon certainly didn't want repatterning.

Thumb and middle finger. "Is it nutritional?"

Of course not. Sharon glowed with organic health.

Thumb and ring finger. "Is it emotional?"

The pendulum jumped.

"Do we need Emotional Stress Relief?" Yes.

"Neurovascular? Verbal?" The pendulum didn't jump, but wasn't entirely inert, either. "Now?" I asked. No.

"Maybe later?" Yes.

Rosetta came by to check. "How are you doing?"

"We're on Emotional Stress Relief."

Rosetta considered. "It's good to say the major indicators out loud, like physical, nutritional, emotional, electrical, spiritual, but you don't need to say all the parts out loud. And you'll find as you practice more that you don't need to go through every indicator. When you've anchored the belief systems in one, just ask if there's anything else. If there isn't, you can start to end the session. Be easy on yourself."

"Okay. Is that okay with you, Sharon?"

"Sure."

Rosetta said, "You don't want to dilute the session with extraneous questions."

I didn't want to start again while she was still there, and she must have picked up on that, because she turned away, promising she'd be back. I hoped that by the time she returned Sharon would be facilitator.

"I'm sorry if I'm doing this wrong," I said.

"Are you supposed to say things like that if you're in the system?" asked Sharon.

"You're right. I'd better start again."

I remembered to close the session before I began again. It was faster the second time. I didn't say everything out loud because we'd already done it, and we soon came again to Emotional Stress Release (ESR), to Future Age (Five Years), and belief systems.

Sharon wanted to anchor "My highest wisdom comes from my heart" and "I am now attuned to the Divine Plan of my life," which I might not have chosen, but she did. For Emotional Replacements (anchoring the belief systems), she wanted verbal, which was a relief, at least for now.

"It's gone to verbal," I said. "Is there anything you'd like to say?"

I tried to solve who Sharon was, looked at her good skin,

dark hair, dark eyes. She had no time to exercise (I didn't either), and it showed, but still a very pretty woman, very much a wife and mother, absorbed in running her household, bringing up her kids.

"I grew up in the North End," she said, "My dad changed jobs a lot, and he and my mum fought a lot, but my mum kept things steady, so we got through school. I worked part-time at St. Mary's, the hospital for chronic and end-of-life care, and I'd just started the early childhood education program at St. Lawrence when I met Jim—so, I married young. He's done well, and we have our own home and our three boys—though I worry about Rory, the middle one, the one who doesn't like school but likes to draw."

"He might be an artist," I suggested.

"You can't really make a living at that."

"How old is he?"

"Eleven."

"Could you get him art lessons?"

"I guess so—but it seems like a terrible waste of money. It's not like hockey or soccer."

I shuddered, suddenly intensely thankful that Davy had never been the least bit interested in either sport.

"It's not as if we're *rich,*" Sharon said. "We're paying off the house. We grow a lot of our own food, but we do have to watch what we spend."

"Maybe an art lesson once a month? See where it goes? At least you'll be honouring what he loves." *And in five years,* I thought, *he'll be in a whole different space.* Even Davy was.

"But is that what this session's about?"

Sharon pressed her lips together. "I think—I think now that the boys are older, I'd like to work a little outside the home. Not that there's not lots to do looking after them and Jim and the animals. But next year Mikey will be in first grade, and they'll all be out of the house from eight until four, and I'm starting to wonder who I am besides a wife, mother, and housekeeper. I'd like to see a little more of what's out there. You're so lucky to have a career. I thought maybe this course would give me some ideas."

"Your work is not totally who you are either. And you've been busy. It takes a lot of work to make your life work, even with a partner." Even though I was worried about Davy and even though I had huge problems with my job, I'd hate not having work of my own. I'd hate staying home and raising kids, even if they all turned out well. *Thanks, Sharon*, I thought. Maybe I *was* lucky.

"What do you think you'd like to do?" Maybe I shouldn't be asking that? Maybe I should let Sharon find out herself? And finding out who you are isn't exactly the same as finding something else to do—but I put that aside.

"I don't know. Maybe I could start by volunteering in Mikey's school? I could help with reading. Or in the library. I could read stories."

"Good idea," I encouraged. I asked my pendulum if there was anything else to say about this, and it said no. I asked if Sharon needed anything else, and it said yes. What? Future Visualization. A meditation. An element. I gulped.

"It says you want a meditation on an element," I said. Sharon nodded.

I scrambled through my book—I would have to sit down with Vivienne some time and get the pages right, but I was embarrassed to let Sharon know how I'd messed up the very first thing we did. But I did find the element meditations toward the back. Sharon wanted a meditation on air that was called Blowing in the Wind.

"Close your eyes," I instructed, "make sure you're comfortable."

I read, trying to give Sharon time to take it in and visualize. "You find yourself outside, and you walk to a comfortable spot. The wind is blowing, and you feel it gently touch your face and hair. As you look around, you see it playing with the leaves of the trees, maybe the smoke from a chimney."

"It's home," said Sharon, "I'm home."

"As you watch the wind, you sense it blowing in and through your heart space, and that, if you are willing, the wind will carry you to your heart's desire .... Feel yourself gently lifted and carried in the wind, feeling safe and secure as you go. See where it is carries you—the knowledge of why you have come here comes to you.... If you have any questions, the wind again lifts you and carries you to another place. This one holds the answer you are looking for.... And finally, you will return where you began ... feeling the ground beneath your feet.... And in your heart, you now know that the wind of your inner knowing will always carry you to the answers....As you open your eyes, you do so with the with the knowledge that the answers are all within you."

It seemed so much shorter reading it than it did when you were doing the meditation.

Sharon opened her eyes. "That was lovely. Thank you, Judith."

Could we conclude the session?

Yes.

"That's it," I said. "Do you want to try?"

"Okay." But just then Rosetta called from the living room. "Time's up. Come on back."

We'd all been very slow. No pair had finished both sessions.

"All right," said Rosetta. "We need to shake things up. You need to be able to work within the system. And at this stage, it's important to experience it as a client, not just as a facilitator. Vivienne, you work with Andrea. James, you work with Elaine. Talitha, you work with Judith. Deirdre, you work with me. This isn't really that complicated. You need to set your intention that healing will come through you, and you just need to follow the book."

Talitha and I stayed in her corner. I slid gratefully into Vivienne's comfortable chair and pulled it a little more toward Talitha.

"Okay, so will you tell me if I'm doing anything wrong?" asked Talitha.

"You're asking *me?* After all, I'm just here by accident. Rosetta foresaw all the rest of you."

"There are no accidents," said Talitha. "Just because Rosetta didn't foresee you doesn't mean you shouldn't be here."

"Thanks! But even if I should be here, it doesn't mean I know what I'm doing. I can't believe that a little over a week from now we'll be about to graduate."

"So what are these frigging hand signals?" Talitha brought her fingers and thumb gracefully together. "Do I have permission to enter the system?" Yes.

"Is it for Judith's highest good to enter the system?" Yes.

"Is there anything physical?" No.

"Can we go on?" She changed her hand from making the circle with her thumb and little finger, bunching her fingers and thumb together. "Thank you." Thumb and middle finger making a circle. "Is there anything nutritional?" Yes.

Not too surprising, since I was addicted to sweets, though this week I'd followed the rules, except for food-combining and coffee with Vivienne.

"It says there's something. Is it water?" No. "But we should probably have some water," said Talitha. "I'll get some." She was back in a flash with two glasses, and we both drank.

"Thank you."

"You're welcome. Can we go on? Is it food?" Her pendulum jumped.

"Does Judith need food now?" No.

"Do we need to discuss food lifestyle?" No.

"Questions, comments, discussion?" Yes.

"Question?" No.

"Comment?" No.

"Discussion?" Yes.

She swung her pendulum a couple more times. "It says you have something to say, Judith."

"I hate being told what to eat and not eat," I said, surprising myself. "It makes me feel confined."

"Why?"

I had to think. "Once I gained weight when I was about twelve, my mother was always watching what I ate. I wasn't supposed to eat anything because I was overweight. Then after Davy was born and we couldn't go out, Henry took over the cooking, and he'd make these huge tasteless stews which weren't ready until ten at night. He'd wake me up for dinner and give me enormous portions that I was too groggy to refuse. Afterwards, I used to sneak out for brownies or cookies."

"What do you *like* to eat?"

"Chocolate," I said ruefully. "I remember once when I was about three and my mother was cooking dinner and having her shot of scotch, I asked her if I could have some M&Ms and she gave me some. I know it's pathetic, but it still makes me happy to remember it. One of the things I loved about Henry was that we'd have chocolate and sherry and coffee in our offices late at night. And we'd go out for great dinners and always have dessert. Anyway, I'm very screwed up about food, and I hate being told what to eat."

"I don't think I've got food issues," said Talitha, "but I really don't like being told what to do."

"Do we need more?" She swung her pendulum. It said yes. "Now or later?" It said later.

"Well, there's more, but it says later," said Talitha. "Should we stay in this indicator or go on?" Her pendulum jumped at "go on."

"Is it emotional?" Her pendulum jumped.

Of course.

"You want Age Regression," said Talitha. "Give me your thumb and little finger."

"How do you keep all this straight?"

"I've been reading the book. And Rosetta said to ask for Age Regression by finger testing."

I offered my thumb and little finger, the rest of my hand behind them.

She pulled. "Something happened when you were seven."

"We moved. I didn't like the house as much. I missed my friends."

"What about food?"

I tried to remember. I remembered casseroles punctuated by Chinese food (which I liked), pot pies from Horn and Hardart (which I liked), and sometimes smoked salmon and scrambled eggs. Smoked salmon is still one of my comfort foods. I couldn't have said that to Talitha. I know it's decadent. One of my other comfort foods is pineapple, probably because we went to Puerto Rico when I was eight and stayed in a hotel with a view of the sea, and they welcomed us with a fresh pineapple—the most delicious thing I'd ever eaten.

I wasn't sure when our meals got silent. I wasn't exactly sure when my mother started watching everything I ate and I started sneaking food so I wouldn't be watched.

If my mother believed that food was love, how could she make it so dingy for me—all those years of hard-boiled eggs and iceberg lettuce wedges for lunch. It didn't "work." What "worked" was when I got away from home—meals became fun and stress wasn't going straight to my hips.

"Okay," said Talitha. "I think you've got it. You don't have to tell me. Let's see what belief systems you want. This one: 'Everything I need is already within me.' Let me finger test you."

Of course I didn't believe it.

"That needs anchoring then," said Talitha, unruffled. "My pendulum says you want this one too: 'I am deserving of and receptive to kindness.'"

My eyes teared up and my voice cracked as I said it. No, I didn't believe it. My mother hadn't been kind once I became a teenager, and Henry had stopped being kind a couple years after Davy was born.

I said, "I think once we got married Henry started turning into my mother."

Talitha swung her pendulum again. "You need a third belief system. Can you say, 'I trust myself for my guidance'?"

That wasn't so bad, but I knew it needed anchoring, especially now that I was single, especially around food and nourishment.

"You want a future visualization," said Talitha. "Two months."

"That's not very long!"

"That's what it says. Close your eyes. Imagine a time when you were loved. Imagine a time when you were loved and comfortable around food."

I saw myself on the screen porch eating dinner with my mother before my father came home. I think we were having canned corn and maybe carrots and chicken. I must have been three or four. My mother was keeping me company—she would eat with my father after he came home from work. Then I thought about being with Henry and having chocolate in our offices, but also grilled cheese sandwiches in a small restaurant near the university. And having lunches and dinners in Boston, London, Oxford, Rome, Amsterdam, eating sea bass or venison or veal saltimbocca. I didn't feel guilty. I felt in tune with the world.

As Talitha took me through the eye positions, I started to feel that maybe what I really craved wasn't sweets, but this being in tune with the world, not having to sneak the right to exist.

"Now picture yourself in two months," said Talitha.

I saw myself in my back garden with Vivienne. The garden was in its last bloom before drying up in August (which it wouldn't do if I were a better gardener). We were eating raspberries and pineapple and drinking coffee—coffee? Or ginseng tea? And feeling entirely comfortable. Then I had a quick glimpse of Brian having coffee somewhere—somewhere I'd never been. I felt at home.

"Whenever you're ready, open your eyes," said Talitha.

"Wow, I felt like I went very deep."

"You did. Now we should drink some water."

"I feel a bit dizzy."

"You let go of something."

She retested my belief systems—now I believed them—but I needed to keep working on them, especially "I am deserving of and receptive to kindness." I was a little better on "I trust myself for my guidance."

"Just keep thinking raspberries and pineapple," said Talitha.

"How did you know that?"

"I saw it."

She swung her pendulum again. "You have a comment."

"Thank you."

"You're welcome. Okay, can we conclude the session? Questions, comments, discussion? Can we close?"

Her pendulum said yes.

"You're really good at this," I said.

"Thanks. Rosetta keeps telling me I should quit my job and do this full-time, but I love what I do. Maybe we should drink the rest of our water. Wait, I'll refill the glasses."

She did, and we both drank. Did water really cement changes?

Rosetta called us back to the circle, and I went back to my usual chair, still absorbed in the visions the session with Talitha had called up.

People shared, but I didn't really want to. I wanted to hang on to the sense of being with Brian, just for that instant, and feeling at home.

Rosetta let us go unusually early. It was just past five. I gathered my dishes and brought them to the car. Once I got home, I slept until Davy got back.

I thought I dreamed of Brian saying, "Your raspberry pie turns me on." And I was pleased because it meant he was drawn to me, even if it was a dream.

I woke with a start and almost picked up the phone, but then Davy came home, so I didn't.

# 13. PENDULUMS

THE NEXT TWO DAYS were uneventful. When we arrived Sunday morning, a cluster of pendulums gleamed in the middle of the circle of chairs. For once we didn't linger too long over tea and conversation, but took our places right away. The pendulums were all colours—deep blue, clear crystal, yellow citrine (I guessed), clear amethyst, opaque green (malachite?), rose quartz, shiny black. They were better made than the practise pendulums, and the stones were larger. James reached for the crystal, but Rosetta appeared, sleek in tan slacks and a white blouse, a no-nonsense intervening angel.

"Not yet!" she said. "Yes, these are your pendulums. They are powerful energy sensors. Use them responsibly."

James raised his hand. "How do you use them responsibly?"

Rosetta gave him a look. "I'm not going to tell you that. Ask for guidance. Pendulums are powerful tools, and any tool can be used for good purposes or bad. Think of any power tool—if you are careless or use it wrong, it can be destructive."

"But energy can't cut off your finger," said James.

Rosetta grew sterner. "You, of all people, should know, James. Energy can cut in its own ways if it is misused. And never, never make the mistake of thinking you are controlling the energy. You are channelling it. It works through you. And you need to be careful of what energies you are summoning."

"Okay," James subsided.

"Now," said Rosetta. "We're going to choose pendulums

one by one. Take your time. Pick one that seems to speak to you. And remember, it may be choosing you as well as you choosing it."

The blue one, I thought. It was definitely speaking to me. If we hadn't been going one by one, I'd have reached out and grabbed it.

"James." Rosetta started on her right.

James pounced on the crystal he'd had his eye on—so, in his case, all was well that ended well. "I love it!" he said. "It's my best pendulum!"

"Deirdre?"

Deirdre took some time to consider, then settled on the malachite pendulum. She warmed it in her hands, then put the chain over her head. The deep green malachite somehow gave her more of a presence.

"Good choice," said Rosetta. "Malachite is a protector and helps you heal from trauma."

"It's beautiful," said Talitha.

"Yes, it's beautiful," echoed Deirdre, warming the stone over her heart in her right hand.

Rosetta didn't need to caution her—I was sure she'd use the energy well. I was still looking at the blue pendulum and willing it to me.

"Andrea?"

Andrea hesitated, then chose a smooth brown stone with yellow glints. *Why would anyone choose brown?* I wondered. Though I loved the silky surface.

"Tiger's eye," Rosetta approved. "Protective and clearing. Grounding. Good for clear thinking. Good for feng shui."

"I just like it," said Andrea. I like the way it glows. I like the feel. Feng shui is something I want to look into."

"It should bring you luck," Rosetta said.

"Good," said Andrea. "I know the luck I want!"

After more than a week together, we did too. A new job. A new man. Somehow now it seemed possible.

"Elaine?" Elaine stepped into the circle, and my heart sank with disappointment as she reached for the lapis pendulum I thought had been calling my name. I wanted to say, *That's mine!* But obviously, it wasn't.

Elaine was delighted. "I love blue. I love lapis."

"A third eye stone," said Rosetta. "Spiritual love. Good for connecting the earthly and celestial realms. I hope you have many good years together."

Elaine looked so happy that I really couldn't begrudge her the stone, but now I had no idea which one I would choose.

"Sharon?"

Sharon, dark-haired, perky, kind, stepped into the circle and settled on the rose quartz.

"Love," said Rosetta. "Relationships. Healing."

"Heureuse rose," said Vivienne suddenly.

Yes, heureuse rose. A good stone for Sharon with her good marriage and three sons. It might ease her worrying, surrounding them all with pink light.

Now it was my turn. I stepped forward, panicking, indecisive. There was another blue pendulum, but I didn't like the stone. There was another crystal, but it didn't draw me. There was the black stone which was a bit scary and reminded me too much of licorice. There were two amethysts, light purple. I liked amethysts. So had my mother, but I wasn't so obstinate as to reject everything she liked. After all, she had also liked Jane Austen and Chagall. Brian had said there was lavender in my aura, and the aura crystal had showed me lavender too. I picked up both stones and chose the one that was smoother and better shaped. It wasn't blue, but I hoped I would learn to love it.

"Amethyst," said Rosetta. "Protects against drunkenness."

Everyone laughed. I wished I'd chosen a stone of more power.

"Vivienne?"

Vivienne didn't hesitate, but went straight for the black stone. Courageous.

"Obsidian," said Rosetta. "Turns evil thoughts back on anyone sending them toward you."

"Good," said Vivienne. She held the stone in her hand, then put it in a hidden pocket in her flowing dress.

"Talitha?"

Talitha considered. I wondered if she would choose the other rose quartz, since her aura had been all pink, but she settled on the other clear crystal.

Rosetta nodded approvingly.

"Now take some time to get used to your pendulums," she advised. "We'll meet back here in about fifteen minutes."

Vivienne and I headed for the balcony.

"Why did you choose black?" I asked.

"I like it. It's absolute. It's dark. I like that it repels negativity. Why did you choose purple? Not that I really need to ask—it suits you."

"It does? I was hoping for blue."

"You don't need any third eye strengthening. Purple is the crown chakra, good for pulling down energy. Ask if it's the right pendulum for you."

"Don't you think it has ideas of its own?"

"That's the point."

I threw it out, and it leapt. "I guess so. I guess it shows that the conscious mind won't always make the best decisions." I definitely wouldn't have thought that a week ago. And getting our pendulums felt like a graduation. Even if we wouldn't finish the course till the end of the week, sometimes the unsung moment is the best.

When we regrouped, all of us were holding our pendulums in our hands.

"I anchored five belief systems," said James.

"Give your belief systems a chance to sink in," said Rosetta. "You're making cellular changes. You don't want to go too fast."

"I didn't anchor any," I said, giving my amethyst a squeeze and slipping the chain over my head. I still looked wistfully at

Elaine's lapis, but I was beginning to like my own pendulum's purple clarity.

"I didn't anchor any either," said Vivienne. "But I think I started to work on getting rid of some that aren't useful to me."

Vivienne was usually subversive, and this sounded almost mellow. Maybe the obsidian was already helping her repel negativity. I wondered if she'd still be so interesting if she didn't resist so hard.

We spent an hour reviewing acupressure—which I sort of liked because it was like massage—and then broke for lunch. Vivienne had made citrus beets and pasta with mushrooms and peas.

"What a great lunch," said James, and we all chorused our thanks.

"We grow beets and peas," said Sharon. "Of course, they won't be ready yet, not even the peas. I could bring in some baby beet greens though."

"If you do, I'll put them in a salad," I offered. "Just let me know when."

"Tomorrow?"

"Sure, why not?"

"Elliot is so interested in what I'm learning here," said Talitha. "He likes finger testing."

"Lily gave me energy last night," said Elaine. "She was good."

"You shouldn't give energy outside of the system," said Rosetta.

"Isn't your intention what matters most?" asked James.

"Your intention matters most, but the system gives you a structure to focus and direct the energy."

"What about the energies in therapeutic touch and reiki?" asked Deirdre.

"They're still systems that give structure and focus."

"I'm not surprised that Lily's a healer," I said. "She's got such a great spirit." Again, I thought of her dancing like a butterfly in the Golden Rooster. Besides, I had a guilty secret: I'd given energy a couple of times to people in Tara, the health food store downtown, right there among the bins of dried beans and chocolate-covered almonds.

"She does have a great spirit," said Elaine. "I just wish I could afford dance lessons for her. And skates."

"Rory is doing great watercolours after I give him meditations," Sharon volunteered.

Elliot, Talitha's son, was five; Lily was seven; Rory was eleven. Davy hadn't been interested in what I'd been learning this past week, except when I told him that silver was had a higher vibration than stainless steel; he thought we should use the family silver every night—so we were.

When other mothers started talking about how great their kids were, I felt left out. Not that I'd had a child in order to have bragging rights, but I wished Davy weren't so far off the scale—it made me worry about him all over again.

"Tomorrow," said Rosetta, "we're going to talk about sacred sex."

"Oh great!" said James. "Can we do it now?"

"No," said Rosetta, with a grim expression I thought I recognized from my own teaching, which might have meant she wasn't yet prepared and would have to work out a lesson plan tonight. I was surprised—the course didn't *seem* prepared, but of course there was so much material that it must be.

"We're going to review body alignment and do a meditation this afternoon," she said crisply.

Sacred sex! I thought of Brian and thought how long it had been since I'd had any sex that wasn't telepathic. If we did have sex in real life, would it be sacred or confused?

Feeling left out on both the sex front and the motherhood front, I gathered an armload of dishes, marched into the kitchen and started to wash.

"Wow, thanks," said Vivienne. "You didn't have to do that."

"I know." Of course, Vivienne had done them for me, and I definitely hadn't done my share of dishes since the course started. I put it down to not being strong on action. "I didn't have anything to say," I explained, "so this seemed like a good idea. I wasn't being nice. Besides, you did them for me."

"It seems nice to me," said Vivienne. "Do you want to switch and dry?"

"Sure." I don't do dishes quickly—I wash one at a time and waste a lot of water, just like my mother did—so I'm better at drying.

Vivienne tactfully removed the dishes from the sink, ran hot water, put in detergent, and started in on them while I dried as quickly as I could, wondering why I was still copying my mother's inefficient dishwashing long after I'd left home, fourteen years after her death. When the dishes were done, we had time for a few minutes on the balcony, turning our faces up to the May sun, listening to the birds.

"Wouldn't it be easy just to leave?" I said. "I don't know if I can absorb another thing. If I never align another body, it will be too soon."

"Ask your pendulum," suggested Vivienne.

"Can I leave now?" I asked hopefully. It jumped. But on second thought: "Is it for my highest good to leave?" It stayed inert. "Is it better to stay?" It jumped.

"Whose side are you on?" I ask, but pendulums only answer "yes" or "no." So I took one last look at the leaves—broader and greener now than they were just a few days ago—and the birds flitting and calling, probably still working on their nests, and the enormous blue sky, and turned toward the door.

We settled into our circle. I thought everyone's energy looked a little clearer after nine days, but maybe we were all just healing.

"This afternoon," said Rosetta, "We'll do Natural Process Plus. It's a way of checking where you are and where you need to go." (Thank goodness, no body alignment for now!)

She handed each of us a laminated card with underlined headings in capital letters and a baffling list of qualities underneath: TUNNEL, HEART, TRUST, LIGHT. On the other side: RECOGNITION OF PERFECTION, GATE TO ONENESS, ONENESS, CARRYING OUT ASSIGNMENT. Looking at the second side, I remembered that Rosetta had said way back in January that Brian and I were stuck at the GATE.

"Natural Process Plus charts your spiritual journey," said Rosetta. "It begins in the tunnel where everything around you is dark and you're just going one step at a time without knowing your true goal."

I could understand that. I'd had dreams of being in a tunnel when I was writing my thesis in a one-room apartment. It had a window that looked out onto a wall and never gave much light. My friends had been busy getting their lives started. I dreamed of the tunnel more than once. There might have been small dim lights in it—and I knew somehow that at the end of the tunnel there was rolling landscape—hills, trees, and sunlight—a vast expanse. But I didn't get there the winter I wrote my thesis.

I looked at the words under TUNNEL: Desperation, Expectations, Sacrifice, Exaggeration, Finality, Lack, Stagnation, Attachment—but also Growth, Change, Vitality, Prominence, Emerging. I might have done some of that. The next section was HEART—that had happened when I met Henry. I wondered where I was now.

"Some people spend all their lives in the Tunnel," said Rosetta. "Tunnel vision, never getting beyond the demands of dailiness. Not that dailiness isn't important, but, as we evolve, we live on several levels at once. Heart opens us, and then we can go on toward Trust and Light."

"Can you ever go backwards?" asked Deirdre.

"Of course. But then you can regain lost ground."

"I think I've been in the oneness and then slid backward."

"That's possible. But you'll have the memory of being in the oneness, and you'll know when you're back there. It's also possible to jump. You don't need to go through all the stages.

Let's see where you are now."

She swung her pendulum. "You're still in the Oneness. You're at reuniting. Before you were at Assignment. You might be reuniting with your purpose. Natural Process Plus is not just a spiritual journey—it's a life map for finding your assignment and manifesting it. Some people never get past Heart, and that's not bad, living in love. But you are all way beyond that,"—she looked at Andrea—"even if you don't have partners."

"But I'd like a partner," Andrea sighed. "I want to be in the twoness, not the O4neness."

"Your most important relationship is with yourself," said Rosetta a bit sternly. Well, she could talk. She had a husband, albeit a husband with Alzheimer's, and a boyfriend.

"Besides," Rosetta added, "if you flip the sheet you'll see that under RECOGNITION OF PERFECTION there's the 'I' and the 'We.' But the 'We' is more about groups than couples."

I looked under "We" in RECOGNITION OF PERFECTION: Integration, Groups, Government, Taxes, Leadership, Uniting.

"Taxes?" I asked.

"Life is about relationships," she said. "Romantic relationships are under HEART. But we also belong to groups. Government and taxes are part of our being in the collective—taxes are one of our contributions to the state. It's important to recognize this. Do you see that?"

I nodded, feeling stupid.

"Once you recognize the perfection of the 'We,' you're ready for the GATE TO ONENESS," Rosetta continued. "Many professionals achieve the GATE, which begins with accountability and ends with output. This is where I was when I was teaching. But it's not like being in the Oneness."

"How do you know when you're in the Oneness?" asked Talitha.

"Ask your pendulum!" Rosetta said triumphantly. "The Oneness is the state we will all be in once we have evolved. It's a state of being connected to everything that is. You can be in the Oneness and in ordinary life at the same time, like when you're doing the dishes or vacuuming."

That was sort of what I was doing with Brian, keeping him with me when I was walking by the lake, even now, a bit, in class. I guess you could do that with the rest of being. I definitely liked the idea of living in two planes at once, of not being alone even if no one else knew I was there.

"Once you have arrived at the Oneness—and not everyone does," Rosetta continued, "you need to do the work of the Training Program which begins with 'Influence' and 'Instruction' and ends with 'Divine Order'."

"Why 'Divine Order'?" asked Elaine timidly.

"We are all part of the Divine Order," said Rosetta, "but you need to be aware of it before you can carry out your assignment. Again, not everyone gets to the point of having an assignment. But each of you will. That's why you're here. And your assignment will be to hold down the vibration of the Divine Order. It may be healing lots of clients"—she looked at Talitha and James, maybe Deirdre too—"or it may be bringing up your kids with grace and then seeing what comes next. Natural Process Plus gives you a checklist of stages for your Training Program, receiving your assignment and then carrying it out."

"How do we know when we've got our assignment?" asked Sharon.

"You'll feel it," said Rosetta.

"I thought I was doing my assignment," I said. Wasn't teaching, bringing up Davy, and trying to write enough?

"You weren't in the Oneness," Rosetta said. "There may be more to it than you think. And you haven't been manifesting much."

No, I hadn't. The thought was like a fishhook in my heart. I felt myself starting to cry and resolved not to say another word.

"And besides," said Rosetta, not particularly at me, "Life is about happiness. When you are truly carrying out your assignment, you'll be happy."

Happiness seemed as far away as Istanbul. But I also felt a surge of anger. It was bad enough having all this grey heaviness in my cells without having depression stigmatized as a moral failure.

"What about evil?" asked Vivienne.

"That can be an assignment too—not an easy one. Evil is also part of the Divine Order."

"I'd hate to be assigned to be evil," said Sharon.

"It's hard," said Rosetta. "That's why Satan has the hardest assignment."

We all thought about that for a moment and I wondered if others were as confused about this as I was. Then Rosetta tested us with her pendulum to see where we were.

James was carrying out the assignment but stuck at Consistency. Quiet Deirdre had her assignment and was in Priorities, which was quite far along. Andrea was at the Gate to Oneness, which turned out to be the furthest back of anyone.

"You were probably much further back when the course started," said Rosetta.

Elaine was in the Oneness at Communication, working on Enthusiasm. It seemed to me very prescriptive to have to be enthusiastic as well as everything else.

Sharon was in the Oneness, getting her assignment, at Focus.

I was afraid I'd be the farthest back of anyone in the class, not in the Tunnel—I'd stopped having those dreams long ago—though I wasn't in the sunlit rolling landscape I'd envisioned at the tunnel's end—but Rosetta's pendulum kept swinging, and I was apparently in the Oneness, in the Training Program, at Learning. Well, that seemed right, although there might be some other things I could be stuck on, like Self-Confidence in Recognition of Perfection and Progressing in the Gate to Oneness. I was relieved, though. I wasn't at the bottom of the class, at least in this.

Vivienne had her assignment and was working on Decisions.

Talitha was Carrying Out her Assignment, at Patience.

"Good," said Rosetta. Then she swung her pendulum for herself. "Manifestation," she said, pleased, in a way that reminded me of Mary Poppins. It did make sense—she was healing people and teaching us, after all—but I couldn't help wondering whether, she might not be just a bit attached to outcome.

Then Rosetta led us through a meditation on Master Technique. I closed my eyes and settled into my inner world.

"Turn your eyes down and to the right, and as much as you can, allow yourself to become a Master," Rosetta read. "Become the highest knowledge, the highest part of universal knowledge that is all-knowing. Truly get a sense of what it is like to become a Master—one that is all knowing, all-loving."

I saw myself sitting on the corner of my worn blue couch, last reupholstered when I was nineteen, when my mother was alive. She had loved that fabric, dark blue shot through with black, but I wasn't wild about it. I liked the couch though. It was really comfortable, and many kittens had clambered over it. Rigel was curled up next to me purring. Morning sunlight was coming over my shoulder. I was writing longhand on unlined paper, but it wasn't quite so slow, quite so agonizing as it usually was, maybe because I wasn't attached to outcome. It was more like when I was in school and university, even grad school, when things just dropped from the sky, and I wrote them down, and they were published in school literary magazines, and people thought they were good. I was writing without this huge weight of failure over me. But really, if you're a Master, don't you keep doing what you're doing whether you fail or succeed?

Rosetta took us through the different eye positions—see yourself from the outside; allow yourself to go into action.

Visualizing writing doesn't make the world's greatest movie. I did see myself sending things out and being prepared to send them out again if they came back—but knowing there might be the odd acceptance. Maybe my jeans were a size smaller.

Eyes up centre: allow yourself to become aware of the results of the action. I had no idea *what* I was writing, but I felt it would have readers. I remembered Brian had liked what I'd written at Banff, even though he was probably that way with all his students. But I didn't want to be the best student he'd ever worked with, I just wanted to be part of the circle, not outside it. I was jumping the gun, though. First, we had to be alone with our Mastery; then we had to be in the presence of others. Brian reached out his hands and pulled me into the circle. We were all dressed in white—it made me worried that I'd died and that this might be heaven. Would I have to die before I saw him again?

Then we brought our eyes down and to the centre and brought this experience into our physical bodies, owned it, made it part of us.

So I hadn't died. I'd just been in the Oneness.

"We all have Mastery, so honour and use it," Rosetta concluded. "And when you're ready, open your eyes."

We all sat for a moment coming back from the visualization to the present.

"Anyone want to share?" Rosetta asked.

"I saw dresses," Vivienne said ruefully. "One was purple with a scoop neck and long sleeves with black lace cuffs and little red hearts along the skirt. Good for fall. Now I've got to make it."

"I told you," said Talitha.

"But what about my painting?"

Rosetta said, "Purple is the crown chakra, so you were connected with the heavenly energies. Hearts are love, so that's connection too."

"I want one," said Talitha. "But could you make mine in red with black lace cuffs and black lace at the hem?"

"Did you see any dresses with short skirts?" asked Andrea.

"No, but I can imagine a short skirt with blue and red poppies, a black background, and a black top—it would look great on you if I could find the material."

"I was in a circle of crystals," said James. "I stepped through them to meet Mama Isis and Auntie Hathor and Papa Zeus, and they welcomed me home."

"You were in the Oneness," said Rosetta. "What did you do when your Mastery swung into action?"

"That was when I stepped into the circle," James said. "Oh, I wish I could bring some of those crystals back with me! Some of them were so tall—they were like soul brothers and sisters."

"Beautiful," said Rosetta, "Anyone else?"

I almost shared—my visioning was so close to James'—but I was afraid of having it cut down. Rosetta had been encouraging to Vivienne and James, but they were truly magical. I realized that I didn't trust. Maybe with some reason.

"I saw myself with Lily maybe about ten years from now," said Elaine. "She was helping me with my practise, even though she was a teenager. We were off welfare. We were living in a nice house with lots of light."

"Did she have a boyfriend?" asked Vivienne.

"I didn't see."

"You were saving yourself some worry!"

"We had our own garden," said Elaine. "We could go out and pick zucchini and tomatoes and peas and radishes."

"Try kale too," said Sharon. "It grows like a weed, and it's really healthy. It's good in stir fries. You could probably plant some where you are—tomatoes, too."

"Or get a community garden plot," said Deirdre, surprising me. "I have one, and I grow a lot of my own vegetables."

We were all so carried away by the thought of Elaine's gardening that we almost forgot we had just done a meditation on Master Technique.

"Nice," said Rosetta. "Gardening is one of the master skills and puts you in touch with the earth." Did Rosetta garden beyond keeping up the extensive grounds of her building?

"Anyone else? Deirdre?"

*Oh, come on, Rosetta*, I thought. *Leave Deirdre in peace.*
Deirdre hesitated. "I was in a forest," she said. "Animals
were coming to me, and I was healing them. There were deer.
Their noses were soft. There were two wolves. I touched them
and gave them energy, and they healed."
"Lovely," said Rosetta.
She tested us all again, and we'd all advanced. James was
carrying out his assignment and was now at Patience. Andrea
was now in the Oneness, in the Training Program, getting the
Whole Picture. Elaine had moved to getting her assignment at
Options—the visualization had allowed her to skip the whole
section of Training Program. Sharon had moved to the end of
getting her assignment at Receptivity. I flinched when I was
touched, but I had jumped to the beginning of Carrying Out
the Assignment, stuck on Success—well, wasn't that the truth?
Vivienne was Carrying Out the Assignment at Rejection—she
seemed so insouciant that I hadn't realized how much she
cared. Deirdre had moved to Carrying Out the Assignment
and was at Maintenance. Talitha was Manifesting—I couldn't
help wondering what her vision had been. But she was healing
people every day giving those great haircuts.
"You've all moved along," said Rosetta. It seemed weird,
but I believed her. We were now all in the Oneness.

WHEN CLASS WAS OVER FOR THE DAY, I helped Vivienne carry
her dishes down to the car. "Your lunch was really good.
Thank you."
"I like to cook."
The elevator came, and we got in. Everyone else must have
been hanging around talking, but I thought nine hours in
Rosetta's apartment was plenty.
"What did you see in the meditation?" asked Vivienne as
we glided down.
"I was writing, not squeezing words out of an empty
toothpaste tube," I said. "And this man I'm so interested in

welcomed me into the circle. It was lovely, but I wondered if I would see him again before we both died." Before I'd noticed, we were outside, at the door of Vivienne's repaired car, the late afternoon sun slanting tenderly on our arms.

"Why didn't you say?"

"I didn't want Rosetta cutting me down. That's what my mother would have done."

"Rosetta's not your mother."

"I think I'm seeing my mother through her."

Vivienne put her dishes in the trunk of her car and then took the pile I had in my arms. "You need a session on your mother," she said as she tucked away the rest of the dishes. "Where do you think she was in Natural Process?"

I definitely felt lighter without the dishes in my arms. I took out my sheet and my pendulum and breathed in deeply. "Not Tunnel. Heart. I'd bet she spent some time being hung up on possessiveness. But when she died, she was at Affection. She certainly didn't make it to Peace—she was always driven."

"See?" said Vivienne. "She needs your understanding. You need to do a session and send her into the light."

"Can you do a session on someone who's been dead fourteen years?"

"Of course. Haven't you been paying attention? She's just discarnate. People don't need a body for you to do a session on them."

"How do you know so much?" I asked, my admiration for her undisguised.

"I've been around the block. See you tomorrow."

She got into her car and roared away, and I turned toward mine, wrung out. I definitely wasn't ready to do a session on my mother tonight. But maybe Vivienne was right; I expected her sort of criticism from the world, and the world gave it to me.

I stopped at Loeb's for undistinguished salad stuff—the market would have been better, but it was too late for the market—and besides, it wasn't even a market day. Olive oil and lemon juice would improve boring greens. And green onions. Chives and cilantro from the garden. Then home to the cats who were waiting patiently, but determinedly, for dinner.

It wasn't quite six. I wanted to call Brian, and, as I thought of him, my soul surged toward him. Wouldn't he be interested in all this? I dialled his number. Even though I hadn't called him very often, I knew it by heart. I got the answering machine in his colleague and housemate Hugh's chill voice, and hung up. Then I thought I hadn't spoken to Claire for what felt like forever, and I dialled her number, which I also—not surprisingly for a left-brainer—knew by heart.

It was reassuring to hear Claire's cool voice. "How's the course going?"

"It's draining. But I'm more than halfway through. We got our pendulums today."

"What are pendulums?"

"You know, the crystal Rosetta had at the Psychic Fair that she kept swinging."

"Yes..." she said, sounding doubtful. Maybe she didn't remember.

"We each got our own today. Mine's an amethyst."

"Nice. What do they do?"

"They're energy sensors," I parroted Rosetta. "They can pull things out of the air you wouldn't know otherwise."

"Can it tell if Josh and I have a future?" Her voice twinkled a little on the "u" of future.

"I'll ask." I let the receiver dangle against the wall, took off my pendulum, and asked, silently. It was inert. I picked the receiver up again.

"It says 'no.'"

Claire sighed. "I'm afraid that's true. We aren't really connecting these days."

All of that seemed very far away.

"Then you should break it off."

"But Rosetta predicted it," said Claire. "Maybe I should stick with it."

"She didn't predict it would last forever." I had told her this before. It seemed she still wasn't ready to hear this.

"He uses porn," Claire said hesitantly, forgetting that she'd already told me.

"Well, you don't want that. And none of us have met him."

"I can't really introduce him to people."

"Why would you stay with someone you can't introduce to your friends?"

"I like being in a relationship."

I understood this. Why else had I stayed so long with Henry? Well, mostly it had been for Davy. But then Henry hadn't been so good for Davy. Maybe it was the memory of what we'd had the first few years we were together.

I said in a voice not entirely mine, "When the drawbacks outweigh the benefits, you'll know it's time to move on."

"Does your pendulum say I'll meet anyone else?"

I threw it out, and it jumped. "Yes."

"When?"

I asked, "Can you give us a timeline?" Nothing.

"It doesn't answer. Maybe it hasn't been decided yet. The future is always changing." I couldn't believe how much I sounded like Rosetta.

"Could I ask it?" Claire was always impatient.

"You have to know how to use it. It's not complicated—you just have to know how. And you can't be attached to outcome. Maybe we can try it some time. How are you otherwise? It feels like ages since we talked."

"It's only been a week."

"A lot can happen in a week." Actually, a lot *had* happened.

"Have you heard from Brian?"

"Of course not." Unless you count telepathic vibes and seeing someone in a meditative vision. I still felt like he was often next to me, but there wasn't much I could talk about in real life.

I remembered at the end of my last class with him that Brian had said, "This is a beginning." Now I thought that maybe it was a beginning with no middle. But maybe real life was only a beginning too. Even so, I could feel Claire's lip curling, even over the phone.

"It's nice going out with someone though," said Claire. "Last Wednesday we flew to Lake Placid for the day and hiked a bit and then had a lovely lunch by the water."

"That sounds great," I said, not without envy.

"It would have been great with someone else. I had to plan the whole thing, except the flying. And even though the trip was beautiful, we didn't have much to say to each other. We were out for dinner last night, and I told him that he'd meet someone else, that I was just practise."

"You *said* that?"

"I think it's true."

"Well it all seems very sudden—flying off to Lake Placid and then having that conversation a few days later."

"It was sort of sudden from the start. And we're not broken up yet. I think I'll end it after my birthday next month."

"Why?"

"I don't want to be alone on my birthday."

"You won't be alone. You've got your kids. You've got your friends. Anyway, is it worse to be alone or to be disappointed?"

"I don't feel like a whole person if I'm not in a relationship."

"Claire!"

"Well, that's how I feel. I don't like managing my life alone. Don't you feel that way?"

"Really, I think my life is easier since Henry moved out. I don't have to worry about anger bursting out of nowhere. I get to sleep through the night. And actually, I felt more alone when he was in the house, than I do now that he is no longer living in it with me." And it suddenly occurred to me how true that was.

"But what about money?"

"It'll be harder now that I'm buying him out of the house, but we'll manage. How are your kids?"

Claire's daughter Megan was about to go on a school trip to Montreal; her son Scott was playing soccer, and his team had won their most recent game.

"How's Davy?"

"He's okay. I think Henry took him birding today—at least I hope so. Usually he just sits Davy down at the piano and tells him to practise for four hours while Henry goes off and does other things. He thinks he's being Leopold Mozart. At least it hasn't ruined piano for Davy yet. But birding would be better."

"Does Henry ever take Davy overnight?"

"Of course not. The once or twice Davy stayed with him, he had to bring his own duvet and pillow. When he goes over for dinner, he has to bring his own pasta. Henry says he couldn't afford to feed him."

"Isn't he a full professor?"

"Of course, but he's just confusing emotional poverty with financial poverty."

Claire was always good to talk about exes with. Her ex was financially more generous, but emotionally just as stingy. He did take their kids for weekends sometimes, but he didn't do much with them. And he asked their daughter to do house-work and dishes as if she were a Claire surrogate, which their daughter, Megan, hated.

Claire gave me a week's worth of news of people we knew. She told me that the downtown fish store was closing—which was sort of a disaster—and that Minaker's Nursery still had lovely blue pansies and always the best roses, so I might want to go when the course was over.

I heard the front lock turn.

"Hi," Davy called loudly.

"Hi," I called back. "Claire, Davy's home—got to go."

"Maybe you could repattern me when the course is over?" asked Claire.

"Sure. Bye for now, we'll speak later."

"Bye."

I hung up and went to ask Davy how his day had been, and if he'd been birding. He hadn't, but he'd played the piano, and they'd planted tomatoes and just hung around. Yes, he'd had a good day.

"Would you like to practise again?" I asked hopefully. I loved hearing him play, and exams were coming up, so any extra practise was good. "Yes," he said, and I settled on the couch to listen to his Bach.

"Lovely," I said, "but remember what they told you at the Kiwanis Festival: play the music inside the music. That way you'll get the phrasing right. Do you want to try it again?"

"Okay." I would never have taken that sort of suggestion from my mother. Mind you, she was tone-deaf, and her suggestions wouldn't have been worth much. And now that I knew I had a brain-hand block, I could see why I wasn't very good at either piano or violin.

Davy played the Bach again.

"Much better," I was emphatic. "What about your other pieces?"

Listening to Davy play was always the high point of my day.

After that, dinner, then reading *Alice in Wonderland* out loud (all wrong for someone who didn't like fiction), homework, and Davy was ready for Monday. Sort of. If it didn't matter that he had no idea what he'd just read.

And I was sort of ready for Monday too, if it didn't matter than I hadn't practised anything and that I hadn't read ahead.

## 14. ENERGY RODS AND AFTER

O N TUESDAY, we got our energy rods. They were brass with nice white handles. "These are very powerful energy sensors," said Rosetta. "More powerful than pendulums. Be careful how you use them. Don't use them just to ask what you should wear today—not even you, Vivienne!" Vivienne was in a flowing, blue, sleeveless dress with purple trim.

"What a great dress!" said Talitha. "I don't think we've seen it before." She seemed to approve of everything Vivienne wore to the class.

"I threw it together over the weekend," said Vivienne. "I was tired of everything else."

"What are you going to call your business?" asked Andrea.

"Aphrodite's Closet!" (James, of course.)

Rosetta clapped her hands to call us back to order. "These are the Cadillacs of energy rods," she said. "Use them carefully. And don't lose them!"

She showed us, more systematically this time, that when the energy rods opened, it meant "no"; when they closed, it meant "yes"; if they stayed straight it meant they refused to answer; when they swerved to one side, it meant you had spirit help. It was the same as the pendulums: you had to let go of your conscious knowing; you couldn't be attached to outcome; you had to accept what they said—if you didn't, they didn't like it.

We tried them out, measuring energies and auras all over the apartment. They were actually easier than pendulums because they were all in one step. There was nothing you had to learn and then unlearn.

After a bit, I went out to the balcony and whispered to them, "Will I ever see Brian again?"

They inclined together, deliberately, with dignity, then bent to one side. Yes, and I'd have spirit help.

"Am I too attached to outcome?"

No. They assured me again I'd have spirit help.

"Can you give me a timeline?" I asked doubtfully.

Yes, but they weren't enthusiastic.

"Within a year?"

Yes. I knew it was time to stop. They'd get irritated. Or whatever was making them move, the forces behind them, would. Besides, Rosetta was calling us back into the circle.

"So what did you think?" asked Rosetta.

"I like them," said Vivienne.

"They're much easier than pendulums," said Sharon.

"I like pendulums better," said James. "They're crystals."

"I can't wait to show them to Lily," said Elaine.

More than finger testing, more than pendulums, I could feel energy rods searching the ether, beyond where I could reach.

"Any questions?" asked Rosetta.

Talitha raised her hand. "Isn't it awkward to do sessions on people when you always need two hands for your energy rods?"

"Good question! Sometimes I just use one energy rod when I'm doing sessions."

"But then you don't know if you have spirit help," said Deirdre.

"Well, it's harder to see, but if it goes to one side, you know. But when you're working with other people, there's a lot to be said for finger testing—that way you know you're communicating directly with their bodyBsoul. And pendulums only take one hand. Also, people can be put off by energy rods. But they are more powerful. You don't always need something so powerful, though. I wouldn't use energy rods for finding the ripest fruit in the market, for instance."

"Can they find water?" asked Vivienne. "They look like divining rods except for not being wood."

"If you ask them," said Rosetta, "and you really let go of your conscious knowing."

It didn't feel so much like a graduation, but it was still nice to get them. By this time I was getting used to the course. I enjoyed the meditations; I could sort of do body alignment, though I still had to look at the book—especially for all the ribs, which you had to be so careful of because you could hurt people. I was getting used to not eating sugar, but I still missed chocolate. I was aware, anyway, of when I was eating fats or meats with starches (a no-no), even if I was still doing it. I was getting used to ginseng and peppermint tea, though I had promised myself a leisurely coffee at The Sleepless Goat the minute the course was over.

I thought I'd be fine if the course ended right here, but we still had belief systems to anchor and meditations to do, and we might do Natural Process for Universal Peace. And we also would be reviewing because Rosetta would be examining us Thursday and Friday. The thought made me sick.

"Put your energy rods away," Rosetta instructed. "Find a partner, and we'll review Herman."

Herman wasn't body alignment, but it was a physical check, going down the body from head to toe, finger testing for wellness or stress. Herman was what Talitha had done on me in the first days of the course, and all my glands had been off—so I wasn't looking forward to it.

Vivienne was working with Talitha; Andrea was working with Sharon; James was paired with Deirdre; I ended up with Elaine.

You could use pendulums or energy rods for this check, Rosetta said, but finger testing was best. But some people had arthritis, she reminded us, and it hurt them to be finger tested. Then it was better to use another method.

"Do you want to go first?" I asked.

"No, you," said Elaine.

I liked Elaine because she had such a great daughter and was obviously a good mother. But she was hard to finger test. Her fingers were weak, and I couldn't tell if they were coming apart because they meant "yes," or if they were just coming apart.

"Put your fingers closer together," I said. "No, looser. They'll come apart when they want to."

I thought Elaine's hormones and kidneys were off, but I couldn't be sure.

Luckily, Rosetta came around to see how we were doing, and she retested Elaine with crisp, decisive fingers. Her hormones weren't off, but her kidneys and adrenals were, and she needed help with iron absorption—apples, apricots, green beans, green leafy vegetables. Rosetta vanished briefly and came back with some core iron tablets and a glass of water.

"Thanks," said Elaine.

"Sorry," I apologized. "I would have given you totally wrong advice." At least mostly wrong advice. That was the trouble with the system—you could be totally wrong.

Rosetta stayed while Elaine tested me. She wasn't confident, but I could feel her clarity.

My adrenals were better after all those days of core adrenals, and my glands were mostly better. My liver was still stressed. My pituitary was stressed. I still had yeast, but not as much. Rosetta went and got me phos drops, a sort of concentrated Vitamin C, for energy. and a combination of milk thistle and dandelion to strengthen my liver. At least the pills weren't too big to swallow, like the core adrenals had been, but I still felt hopeless with so much wrong with me.

"Read the book," said Rosetta before she left us to check another group.

"Okay," I said, feeling abandoned.

We'd all been slower than Rosetta expected on Herman— we'd been through a lot of material since we'd done it last, and there were a lot of things to check off.

Talitha got it, and so did Deirdre—who after all did massage and knew the body—but the rest of us had struggled.

"What do I care if someone has hiatus hernia?" Vivienne whispered to me when someone else was talking, but Rosetta must have heard or picked something up, because she said, "This is a complete system of stress management. The more of it you master, the more you have to offer. I didn't use to like body alignment, for instance, but then I realized that I was limiting what I had to offer my clients, and now I use it a lot."

I couldn't imagine that I would ever have clients, and I couldn't imagine that they'd want me to tell them that their liver was stressed when they could go to a doctor or herbalist.

"How do you learn about all the supplements?" asked Deirdre. "That's something I'd like to be able to offer my clients."

"That's not really part of the system," said Rosetta. "You'd have to study with a nutritionist or herbalist. Either or both would be valuable."

"Do you have any names?" asked Deirdre.

"Yes, but I'll tell you after class."

"But there are some that you just need to look on a chart," said Deirdre. "Like Bach's flower essences—they tell you what each is good for. And there are essential oils, which are good for massage."

"They'd probably be good for reflexology too," said Elaine.

"You know what's great with reflexology?" said Vivienne. "Ion foot baths. They pull toxins out through the feet and then you can set the healing with reflexology. I had them in Vancouver. They were great."

"That's a good idea," said Elaine hopefully. "But I'd probably have to get the equipment."

"It's not that complicated," said Vivienne, "And once you had it, you'd be able to set yourself apart from other reflexologists. I don't think anyone else in Prince's Harbour offers it."

"There's so much to learn," sighed Sharon. I felt exactly the same way—overwhelmed. I thought I was making a start on this stuff, but I suddenly understood that there was so much else out there that I needed to learn.

"Elaine, Deirdre, and James already practice healing modalities," said Rosetta. "This system gives you a lot. When you're comfortable with it, you can add other modalities. But don't do it too fast"—she looked pointedly at James. "You'll get things confused."

*I don't want to learn a single other thing*, I thought. *Why did I get into this in the first place?* I had simply wanted to heal myself and maybe clear away some blocks between myself and Brian, and now there was all this other stuff to learn and make things complicated.

Rosetta looked at me. "Don't forget," she said, "When you heal your clients, you heal yourself. Especially at the beginning, your clients are your mirrors."

Well, if my clients were my mirrors, I shouldn't have to worry about hiatus hernia for a while. Whatever my problems were, that wasn't one of them. Mine were liver, yeast, and adrenals—I had physical problems that needed correction, and nutrition was a start.

WE DID SOME REVIEW, had lunch, did some more review, and finished the day with a meditation on brain expansion. It reminded of the first time Brian met with our group at Banff. He had us throw our minds way beyond—beyond the atmosphere, past the moon, to the edge of the solar system, to the edge of the galaxy, to the edge of the universe. I had no idea then that I'd fall in love with him, but I loved the meditation, loved the idea that the brain can contain the stars. This was like that, except now we were consciously trying to expand our brains. It felt relaxing not to have to deal with clutter or misaligned ribs or clothes that didn't fit or mere confusion about what to do next. I think my brain expanded—I soared and saw planets and pillars of galactic dust that looked like ancient gods. Vast space—*Brian would like this!* But when I got to the edge of the universe, I didn't know what I saw. More space? I've always been puzzled about what was at the edge of the universe, and this meditation didn't give me any answers.

Rosetta brought us back past the outer planets, past the moon, and said that when we were ready, we should open our eyes.

"That was wonderful!" I said.

"What did you see?" Rosetta asked.

"Oh, just lots of space and stars and galactic dust—I felt like I was seeing into the core of being."

"I didn't like it," said Andrea. "I felt so small."

"I saw purple, nothing but purple," said Sharon. "Oh, I'm so lucky. So lucky!"

You couldn't really follow that, so Rosetta let us go fifteen minutes early, telling us to be on time tomorrow because the course was coming to an end. Then she remembered that we'd forgotten to sort out lunch, so we did that, chipping in again for a potluck.

"What did you think of that?" asked Vivienne as we were leaving.

"As I said in class, I loved it. And I also love your dress. I can't believe you made it so quickly! You must have had an expanded brain even before the meditation to think of it."

"Thanks, but there's always more you can do for your brain. I meant, what do you think about about Sharon."

"I think it's great to feel lucky. Maybe marriage and motherhood and owning a home and some land are great blessings after all."

"Would you want that?"

"I couldn't," I said. "I was glad to see my ex go; the man I'm interested in is a thousand miles away, and I can barely manage the house I have. Especially since it's a heritage house. I'm always afraid I'll ruin it."

"It all seemed too nice-nice to me," said Vivienne, "Not you,

Sharon. Like she took this whole course to realize how happy she is. Little ray of sunshine."

I laughed. "You can't tell where Sharon will go from here. There's something to be said for happiness with where you are. Of course, there's also something to be said for divine discontent, which you've got in spades, by the way. I like it in you."

"I just want more."

"That's what I mean by divine discontent. "

We reached our cars. "See you tomorrow."

"*Ciao.*"

## 15. THE GOD THING

WEDNESDAY AND THURSDAY were mostly review. "We haven't done much with the spiritual," said Rosetta on Friday morning when we'd reassembled.

*Oh no!* I thought. I had enough trouble dealing with my life as it was without trying to include spirituality. I liked James' Mama Isis and Auntie Hathor—but I couldn't stand books where people struggled and struggled and the answer was simply God. Yes, I knew if I were attuned to the Divine, I'd accept things the way they were, but would I still be me? It just seemed too easy an answer.

First, Rosetta showed us the God Thing She took the three middle fingers of her right hand, middle finger above, index and ring finger below, and pressed them into the middle of her forehead, maybe into your third eye? We tried it on ourselves. It felt centring, but it didn't feel like anything particularly divine.

Rosetta said, "Sometimes this will be the only thing your clients need. It will reset them, and you can test to see if their stress is relieved."

Now that we knew how to do it, we left the God Thing and started to talk about addictions. "Addictions are all due to lack of love," said Rosetta. "If you feel perfectly loved, you don't need extra food or cigarettes or too much wine or drugs. Or coffee." She looked at James.

"I couldn't LIVE without my addictions," said James.

219 A SEASON AMONG PSYCHICS 219

"When you feel perfectly loved, you won't need them," said Rosetta.

"Okay," said James, "but until then I'll keep going on coffee and cigarettes. And chocolate. Don't forget chocolate."

"Can you be addicted to things that aren't substances?" asked Talitha.

"Of course," said Rosetta. "Sex. Power. But addiction is compulsion. When you are truly free, you're past choice," said Rosetta. "You are impelled toward the light. And when you are truly enslaved, you are impelled toward the dark, but at each stage you have the choice to turn back toward the light."

"What about free will?" asked Vivienne.

"Your free will gets you started. When you are truly on the path, you are drawn to it as if by a magnet." Rosetta sighed. "Oh, I should have left more time for this. We'll never get through it by the end of the course. Okay, we'll do a meditation." She turned toward James. "Can you say, 'My highest wisdom comes from my heart'?"

Rosetta went around the circle, finger testing, then started with James again. "Can you say, 'I am grateful for Divine restoration in mind, body, financial affairs, and in all my relationships'?"

"I can't even remember it," said James.

Rosetta broke it down, testing each part separately. "You don't believe it." None of us really did.

"This is advanced," said Rosetta. "When you anchor this belief system, really anchor it, not just a beginning, you will realize that you are not single people. You are connected to the Divine, and so to others. Divine restoration comes in many forms. But if you believe in it, it will be there. You are not just living your own life; you are part of something larger."

I closed my eyes and went so deep into my own life that I didn't really hear the meditation. And I didn't come back healed. I came back feeling like I didn't belong and alone—I felt the depths of my aloneness; I felt like I was alone inside a great luminous circle. I liked Vivienne and Talitha, but they weren't there. I wasn't a radiant light of love. I didn't believe in Divine restoration. I just felt depressed.

I didn't anchor either belief system, and I slid into isolation for the rest of the day.

"Are you okay?" asked Vivienne after lunch when we were on the balcony.

"I'm okay, but I feel awful," I said. "I don't feel spiritual at all."

"Well, it is a bit *rah-rah*."

"You don't feel all grey and outside the circle?" I asked.

"I don't feel all grey, but I'm a professional outsider. I was brought up Catholic, so I got all this stuff with my mother's milk."

"But, you don't feel as if you don't belong anywhere?" I persisted.

"Well, you know the Pete Seeger song: *'I've got a home that's so much better I'm going to go to sooner or later. I don't want to get adjusted to this world.'*"

"I guess so," I said wanly. "I'm not sure I've got a home that's so much better waiting for me." Although, as I spoke, I remembered my vision of robed figures on an island in the middle of the sea. "But I'm so imperfect I think I'll never get there. I can't believe Rosetta anchored 'I love myself' when I was repatterned. It's as if it never happened."

"You just need to keep nurturing that seed," said Vivienne.

"I guess so," I said. "I guess I can do the rest of the afternoon."

But I could feel myself slipping. When the day was over, I still felt as if I were flickering on and off like a lamp, like the consciousness of a patient in mid-Alzheimer's. They're there and then they're not. It has to do with neurons firing. Sometimes they connect, and sometimes they don't. As though the brain's wires are frayed.

"I don't think I'm spiritual at all," I said to Vivienne at the end of the day.

"You believe in magic, don't you?"

"Yes, but that's fun."

"You believe in the other world."

"Yes. I really like other world journeys, but I sort of take the Christianity out of them, even Dante. And I've got to say, when I got to the Paradiso, I thought if I never saw another angel again, it would be too soon."

But Brian believes in angels. I know that. At the end of the one letter he'd sent me, he said, "Angels surround you." Even at Banff he'd talked about angels and guides, a little like James. Brian was way ahead of me. How could he ever like anyone who couldn't even keep up with him in the other world?

"Okay, thanks," I said to Vivienne, and I drove home crying.

AT HOME, I LISTENED TO DAVY practise—his Bach Prelude was especially good; the Diabelli a little perfunctory. "Davy, remember what your teacher said about playing the Diabelli a little more brightly, letting the wrists and fingers bounce?" He played it again—better—and once again—better still.

Now that the course was nearly over, I remembered that he'd have his Grade 6 piano exam in a couple of weeks, and I wanted to make sure he was prepared.

Dinner, homework. It wasn't until Davy was in bed that I returned to feeling that all I wanted to do was cry.

Oh, if only I could call Brian. But that was part of the trouble—I couldn't. I'd get his partner's frigid voice on the answering machine, and I'd be throwing my anguish into a void.

I didn't call anyone; and no one called me. I was alone with my grief. My life was so far from being what I wanted it to be. It felt like years of inner ice were melting and pouring out of me, hot and salty. It was a relief to fall asleep, cats curled comfortingly at my feet.

*Thank goodness that's over*, I thought the next morning. It was Saturday, the last full day of the course. Davy was asleep.

I took a quick shower and bundled into the car with my book, my notebook, and my energy rods. I was wearing my pendulum. I drove the long way, past the market, and got a glimpse of massed spring flowers—tulips and hyacinths and daffodils.

If I hadn't noticed before, the market told me it was spring. No more fog. Sunlight. Flowers. New leafy green trees. No more sweaters. Almost in my sleep I'd reached for a blue shirt and bright flowered skirt and sandals. There would be life after the course. Just one day to get through.

I found out on the car radio that Jacqueline Kennedy Onassis had died at only sixty-four. I don't always feel public people as a loss, but I felt her death as a loss. I remembered her great beauty and grace, and even though I'd never met her, I felt the world was diminished without her. So, she was the famous person who had died after the eclipse. I cried as I parked, then started to panic about being late.

I was late. I rang and rang the doorbell, but everyone must have been doing something, and no one answered. What could I do? I couldn't miss the whole day, not the last day. I pointed my thoughts toward Rosetta. *I'm here*, I thought. *I'm here. Please let me in!*

The buzzer didn't ring, but a man came out, and I grabbed the door and headed for the elevator. I glided up to the top floor, past the scrawny plants and spent boots.

When I stepped into the apartment, I could see why no one had heard my ring. Everyone had gathered in the sunroom, on the light-filled landing below the stairs

"I'm sorry I'm late," I began, feeling suddenly shaky, my feelings about Jackie Kennedy, emblem of my youth, joined to everything else. .

"Hello Judith!" said Talitha, and then Vivienne and everyone chorused hello, not at all furious that I was late and had held up class. Rosetta wasn't there.

But all the kindness unleashed something and I just started sobbing.

Rosetta came in, took one look at me and said serenely, "It's a healing crisis. Talitha, when you have a moment, could you come and trim my bangs?"

I wanted to slug her, but I also couldn't stop crying. Talitha, Vivienne, and James all gathered around me. Talitha was holding my hand, James was giving a sort of reiki treatment, and Vivienne was doing some sort of magical passes with her pendulum.

"What's the matter?" asked Talitha.

"I don't know." I couldn't stop sobbing. Again, I felt as if I were being carried down to the bottom of the sea in a whirlpool full of bubbles. It was loneliness. I was missing Brian, worrying about Davy, feeling like I didn't have any right to exist because I couldn't do anything, regretting I hadn't made anything of my life. .

"It's old grief," said Vivienne. "It's not just you. It's ancestors before you. You're crying for a lot of people."

"I am?" I was so surprised that I almost stopped sobbing. My parents had never talked much about their families; they thought they could leave the past behind and live in the now, and, mostly, they did.

"Probably."

"What else?"

"I don't know. But you sure had a lot of stored up tears."

It made me cry that people cared. Mostly when I cried, I cried alone. Eventually I sat up and said, "Thanks, I'm okay. Just thanks."

Talitha went to trim Rosetta's hair, and James went back to his seat. Vivienne stayed next to me on the couch.

"I think I'm okay," I said again. "Thanks for caring."

Vivienne stood up. "I think we need a change of scene." She led us toward the living room.

"Do you think Rosetta and Talitha will be able to find us?" I asked.

"You think Rosetta doesn't know her way around her own apartment?" asked Andrea.

"I guess." I picked up my binder and followed everyone weakly into the living room. Rosetta and Talitha joined us a few moments afterwards. Rosetta looked shinier with her hair trimmed. She was wearing a fitted white shirt and khaki shorts, and she looked serene. I still wanted to slug her.

I appreciated Talitha's careful glance toward me, but it made me weepy all over again.

Rosetta began to speak. "Become ever more aware of the vibration of the places you put yourself in. Create a sacred space in your home; be aware of the things you surround yourself with. Seek out mentors—people or books. Books can be mentors. Spend more time in nature"—she said *nature* reverently, as usual—"listen to music. Music raises the vibration. If you find yourself growing apart from a group you're in, eat some of the foods they eat...."

"What if they're incorrect?" asked James.

"You need to decide whether it's more important to be part of the group or to choose correct foods every single time. Some foods restore balance. Three almonds a day, especially eaten on an empty stomach before bedtime, will destroy parasites, and that's a good start to being part of a group. Parasites make you needy or needed too much...."

This was the last morning. We had been together so intensely for two weeks, and we would never be in this circle again, even if we did join the Advanced Results training, which I certainly didn't plan to.

Whatever had or hadn't happened in these two weeks, I could see that there had been transformation. Although, it had not been enough for me. But if you needed a lot, I thought, you simply couldn't do it all at once.

We spent a lot of the day reviewing body alignment, acupressure, transformers, and meditation, and doing a practise session with a partner. Rosetta touched base with all of us to see how we were doing, and, so, it was a final exam of sorts.

Toward the end of the day, Rosetta gathered us together

and told us how hard it was to break old patterns. She told us about NLP, neurolinguistic programming, which was not in the system. Your body had set points for bad habits, and you could move the set points down in moments. She showed us how to do this using James as an example, helping him to focus on his smoking and and his weight, and moving his set points for these behaviours down.

She worked on Vivienne's smoking as well and deftly moved her set point for smoking down a lot.

"I'd like to stop smoking," said Vivienne. "I just need less stress. I need to start selling paintings."

Rosetta turned to me, "And you, Judith. You need to lose weight, too. You've been heavy for a very long time." She put my set point down about twenty pounds, which still left me overweight, and I wanted to tear myself apart. Maybe I'd love myself if I were thinner, I thought, but maybe I'd hate myself too much to get there. The membrane that had formed over my tears burst again, and like a wound breaking open, they spilled uncontrollably down my cheeks.

At the end of the day, we stood in a circle and had people of our (unspoken) choice give us end-of-course wisdom or blessings. James wanted words from all of us. Brushing my tears away, I said, "You're so gifted. I can see you at forty, a master healer."

James grinned and said, "The next step is reiki!"

Rosetta didn't caution him, for once, about too many specialties, but went on to the next person.

Everyone wanted different people to talk about them. Almost everyone wanted Talitha. No one except James wanted Andrea. I just wanted Rosetta.

She said, "I hope this course did as much for you as it did for me."

"Thank you," I said, sniffling a little. I was grateful, but also skeptical. It didn't feel like a graduation, but then graduations don't always. The best graduation I ever attended was Davy's from kindergarten. On that day, I was shot with joy. I knew that it might, so easily, not have happened at all.

Of course, we had all passed. We were all Results Facilitators. Watch out world!

Rosetta said, "People ask me why I offer so many classes. They think there will be so many facilitators that no one will get work, especially in a small place like Prince's Harbour. But look at how many hairdressers there are here. Just as everyone needs to cut their hair, so too, do people—all kinds of people everywhere—search for help, for answers, for healing. Each of you will find people who follow you."

She said she had sent for certificates. She would call us all when they arrived, and gather us to present them to us.

I DIDN'T WAIT FOR VIVIENNE to leave. I just dashed for my car, drove home, and called Claire. "Well, I did it," I said.

"How do you feel?"

"Terrible," I said. Really, I thought, if I never saw a psychic again, it would be too soon.

But, of course, I'd see Talitha the next time I needed my hair cut, and that would be in a couple of weeks. And I hoped Vivienne would make me a dress.

## 16. THE WEEK AFTER THE COURSE ENDED

I WAS OUT EARLY SUNDAY MORNING pruning the roses, dead-heading the lemon lilies and white peonies, checking in on the scarlet Sweet William and the lupines, pulling the odd irritable weed, when the phone rang. I thought it might be Vivienne, or possibly Elaine, who had called me once or twice since the course had ended. I ran for the phone, pruners still in my hand.

"Hello?" I was breathless.

"Hello. Is this Judith? You sound like a little girl."

"And, you can you tell that from one hello?"

"I've got a good ear. Do you know who this is?"

How many men with voices like silky polished wood would call me early on a Sunday morning? Besides, I could feel all my cells leaping to attention. I was astonished to hear Brian's voice, surging through me like a jolt of electricity.

"How are you?" I was practically panting, trying to catch my breath and thinking of something important and profound to say.

"My friends and I are envisioning a theatre. We bought an old hockey rink from the university for a dollar, so now we're planning to renovate the whole thing. We got a five-million-dollar grant—maybe you read about it?" he asked hopefully.

'No, I didn't read about it," I said regretfully. "I've been taking a healing course for the past fifteen days, and I'm just coming back to the land of the living."

"How was it?"

"Well, I am not sure that I actually liked it, but I have been running into a lot of people in the week since it ended and giving them energy or telling them to come back for repatterning. So I did learn something."

"Are you making any money?" I had thought of Brian as being wildly impractical, living about two feet off the ground, so his interest in money surprised me.

"No, of course not. I'm just learning." I was going to add that it seemed tacky to offer something and then to charge for it, but Brian interrupted.

"I don't tmake any money either," he crowed. "I'm always giving people sessions for free. I might be *rich if*—"

"No one would like you any better if you did," I interrupted him. "I went out with someone who bought four orangeades at a really crowded performance of Shakespeare in the Park and sold two of them at a profit. I found it so off-putting that I never went out with him again."

He chuckled. Then, "What play did you see?"

"It was thirty years ago, Brian! Do you think I remember?"

"You'll remember the plays we'll do at the Festival even after thirty years."

"If I live that long," I replied.

"You'll live long—and I hope I will too—pity the poor planet with the two of us roaming around and wreaking our own havoc! Don't you want to be rich?"

"I want to be published. How could we ever get rich? And, anyway, what would you do if you were rich?"

"Buy an enormous house—well, actually, I've got a big house, but it needs a lot of fixing up—and I'd put money into the theatre."

"The theatre? Five million dollars is a huge grant. You have that."

"It's a start, yes, but we're going to have do to constant fundraising to get the festival up and running, let alone put on the plays we'd love to see performed. "

"I never dreamed you did things like start theatres," I said.

"That's my real work," he replied, unusually serious. "I have the vision; Hugh is great on detail and raising money."

No wonder Brian was so busy! Starting a theatre in his spare time after teaching drama at his university and teaching at Banff, I realized how little I knew him, realized his outstanding teaching rested on a large, ambitious vision, well beyond the various classes he taught.

"I want to do classics," Brian said. "Shakespeare, Chekov, Sophocles. There's nothing like that in the Maritimes. Theatre is the most transformative thing there is. Actors carry emotions for everyone, things people might not otherwise let themselves feel."

"Writers do too—" I ventured, somewhat hesitantly.

"Yes, but there's something about being in a theatre, the whole imaginative experience, hearing the words spoken out loud. I want it to be *charismatic*."

He was so persuasive that I thought I knew what he meant, even though I couldn't have explained it to anyone else. I'd never thought about making more money than I needed to pay my bills and run my life, but now I realized that if I had more, I could give a lot to Brian's theatre. I could start a publishing house. I could redo my kitchen. I hadn't let myself imagine the possibilities having money might bring.

"Of course, right now it's just an old hockey rink, but we're making plans, designing the space, preparing for the necessary renovations. We'll start work on it this summer. I think a thrust stage, like the one at Stratford, would be good, and seats that slope gently up so that every seat in the house has a great view. And the aisles should be wide enough so that the plays can spill out into them if necessary."

I listened, rapt, and, as at Banff, I felt that the sky had opened up and let in a huge slice of universe.

"Drama carries the mysteries," he continued, the words rushing out, "but right now we're at the nuts and bolts stage.

You know, if you have a spare million, we could find a good use for it.'"

"Oh, sure! I won't make that in my lifetime," I said, wishing I could have offered him everything he wanted, or needed, to make his dream unfold.

"Just thought I'd ask," he laughed. "How's your writing?"

"Don't ask," I replied, ashamed of my lack of accomplishment. "I finished all my marking and then dove head-first into this healing course. I haven't had a moment to breathe." Wrong thing to say. I'd forgotten that for Brian, breath was the foundation of everything. He and Rosetta had that in common. He didn't exactly chew me out—he was too much of a trickster for that—but he did remind me that everything depended on the breath. Without the breath, there were no words and not much of anything else either. And I couldn't help thinking—as he talked about my poor little stories when we were in Banff, which absolutely weren't charismatic and which did not, in any way, embody the mysteries of the universe—did writing have to? But at least they could have breath.

"I've been busy too," he said. "I was at Banff...."

"How was it?"

"It's always such a privilege to work with the writers. It was an extraordinary group. Of course, they're all extraordinary...."

"As good as ours?"

"Oh, well..." I could almost hear him mugging, "...it was missing one special person."

I wanted to ask, "*Did you connect to anyone else telepathically this year?*" But instead I prompted, "So then you got back..."

"We've been having non-stop meetings. We've assembled a good board—some local people, some from Halifax, some from Toronto and Montreal—and we're starting to make offers to actors. We're breaking ground for the theatre over the long weekend."

"You aren't wasting any time."

"Not now. But I've been thinking about this since I came here to teach eight years ago. I knew this was the right space for a special theatre. It's finally starting to happen."

"Do you know what plays you will be doing?"

"We're tossing out possibilities. I've always wanted to do *Oedipus*."

"I'm really impressed." And I was. Completely.

"Well, it's not started yet, not really."

"But it will be."

"Yes, it will be. Then the problem will be to keep it going. As always, money is a crucial issue..." he sighed loudly. "So, how's your son?"

"He's fine. He's practising for his Grade 6 piano exam. He's playing well." I didn't want to tell Brian that I was always so worried about Davy, worried about his end of year school exams, and even about his piano exam.

"He'll be fine," Brian said. "I can see it. Especially his piano."

For now, I believed it.

"Can you see what's going to happen with your theatre?"

"I can see the theatre with people in it. I can see the first season. I don't know about after that—and that's worrying. Hugh and I have started six companies together, and none of them have lasted. But sometimes you just have to keep going on faith. I'm sorry, Judith. I've got to go. We have a meeting. I'll call you back. All my love to you."

"And mine to you," I said, so surprised that I nearly dropped the phone. Then he hung up.

On the one hand, he'd called, and, while we were speaking, my heart was at rest. I was comforted. He believed in Davy and in my writing. On the other hand, I felt as if I'd been cut off in mid-conversation. But if you're going to have meetings Sunday mornings, you've got to get to them.

*All my love?* Did he mean what he said? Or was it just a theatre thing to say? Did he say the same thing to everyone?

I couldn't go back to pruning and weeding just yet. I poured myself another cup of coffee—one of the best things about the course being over was that I could have coffee—and dragged myself into the living room, collapsing on the old blue couch. I reached for my black cat, Rigel, who was curled in the corner, and whose purr was so loud it made me see blackberries.

Then it hit me—was it me or was it Brian? It was always after his phone calls (and there hadn't been so many of them)—that wave of desire coursed through me, a feeling of intense love rushing from head to toe. I wanted to jump on a train or a plane or a magic carpet and just arrive. But Brian was complicated—he probably didn't even know he was sending out vibes like that. Was it real or was it imagined?

I let Brian inhabit every cell of my body for a while, then took a deep breath—several breaths—then went back out to the peonies, the roses, the lemon lilies, grounding myself in their literal nearness.

FOR THE NEXT FEW DAYS, I stayed near the phone and dashed to answer when it rang, but there weren't too many calls, and none of them were from Brian.

I did see Claire. I showed her my pendulum and energy rods and repatterned her, and, although she liked it, I think she just thought it was a bit of a hoot, like trying perfume or lipsticks in Shopper's Drug Mart. But she was very perceptive about people, and I loved that about her.

"I don't know why Brian hasn't called," I said wistfully.

"Why don't you just call him?"

"I either get his partner or his partner's voice on the answering machine," I said, "and I just want to go through the floor. I feel like a groupie."

"Judith, don't you want someone real?"

"Yes, but not if it isn't him."

A FEW DAYS LATER, I called Vivienne and asked if she would make me a dress.

"Okay," she said. "I'll concentrate on your measurements, and then I'll start it."

"Don't you have to *take* my measurements?"

"I'll dream them," she said. "Like Set dreamed of Osiris and then made a perfectly-sized coffin. There's a lot of information in the air if you just tap into it."

"I don't want a coffin," I said. "I want a dress. If I ever see Brian again…"

She stopped me before I could finish my thought, "He sounds as if he can pull things out of the air too."

"Yes, but not me. If I ever see him…"

Again, she interrupted me. "Give me a couple weeks," said Vivienne. "I need to settle down from the course. Then we can do a few sessions on each other. Remember, I said you needed one around your mother. And I'd like to know where and when I'm going to meet my shaman."

"And you think *I* can tell you?"

"Not you. Something working through you."

"How does the course look now that you're done?"

"It wasn't what I wanted. But I'm still tired from it. Something must have happened. What did you think?"

"You mean now that I've stopped crying? I guess I learned a lot. But it didn't help me with my writing, or my dreams of love, or my worries about Davy or my job or my weight, in spite of Rosetta going at me about it. The one good thing that happened was that Brian *did* call. But then again, he said he'd call back, and he hasn't."

"He didn't say when, did he?"

"No…. I guess it could be next year." I sighed. "Anyway, the course didn't make me feel better about myself either. I only have more to offer other people."

"That is a good thing."

"But the first belief system Rosetta anchored, when she repatterned me, was 'I love myself.' I don't think I love myself any better."

"Are you sure? Ask your pendulum."

I took the amethyst from around my neck and asked, "Out of ten, how much did I love myself before I was repatterned?" I swung it. It said four. "How much do I love myself now, out of ten, please?" I swung it again. "It says seven."

"See? You can't always tell about yourself."

"Okay," I said, "But why hasn't Brian called me back?"

"He doesn't have much privacy."

"How can you *say* that?"

"I asked my pendulum. What colour dress do you want?"

"Blue. Not navy. Sort of a night-sky-in-moonlight blue. Sort of starry. With some silver. Is that possible?"

"Flowing, right?"

"Yes, flowing."

"I'll need to find the right material. Let's say three weeks. I'll come over and bring it. And my book and energy rods. If I can't find the material, I'll come anyway."

"Great, and yes, come even without the dress. We should have gotten our certificates by then, and the course will be really behind us. And, thanks Vivienne, you are a good friend."

"Well, I want a session from you too, remember. And I wouldn't stay too near the phone. Watched phones never ring."


"IT'S DEFINITELY OVER," said Claire a few days later. "I'm going to Montreal to listen to some jazz. Do you want to come?"

"I can't leave before Davy has his exams," I said, sighing for my lack of freedom. "He's got his piano exam next week and then his school exams."

"Can't he stay with Henry for a couple days?"

"Henry couldn't take care of a gerbil."


TOWARD THE END OF THE WEEK, my lawyer called. Henry had finally signed the separation agreement. I would keep what was mine; he would keep what was his. I would buy him out of the house. I would have a hefty mortgage. Maybe now Henry would feel he could buy Davy's pasta. I was afraid I wouldn't be able to afford toothpaste.

Henry had promised Davy that if I settled and bought him out of the house, he would take Davy to Iceland. Davy actually thought this might happen, but keeping promises wasn't one of Henry's strong suits. It soon became clear that I would have to spin a summer holiday out of thin air, and it was already June.

I vented about this to people I ran into while I was doing errands. One of them, a former student, now a friend, who was also going through a divorce, asked if I wanted to rent her cottage on the Northumberland Strait for a couple of weeks, maybe at the end of July, beginning of August.

I didn't usually do things like that. But I didn't have a lot of choices. It was on the water, and Davy loved water. It was Nova Scotia. We could drive through Brian's town on the way home. I wasn't a great distance driver, but my finger testing said we should go, so I thanked her, and we booked the last week in July and the first week in August.

She said she'd give me directions and that there would be instructions at the cottage itself, including directions to the best place to buy lobster.

"We're going to Nova Scotia," I told Davy so he wouldn't be too disappointed about Iceland. "We're renting a cottage. It's right on the water, and there will be raspberries."

"Okay." Davy always held his cards close to his chest, so I couldn't tell how he felt. But at least he was thinking about Nova Scotia and not Iceland.

## 17. REPATTERNING DAVY

THE COURSE WAS OVER; Davy's piano exam was over. He'd played really well, especially the Bach. And I had time to face the neglected crisis of Davy's English. It *would* be English.

We somehow got through the last two book reports on Emily Carr's *Klee Wyck* (Davy liked it. There was a lot of description and not too much plot, and we could look at reproductions of Emily Carr's pictures) and *Alice in Wonderland* (Davy didn't have a clue, though I think he liked the Cheshire Cat). I had never imagined that I would be all but writing my son's book reports for him: "Davy, do you want to say this? Or do you want to say that?" But motherhood leads you to places you never expected to go.

Now it was June, and Davy was studying for his English exam, mostly on *Julius Caesar*. It was as if we'd never read it the past winter. When I'd read it in tenth grade, I had thought that Shakespeare had concocted it and its elaborate language solely for the confusion of teenagers. Thirty-five years later, it all made sense—I could see that it was a good play—but Davy couldn't understand why Mark Antony didn't just say what he meant. And why did you need the distraction of a ragged old soothsayer? (I remembered thinking that he was a distraction too, just when things were getting started.)

"The point is," I said to Davy, "all the omens say that Caesar is going to die."

"What are omens?"

"They're signs of something that's going to happen. Like when we were flying back to England when you were a baby and the gold pin my mother gave me slipped off in Heathrow Airport. I wanted your grandmother to get better, but when I realized I'd lost that pin, I knew she was going to die."

Davy fidgeted. "I need better notebooks."

"You don't need notebooks now, Davy, the year's over. After the exam we can get you next year's notebooks, if you want. Now look at Brutus."

"I need better notebooks," insisted Davy.

It was a beautiful sunny June day, the sort of day you summoned when you did meditations, and we were wasting it with *Julius Caesar* and loops about notebooks. In spite of its being a good play, I was starting to go back to my original idea—that Shakespeare had concocted it solely for the torment of teenagers.

And it was a crisis because Davy's English teacher didn't really believe in him and thought he should be in the General Stream or even Basic. Luckily, a student's assignment to streams required the consent of the parent, and I'd put my foot down. I had argued that two of my own students who had gone through teacher training said that Davy would be bored silly in the General Stream, but if they'd seen him that morning, being tied into knots by *Julius Caesar,* they might have thought otherwise. Why didn't Shakespeare ever say anything directly? Everything had to be translated. "I have not from your eyes that gentleness and show of love that I was wont to have," says Cassius. And that's fairly direct, but Davy didn't think about looking into peoples' eyes to see what they thought about him, and it needed explaining. And that was only one detail of the play, and then we had to go on to the next thing. I was wrung out, and the exam was tomorrow.

"Davy, I think you're worried about the exam, and that's why you're going around in loops."

"I just need new notebooks."

"It's better to admit you're worried instead of pushing it away. Then you can start. You're just wasting all your energy going into a loop."

Davy's eyes glittered, a sign that he wasn't going to be distracted. "No, I'm not! I just don't have the right notebooks!"

I took a few breaths. Davy was throwing up a wall that I couldn't get through.

I remembered in high school they told me Shakespeare didn't believe in all that supernatural stuff, but now I wasn't so sure. All the warnings were there, but no man of action, no hero, would pay any attention to them and change his course, not in the Renaissance, and not today. But the older wisdom—in Roman times and maybe today if you'd just taken a two-week course that included energy work, telepathy, and guided visioning—was to heed the omens and to acknowledge the limitations of the single being. Caesar could have heeded the omens at any point, could have stayed home, but heroism told him to go forward, even if it was to meet a destined, tragic death.

I ran my fingers through the soft, too-long grass and looked up at the willow, still tender green under the blue sky. There was no point spending all morning in a standoff like this. "Davy," I said, "do you want to be repatterned? It's some of the stuff I was doing while I was taking that course."

"Yes," he said firmly, and I had to laugh—anything was better than studying for an English exam.

"Okay," I said. "Now just forget about the English class, forget the notebooks, and just be in the sun, with the lemon lilies, the first roses, the willow tree. Just be in the moment."

Davy looked more relieved already, and his eyes stopped glittering.

I went inside to get my book and energy rods. "This is a rebalancing of the space in your cells," I said, the way Rosetta did, when I came back outside. "It releases stress and substitutes positive belief patterns for negative ones."

"Okay." Davy was with me now, and the wall around him was gone.

"We'll start with your brain pattern. I know you're right-handed." Davy had been obviously right-handed since he was a few weeks old. "Now if I rolled a ball between your feet, which foot would you kick it with?" (Not that Davy kicked balls much.)

"Right."

"Now make a small triangle with your hands"—I showed him. "No, smaller. Good. Look at my nose through it."

Davy's left eye, bright and brown, stared through the triangle at me.

"Close your left eye." He did. "And my nose disappears."

"Yes."

"You're left-eyed. Now I need your fingers for muscle testing. Make a circle with your thumb and little finger."

People usually made the circle with their thumb and index finger at first, and Davy did too. "No, your little finger." I showed him. "Hold your fingers firmly together but not too tight—I need to see if you're testable. No, looser than that. Tighter than that. Good. So I don't have to pry your fingers apart, but they're together enough that I can tell when they're speaking to me. Think of something you really, really like."

Once he got it, Davy's fingers were nice and strong. I wondered what he'd been thinking of.

"Now think of something that stresses you." I pulled. "See, they come right apart. Now, with the other hand, hang onto an ear."

Davy was left-eared, left-eyed, left-brained, right-handed, right-footed. Strong on action. That made perfect sense. Davy wasn't hyperactive, but he didn't like sitting still too long either.

"When you're stressed, action's good for you," I said. "Running, walking, swimming." I didn't add: hopping, fidgeting, pushing buttons. I noticed the brain-eye block that might contribute to problems in reading. But that didn't explain Davy's gift for photography. Davy's logic was in his left brain, where it should be, so he should be strong on logic, which he was. His gestalt, or feelings, was in the right brain. Davy had terrible problems synthesizing (witness *Julius Caesar*) and had trouble accessing his feelings, especially when he was stressed, like all of us left-brainers. Of course he'd frozen at the prospect of an exam on material he couldn't begin to understand.

"Without moving your head, turn your eyes right," I said, still hanging onto his hand for finger testing. His eyes were strong going to the right, weak going to the left, weak looking up (spiritual?), strong looking down (grounded?). I still had no idea what the eye positions meant, so I didn't say anything.

I silently asked if we were ready for concrete base. His finger testing said no. I asked the energy rods. They said no. "You want optional testing," I told him. Optional tests included reading stress, reading brain, attitudes.

"Okay."

Reading stress? Yes, definitely. No surprises there.

Reading brain? His left brain, which recognized words and music, was strong; his right brain, which synthesized, was weak.

Attitudes: well, he didn't want to learn to read—again, no surprise there. Brain-eye block wouldn't help. Reading stress and weak right reading brain wouldn't help.

Surprisingly (to me), he did want to succeed. Maybe that's what had kept him going through school even though it was so hard. But he had also wanted to fail—there had been plenty of that too. But he wanted to be well; he didn't want to be sick. He was stressed with ABCs, but fine with breathing, focus (take that, Therapeutic Nursery School!), and numbers. His peripheral vision was narrow, but not as narrow as mine had been when I was repatterned.

Anything else? I checked with the energy rods. No. Can we go on? Yes.

"We're ready for concrete base," I said. "Your concrete base is a belief system you formed during a stressful period of your life that helped you get through that time, but now it's limiting you. I'll finger test you for when yours was formed."

Between zero and five. I should have known. I asked for specific years. Between two and three. My fault. Uncomfortable as it was, I had to face it.

"Yours was formed between age two and three," I said. I knew what it was, but Davy had to know too. "Do you remember what was going on in your life then?"

"Daycare," said Davy.

"And how did that make you feel?"

"Bad."

"Why didn't you say anything?"

"Didn't think it would do any good."

*Ouch.*

"That's probably your concrete base." I tried to be professional. Anyway, I was left-brained and pretty adept at carrying on despite feelings. "That you were unhappy and you didn't think anyone would help you. Is that right?"

"Yes."

I held out my energy rods to check and they swept together. *Oh, that he should have had to go through that at the age of two!* I cringed.

"I am so sorry, Davy. I should have taken you out of daycare much, much sooner. I didn't mean to hurt you so badly. I'm sorry."

"Okay." Sturdily.

"Well, it's not okay, but this should be a path out. Daycare is long behind you, and it's time to get over it. This should break that belief system and replace it with more positive belief systems." I looked at the sheet of belief systems and held out my energy rods. They swung in at "I am open to and worthy of all the abundant blessings of this universe."

I had to break it down for Davy bit by bit, and he repeated after me.

"I am open to and worthy of..."

"...all the abundant blessings..."

"...of the universe."

Davy repeated obediently, and I finger tested. Of course he didn't believe it. Did he even know what it meant? It probably didn't matter. So much of Results was non-verbal, at the cellular level, even if words were the door. You didn't need to understand them to go through it.

"That needs anchoring," I said. "Repatterning will do that."

I held my energy rods over the belief system sheet again and turned the page. They swung together at "I trust my future."

I wasn't at all sure about Davy's future. Davy didn't believe it either.

"That needs anchoring too." For both of us. But Rosetta had impressed on us that creating a healing space changed both people in it. I added, "The energy rods wouldn't have chosen things you already believed. The point is to change your belief systems."

The energy rods said that Davy wanted to be repatterned by meditation and that he'd chosen The Ultimate Self, the meditation I'd liked best when we did it in the course.

"Just sit back in the chair," I said to Davy (we'd both been standing). "Close your eyes. See what images come to you. There are no right answers. Just say what you see."

Would this work? I brushed doubt aside and began to read. "Observe your Ultimate Self, whatever form the Self may take for you. You may see a visual picture. You could heal that Self, or you might just 'feel' or 'know' that Self. Whatever form it takes, be aware of what comes to you." I gave him a few minutes. "Do you want to say or do you want to write it down?"

"Red, blue, green, orange."

"Nice," I said, although probably I shouldn't be commenting. "Now turn your eyes down and to the centre. What does your Ultimate Self feel like?"

"I see elevator panels. It feels like going up and down in an elevator."

"And with your eyes down and to the left, let your Ultimate Self go into action. What action do you see yourself doing?"

"Math sheets."

Who would have thought? But Davy had always liked numbers ever since he did number cookies in kindergarten, and he usually got As on his math sheets.

"Now turn your eyes up and to the right. What music do you hear as part of your Ultimate Self?"

"Classical."

I didn't ask for a composer, but I would have guessed Bach. Possibly followed by Mozart.

"Turn your eyes up and to the centre, and bring the experience of intellect to your Ultimate Self. What do you see?"

Davy considered. "A road going down to a lake."

"Lovely." I couldn't help it. "Turn your eyes up and to the left—what smell do you associate with your Ultimate Self?"

"A rose." I remembered walking with Davy in England when he was little, about up to my knee, and we would always stop to smell roses. And a heavenly scented deep pink rose in our garden still survived our patchy gardening skills.

Davy was starting to fidget.

"Just a little more," I said.

Davy's Ultimate Self intuition was our backyard, and his logic was a midsummer day, a really strong light.

"Now with your eyes up and to the centre, combine acting with feeling, logic, knowing, sound, smell, and intellect. Allow all of these to join together in your experience. What is this like for you?"

"It's a sunny summer day—a backyard with a lake at the end," said Davy. "It feels good."

"Great. Now with your eyes still up centre, bring the highest energy form you can think of to your Ultimate Self."

"Lightning," said Davy. "It's bright. Scary. Lovely."

Agent of change.

"What colour is associated with your Ultimate Self?"

"Red." Davy's favourite colour since he was a baby.

"Allow this colour to join the experience of your Ultimate Self. Turn your eyes down centre, and bring that whole experience into your physical body, filling your body with that calm. Just experience what it's like."

I gave Davy a few moments. "Then when you're ready, open your eyes."

Davy's eyes opened wide—bright, brown, clear.

"How did you find that?"

"*Good.*"

"That's what I did those two weeks in the course."

"I'll just retest you." I remembered what Rosetta had said about not leaving loose ends hanging. The backyard was a little unkempt, but green and full of flowers. The willow fronds fluttered.

The reading stress was better, though Davy still had trouble following my finger as it went back and forth in front of his nose—so one of Davy's troubles with reading was that it was physically hard for him. Next, peripheral vision: my arms opened wider, which meant that Davy was taking more in. The thing about the peripheral vision test, Rosetta had impressed on us, was that you could see how much you'd changed in a short time.

The belief systems were anchored, maybe for me as well as Davy. It was a very sound healing. I began to let myself believe in Davy's future.

"I'm afraid we should go back inside," I said. Even though I ought to have given the repatterning a chance to sink in, there was still Davy's English exam tomorrow. But then I also remembered we should be drinking water to consolidate the changes, so I brought out two glasses, and we drank them.

Then we did go in, laden with glasses, *Julius Caesar*, my big blue binder and energy rods, and Davy's English notebook. But as we passed from sun to shade, I thought maybe Davy needed energy. Why not just throw some in? A little more time away from English probably wouldn't make the least bit of difference, and it might get him away from obsessing over notebooks.

I put the glasses in the sink, my results stuff on the counter, and suggested Davy take *Julius Caesar* and his English notebook to the dining room so their vibes didn't distract him. I think he would have been happy to take them to China.

"Just relax and be ready to receive," I said. Before I closed my eyes, I was aware of the kitchen door—we were just inside, on a threshold, summer light made neutral by walls and windows. I stretched out my arms, making sure not to touch Davy. In Reiki, you touch, but giving energy depends on the space in between, just as repatterning rebalances not the pattern of the cells, but the space in them. I asked that healing energy flow through me. I pulled down white light. Davy's heart felt fine— he'd always had a stout heart, even as a baby. His shoulders felt fine, not overburdened by responsibility, even with the prospect of this exam. His power centre was a bit down—no wonder!—but not seriously, and I visualized orange poppies for it. His legs and feet were fine. Then I came back up. His throat chakra needed attention, and I flooded it with lemon lilies.

Then I ran my hands above Davy's head and felt with a shock: his left brain was strong, but his right brain was incredibly weak—almost entirely turned off! No wonder Davy had trouble with synthesis! No wonder his right reading brain was weak—it was practically dormant! How could all these professionals have missed this? They'd been fine slapping on a label, but hadn't wrapped their minds around a possible cause, a possible remedy.

I gave a lot of attention to Davy's right brain, poured energy into it, then moved my hands over his head with the intention of bringing right brain and left together. I remembered what Rosetta had said about men having more slender corpus callosums than women, and a more tenuous connection between left and right brain. I also remembered how James had needed his parts brought together—maybe not so much his brain, but other things. Healing is timeless time: a few moments or minutes can make lasting change. I don't know how long we were there in front of the kitchen door. I gave Davy's head energy until I was spent, then opened my eyes. Davy's were still shut. Now that he was a teenager, I didn't see his eyes shut so often, but I remembered his sleeping when he was younger—his closed eyes were delicate as seashells, a whole world of sleep or thought behind those slight doors.

"Whenever you're ready, you can open your eyes," I said softly.

Davy opened his eyes, totally present, and I gave him a light hug.

The light was the same; the tawny pine of the jam closet was the same, but there was a difference. "How did that feel?" I asked.

"*Good.*"

I took a deep breath, "Davy, I thought your right brain was almost totally turned off. Is that possible?"

He considered. "It might be possible."

"Do you think that's true?"

"It's probably true."

I had to catch my breath. I had *felt* Davy's autism—or disability—whatever it was. No wonder he twitched and hopped. He was trying to correct that brain imbalance, though probably twitching and hopping weren't enough to give him the balance he needed. But if a problem could be felt, then it could probably be improved. And it had happened here in our kitchen, in a spot we had passed through thousands of times. I was moved and exhilarated and more hopeful than I had felt in a long time.

"Let's have some more water." I refilled our glasses. "Repatterning is the beginning of change, but it's just a beginning. Water will help make the change stick, and you'll be able to grow from it.

"Okay." It was hard to tell what Davy was thinking, but

he seemed calmer, less fidgety, more stable. Not talking about notebooks.

We went into the living room—the most healing place in the house with its high windows, high ceilings, good light, good fireplace—and drank our water.

I thought of *Julius Caesar*, but decided against it, at least for now. We were at a crossroads—the English exam, which was probably hopeless, or the rest of Davy's life, which might not be.

"Did you see anything when I gave you energy?" I asked.

"Blue and green. Maybe a lake."

"Hang onto that lake—it's the beginning of new growth. Think of it when you drink water."

We drained our glasses. (Rosetta had impressed on us that we must always drink when our clients drank.)

I sent Davy back outside to play, and I settled on the couch with a purring cat. Cats are healing too, and Rigel cared a lot about Davy.

If I'd taken that course for no other reason, I'd have taken it for this.

# 18. GRADUATION

THE CERTIFICATES TOOK A LONG TIME to come, so we didn't formally graduate until a Sunday afternoon in the third week of June, after Davy's English exam.

It was weird—confining—to be back in Rosetta's penthouse. I hadn't liked the course very much. But at least I'd passed. We'd all passed. And I did like the bronze statue of the girl at the top of the stairs, with the living room and the light from the windows behind her. I nodded to her—for the last time? My finger testing said no. The apartment looked as usual—no flowers to mark the occasion. After all, Rosetta was giving four classes a year, and this graduation wouldn't be that special to her.

Vivienne had phoned me in the morning. "I'm not going," she had said. "Can you pick up my certificate for me?"

"Why aren't you going?"

"Ceremonies don't do it for me. It's not like this is an initiation into the Hermetic Order of the Golden Dawn."

It was nice to see everyone though— all of us a bit dressed up, all of us less stressed,. Talitha looked more like her almost-model self; Andrea, like someone fresh from an office; Elaine, a little droopy. Lily was better, but Elaine still worried about her daughter's health. James looked a little aimless—he was likely the one who missed the course the most.

"Judith! You look wonderful!" said Talitha.

I was pleased, but it was really just my clothes—a red skirt, blue t-shirt, and a matching red jacket in a light summery material. I tended to use my clothes as armour, so I could lurk invisibly behind them. Well, and I also wasn't crying my eyes out.

"Thanks. So do you." Talitha always looked wonderful, but then everyone seemed to be looking better than they had during the course.

Rosetta made her entrance, looking like a priestess in a white , jump suit and gold necklace. Her hair was newly trimmed and very shiny. She held a large envelope in her hand.

"I don't know why it took so long for these to come," she said. "But they're here now. Congratulations. You have all earned them. Good work."

I didn't think my work had been very good, especially in body alignment, but now it was all in the past.

"Let's form a circle," said Rosetta. "I'll give you each your certificate, and you can tell us what you've been doing since the course ended last month."

We formed our circle, taking the same chairs—except that since Vivienne wasn't here, I slid into hers. Comfort at last.

"James?"

"I've been hanging out a lot in Treasure Garden," said James. "They have a space curtained off in the back where I can do energy work. I've been reading a lot. And I did a session on Trish and got this GREAT crystal," which he promptly waved in the air.

"Good," Rosetta handed James his certificate. "Congratulations, James. This is an important step in becoming the healer you were meant to be."

"Deirdre?"

"I've added Results to my massage practice," said Deirdre. "I've had some clients. And I'm hoping to go to Lilydale."

"Oh, I'd like to go there!" said Talitha.

"What's Lilydale?" asked Andrea.

"It's a spiritual place in western New York where there are lots of mediums," said Talitha. "Take me with you if you go, Deirdre."

"And are you being careful with food and exercise?" Rosetta asked Deirdre.

"Yes. I feel the course gave me a lot of healing. Thank you."

"You're welcome. Congratulations." Rosetta looked pleased, even affectionate for an instant, as she gave Deirdre her certificate.

"Andrea?"

"I've quit my job," said Andrea. "I'm not staying in a toxic situation. I'm looking for work."

We all chorused congratulations.

"Nice," said Rosetta. "Congratulations. Elaine?"

"I've been doing food combining with Lily. She's gained a couple pounds and hasn't been sick since the course ended."

"Good," said Rosetta. "And are you using Results at all with your reflexology clients?"

"A little. I've been doing some aura cleansing. But I really need a massage table so I can do body alignment."

"Set your intention," said Rosetta. "As you have more to offer, you'll get more clients."

"I know where you can get second-hand massage tables," said Deirdre. "They're not expensive. I'll take you there next week."

Elaine looked surprised, then gave one of the first smiles I'd seen from her. "Wow, thanks, Deirdre!"

"Sharon?"

I've mostly just been home with my family," said Sharon. "But I also volunteered in Mikey's school a few times before the year ended. And I think I'll go back once or twice a week in the fall."

"Good," said Rosetta. "Congratulations." She turned to me.

I got that sinking *everyone but me* feeling. I didn't really want to talk about repatterning Davy, even though I was removing myself from the group by not being honest.

"I've repatterned some people," I said. "That's about all."

"And Vivienne," I added, "is painting and making me a

dress. I'm sorry it's not ready for today. She asked me to carry her spirit."

"Congratulations to both of you," said Rosetta, handing me two certificates. She turned to Talitha.

"James and I have done some sessions. He saw that my house and yard were full of ghosts—we live right next to a graveyard—and we spent two afternoons asking them to sit in a chair and sending them into the light."

"That's amazing!" said Sharon. I was very impressed too.

"Why didn't you say anything about that, James?" asked Sharon.

"I feel like I'm sending ghosts into the light all the time. It's just something I do. It doesn't pay."

"It's a very good deed," said Rosetta. "Congratulations, Talitha. You were born to do this work."

She led us toward the dining space where lemonade, rice crackers, and cheese were set out in addition to the apples and almonds. I gulped a glass of watery lemonade, then drifted over to the side wall where the books Rosetta had set out during the course were still on display. I remembered Rosetta had said something about brain gym exercises, and I found the book.

I didn't really have time to read it, but I found some exercises for stiff eyes—have the client follow your finger from one side to another and see if his eyes stop at the midpoint. Have the client follow your finger as you make small figure eights and then big figure eights. Try to work up to a hundred. It didn't sound like much of an exercise to me, but then I had a brain-eye flow, and, despite the many things I couldn't do, I was a good reader.

And then I remembered that Rosetta had told us about brain buttons—put one middle finger on your belly button and the other on the top of your head. This somehow balances your brain better—I don't know why. Maybe it creates a connection between two centres.

I read the pages over a few times so I would remember and could use them for Davy.

I went for another gulp of lemonade and then said my good-byes. Not final goodbyes—Prince's Harbour is too small for that. People run into one another all the time. And Talitha would cut my hair next week.

"Did you really see ghosts?" I asked her before I left.

"I didn't see them until James was with me, but then I did. We summoned them one by one, sat them in a chair in the kitchen, and sent them into the light."

I was really impressed.

"That's amazing."

As I left, I thought that it really was all amazing. People had changed and moved their lives along. The course had seemed organized on a shoestring budget and had offered what I thought of as bandaid solutions. At times, it was so chaotic; at other times, people slept while Rosetta talked. But it had worked.

ONE OF THE REASONS I'd left the graduation so promptly was that Davy was at home. I hadn't been gone so long that he'd gotten jangled, thank goodness. But the truth was also that I didn't have much to say, and I was just as glad to slip out and get back home.

"Davy," I said. "I saw some exercises that might be good for your reading. Do you want to try them?"

"Okay."

I did a few figure eights, but I could see that after two or three that they were really a strain. Well, that meant that Davy needed them. "Do those bother you?" I asked.

"They're hard."

"We'll do a couple more tomorrow. Let's go out in the garden and do some weeding."

Davy liked gardening—he had more staying power for that than I did—and we got through a bunch of weeds before we came inside to read—Davy had been allowed to stay in the

Advanced Stream on the condition that he work on his reading all summer—and have dinner.

VIVIENNE CAME OVER THE NEXT THURSDAY, bringing the gorgeous dress she'd made for me, with a shawl to match. It was deep electric blue with silver stars scattered over it, long skirted, and sleeveless. It even fit, not so usual with me and dresses.

"You must be psychic," I said. "It's perfect and I'll love wearing it."

We quarrelled over price—I wanted to pay more; Vivienne thought it was too much.

"You're not counting your time and your artistic gift." I objected.

But we didn't agree, and I realized I would have to win by stealth.

"Let's leave it for now," I said. "Let's start the sessions. You did the dress; I'll facilitate first."

We sat at the picnic table, the tall willow bending gracefully at the side of the yard, the large maple spreading over the back corner. The garden was at its best in spring, but even now there were still white roses and foxgloves. The air was sweet with mock-orange. The leaves had their full growth, and everything was very green.

I asked my energy rods if it was for Vivienne's highest good to ask about her shaman and if we should enter the system. They said "yes."

We went through the indicators to emotional, and suddenly I *saw* him—tall, skinny but strong, long grey hair, dark eyes. He was wearing some sort of robe—skins? Cloth?

"I see him," I told Vivienne. "He looks nice. Powerful. He could probably keep up with you."

"Okay, but *where* is he?"

I faced each of the directions, my rods in hand. West, they said, northwest.

"You already sort of knew that."

"But I can't travel yet. Can I contact him in dreams or by astral travel?"

I concentrated. "Can you see him?"

"A little. I think I can hear him chanting."

First dreams, the energy rods said. Then astral travel.

"Do we need a belief system?" I asked. The energy rods stayed straight, not answering.

"I think it's just a belief in him," said Vivienne. "A belief that he exists and that even if I haven't met him in real life, he's still there."

The energy rods slanted together. Yes.

"Do we need anything else?" I asked. Yes. From Vivienne? No. From me. Yes.

"Your clients are your mirrors, even when they're friends," I said. "I need to remember that about Brian—and I've even met him and been in the same place with him for two weeks. But I don't know if it was real or if I was making it all up. There wasn't much between us on the surface, but it seemed like there was a lot underneath—*if* I wasn't making it all up."

"Well, that was a long comment," said Vivienne.

"Is that enough?" No. We both needed to say thank you.

"I love how polite the energy rods are," I said.

"It's not just to be polite—gratitude is part of the healing."

The air felt as if it had turned over. I was starting to realize that was the signal that a session had ended. Again, I'd forgotten about the water. I went inside for some, gave a glass to Vivienne, and we both drank.

"That was *weird*," I said. "I actually *saw* your shaman. I'd recognize him if I saw him again."

"Well, I'd recognize him if I heard him chant. I'd know that voice anywhere. You can't explain this stuff. It just is. Hey, thanks, Judith—you created a powerful space."

I was so surprised that I nearly fell off the picnic table bench. But I just said, "Let me know what you dream." I picked up my glass. "Here's to the inexplicable and the long distance."

We clinked glasses and both drank again.

"I could make coffee too," I said. "Even if it interferes with the energy."

"Maybe after your session," said Vivienne. "I'll just go refill the glasses."

While she was inside, I slipped money for the dress into her purse. That way we wouldn't have to argue.

When she came back out, I said, "It's not so scary doing a session with you."

"Okay, now your mother."

I looked at the light. "Do you have time?" I looked at my watch. It was nearly three, the witching hour for mothers—the time when your kids get home from school.

"Oh my god—I've got to get home! We'll do it soon, though."

When your kids are school age (or even older, ain Davy's case), motherhood trumps all.

I understood, but could help but plead "Can you just tell me if I'll see him again?"

Vivienne held her energy rods. They bent together, then swept to the side. "Yes, you'll see him again. And you'll have spirit help. But don't ask too often—the energy rods might get annoyed at being nagged. I'll just use your washroom before I go, if that's all right. All that water."

"Thanks, Vivienne!" we hugged.

After a quick washroom stop, Vivienne dashed to her car and roared home.

## 19. REPATTERNING MY MOTHER

"YOU'RE SURE THIS IS ALL RIGHT?" I asked Vivienne a few days later, The weeping willow was tender green against intense blue sky, white peonies were starting to droop, the weigela bush was a mound of raspberry sherbet pink. The air smelled sweet, maybe because traces of mock orange blossoms wafted through the air. We were out in my backyard again, with water and, wickedly, with some forbidden coffee as well. After all this was a spirit session.

"We'll ask her," said Vivienne. "Maybe you should put a glass or mug of something out for her. What did she like to drink?"

"Hot water," I said with a grimace. It seemed so joyless.

"You'd better put some out," said Vivienne. She was wearing her purple galabia and blue jeans.

I went inside, boiled water, and poured it into a mug my mother would recognize—she'd given it to me during my first year in university as part of a tea set. It occurred to me that she also liked scotch on the rocks, but if we weren't supposed to drink, we probably shouldn't put out scotch for a Results session, even for someone discarnate.

"Good," said Vivienne, drinking her water. I followed suit.

"I still don't see how you do this."

"Just hold her in your head. Do we have permission to enter the system? Yes.

Is it for Judith's mother's highest good for us to enter the system? Yes. Is it physical? Yes. She swung her energy rods.

yourself. You lived your life and you were successful. Judith needs you to forgive yourself so that she can forgive herself."

To me, she said, "I told you your tears weren't just for you."

To the air, she said, "Ruth, you need just one belief system: 'I am grateful for Divine Restoration in my afterlife.' Is that right?"

The energy rods swung inward.

"How do you want to be repatterned?"

"Well, I'm sure it's not cross-crawl," I said. Magnetic field was the best, but how did you give magnetic field to a spirit?

"Meditation," said Vivienne. "Judith and I will both meditate on forgiveness and healing."

So we did. I thought of my mother losing her mother at fourteen and her brother six months later, blaming herself, and my heart broke. I wish I'd known. And I felt even more admiration for her working her way through Barnard and, graduating magna cum laude, in spite of ill health; able to find good jobs, even during the Depression, marrying, and travelling. Once things went bad between us, I must have been a sore trial to her, alternately losing my temper and withdrawing, even though she was also a sore trial to me, with her anger and criticism. But I didn't know she'd had a brain tumour all those years, and I didn't know the burdens she'd kept to herself. Maybe I couldn't have given her healing in her lifetime, but I could have given her understanding.

"I think that's done it," said Vivienne. "Ruth, I send you into the light." I opened my eyes and found I was crying. I wiped my eyes on my sleeve.

"That's anchored," said Vivienne. "We should both drink some water."

"What about the tea?"

"Maybe pour it out on the roses. Did she like roses?" I nodded.

Vivienne retested everything that she could (it's harder with spirits) and asked for questions, comments, discussion. From my mother? No, from me.

"I wish I'd known what I was dealing with. I would have been less difficult myself."

"Well, you're making it up to Davy," said Vivienne. "He inherits that too. You're changing old patterns, and when you do that, you do it for everyone who came before. Are you okay?"

I was still crying. "I might need a session for me," I said.

"Another day," said Vivienne. "Are you okay?" she asked again. "I'm going to have to leave soon."

"I'm okay. I'm just going to get a Kleenex."

"Get some more water too."

I did, and thought, *forgiveness isn't that hard when you're ready for it.*

I brought the water out, we drank it, we hugged, and I said, "Thank you!"

"Oh my God!" said Vivienne. "I don't think I closed the session. Can we close the session?" she asked. "Questions, comments, discussion? Yes. Who? Judith? No. Ruth? No. Me? Yes. Question? Comment? Yes."

She thought for a bit. "I really didn't like the course, but it's sort of spooky the way this stuff works. Is that it?" The energy rods swooped shut. "Okay, can we close the session?" The energy rods swung shut, and then to one side. "And you'll have spirit help," said Vivienne. "Okay, I have to go. I'll call you tonight."

We hugged and she left, leaving me to think about my shadowed past and about the difficult road my mother had walked with her burden of guilt, now hopefully dissolved by her finally forgiving herself, and also by my forgiving her. But I was shaken, as if something dark and sad had escaped from me, and maybe some of the ice inside me had melted too. I needed to readjust without its usual heaviness inside.

## 20. ANOTHER PHONE CALL

I HADN'T FORGOTTEN ABOUT BRIAN—that was impossible with the way he was in my head. I tried to call him and, as usual, got the off-putting voice of his partner, Hugh.

But he dropped into my dreams once or twice, and for a change, he wasn't going out one door when I was coming in another. We were in the same place in these dreams, but not interacting. These dreams made me think that although part of him was drawn to me, another part absolutely wasn't, and that I therefore couldn't count on much from him in real life, My only consolation was that I wouldn't have designed my dreams that way, so, there must be a truth in them beyond my conscious knowing. At the very least, we were connected in dreams, even if they weren't romantic. And, at least for now, he wasn't always leaving.

I'd just about finished planning our trip—two nights on the road each way so the driving wouldn't be gruelling. Ten days at the cottage. Two nights in Halifax. One night in Saint-Loup, where Brian lived. I didn't plan more than one night there because I had reservations on the Digby Ferry the next morning. It was all travel into the unknown.

I was in the backyard nursing my coffee the Sunday morning of the long weekend when the phone rang. *It couldn't be*, I thought as I ran in to get it on third ring. But it was.

"Hi." His voice was instantly recognizable.

"Hello." And we were back in our own space, whatever that

was, completely together, ear to ear, even though a thousand miles apart.

"How are you?"

"I'm fine—Davy passed his year, in spite of his dreadful English exam, thank goodness."

"He'll be fine—I can see it."

"Oh, I hope so." The knot of worry that was always there was loosening a little. "How are you?"

"The festival's coming along. But we're breaking ground for the theatre in a couple of hours, and Hugh's gone off to England. Someone should be saying something."

"Can't you say something?"

"I suppose I'll have to. I wasn't expecting this. He just left last night."

"You have a lot of vision for the festival. It might be the perfect way to break ground for it."

"I don't know if people want to hear about charismatic theatre," Brian said doubtfully.

"Why not?"

"Some things should be invisible—stitched into the fabric of things. When I iron the sheets for guests, I kiss them, and the guests never know it, but the love is there."

I never ironed sheets. I felt I had a lot to learn about love.

"I dreamed about you a couple times," I said. "It felt as if you were right there in the dream with me."

"I probably was," he said. "I have many bodies—well, we all do—that's Egyptian. My ba could have come to you on the wings of a bird."

"What are the other bodies?"

"The ba, the ka, the name, the heart—I forget them all, but I like the idea of being so multiple."

I wasn't surprised. I thought of James. He was multiple too. I made a mental note to look up Egyptian ideas of body and soul.

"What are you doing for the summer?" I asked.

"I'm going to Australia."

"When?"

"Oh, late July, early August." My heart sank.

"Then you won't be in Saint-Loup when we come through."

"You're coming *here*?"

"Just for one night. August 8. We'll wave at you in your absence as we pass through."

"I'll check to see when I'm going—I'm not sure exactly when it is. Can you change your plans?" As if he might really want to see me. Also, as if he didn't find it the least bit improbable that I'd just happen to be in his neighbourhood a thousand miles from home.

"I've made reservations." Should I change my plans? I held the phone between my ear and chin and finger tested. It said no. "How's the festival coming besides Hugh going off to England at the wrong time?"

"It's coming together. It's exciting. We've got a board. We're starting to talk about plays and possible actors. We're starting to get press in the Halifax paper, and we're hoping for *The Globe and Mail* once things are a little more firmed up."

"That's amazing," I said. But amazing was inadequate. I couldn't imagine that I knew someone who could actually make things happen like that. Then I remembered that he'd given me a new life, something I'd thought impossible. Maybe he could make this happen too.

"It's a start. I *wish* you could see some of the plays. At least the theatre."

"I'd love to." But this was all far in the future, and even though I'd fished for an invitation, he didn't offer one.

"It will be a wonderful opportunity for our students to work with really professional actors."

"They've got you, though." I hoped I wasn't sounding gushy, but I knew Brian was a terrific, if unorthodox, teacher.

"I try to get them ready for drama schools, but it's not the same as being in real theatre—and it's good for Saint-Loup to have something world class right here."

"I can't believe you envisioned this, and now you're making it happen."

"Well, the vision part is easy. I've been dreaming of this since I came here I was sure it was the right place for a special theatre. But it wouldn't be happening without Hugh, even though I'm annoyed at him right now."

"Why?"

"Why am I annoyed?"

"No, why wouldn't it happen without him?"

"He works non-stop. And he's a genius at getting money. You wouldn't come into money since we last talked, would you?"

"Oh sure, I just found a million dollars on the street. I'll put the cheque in the mail."

"I've told you this before, I think. Hugh's great on detail. He just goes straight ahead. He's very *linear*. We've started other theatre companies, but I hope, this time, this one will last. We do have the community behind us, and that's important. And the university. And the drama department, even though it's small. So, we've got a committed group of students and former students who will help."

"So, in your speech you just have to thank everyone, ask them for their good wishes and support going forward, and look forward to the finished theatre and plays."

"That's right," he sounded relieved. "I don't really like doing stuff like that in public. I can. I just don't like it."

"What are you doing when you're not working on the festival?" I asked. It seemed like a chance to find out something more about him.

"We're building a deck behind the house. We'd like to wrap it around the entire side of the house, but we don't have the money, so we're doing it a bit at a time. I have a former student who's a carpenter. He gives us a good deal."

I was almost intimidated into silence, but I asked: "What are you doing with the rest of the day?"

"I'm not sure. Meditate. Maybe go look at antiques—there

are a lot around here, and I love them. Maybe take the cats for a walk. I do like having the house to myself, but, after all the activity, I need some time to get a rhythm. What about you?"

"Work on a story, I hope. Listen to Davy practice. Do some reading. He nearly failed ninth grade English, and his teacher let him go on to Grade 10 on the condition that he read widely—as if!"

"Doesn't he like to read?"

"He hates it. He's fine with music and manuals, but he doesn't like imaginative literature. But I just discovered he has stiff eyes, and his right brain is almost totally turned off, so we're doing brain gym exercises. After that and reading, we'll go swimming."

"Sounds nice."

"Brian, I know you're a great teacher, but I wouldn't wish Davy's reading on you. It's excruciating."

"What about writing?"

"He likes writing. He likes writing letters to newspapers about things he thinks should be changed—and sometimes they are. Like he wanted recycling bins placed at the university, and they were. And he wanted the city to recycle plastic cider jugs, and they did."

"I'll include Davy in my meditation," Brian said with that surprising sweetness, which was one of the things I loved about him. "He'll get the reading—you'll see. Not today. Keep working on the exercises. I'll hold him in my thoughts."

"Thank you!" Often I felt alone with Davy. But, just for a moment, I felt companioned, and I felt a rush of gratitude. And even though Brian had never met Davy, I didn't doubt that it would make a difference.

After a breath or two, I asked, "How do you take your cats for a walk?"

"I have them on leashes."

"My cats would never stand for that."

"Well, I have them on leashes when they're outside. We're

on a main street, and I don't want them running out onto the road."

I had a vision of Brian leading me around on a leash. Part of me found it sexy, and part of me found it repulsive. I reminded myself that I scarcely knew him—after all, we'd never even walked down a street together. Would he like me better if I were a cat? I'd never even half-wanted that sort of submission with a man, and I knew I'd have to be careful.

"What do *you* do to make sure your cats don't run away?" he asked.

"I spend a lot of time outside with them when they're little so they know the yard and the neighbourhood. I try to warn them about streets, but we're not on a main road."

Then, out of nowhere, he said, "Well, I should go."

I suddenly panicked. He always seemed to end our phone calls so abruptly, and he was always the one to end the call. "I'm sorry you won't be there when we come through Saint-Loup," I said.

"Well, I might be. I'm not sure when I'm leaving. I'll check and call you back."

"Okay," I almost believed he might.

"I've really got to go. I've got to figure out what I'm saying. I don't want it to be a formal speech."

"Good luck." Maybe you didn't say that to theatre people? But I couldn't say break a leg.

"Goodbye, darling." A flash of sweetness again. And he was gone.

A wave of pure desire washed over me. I still didn't know if I'd imagined our connection, or if it was real. But it felt real, and I gave in to it.

Then I went outside, still a little enveloped by the feeling of connection between us, and pruned and weeded. Our house had a big garden, considering it was in the middle of town, and I was always behind with it. I thought of Brian at eleven (noon his time) and wondered how the speech had gone.

## 21. COTTAGE

O F COURSE, BRIAN DIDN'T CALL BACK, which meant that
he'd probably be gone when we drove through Saint-
Loup. I wondered how his talk had gone. Although I could still
feel him at the end of the telepathic line sometimes (again, if
I wasn't all in my head!), I wasn't dreaming about him. I was
busy. Davy's birthday was right before we left, and what he
always wanted more than anything else for his birthday was
a party. It was always a mix of neighbours, family friends,
and a few scattered friends of Davy's from grade school. We
decorated the back yard with balloons, played games, and
had cake and ice cream with raspberries and wild blueberries. And then there was getting ready to go—getting the car
ready, packing bedding, and squeezing in the last of supplies
we might need. The car was packed to the edges by the time
we left and rolled down the 401 to Montreal.

We stopped overnight and took a whale watching tour. It
was foggy, but we got memorable glimpses of ghostly whales
in that vast expanse of the St. Lawrence near Saguenay. In
Fredericton, we walked by the river and along the leafy streets.

The cottage itself was right on the Northumberland Strait,
on a cove. Sometimes herons hung out along the curve of the
shore, sometimes a seal or two. Wherever we walked we saw
wild pink roses with white centres. Behind the cottage, an
enormous raspberry patch was luxuriant with ripe and ripening
raspberries—we picked them for breakfast and dinner every

day, and there were still more. The sand on the beach in front of the cottage was red, and the tide left it looking rippled. There were jellyfish, but Davy watched other people scooping them up and throwing them to one side, and he soon got good at clearing them out of our swimming space.

We had a breakthrough with brain gym exercises: Davy began to follow thirty, forty, fifty figure eights at a time. We were also reading a book a friend of ours had written about an injured red-tailed hawk she and her husband had taken in and brought up. Davy had met the hawk—she had rested on his arm—and we both liked the author. For whatever reason—the more flexible eyes, the slightly-awakened right brain, a more suitable book, maybe even the sea and the raspberries—Davy's reading became less tortured. He could read more at a time, didn't try to skip the middles of words to make it go faster, and had less trouble putting together the pages he'd read.

I'd brought my Results binder with me and did some sessions. I asked the energy rods: "Will I see Brian this trip?" They said Yes, and that I'd have spirit help. I remembered Vivienne saying not to ask too often, so I limited myself to asking once every few days and working on other things in other sessions. As a vacation, it was a little too relentlessly domestic for my taste. There was no putting off shopping, cooking, cleaning, going to the dump, which we combined with trips to the lobster pound. In between chores, I was charmed by the wild roses and the red sand and the lighthouse—really, it seemed like we were inside a postcard here. I read a little, wrote a little, thought about Brian.

It rained when we left; Davy hated to leave, but the rain helped persuade him. The drive to Halifax was surprisingly long for what looked like a fairly short space on the map. The roads were slow: the visibility poor. Davy's navigation had jumped a notch with his reading—he was great with road signs now but still slow with maps. We left in the early afternoon, got to Halifax in the early evening, and snuggled into our room at the hotel, glad to be out of the rain. We had a light supper (dinner was over by the time we got to the dining room), a short swim in the hotel pool (no jellyfish, but no herons or seals or red sand either), and collapsed in the very comfortable hotel beds. We walked in the Halifax Public Gardens, admiring the imaginative mix of colours—orange lilies, pink phlox, roses of all sorts, pruned, but still riotous. We checked out the stores on the Halifax pier and had lunch at a pub that seemed as if had sailed straight from New England. We walked around the Citadel.

One by one the days between the beginning of the summer and our arrival in Saint-Loup had worn down to a sliver. Whether or not Brian was there the next day, I'd see where he lived, walk the streets where he walked.

## 22. REPATTERNING BRIAN

MY HANDS WERE SHAKING so badly when I called Brian from the payphone that I could barely put the money in. I could barely dial his number—in fact, I dialled wrong the first two times, in spite of having his number memorized. The phone booth was in the parking lot of a tacky pizza parlour. As my hands trembled, I was aware of my surroundings: the parking lot with some broken glass shards twinkling in the sunlight, the road we'd come in on, and a strip of green beyond.

When Brian did answer the phone on the fourth ring, I stammered, "Hello Br-Brian. It's Judith. I told you we'd be here today, and we are. I thought you might be in Australia, so I'm happy to hear your voice."

"Where are you exactly?"

"Outside the pizza parlour on the main drag."

"Well, you can't stay here."

I felt slapped, but since I hadn't expected him to be there anyway, I went for plan B.

"Okay," I said. "We'll just walk around and roll on down the road."

"Well, you're here, you might as well come for lunch."

"Are you sure?" I didn't feel exactly welcomed. "I don't want to intrude."

"Yes, you're very close."

"Where are you exactly?"

"You came from Halifax, right?"

"Yes."

"Turn around and go back the way you came. It's a big white house. I'll be on the front porch."

*What if I don't recognize you, Brian?* I thought. *It has been two years.*

"Does your house have a number?"

He told me.

"We're going to see Brian," I told Davy. So we got back in the car, retraced our route, and looked at numbers. Just before the road bent out of town, there was a big white house. I saw the number (left-brained) before I saw Brian. He was sitting on the porch railing, his back against a white column, like a caryatid. But I also recognized the house from the time I'd gone there by astral travel. But I'd gone in the side windows, not the front.

I teetered into the driveway at the side of the house. I thought of Leopold Bloom toward the end of *Ulysses:* "He had travelled."

Brian bounded around from the front of the house. I extricated myself from the car and introduced Davy. "Hi Davy," he said, and then, to my surprise, he went to the grass and did a cartwheel. "Can you do that?"

"A little." Davy's cartwheels weren't great, but he tried, and Brian applauded.

I thought almost enviously, *Davy should have come without me!* I felt awkward as Brian led us into his kitchen and scrounged through the refrigerator for lunch. There was enough chicken for one sandwich. I earmarked that for Davy. There was cheese. There were fresh tomatoes for all of us—Brian plucked them from the windowsill. "We've been growing them," he said. He poured juice for Davy, coffee for us.

"I wasn't supposed to be here," said Brian over lunch. "I was supposed to be flying to England. I had my ticket. I ironed my shirts last night. And then I had this terrible feeling that

I shouldn't go, and I cancelled. I've never done that before."

So the energy rods were right. I was seeing Brian, and I had had spirit help. But it still felt awkward.

We ate outside on the patio. The two Siamese cats were on leashes, but they were very long leashes, and the cats seemed contented. One of the cats glided over to and curled itself around my legs. I dangled my pendulum and let him play with it.

"He's friendly," said Brian. "The little girl cat's frightened. She was abused."

I picked up the cat and felt his purr, put him down, then tried the coffee. "This might be the best cup of coffee I've ever had," I said.

"I make it strong. And the water here's good."

"I like it strong." At least we had that in common.

Davy started talking about the cottage and our trip. I chimed in, still dangling my pendulum in front of the cat. Gradually I felt more at ease and less as if this had been the world's worst idea.

As Brian and I brought the dishes in, and he cleared up with twinkling speed, he said, "Your son has a speech impediment."

"He was assessed with autistic elements," I said.

"He's got a good energy."

My heart swelled just then, and I could have kissed him.

Instead, I said, "I love your house," looking up at the high ceilings and admiring the large windows open to the garden.

"It was built in 1792."

Even from the kitchen I could see that it had that eighteenth-century look of reason infused with light. "I'll show you the rest later," he said.

Later. So he wasn't throwing us out in the street—yet.

"Do you want to see where the theatre's going to be?"

"Sure."

Brian brought the cats inside. We gathered Davy, bundled into Brian's car—one of those wide Chevies—and drove down the road. We didn't go very far, though past the pizza parlour

I'd called from—we could have walked it—but I could see already that Brian liked to fly. When we got to the parking lot, he sped around the car and opened the door for me, something no one had done for decades. Henry wasn't ever that polite.

The theatre was in the very beginning stages of its new life. The outside wall of the hockey rink was still there, but, behind it, everything had been torn down, and there was mostly dirt. But there was a walkway and a platform with a display on makeshift walls—a history of theatre, a vision statement, and a drawing of what the theatre would look like inside and outside, complete with shrubs and flowers. I read the vision statement.

"It's very well-written," I said, wondering if Brian had written it.

"It's Hugh's."

"But there's no mention of you."

"Well, Hugh tends to take things over," Brian said drily.

"Don't you mind? Especially since he flew off to England and let you give the speech?"

"I do mind. But the important thing is to get the Festival up and running. We'll sort it out later. Anyway, everyone around here knows what I've done."

I wondered if he might have trouble sorting things out. But it did look splendid, and I said so. But I could also see that a lot of it was Brian's vision, and I was troubled that he wasn't getting the credit he deserved.

"Do you have a theme of betrayal in your life?" I asked.

He looked startled. "Yes."

"I do too." I'd learned about it when Theadora at Treasure Garden did a crystal ball reading for me. That explained Henry not standing up for me and my job collapsing on me, maybe even Dottie. But there wasn't much else to say right then, and we let it go.

"That's where the stage will be," said Brian, gesturing to an expanse of mud. "And the seats back there. There will be an entrance at street level and a bar underneath. And behind and to the side, the dressing rooms. The Young Company will be in that building," he said, pointing to a dingy boarded-up brick building toward the back of the site. "That's what I'm particularly interested in."

"You really have a transformative vision," I said. I'd almost forgotten about Davy. "What do you think about this, Davy?"

"I think it's interesting." Davy liked buildings.

"You'll have to come back and see it when it's built," said Brian, but I thought he might be talking to Davy.

We walked back through the dusty parking lot to Brian's car. "I've got some things to do," he said. "Do you want to meet me back at the house in an hour? Or I could pick you up here?"

"We'll look around and walk back," I said. "It's not that far. Davy has his camera, and he'll want to take pictures."

"See you then." He jumped in his car and sped off, a cloud of dust behind him.

Well, being with Brian was certainly not like anything I'd imagined. Unlike the telepathy, it wasn't sexy, or romantic, at all. But now that the awkwardness was wearing off, I was starting to feel very comfortable. It felt as if we'd known each other for ages.

Davy and I browsed along the main street and side streets. Saint-Loup was a pretty, very eighteenth-century white frame town,. We walked along the dike. Herons were nesting and flying. The tide was going out. Davy got some good pictures of a white frame church steeple and orange sumac berries. Then we went back to Brian's house.

"I hate to say this," I said when we were settled in the living room. "But we need to make some decisions. We need to find some place to spend the night."

"You can stay here," said Brian. "I hope you'll stay for dinner. I bought *corn*." He said it with a sense of wonder, as if it were precious.

"Okay," I said, happy he wanted us to stay.

After we got our stuff out of the car, Davy went outside, possibly to play with the cats, and I said to Brian, "I could repattern you."

He agreed, and I found my belief system sheet, a repatterning sheet, and my energy rods. We sat at his dining room table, tender afternoon light slanting in through the high windows. "You don't really believe in this stuff do you?" Brian asked after I'd gotten permission to go into the system and the energy rods had gone to repatterning.

"Well, yes, I do."

I thought, *You, of all people, are asking me that?* Out loud I said, "If you think it seems all wrong, you can just ignore it, and it's only wasted an hour of your time."

He nodded. "Okay."

Brian was right-handed, right-footed, right-eyed, right-brained, and left-eared, with his logic in his left brain, where it is for most people, and his gestalt was in his right.

"You have a very inward brain pattern," I said. "A lot of creative people have this pattern."

"Well, I'm definitely right-brained. Hugh is extremely left-brained."

"I think we tend to be drawn to people with complementary brain patterns," I said. "I have a very inner brain pattern too. I'm sure Henry was strong on action. Davy's strong on action."

"Right-brained people are more creative, though."

"Left-brainers can be creative too," I said. I hoped so, anyway! "I'm left-brained. I'd bet anything that Sylvia Plath was left-brained. Left-brainers go for the significant detail. Right-brainers tend to see the whole picture. Anyway, you have an inner brain pattern. You were probably shy as a child."

"I'm still shy. Sometimes I can be the life of the party, though."

"When you're not stressed," I said. "When you're stressed, you tend to go inside. I do too. When you're stressed, your outer life tends to fall apart."

"Does it ever!"

"But you can keep your inner life going. If your inner life falls
apart, you're extraordinarily stressed. Your gestalt is in your
right brain, so you're very strong on intuition and feelings."

He nodded.

"When you're stressed, you have a harder time getting to
your logic."

"I don't really like linear. I like to work in many dimensions
at once. Not that linear doesn't have its place."

"You have a great ear," I continued. "When you're stressed,
you can always take things in through your ears."

"That's true! The wrong cough can ruin my day."

"And you might be clairaudient, healing things from afar or
picking them out of the air."

"Yes."

"When you start a project, you need to visualize the whole
thing. You don't go step by step. But once you start, you can
go straight through to the end."

He nodded.

I already knew him better than I had before—and that was
only his brain pattern! I wasn't sure that two people with inner
brain patterns made a good team, especially when one of them
wants to start a theatre company. But I tucked that caution
away to think about later.

The energy rods said we could go on.

Brian's eyes were weak down and to the right, strong up
and to the left. I thought that might mean that he was more
comfortable with the world above than this world, but I wasn't
sure, so I didn't say anything. I still had no idea what it meant
when eyes were weak or strong to the left or right.

I'd wanted to touch him for so long, and here I was finger
testing him. But it was a professional situation, and I couldn't
let sex get in the way of healing. I was aware of the fine dark
hairs on the backs of his fingers and on his arms, and I also
tucked those away to think about later.

The energy rods went to Latissimus Dorsi.

"Do you have a sugar sensitivity?" I asked. The test was to push his arm down, and I really didn't want to. I felt like I was on a knife's edge as it was.

"I'm very allergic to sugar. My mother used to bake all the time, and she wrecked my immune system. I'm allergic to white flour too. I get mood swings."

"Well, you're very high-vibrational," I said. "I'm not surprised you've got sensitivities. You've got to honour them."

He looked at me ruefully. "I really do love cheesecake. Do you?"

"Sorry, it's too heavy for me. I don't think repatterning can correct your food sensitivities—you just have to pay attention to them."

"I hate being told what to do."

"I hate it too. But I'm not telling you. Your body's telling you." I thought of adding, *It's a small price to pay for such a great body.*

We went on to attitudes. I wasn't surprised that Brian didn't want to fail. But he was weak on wanting to succeed. And though he didn't want to be sick, he didn't particularly want to be well. Maybe my finger testing was wrong? I re-checked. People are complicated. What we perceive is only a beginning.

"Well, repatterning will correct that," I said confidently, hoping my faith in the system wasn't misplaced. But maybe I shouldn't have been so surprised. Healers need healing—that's why they go into it.

"We're ready for concrete base," I said and explained it to him. I finger tested. Not between zero and ten. "Yours was formed between ten and twenty. Do you remember what happened then?"

"The accident."

I didn't have to ask about the accident. I had heard about it from the poet at Banff, someone else who'd needed lots of healing. Brian had spent a lot of time with her. The accident had happened in mid-December. Brian in the back seat of the car, his parents in the front. A car going the opposite direction skidded out of control. And then the crash. Brian's parents had been killed; he had been in a coma for days, in the hospital for six months. His left hand had been almost severed from his arm and had had to be reattached surgically. His right leg had been smashed and never grew to the full length of his other leg. He'd had a concussion. Sylvia Fraser said that head injuries open the brain, make you more psychic. Brian was psychic in spades, in spite of his scepticism about the Results system.

He had told me that rabbis had prayed over him and that he had studied with them and learned some of their mystic knowledge.

"Is there more?" I asked the energy rods. They said there was. Age sixteen? Seventeen? "What happened when you were sixteen or seventeen?"

"I started sleeping with my ex-wife and got her pregnant. She was my teacher."

"She shouldn't have let it happen," I said without thinking. No wonder he hadn't wanted to get involved with a student, even an adult student. "You wouldn't have let it happen if you were the teacher."

"My ex-wife was brilliant. She spoke six languages. She was an opera singer."

"Still, you don't do that with students," I said. I might have just done myself out of any chance I'd had of sleeping with Brian, but I was inside the system—I had to be honest. "You formed a belief system then," I said. "It got you through at the time, but it was limiting. Do you have any idea what it was?"

"Oh, maybe that love is a disaster." He was joking, but the energy rods swung in.

"That's it," I said. "Now we need to find belief systems that will replace it." I swung my energy rods again. "You want three. Let's see…. 'I allow myself to grow in my own space and time'—let me finger test you—yes, that one." I could never have guessed Brian might not allow himself to grow in his own space and time. But how well did I know him? I kept going down the belief system sheet. "'I have everything to give and receive through love,'" I suggested. Of course he finger tested weak.

"It's true," he said. "I have so much love to give, and I've been giving it to the cats."

*Throw some my way*, I thought, and went back to the list. "Can you say 'I now recognize, accept, and follow the Divine Plan of my life as it is revealed step by step'?"

"I can't even remember it!"

I understood that! I broke it down and finger tested it part by part. It probably needed anchoring for me too. I'd never thought about there being a Divine Plan for my life, let alone it being revealed to me step by step. I thought I was just stumbling through without any pattern at all, sort of like making my way through the raspberry patch we'd left so recently—lots of raspberries, but no path.

I wasn't surprised that his body/soul wanted to be repatterned by the magnetic field. He was an energy worker, and Rosetta had said that magnetic field was the best, most powerful way of being repatterned.

"Stand in a place where you're comfortable and be ready to receive," I said. I'll walk into your magnetic field. I'll ask that energy come through me without my touching you. I'll close my eyes, but you don't have to. "

He stood by the window, and I walked into his magnetic field and closed my eyes.

I could feel the unhappiness in his heart and his power centre, and I tried to pull out the negative energy and stream in golden light, white light, purple light. His crown chakra was clear; his third eye was clear. James had said that healers needed their root and crown chakras open to be able to heal—in between they could be as messed up as they pleased.

How easy it would be to slip and touch him, but the healing would shatter and so would his trust, so I gave light and energy—lilacs to his heart, waterfalls to his power centre—until

I felt drained. His eyes were still closed—he probably needed more energy. He gave so much healing—how often did he get it back?

As I looked at him with his eyes closed, I thought his face could have been painted by Rembrandt, or like someone who would have been well cast in a play by Molière. Some peoples' faces are nothing without their eyes. Brian's face was still strong, but it was different. I suspected that if I saw him at a different time, his face, even with his eyes closed, would have been different still.

"When you're ready," I said softly, "open your eyes." Good timing, because we'd just hugged lightly when Davy came bursting in.

"One of the cats got out of his leash!"

Brian was halfway out the room "Which one?"

"I don't know."

We were out the back door. "Misha! Misha! Come to Daddy." He circled the bushes, and a lean Siamese cat appeared from behind one of them, purring. Brian picked him up and carried him inside.

"You'd better stay inside for a little while before you go out again." He looked at the other cat, still peacefully leashed. "You'd better come too." He scooped her up and brought them both in.

I said to Davy, "We're just at the end of a repatterning. Can you stay outside just a little longer?"

"Weren't we done?" Brian asked.

"No, we have to recheck everything. It won't take long. We have to close the session."

Everything was stronger; the belief systems were anchored. I wrote them down for him and told him anchoring these belief systems was just a seed. You had to nurture them so that they grew. That must have been what he meant at Banff when he said, "This is a beginning."

I asked the energy rods for questions, comments, and discussion. He had a comment.

"It would be great if actors had access to this."

I had a sudden vision of working with actors, repatterning them—watching rehearsals—but then what would I do with Davy? I swung the energy rods again. "You have another comment."

"I do? Just thank you."

I gave silent thanks that I hadn't shattered the moment with touching and had let the space between us do its healing work.

"We should drink some water," I said.

"Okay." Brian brought us glasses, and we drank, and then he swung into action. "I should start dinner."

I couldn't have told from his teaching how fast-moving he was, how impatient he was.

"I could make a salad. I'm good with salads."

He flew around the kitchen getting everything ready while I washed and spun dry the lettuce, cut the tomatoes and green onions and cucumber. "Do you grow any herbs?" I asked. "Chives? Oregano?"

He looked surprised. "Nooo. Maybe I should?"

"That won't do any good for *this* salad. What about garlic and olive oil?"

He found a couple cloves of garlic and a small bottle of olive oil. I felt extravagant using half of it, but you can't make salad dressing with just a few drops of oil.

"Vinegar?" I asked hopefully. "Lemon juice?"

There we were, cooking together as if we'd always done it. Dinner was just on the table when the back door opened and Hugh appeared—it had to be Hugh. He was in his mid-fifties (I knew this from the newspaper article about the festival), white-haired, with bright but chilly blue eyes and an understatedly rosy complexion that might suggest heart trouble later on.

Brian introduced us and added, "Judith's made a lovely salad."

I tried to look as if I deserved the compliment, but thought wistfully of chives, good vinegar, heads of garlic.

Hugh was perfectly polite to me. We'd been travelling, so there was a lot to say. He was a little more cordial to Davy, asking him adult questions and being respectful of his answers.

After dinner Brian did the dishes and wiped the counters with the same twinkling speed. I dried. Then we all sat in the living room, and Brian suggested that we each perform something. They had a piano, so Davy played his Bach, very creditably. He liked performing and rose to the occasion.

"Judith?" I shook my head. I wasn't a performer. I liked singing, but I couldn't think of a single song. The idea of singing in front of Brian, of all people, and chilly Hugh made me shrivel.

Hugh also played something on the piano; it was accomplished, flowing, and forgettable.

Then Brian started to sing "The Way You Look Tonight." It might have been romantic, but with Davy twitching a bit and Hugh making me feel intrusive, it was just awkward. Brian stopped singing in the middle. Hugh sang along with him.

Hugh went upstairs to pack. He was leaving in the middle of the night to get to an early morning meeting in New Brunswick to get support for the festival. Davy went upstairs to get ready for bed.

"I wish Hugh wouldn't do that," said Brian. "He just makes it worse."

"At least you sang," I said. "I have terrible performance anxiety."

"So do I."

"Inner brain pattern," I said. "That's probably what makes you such a great teacher."

He gave me a hug, and we drifted out back and sat under the stars. It was one of those extravagantly starry summer nights, when the stars are so dense and generous that they practically pour into you. We were just starting to talk, not awkwardly, as if we were beginning to be comfortable with each other, when Hugh rushed out the back door—perfect stage entrance.

"I don't want to interrupt anything," he said, and we both jumped to assure him he wasn't. But he couldn't find something. Brian suggested where it might be.

"Do you need gas in your car?" Brian asked.

"Yes, I think I do."

"Give me your keys, and I'll go get some." Hugh extracted his car keys.

"I'll come with you," I said.

"You don't have to."

"No, I want to." Besides, what was I going to do in a strange house with a strange man packing upstairs and Davy on his way to bed? Even the cats seemed to have disappeared.

So there I was, driving under the stars with Brian—a dream come true, except it was only to a gas station. After we got gas, Brian said, "We could go to a beach!"

I wanted to go! But I'd left Davy behind in a place he'd never been before. He might worry if he woke up alone in a strange place. "It sounds wonderful," I said, "but I don't think I should leave Davy for that long. And Hugh will want to start off with a full tank of gas. Isn't he leaving in a few hours?"

"You're right," Brian said. "We shouldn't."

I finger tested. "Anyway, my finger testing says no. Too bad. It would have been lovely."

We drove back, he sped around and opened the door for me, and we hugged—maybe the hug that might have happened on the beach? Then we both went inside.

The house was quiet, quiet for a short time, because Hugh would be up at one-thirty to start off for his morning meeting in Fredericton. "Good night," I said before I started up the stairs.

"Good night." We hugged as if we were family, and I noticed an old grandfather clock on the first landing—I almost recognized it. This was the place where my heart had gone.

Both Brian's cats came and slept with me, at least for part of the night. Whatever else, I could say I'd slept with the cats who slept with the man I loved.

THE NEXT MORNING WAS BRIGHT, clear, and perfect. I woke early, but Brian was ahead of me and had already made coffee. We went out on the deck, and being with him was was suddenly very easy. Maybe it was because even the outside of the house seemed lighter with Hugh gone. Yes, he'd gotten off all right. He'd probably call later to tell Brian about the meeting. He'd stay overnight in Fredericton and be back tomorrow.

"We'll be in Fredericton tonight," I said.

"You might see him."

What were the chances? "I'll keep an eye out," I said.

AFTER BREAKFAST, I asked Davy to take pictures of us. "I don't take good pictures," said Brian.

"I don't either."

We sat on a bench in front of two of the tall evergreens, and I tried not to show what I felt.

"I've got one picture left," Davy announced after he'd taken a few.

"I know," said Brian. "You look at the camera, Judith. I'll look at you. Okay, Davy."

"That's going to be good," said Brian, "I know it."

As we packed our overnight stuff in the car, Brian gave us three of the tomatoes that were ripening on the windowsill. "Will you let me know if you get home safely?" he asked, with the same care he showed his cats.

I promised to call and reminded him that we wouldn't be home till three days from now.

We hugged goodbye and then Davy and I were gone.

ABOUT TEN MILES DOWN THE ROAD, I felt a wave of longing so strong that I almost turned around and went back. But I couldn't. We had ferry reservations, and, since it was August, they wouldn't be easy to reschedule. Besides, what if we did turn around and go back?

But the longing enveloped me all morning—as we waited for

the ferry, as we rolled over the blue swells of the Bay of Fundy, even when we saw dolphins. Davy, who was luckier than I, saw a whale. The feeling of longing persisted, but lessened once we hit the shore of New Brunswick and headed north toward Fredericton. I looked for Hugh, but it wasn't likely I would see him, and I didn't.

I thought of Brian as we drove to Quebec City the next day and strolled the promenade listening to buskers. I imagined him standing beside me—I could feel his presence, solid, at my shoulder, until I turned and saw he wasn't there. Would Brian ever take a night off work to watch buskers? Probably not. But if he had, he might have liked it.

The only other incident on our way home was that the car broke down on the Mercier Bridge just outside Montreal. Shifting had been sluggish since Fredericton, and all the construction along the route hadn't helped it much. The nearest Subaru place was on the far side of Montreal. We had to be towed home. When we got to our door. I nearly kissed the ground.

I called Brian, as I'd promised. Of course I got the answering machine. It was as if nothing had changed.

But something had changed. I had the three tomatoes—which I put on my windowsill to finish ripening—and in a few days I had Davy's photographs. The last one, which Brian had promised would be good, wasn't great of me, but in the photo, Brian was looking at me in the way I'd always wanted to be looked at. Whatever might or might not happen between us, there we were together on an August morning in a lush green back garden.

## 23. COMING HOME

I SHOWED THE PICTURES of Brian to Claire. "They're nice," she said. "He's attractive. But they're only a moment. You need someone real."

Claire had met someone real, someone who liked music, who liked to travel—they had already been to New York. They weren't sleeping together yet, but all Claire's friends, and probably Claire too, knew they would be. Claire was receding into her new bright and shiny life and was less interested in all things psychic. She was also less interested in a friend who didn't have a new bright and shiny life. Still, I wished she had been less dismissive.

I showed the pictures to Vivienne. "He looks beautiful but difficult," she said.

"I can do difficult," I said. "Henry was difficult."

"But you're divorced."

"That's not because he was difficult. It's because he was unkind."

Vivienne looked at one of the pictures, which wasn't good of either of us. "I've never seen anyone look so scared," she said.

"Of *me*?"

"Of something."

She looked at the last picture, the one Brian said he knew would be good, where Brian was looking at me affectionately.

"Nice picture," she said. "But what's really beautiful is the distance between you."

*Oh, fine.* "If I'd brought your dress, he'd have been dazzled and it might have worked out."

"Maybe it did work out. Maybe what happened was meant to happen."

"Now you're sounding like Rosetta."

VIVIENNE HAD PLACED several of her dresses on consignment in a store on Brock Street. They were selling for two and three hundred dollars. After all, they were designer dresses, just a designer no one had heard of. So she had money for art supplies. If this kept on, she'd be able to mount a show.

We had started doing sessions once a month, sometimes adding Tarot cards. So far, there was nothing to suggest that Brian would be part of my outer life. I still felt a telepathic connection to him. But I had written him a thank you note, and I still hadn't heard back.

The sessions also weren't optimistic about Vivienne meeting her shaman within the next year, but the sessions indicated that her daughter had a great future.

Whatever else, Davy's school was going well. He was doing an Environmental Studies course, and his teacher told me on parents' night that Davy was first in the class. He had a more sympathetic English teacher. His eyes weren't so stiff after a summer of doing brain gym exercises, and his right brain felt more alive when I gave him energy. I found a good craniosacral therapist, and Davy was twitching and jerking less.

He still talked a little jerkily, still didn't have friends his age, but he was more sociable with teachers and with my friends, and I wasn't worrying about him quite so much. I remembered that Brian thought he'd be fine (whatever fine was), and, even though Brian was absent, he was still psychic.

A story I'd written was published in a literary magazine, and I started sending out others. But I still missed Brian.

"It's crazy-making," said Claire. "You should clarify things."

I wasn't sure this was good advice, but as the days grew

shorter in November, I finally wrote Brian a card saying that I felt like there was nothing between us, and this would likely be the last letter he'd get from me. I cried when I mailed it, but I needed closure.

I'D ALMOST FORGOTTEN ABOUT IT when the phone rang about ten days later and I heard an angry male voice say, "What do you mean this is the last letter I'll ever get from you?"

"I didn't hear from you. I thought I was bombarding you with letters and phone calls and you didn't answer because you wanted me to stop."

"I've been busy! I've been doing the fall production of *Under Milk Wood*—"

"Great choice—"

"—And we're still forming the Festival. We've decided on our plays. We're doing *Uncle Vanya* and *The Winter's Tale* and one other, probably a comedy, and we're starting to hire actors."

"Sounds wonderful."

"Maybe you could come see them?"

"Would you really want me to?"

"Yes." He sounded surprised. "How could you write me a letter like that? It ruined my day! I nearly crossed you off my list! But thought before I did, I'd call."

*So much for clarifying. Thanks, Claire.*

"It's very confusing," I said.

"How is it confusing?" He still sounded like a smoking dragon.

I hesitated. "In my perception, we were joined telepathically at Banff. So in an inner way, we're very close. But we hardly know each other in an outer way at all."

"Yes," he said slowly.

"We can't help the inner stuff. It's a bit scary to be so close to someone you hardly know. But we have to decide if we want to know each other in an outer way or not."

"It won't be easy."

"No."

We were both quiet for a minute.

"I don't know what to say," I said.

"Don't say anything." I could almost see scarlet and gold hanging in the air around his voice. "Just feel. When you hang up, just feel what I'm sending you."

After I hung up, I was overwhelmed. It was a wave, definitely from Brian—sweet and protective, but also pure Eros, Eros in every cell, heart, soul, mind, body. Honey. Even though he was a thousand miles away, Brian was totally with me.

Just for now, I knew that Brian loved me.

H.D. says, "You can have a thousand loves, but not one Lover."

I had a Lover—someone I had a heart and soul and cellular connection with beyond the realm of the physical. I would have to remember that after Brian stopped flooding me with feeling.

Just because there's no word, no reason, no proof, doesn't mean it isn't true.

## 24. HAIRCUT

IT WAS MY FIRST HAIRCUT in Talitha's new shop, a small space with a front wall of glass letting in swaths of sun. There were wreaths with dried flowers and casual bows, old candlesticks, and a few vases with dried flowers in them. I'd bought purple tulips from the market. "It's a lovely space!" I said. "Congratulations!"

I knew she'd worked very hard over the past month to get the space ready, and, by a miracle, here she was. "Thank you, Judith," Talitha said serenely. "It's nice to have my own place."

She put my tulips in a vase. They weren't the only flowers— there were also orchids, some beautiful florist arrangements with stargazer lilies and white double chrysanthemums, and one arrangement of pink roses.

"I'm really glad Rosetta was wrong about your quitting your job and doing nothing but healing," I said, stretching my neck over the sink so Talitha could wash my hair.

"Just because you're psychic doesn't mean you're always right." Talitha dried my hair, combed it, and led me to her chair. "How much off, Judith?"

"Not too much. I don't want it too short. Anyway, haircuts are healing too. I've had some bad ones where I cried for a month until they grew out."

Talitha considered, then started snipping.

"Have you seen anyone from the class?"

"I ran into Andrea on the street the other day. She looks

great. She's got a new job and she's started seeing someone. And I saw Sharon in Tara last week. She's volunteering at her youngest son's school a couple mornings a week, helping kids read, and she really likes it." (I gave an inner shudder thinking how hard it had been with Davy, but his long-ago kindergarten teacher had said, "There are no problem children; there are only opportunities for growth.")

"Rosetta came in a couple weeks ago to get her hair cut," said Talitha. "Deirdre has moved in with her."

"Yikes, do you think that's good for Deirdre? Rosetta can be pretty overwhelming."

"It's hard to tell. Rosetta seemed happy. .She's broken up with her guy. I think they were both lonely—Deirdre and Rosetta, I mean."

Yes, now that I thought of it, Rosetta had been lonely. I thought of the wide spaces between her words when she wrote out belief systems. Deirdre might have been lonely too. She'd never talked about her friends—not that any of us had talked about friends, but she didn't seem to have much in her life besides work. Loneliness had been a streak running through the class, truer of some of us than others. Maybe it was just as well that Rosetta and Deirdre had found each other.

"What about Elaine?" Talitha asked.

I cast my mind back. I hadn't seen Elaine in a while. Davy and I didn't go to the Golden Rooster much any more. Davy had his pasta, and sometimes I made hamburgers or a substantial salad for both of us.

"I saw her a couple months ago buying supplements at Green Door. She's still scrambling for money, but Lily is much healthier and doing well in school. What about James?"

Talitha looked troubled and hesitated before she spoke. "He came over for a session a couple weeks ago. He's got his first level reiki, but he's been hearing these voices."

"You mean like Mama Isis?"

"No, dark voices. Just sometimes. But when he hears them

he feels as if he's split apart. When he's on medication, they go away. But then he says he loses his healing touch and his visions."

"That's awful!" I was very worried for him. "Did the session help?"

"A little. It was big on diet and exercise. Water. Lots of water. And the God thing."

I know I wasn't supposed to know, but maybe it counted as professional consultation.

"What belief system did he anchor?"

"'I am physically, mentally, and spiritually whole.' He'd probably anchored it before, but sometimes you need them again."

"That's tragic. I hope he heals. I'll send him white light." Though how many people get past hearing schizophrenic voices? I thought of the healing James had given me during the course. This seemed all wrong.

"What about Vivienne?" Talitha changed the subject.

"I see her quite a bit. Her dresses are still selling at Shannon's, and she's moving into palazzo pants. She's having a show at the library next year. For her paintings, not her dresses."

"I should go check them out," said Talitha. "Her style isn't my style, but I'd like to see them. And remind me about her show at the library next year. I'd like to go."

"She still hasn't found her shaman, though. She hasn't even dreamed about him."

Talitha had finished cutting my hair and started blow-drying it, fluffing it with her fingers as she went.

"Do you think Rosetta was right about your marriage?" I asked.

"She might have been, but I'm still in love. And I don't like being told what to do."

"I hadn't noticed!"

"What about your guy in Nova Scotia?"

"We're talking on the phone fairly often. A couple weeks ago, he asked me to come see the plays at the festival this summer, but I don't know if it was a real invitation or just a dramatic flourish. I've called, but he hasn't called back. I'd give a lot to see those plays. There was an article in the *Globe*. Hugh is getting all the credit, of course."

Talitha pulled her pendulum out from behind her blouse and swung it a few times.

"It says you'll go," she said. "You may not hear from him, but you'll go."

"Do you think I'll see him again?"

Talitha swung her pendulum. "Oh yes, you'll see him again."

"When he's there, he's totally there, even though he's a thousand miles away. But then when he's absent, he's totally absent. My friends are all tired of hearing about him."

He's a soulmate," said Talitha. "Soulmates don't grow on trees. I think you've got to believe."

"I guess it's like Cupid and Psyche," I said. "She never saw him; he only came to her at night. I've *seen* Brian, but we're only together in the astral plane."

"That gives me goosebumps." Talitha straightened my hair with a curling iron, combed it again, and sprayed it.

It looked wonderful. Anyone who doesn't believe in transformation has never had a really good haircut. "Thank you, Talitha!" I said.

"Thank *you*, Judith."

I paid, left a tip, and walked out into the warm May sun.

# ACKNOWLEDGEMENTS

THIS BOOK TOOK MANY YEARS to come into being. I had hoped to begin it when I went to Banff in 1998, but it wasn't ready to form until I did a workshop with Helen Humphreys at Wintergreen Studios in July, 2010. Helen assigned in-class writing exercises, which I found agonizing, but bits of the novel surfaced during them. My thanks to all the workshop participants for their response to these bits of unwritten novel, but particularly to Lindy Mechefske, who kept reminding me how everyone had laughed and encouraged me to continue. Helen also encouraged me to continue and helped bring the novel into being by asking about it over the next few years.

Thanks to Cynthia French for reading a draft of the first chapter in the fall of 2010 and encouraging the rest to happen. Thanks to the Saskatchewan Writers' Guild for two wonderful retreats at St. Peter's Abbey in Muenster, Saskatchewan, in 2012 and 2013. I went back to the book, more or less in earnest, at the retreat in 2013. I am grateful to Barbara Langhorst for sharing her experience writing her own novel, and for convincing me to apply to the Humber School of Writers.

Many thanks to the Humber School of Writers for giving me the opportunity to work intensively with Helen Humphreys during the winter of 2014-15.

My greatest thanks to Helen Humphreys for her careful reading and for her generosity in continuing to read drafts after the course was finished. Helen, you made this novel's completion possible, and I am beyond grateful.

Special thanks for Barry Dempster for his friendship, his belief in my writing, and for the inspiring example of his own writing and his own achievement.

Great thanks to the friends who accompanied me in various ways through the writing process and after: companions in poetry Clara Blackwood, Carol Gall, Jennifer Londry, Rebecca Luce-Kapler, Jeanette Lynes, Kath MacLean, Peter Sims, Sheila Stewart.

Thanks to other friends: Heather Buchan, Karen Dempster, Carla Douglas, Mary Lou Dickinson for her advice about novels and her example, Tara Kainer, Barbara Langhorst, Lindy Mechefske, Lisa Morriss-Andrews, David Murakami Wood, Susan Olding, Gail Scala, Susan Siddeley for all their friendship, support and encouragement. Thanks to my lovely book club: Marg Conacher, Val Hamilton, Julia Kalotay, Elva McGaughey, Marguerite Ven Die, and Linda Williams, who listened to parts of this novel as it was in progress.

Thanks to Kellye Crockett for her tarot readings and for continued psychic inspiration.

Many thanks to my editor at Inanna Publications, Luciana Ricciutelli, for her belief in this book (as well as my two earlier poetry books) and for her work in seeing it through press. Thanks also to Inanna publicist Renée Knapp and to Val Fullard for her psychic cover.

My son Alan Clark lived with the demands of writing this novel with great patience and good humour. Thank you, Alan! You are at the centre of my dailiness.

The Results System, though no longer current in this form, was channeled by Margaret Fields Kean (1940-2009) after a near-death experience in 1978. Results was an entire system of stress management, from the cellular to the spiritual. The technique of repatterning, which is central to this book, is Margaret Fields Kean's, as are the belief systems and meditations.

*Photo: Bernard Clark*

Elizabeth Greene has published three volumes of poetry: *The Iron Shoes* (2007), *Moving* (2010) and *Understories* (2014). Her poems, short fiction, and essays have appeared in journals and anthologies across Canada. She has also edited/co-edited five books, including *We Who Can Fly: Poems, Essays and Memories in Honour of Adele Wiseman*, which won the Betty and Morris Aaron Prize (Jewish Book Awards) for Best Scholarship on a Canadian Subject in 1998. She lives in Kingston with her son and two cats. *A Season Among Psychics* is her debut novel.